ANNE ENRIGHT has published essays, short stories, a non-fiction book about motherhood, *Making Babies*, five novels and two books of short stories, *The Portable Virgin* and *Taking Pictures*. Her novel *The Gathering* won the Man Booker Prize in 2007.

The Granta Book of the Irish Short Story

Edited and with an introduction by
Anne Enright

GRANTA

Granta Publications, 12 Addison Avenue, London W11 4QR

First published in Great Britain by Granta Books 2010
This paperback edition published by Granta Books 2011

A CIP catalogue record for this book
is available from the British Library.

9 10

ISBN 978 1 84708 255 8

Typeset by Avon DataSet Ltd, Bidford on Avon, Warwickshire

Printed and bound by CPI Group (UK) Ltd, Croydon, CR0 4YY

MIX
Paper | Supporting
responsible forestry
FSC® C171272

This anthology, and the work of many of the writers in it, owes a huge debt of gratitude to David Marcus, who is sadly missed.

Contents

INTRODUCTION

Anne Enright

The short story is, for me, a natural form, as difficult and as easy to talk about as, say, walking. Do we need a theory about going for a walk? About one foot, in front of the other? Probably, yes. 'I made the story just as I'd make a poem;' writes Raymond Carver, 'one line and then the next, and the next. Pretty soon I could see a story – and I knew it was my story, the one I had been wanting to write.'

It is the simple things that are the most mysterious.

'Do you know if what you are writing is going to be a short story or a novel?' This is one of the questions writers get asked all the time. The answer is 'Yes,' because the writer also thinks in shapes. But it is foolish asking a writer how much they know, when they spend so much time trying not to know it.

This is what the American writer Flannery O'Connor did not know about her iconic story 'Good Country People'.

When I started writing that story, I didn't know there was going to be a PhD with a wooden leg in it. I merely found myself one morning writing a description of two women I knew something about, and before I realised it, I had equipped one of them with a daughter with a wooden leg. I brought in the Bible salesman, but I had no idea what I was going to do with him. I didn't know he was going to steal that wooden leg until ten or twelve lines before he did it, but when I found out that this was what was going to happen, I realised it was inevitable.

x   Anne Enright

She does not say when she knew she was writing a short
story, as opposed to the first chapter of a novel – or a radio play,
or the rough draft of an epic poem – at a guess, it was quite early
on. The writer's ignorance may be deliberate, but it plays itself
out in an established space. The sentence is one such space;
the story is another. In both cases, form and surprise are the same
thing, and the pleasures of inevitablility are also the pleasures of
shape.

This is not an argument for a lyrical as opposed to a social theory of
the short story: characters are part of it too; the way people do
unexpected things, even if you have invented them yourself. The short
story delivers what Flannery O'Connor calls 'the experience of
meaning'; the surprise that comes when things make sense.

Much of what is said about the short story as a form is actually
anxiety about the novel – so it is worth saying that we do not know
how the novel delivers meaning, but we have some idea of how the
short story might. There is something irreducible about it: 'A story is
a way to say something that can't be said any other way,' says Flannery
O'Connor, 'and it takes every word in the story to say what the
meaning is.' The novel, on the other hand, is not finished by its own
meaning, which is why it must grow a structure or impose one; making
the move from story to plot.

Short stories seldom creak, the way novels sometimes creak; they
are allowed to be easy and deft. Some writers say that the short story
is too 'easy' to matter much, some say it is the most difficult form of all.
But if the argument is about ease as opposed to difficulty, then surely
we should not undervalue ease. And though it may be easy to write
something that looks like a short story (for being not long), it is very
hard to write a good one – or to be blessed by a good one – so many of
the ones we read are fakes.

The great Irish short story writer Frank O'Connor thought it a
pure form, 'motivated by its own necessities rather than by our convenience.' I am not sure whether the novel is written for our
convenience, but it is probably written for our satisfaction. That is what
readers complain about with short stories, that they are not 'satisfying'.
They are the cats of literary form; beautiful, but a little too self-
contained for some readers' tastes.

Short stories are, however, satisfying to write, because they are such achieved things. They become themselves even as you write them: they end once they have attained their natural state.

Or some of them do. Others keep going. Others discard the first available meaning for a later, more interesting conclusion. In the interests of truth, some writers resist, back-pedal, downplay, switch tacks, come back around a different way. Poe's famous unity of impulse is all very well, but if you know what the impulse is already, then it will surely die when you sit down at the desk.

There are stories in this anthology that are beautifully made, like Seán Ó Faoláin's 'The Trout', and there are some that are slightly untidy, but good anyway. This is what Ó Faoláin himself called 'personality', saying that what he liked in a short story was 'punch and poetry'. The tension is always between the beauty of the poem and the felt life of the novel form.

Frank O'Connor bridged the gap between the aesthetic and the cultural in a more romantic way. 'There is in the short story at its most characteristic,' he writes, 'something we don't often find in the novel, an intense awareness of human loneliness.' His book *The Lonely Voice*, which was published in 1963, is still a touchstone in any discussion of the short story form. The question he asked – as this collection also asks – was why Irish writers excel at the short story. The answer, for him, lay in the loneliness to be found among 'submerged population groups'. These are the people on the margins of society; the outlawed, the dreaming and the defeated. 'The short story has never had a hero,' says O'Connor, offering instead a slightly infantilising idea of 'the Little Man' (as though all novels were about big ones). Americans qualify, because America is made up of immigrant communities, but the proper subjects of the short story are: 'Gogol's officials, Turgenev's serfs, Maupassant's prostitutes, Chekhov's doctors and teachers' and, we might note, not a single English person of any kind. The novel requires 'the concept of a normal society', and though this, O'Connor seems to say, is available to the English, there is in Irish society a kind of hopelessness that pushes the artist away. The resulting form, the short story, 'remains by its nature remote from the community – romantic, individualistic and intransigent.'

In his useful essay on the subject, 'Inside Out: A Working Theory of the Short Story', John Kenny says that the short story has flourished 'in those cultures where older, usually oral forms, are met head on with the challenge of new literary forms equipped with the ideology of modernisation.' O'Connor's theories place the short story as the genre of the cusp between tradition and modernity. The story is born from the fragmentation of old certainties, and the absence of any new ones, and this produces in the writer a lyric response, 'a retreat into the self in the face of an increasingly complex . . . reality'.

The first thing to say about O'Connor's ideas is that they rang true at the time. Whether or not the short story is, in essence, an assertion of the self – small, but powerfully individual – to the writer it certainly felt that way. It is interesting to test that sense of 'the Little Man' against a new, more confident Irish reality; one in which good writing continues to thrive. Is 'submerged' just another word for 'poor'? Is the word 'peasant' hovering somewhere around? There is so much nostalgia about Ireland – it is important to say that this is not always the fault of its writers. They may be closer to the oral arts of folk tale, fable, gossip and anecdote, but speech is also a modern occupation. Irish novels may often reach into the past, but the stories gathered here show that the form is light and quick enough to be contemporary. If you want to see life as it is lived 'now' (whenever the 'now' of the story might be), just look at the work of Neil Jordan, Roddy Doyle or, indeed, Frank O'Connor. Meanwhile, whoever thinks the short story somehow harmless for being closer to a 'folk' tradition has not read John McGahern, whose stories are the literary equivalent of a hand grenade rolled across the kitchen floor.

Seán Ó Faoláin, that other pillar of the twentieth-century Irish short story was wary of the lyrical view. In his book *The Short Story*, published in 1948, he writes, 'Irish literature in our time came to its great period of efflorescence in a romantic mood whose concept of a writer was almost like the concept of a priest: you did not just write, you lived writing; it was a vocation; it was part of the national resurgence to be a writer.'

Indeed, the number of stories about priests and the sadness of priests that have not made it into this volume are legion – parish priests, curates, bishops; all lonely, all sad as they survey the folly of their congregations, and ninety-nine per cent of them celibate. I left most of them out for seeming untrue, and offer instead a couple of stories, by Maeve Brennan and Colm Tóibín, about the more interesting loneliness of the priest's mother.

In the same way that it might be said that much of what is written about the short story form is actually anxiety about the unknowability of the novel (which we think we know so well), perhaps much of what is written about Irish writing is, in fact, anxiety about England. Sometimes, indeed, the terms 'England' and 'the novel' seem almost interchangeable.

Perhaps it is all a yearning for what O'Connor called 'the concept of a society' – in its absence, we must do what we can. And if we can't be as good as them, we'll just have to be better, which is to say, more interesting. Ó Faoláin says it pretty much straight out: what he likes in a short story is personality, and the problem with the English is that they don't have any. 'The fact is that the English do not admire the artistic temperament: they certainly do not demonstrate it.' Dullness is their national ambition and preoccupation. 'In short, the English way of life is much more social and much less personal and individual than the French.'

Ó Faoláin can't quite fit America into this scheme. 'Why America should produce interesting personalities in the short story I simply do not understand unless it be that American society is still unconventionalised.' Even O'Connor's 'submerged' Americans surface with some rapidity. I don't want to dishonour O'Connor or Ó Faoláin, who are heroes to me now as they were to my youth, and I am certainly not saying that the English are interesting, in any way – God forbid – I am just saying it is there, that's all: that national prejudice is still prejudice, even if you come from a plucky little country like Ireland, where it's only endearing really, apart from when it's not.

What interests me is the way O'Connor and Ó Faoláin talk, not about how wonderful the Irish are as artists, but how vile they are as critics. Ó Faoláin describes the conditions for the Irish artist as 'particularly difficult . . . complicated by religion, politics, peasant unsophistication, lack of stimulus, lack of variety, pervasive poverty, censorship, social compression and so on.' An ambitious Irishman, O'Connor writes, 'can still expect nothing but incomprehension, ridicule and injustice.'

Of course, things are different in the twenty-first century, now that poverty has been banished (or was, for a whole decade) and the success of our writers is officially a matter of national pride. But it is perhaps still true that if Ireland loves you, then you must be doing something wrong. There is a lingering unease about how Irish writers negotiate ideas about 'Ireland' (the country we talk about, as opposed to the place where we live), for readers both at home and abroad. We move, in decreasing circles, around the problem Ó Faoláin voiced in 1948. 'There was hardly an Irish writer who was not on the side of the movement for Irish political independence; immediately it was achieved they became critical of the nation. This is what makes all politicians say that writers are an unreliable tribe. They are. It is their métier.'

I first read O'Connor when I was maybe ten, maybe twelve years of age. I chose his story 'The Mad Lomasneys' for the way it stayed with me, quietly, ever since. If you wonder whether this is the selection of a twelve year old, I admit she is certainly here too, that the reason the short story remains an important form for Irish writers of my generation is because the work of O'Connor and Ó Faoláin and Lavin were commonly found on Irish bookshelves, alongside, in my own house, *The Irish Republic* by the nationalist historian Dorothy McArdle, and *Three to Get Married* by the reverend Canon Sheehan (the third in question, I was disappointed to discover, being God). Our sensibilities were shaped by the fine choices of Professor Augustine Martin who set the stories for the school curriculum, among them 'The Road to the Shore', a story that revealed as much to me about aesthetic possibilities and satisfactions as it did about nuns. We were taught French by reading Maupassant and German through the stories of Siegfried Lenz: though if the short story is a national form it did not seem to flourish in the national language of Irish, where all the excitement – for me at least – was in poetry. The fact remains that I grew up with the idea that short stories were lovely and interesting and useful things, in the way the work of Dorothy McArdle and the Canon Sheehan was not.

This may all be very 'submerged' of me, but that is to patronise my younger self. I still find the modesty of the form attractive and right. How important is it to be 'important' as a writer? The desire to claim a larger authority can provoke work, or it can ruin it. In fact, writers claim different kinds of authority: these days a concentration on the short story form is taken as a sign of writerly purity rather than novelistic incompetence, though it still does not pay the bills. (This was not always the case. Ó Faoláin lamented the popularity of the form which 'is being vulgarised by commercialisation'. 'Readers and editors,' he writes, 'must often feel discouraged.')

'The Mad Lomasneys' is a story by O'Connor that is not much anthologised. This may be, in part, because it does not present a recognisable idea of 'Ireland'. It does not deal with the birth of the Irish Free State, like 'Guests of the Nation', or with childhood innocence like 'My Oedipus Complex' or 'My First Confession'. I did not reject these stories for being too 'Irish': so many of O'Connor's stories are good, I just wanted to see what happens when you give the bag a shake. I realised, when I did this, there are even more stories about choice and infidelity in the Irish tradition than there are about priests. I don't know what this means; why both Sean Ó Faoláin and William Trevor, for example, write endlessly about love and betrayal or, to take the problem further, why 'either/or' is a question asked by the work of contemporary writers like Keith Ridgway and Hugo Hamilton, who then answer 'both'.

Is choice a particularly Irish problem? What about shame – a streak of which runs through the work collected here? Humiliation, perhaps? Maybe we should call that 'the problem of power'. There is also the problem of the family, which is the fundamental (perhaps the only) unit of Irish culture, and one which functions beyond our choosing. Until very recently, you could only marry once in Ireland – though this does not answer the question of how many times you can love, or what love is. Catholicism may give Irish writers an edge when it comes to talking about the larger questions, but you could say the adulteries in Trevor owe as much to Shakespearean comedy as to the problem of the Catholic Church. In fact, I think Trevor owes much to the English short story tradition (as does the work of Clare Boylan), but let us not confuse things here. Let us keep everyone in the one box, and then talk us about the box, its meaning and dimensions, and then let us paint the box green.

Perhaps we should move beyond the box to ask: are all short stories, Russian, French, American and Irish, in fact about loneliness? I am not sure. This may be part of writers' nonsense about themselves, or O'Connor's nonsense about being Irish, or it may just be the general nonsense of being alive. Connection and the lack of it are one of the great themes of the short story, but social factors change, ideas of the romantic change, the more you think about literary forms the smaller your ideas become. Life itself may be a lonely business (or not): the most I have ever managed to say about the short story is that it is about

a change. Something has changed. Something is known at the end of
a story – or nearly known – that was not known before. 'We are on our
own' may be one such insight, but others are surely possible.

I put this selection together as an Irish writer – which is to say, as one
of Ó Faoláin's 'unreliable tribe'. Some of these stories made me close
the book with a slam. 'Music at Annahullion' by Eugene McCabe, for
example, defied me to read anything else that day, or that week, to
match it. I found it difficult to finish Maeve Brennan's 'An Attack of
Hunger', because it came so close to the pain it described (is this a good
way to whet the reader's appetite, I wonder?). The world in Claire
Keegan's 'Men and Women' stayed with me from the day I first
encountered it. I looked for stories that had made me pause when I
read them the first time around: stories like Colum McCann's
'Everything in this Country Must' that I finished in the knowledge that
I could not, in any conceivable universe, have written such a thing
myself.

Perhaps Irish writers, like Irish actors, rely more than is usual on
personality in that balance of technique and the self that is the secret of
style – the trick might be in its suppression, indeed, an effort that must
fail over time. Banville, O'Brien, McGahern, Tóibín – these writers
become more distinctive as people, even as their sentences become
more distinctively their own. It is a jealous kind of delight to find on
the page some inimicable thing, a particular passion, and if the writer
is dead, it is delightful and sad to meet a sensibility that will not pass
this way again. The shock of recognition runs through this anthology.
As much as possible I have tried to choose those stories in which a
writer is most himself.

A writer has many selves, of course, and an editor has many and
mixed criteria – some of them urgent, as I have described, and some
more easy. The selection is from writers who were born in the twentieth
century (cheating a little for Bowen, who was born in 1899). I wanted
to put together a book that was varied and good to read, with a strong
eye to the contemporary.

If this selection has anything to say about Irish writing, then it does
so by accident. I chose the stories because I liked them, and then
stood back a little to see what my choice said – about me perhaps, but
also about how tastes change over time. There is a deal of what
Ó Faoláin called 'personality' at play in the stories chosen here, but,

at a guess, not much that he would recognise as 'charm', or even (God save the mark) as 'Irish charm'. It is too easy to move from 'personality' to a mannered version of the self, and this can seem a little hokum to us as the years pass.

It is possible that, as truths emerged about Ireland, or refused to emerge, Irish prose writers became more blunt or more lyrical, or both at the same time. Folk tale and short story pulled apart over the years – a split made radical in Éilís Ní Dhuibhne's 'Midwife to the Fairies' – only to rejoin in the recent work of Claire Keegan. Fashions are darker now. New work is sometimes tainted by misogyny, and this seems to me as lazy a reach as sentimentality was to the writers of the 1950s and – who knows?– as likely to look a bit stupid, in years to come (perhaps this is what makes Patrick Boyle's 'Meles Vulgaris' so amazing, for being out of joint with his time). But these are all trends rather than truths, and only to be noted in passing. Time makes some stories more distant, while others come near, for a while. What I wanted to do was to select work that would bring a number of Irish writers close to the reader, today.

Some great Irish writers – Sebastian Barry, Patrick McCabe, Dermot Healy – love the stretch of the novel or they love misrule. Some, like Deirdre Madden or Clare Kilroy need space to think or to plot. But this book celebrates a fact which I have so far failed to explain, that so many Irish writers also love the short story. They defy current wisdom about the book business and, in their continuing attention to the form, refuse to do what they are told. This may be partly because of the small but crucial distance Irish writers keep from the international publishing industry. The stories in this collection were written for their own sake. They were written in rooms in Monaghan or Dublin, in New York, Dún Laoghaire, Devon, Wexford, Belfast, Bucharest. It seems to me remarkable that the members of this scattered tribe, each in their solitude, has managed such a conversation. The stories in this anthology talk to each other in many and unexpected ways. Is this another aspect of the short story that we find unsettling: its promiscuity, its insistence on being partial, glancing and various?

My romantic idea of Ireland did not survive the killings in the North, and the realisation, in the 1980s, that Irish women were considered far too lovely for contraception: it foundered, you might say, between Dorothy McArdle and Canon Sheehan. Perhaps, as a result,

I found it difficult to lose myself in the dream that was the recent economic boom. My romantic idea of the writer, meanwhile, did not survive the shift into motherhood. I might have felt lonely and wonderful, but with small children, I just never got the time. But though I am not a romantic, I am quite passionate about the whole business of being an Irish writer. Ó Faoláin was right, we are great contrarians. When there is much rubbish talked about a country, when the air is full of large ideas about what we are, or what we are not, then the writer offers truths that are delightful and small. We write against our own foolishness, not anyone else's. In which case the short story is as good a place as any other to keep things real.

Anne Enright
July 2010

The Granta Book of the
Irish Short Story

THE ROAD TO THE SHORE

Michael McLaverty

''Tis going to be a lovely day, thanks be to God,' sighed Sister Paul to herself, as she rubbed her wrinkled hands together and looked out at the thrushes hopping across the lawn. 'And it was a lovely day last year and the year before,' she mused, and in her mind saw the fresh face of the sea where, in an hour or two, she and the rest of the community would be enjoying their annual trip to the shore. 'And God knows it may be my last trip,' she said resignedly, and gazed abstractedly at a butterfly that was purring its wings against the sunny pane. She opened the window and watched the butterfly swing out into the sweet air, zigzagging down to a cushion of flowers that bordered the lawn. 'Isn't it well Sister Clare wasn't here,' she said to herself, 'for she'd be pestering the very soul out of me with her questions about butterflies and birds and flowers and the fall of dew?' She gave her girdle of beads a slight rattle. Wasn't it lovely to think of the pleasure that little butterfly would have when it found the free air under its wings again and its little feet pressing on the soft petals of the flowers and not on the hard pane? She always maintained it was better to enjoy Nature without searching and probing and chattering about the what and the where and the wherefore. But Sister Clare! – what she got out of it all, goodness only knew, for she'd give nobody a minute's peace – not a moment's peace would she give to a saint, living or dead. 'How long would that butterfly live in the air of a classroom?' she'd be asking. 'Do you think it would use up much of the active part of the air – the oxygen part, I mean? . . . What family would that butterfly belong to? . . . You know it's wrong to say that a butterfly lives only a day . . . When I am teaching my little pupils I always try to be accurate. I don't believe in stuffing their heads with fantastical nonsense however pleasurable it may be . . .' Sister Paul turned round as if someone had suddenly walked into the room, and she was relieved when she saw nothing only the quiet vacancy of the room, the varnished desks with the sun on them and their reflections on the parquet floor.

She hoped she wouldn't be sitting beside Clare in the car today! She'd have no peace with her – not a bit of peace to look out at the countryside and see what changes had taken place inside twelve months. But Reverend Mother, she knew, would arrange all that – and if it'd be her misfortune to be parked beside Clare she'd have to accept it with resignation; yes, with resignation, and in that case her journey to the sea would be like a pilgrimage.

At that moment a large limousine drove up the gravel path, and as it swung round to the convent door she saw the flowers flow across its polished sides in a blur of colour. She hurried out of the room and down the stairs. In the hall Sister Clare and Sister Benignus were standing beside two baskets and Reverend Mother was staring at the stairs. 'Where were you, Sister Paul?' she said with mild reproof. 'We searched the whole building for you . . . We're all ready this ages . . . And Sister Francis has gone to put out the cat. Do you remember last year it had been in all the time we were at the shore and it ate the bacon?' As she spoke a door closed at the end of the corridor and Sister Francis came along, polishing her specs with the corner of her veil. Reverend Mother glanced away from her, that continual polishing of the spectacles irritated her; and then that empty expression on Sister Francis's face when the spectacles were off – vacuous, that's what it was!

'All ready now,' Reverend Mother tried to say without any trace of perturbation. Sister Clare and Sister Benignus lifted two baskets at their feet, Reverend Mother opened the hall door, and they all glided out into the flat sunlight.

The doors of the car were wide open, the engine purring gently, and a perfume of new leather fingering the air. The chauffeur, a young man, touched his cap and stood deferentially to the side. Reverend Mother surveyed him quickly, noting his clean-bright face and white collar. 'I think there'll be room for us all in the back,' she said.

'There's a seat in the front, Sister,' the young man said, touching his cap again.

'Just put the baskets on it, if you please,' said Reverend Mother. And Sister Clare who, at that moment, was smiling at her own grotesque reflection in the back of the car came forward with her basket, Sister Benignus following. Sister Paul sighed audibly and fingered her girdle of beads.

'Now, Sister Paul, you take one of the corner seats, Sister Clare you sit beside her, and Sister Benignus and Sister Francis on the spring-up seats facing them – they were just made for you, the tiny tots!' And they all laughed, a brittle laugh that emphasised the loveliness of the day.

When they were all seated, Reverend Mother made sure that the hall door was locked, glanced at the fastened windows, and then stood for a minute watching the gardener who was pushing his lawnmower with unusual vigour and concentration. He stopped abruptly when her shadow fell across his path. 'And, Jack,' she said, as if continuing a conversation that had been interrupted, 'you'll have that lawn finished today?'

'Yes, Mother,' and he took off his hat and held it in front of his breast. 'To be sure I'll have it finished today. Sure what'd prevent me to finish it, and this the grandest day God sent this many a long month – a wholesome day!'

'And, Jack, I noticed some pebbles on the lawn yesterday – white ones.'

'I remarked them myself, Mother. A strange terrier disporting himself in the garden done it.'

'Did it!'

'Yes, Mother, he did it with his two front paws, scratching at the edge of the lawn like it was a rabbit burrow. He done it yesterday, and when I clodded him off the grounds he'd the impertinence to go out a different way than he came in. But I've now his entrances and exits all blocked and barricaded and I'm afraid he'll have to find some other constituency to disport himself. Dogs is a holy terror for bad habits.'

'Be sure and finish it all today,' she said with some impatience. She turned to go away, hesitated, and turned back. 'By the way, Jack, if there are any drips of oil made by the car on the gravel you'll scuffle fresh pebbles over them.'

'I'll do that. But you need have no fear of oil from her engine,' and he glanced over at the limousine. 'She'll be as clean as a Swiss clock. 'Tis them grocery vans that leak – top, tail and middle.'

Crossing to the car, she heard with a feeling of pleasure the surge of the lawnmower over the grass. Presently the car swung out of the gate on to a tree-lined road at the edge of the town. The nuns relaxed, settled themselves more comfortably in their seats and chatted about the groups on bicycles that were all heading for the shore.

'We will go to the same quiet strip as last year,' said Reverend Mother, and then as she glanced out of the window a villa on top of a hill drew her attention. 'There's a house that has been built since last year,' she said.

'No, no,' said Sister Francis. 'It's more than a year old for I remember seeing it last year,' and she peered at it through her spectacles.

Reverend Mother spoke through the speaking tube to the driver: 'Is that villa on the hill newly built?' she asked.

He stopped the car, 'A doctor by the name of McGrath built it two years ago,' he said. 'He's married to a daughter of Solicitor O'Kane.'

'Oh, thank you,' said Reverend Mother; and the car proceeded slowly up the long hill above the town.

Sister Francis took off her spectacles, blew her breath on them and rubbed them with her handkerchief. She took another look at the villa and said with obvious pride: 'A fine site, indeed. I remember last year that they had that little gadget over the door.'

'The architrave,' said Sister Clare importantly.

'Aye,' said Sister Paul, and she looked out at the trees and below them the black river with its strings of froth moving through the valley. How lovely it would be, she thought, to sit on the edge of that river, dabble her parched feet in it and send bubbles out into the race of the current. She had often done that when she was a child, and now that river and its trees, which she only saw once a year, brought her childhood back to her. She sighed and opened the window so as to hear the mumble of the river far below them. The breeze whorled in, and as it lifted their veils they all smiled, invigorated by the fresh loveliness of the air. A bumble bee flew in and crawled up the pane at Reverend Mother's side of the car. She opened the window and assisted the bee towards the opening with the top of her fountain pen, but the bee clung to the pen and as she tried to shake it free the wind carried it in again. 'Like everything else it hates to leave you,' said Sister Benignus. Reverend Mother smiled and the bee flew up to the roof of the car and then alighted on the window beside Sister Paul. Sister Paul swept the bee to safety with the back of her hand.

'You weren't one bit afraid of it,' said Sister Clare. 'And if it had stung you, you would in a way have been responsible for its death. If it had been a queen bee – though queens wouldn't be flying at this time of the year – you would have been responsible for the deaths of potential thousands. A queen bumble bee lays over two thousand eggs in one season!'

'Tis a great pity we haven't a hen like that,' put in Sister Francis, and they all laughed except Sister Clare. Sister Francis laughed till her eyes watered and, once more, she took off her spectacles. Reverend Mother fidgeted slightly and, in order to control her annoyance, she fixed her gaze on Sister Clare and asked her to continue her interesting account of the life of bumble bees. Sister Paul put her hands in her sleeves and sought distraction in the combings of cloud that streaked the sky.

Reverend Mother pressed her toe on the floor of the car and, instead of listening to Sister Clare, she was glaring unconsciously at Sister Francis who was tapping her spectacles on the palm of her hand and giving an odd laugh.

'Your spectacles are giving you much trouble today,' she broke in, unable any longer to restrain herself. 'Perhaps you would like to sit in the middle. It may provide your poor eyes with some rest.'

'No, thank you,' said Sister Francis, 'I like watching the crowds of cyclists passing on the road. But sometimes the sun glints on their handlebars and blinds me for a moment and makes me feel that a tiny thread or two has congregated on my lenses. It's my imagination of course.'

'Maybe you would care to have a look at *St. Anthony's Annals*,' and Reverend Mother handed her the magazine.

'Thank you, Mother. I'll keep it until we reach the shore, for the doctor told me not to read in moving vehicles.'

The car rolled on slowly and when it reached the top of a hill, where there was a long descent of five miles to the sea, a strange silence came over the nuns, and each became absorbed in her own premeditation on the advancing day. 'Go slowly down the hill,' Reverend Mother ordered the driver.

Boys sailed past them on bicycles, and when some did so with their hands off the handlebars a little cry of amazement would break from Sister Francis and she would discuss with Sister Clare the reckless irresponsibility of boys and the worry they must bring to their parents.

Suddenly at a bend on the hill they all looked at Sister Paul for she was excitedly drawing their attention to a line of young poplars. 'Look, look!' she was saying. 'Look at the way their leaves are dancing and not a flicker out of the other trees. And to think I never noticed them before!'

'I think they are aspens,' said Sister Clare, 'and anyway they are not indigenous to this country.'

'We had four poplars in our garden when I was growing up – black poplars, my father called them,' said Sister Paul, lost in her own memory.

'What family did they belong to? There's *angustifolia, laurifolia,* and *balsamifera* and others among the poplar family.'

'I don't know what family they belonged to,' Sister Paul went on quietly. 'I only know they were beautiful – beautiful in very early spring when every tree and twig around them would still be bleak – and there they were bursting into leaf, a brilliant yellow leaf like a flake of sunshine. My father, God be good to his kindly soul, planted four of them when I was young, for there were four in our family, all girls, and one of the trees my father called Kathleen, another Teresa, another Eileen, and lastly my own, Maura. And I remember how he used to stand at the dining-room window gazing out at the young poplars with the frost white and hard around them. 'I see a leaf or two coming on Maura,' he used to say, and we would all rush to the window and gaze into the garden, each of us fastening her eye on her own tree and then measuring its growth of leaf with the others. And to the one whose tree was first in leaf he used to give a book or a pair of rosary beads . . . Poor Father,' she sighed, and fumbled in her sleeve for her handkerchief.

'Can you not think of what special name those trees had?' pressed Clare. 'Did their leaves tremble furiously – *tremula, tremuloides*?'

'They didn't quiver very much,' said Sister Paul, her head bowed. 'My father didn't plant aspens, I remember. He told us it was from an aspen that Our Saviour's rood was made, and because their leaves remember the Crucifixion they are always trembling . . . But our poplars had a lovely warm perfume when they were leafing and that perfume always reminded my father of autumn. Wasn't that strange,' she addressed the whole car, 'a tree coming into leaf and it reminding my poor father of autumn?'

'I know its family now,' said Clare, clapping her hands together. '*Balsamifera* – that's the family it belonged to – it's a native of Northern Italy.'

'And I remember,' said Paul, folding and unfolding her handkerchief on her lap, 'how my poor father had no gum once to wrap up a newspaper that he was posting. It was in winter and he went out to the poplars and dabbed his finger here and there on the sticky buds and smeared it on the edge of the wrapping paper.'

'That was enough to kill the buds,' said Clare. 'The gum, as you call it, is their only protective against frost.'

'It was himself he killed,' said Paul. 'He had gone out from a warm fire in his slippers, out into the bleak air and got his death.'

'And what happened to the poplars?' said Clare. But Sister Paul had turned her head to the window again and was trying to stifle the tears that were rising to her eyes.

'What other trees grew in your neighbourhood?' continued Clare. Sister Paul didn't seem to hear her, but when the question was repeated she turned and said slowly: 'I'm sorry that I don't know their names. But my father, Lord have mercy on him, used to say that a bird could leap from branch to branch for ten miles around without using its wings.'

Sister Clare smiled and Reverend Mother nudged her with her elbow, signing to her to keep quiet; and when she, herself, glanced at Paul she saw the sun shining through the fabric of her veil and a handkerchief held furtively to her eyes.

There was silence now in the sun-filled car while outside cyclists continued to pass them, freewheeling down the long hill. Presently there was a rustle of paper in the car as Sister Francis drew forth from her deep pocket a bag of soft peppermints, stuck together by the heat. Carefully she peeled the bits of paper off the sweets, and as she held out the bag to Reverend Mother she said: 'Excuse my fingers.' But Reverend Mother shook her head, and Clare and Benignus, seeing that she had refused, felt it would be improper for them to accept. Francis shook the bag towards Paul but since she had her eyes closed, as if in prayer, she neither saw nor heard what was being offered to her. '*In somno pacis*,' said Francis, popping two peppermints into her own mouth and hiding the bag in her wide sleeve. 'A peppermint is soothing and cool on a hot day like this,' she added with apologetic good nature.

A hot smell of peppermint drifted around the car. Reverend Mother lowered her window to its full length, and though the air rushed in in soft folds around her face it was unable to quench the flaming odour. Somehow, for Reverend Mother, the day, that had hardly begun yet, was spoiled by an old nun with foolish habits and by a young nun unwise enough not to know when to stop questioning. Everything was going wrong, and it would not surprise her that before evening clouds of rain would blow in from the sea and blot out completely the soft loveliness of the sunny day. Once more she looked at Paul, and, seeing her head bowed in thought, she knew that there was some aspect of the countryside, some shape in cloud or bush, that brought back to Paul a sweet but sombre childhood. For herself she had no such memories – there was nothing in her own life, she thought, only a mechanical ordering, a following of routine, that may have brought some pleasure into other people's lives but none to her own. However, she'd do her best to make the day pleasant for them; after all, it was only one day in the year and if the eating of peppermints gave Sister Francis some satisfaction it was not right to thwart her.

She smiled sweetly then at Francis and as Francis offered the sweets once more, and she was stretching forward to take one there was a sudden dunt to the back of the car and a crash of something falling on the road. The car stopped and the nuns looked at one another, their heads bobbing in consternation. They saw the driver raise himself slowly from his seat, walk back the road and return again with a touch of his cap at the window.

'A slight accident, Sister,' he said, addressing Reverend Mother. 'A cyclist crashed into our back wheel. But it's nothing serious, I think.'

Reverend Mother went out leaving the door open, and through it there came the free sunlight, the cool air and the hum of people talking. She was back again in a few minutes with her handkerchief dabbed with blood, and collected other handkerchiefs from the nuns, who followed her out on to the road. Sister Paul stood back and saw amongst the bunch of people a young man reclining on the bank of the road, a hand to his head. 'I can't stand the sight of blood,' she said to herself, her fingers clutching her rosary beads. She beckoned to a lad who was resting on his bicycle: 'Is he badly hurt, lad? He'll not die, will he?'

'Not a bit of him, Sister. He had his coat folded over the handlebars and the sleeve of it caught in the wheel and flung him against the car.'

'Go up, like a decent boy, and have a good look at him again.'

But before the lad had reached the group the chauffeur had assisted the injured man to his feet and was leading him to the car. The handkerchiefs were tied like a turban about his head, his trousers were torn at the knee and a holy medal was pinned to his braces.

'Put his coat on or he'll catch cold,' Reverend Mother was saying.

'Och, Sister, don't worry about me,' the man was saying. 'Sure it was my own fault. Ye weren't to blame at all. I'll go back again on my own bicycle – I'm fit enough.'

Reverend Mother consulted the chauffeur and whatever advice he gave her the injured man was put into the back of the car. Sister Francis was ordered into the vacant seat beside the driver, the baskets were handed to Paul and Clare, and when the man's bicycle was tied to the carrier they drove off for the hospital in the town.

The young man, sitting between Reverend Mother and Sister Paul, shut his eyes in embarrassment, and when the blood oozed through the pile of handkerchiefs Reverend Mother took the serviettes from the baskets and tied them round his head and under his chin, and all the time the man kept repeating: 'I'm a sore trouble to you, indeed. And sure it was my own fault.' She told him to button his coat or he would catch cold, and when he had done so she noticed a Total Abstinence badge in the lapel.

'A good clean-living man,' she thought, and to think that he was the one to meet with an injury while many an old drunkard could travel the roads of Ireland on a bicycle and arrive home without pain or scratch or cough.

'Tis a blessing of God you weren't killed,' she said, with a rush of protectiveness, and she reached for the thermos flask from the basket and handed the man a cup of tea.

Now and again Sister Paul would steal a glance at him, but the sight of his pale face and the cup trembling in his hand and rattling on the saucer made her turn to the window where she tried to lose herself in contemplation. But all her previous mood was now scattered from her mind, and she could think of nothing only the greatness of Reverend Mother and the cool way she took command of an incident that would have left the rest of them weak and confused.

'How are you feeling now?' she could hear Reverend Mother asking. 'Would you like another sandwich?'

'No, thank you, Sister; sure I had my good breakfast in me before I left the house. I'm a labouring man and since I'm out of work this past three months my wife told me to go off on the bike and have a swim with myself. I was going to take one of the youngsters on the bar of the bike but my wife wouldn't let me.'

'She had God's grace about her,' said Reverend Mother. 'That should be a lesson to you,' and as she refilled his cup from the thermos flask she thought that if the young man had been killed they, in a way, would have had to provide his widow and children with some help. 'And we were only travelling slowly,' she found herself saying aloud.

'Sure, Sister, no one knows that better than myself. You were keeping well in to your own side of the road and when I was ready to sail past you on the hill my coat caught in the front wheel and my head hit the back of your car.'

'S-s-s,' and the nuns drew in their breath with shrinking solicitude.

They drove up to the hospital, and after Reverend Mother had consulted the doctor and was told that the wound was only a slight abrasion and contusion she returned light-heartedly to the car. Sister Clare made no remark when she heard the news but as the wheels of the car rose and fell on the road they seemed to echo what was in her mind: *abrasion and contusion, abrasion and contusion.* 'Abrasion and contusion of what?' she asked herself. 'Surely the doctor wouldn't say "head" – abrasion and contusion of the head?' No, there must be some medical term that Reverend Mother had withheld from them, and as she was about to probe Reverend Mother for the answer the car swung unexpectedly into the convent avenue. 'Oh,' she said with disappointment, and when alighting from the car and seeing Sister Francis give the remains of her sweets to the chauffeur she knew that for her, too, the day was at an end.

They all passed inside except Reverend Mother who stood on the steps at the door noting the quiet silence of the grounds and the heat-shadows flickering above the flower beds. With a mocking smile she saw the lawnmower at rest on the uncut lawn and found herself mimicking the gardener: 'I'll have it all finished today, Sister, I'll have it all finished today.' She put a hand to her throbbing head and crossed the gravel path to look for him, and there in the clump of laurel bushes she found him fast asleep, his hat over his face to keep off the flies, and three empty porter bottles beside him. She tiptoed away from him. 'He has had a better day than we have had,' she said to herself, 'so let him sleep it out, for it's the last he'll have at my expense . . . Oh, drink is a curse,' and she thought of the injury that had befallen the young man with the Abstinence Badge and he as sober as any judge. Then she drew up suddenly as something quick and urgent came into her mind: 'Of course! – he would take the job as gardener, and he unemployed this past three months!' With head erect she sped quickly across the grass and into the convent. Sister Paul was still in the corridor when she saw Reverend Mother lift the phone and ring up the hospital: 'Is he still there? . . . He's all right? . . . That's good . . . Would you tell him to call to see me some time this afternoon?' There was a transfigured look on her face as she put down the receiver and strode across to Sister Paul. 'Sister Paul,' she said, 'you may tell the other Sisters that on tomorrow we will set out again for the shore.' Sister Paul smiled and whisked away down the corridor: 'Isn't Reverend Mother great the way she can handle things?' she said to herself. 'And to think that on tomorrow I'll be able to see the poplars again.'

THE PRAM

Roddy Doyle

1

Alina loved the baby. She loved everything about the baby. The tiny boyness of him, the way his legs kicked whenever he looked up at her, his fat – she loved these things. She loved to bring him out in his pram, even on the days when it was raining. She loved to sit on the floor with her legs crossed and the baby in her lap. Even when he cried, when he screamed, she was very happy. But he did not cry very often. He was almost a perfect baby.

The baby's pram was very old. Alina remembered visiting her grandmother when she was a little girl. She had not met her grandmother before. She got out of the car and stood beside her father in the frozen farmyard. They watched an old woman push a perambulator towards them. The pram was full of wood, branches and twigs and, across the top of the pram, one huge branch that looked like an entire tree. This old woman was her grandmother. And the baby's pram was very like the old pram she saw her grandmother push across the farmyard. Her father told her it had been his pram, and her aunts' and her uncle's, and even the generation of babies before them.

Now, in 2005, in Dublin, she pushed a pram just like it. Every morning, she put the baby into the pram. She wrapped him up and brought the pram carefully down the steps of the house. She pushed the pram down the path, to the gate. The gateway was only slightly wider than the pram.

– Mind you don't scrape the sides, the baby's mother had said, the first time Alina brought the pram to the steps and turned it towards the gate and the street.

Alina did not understand the baby's mother. The mother followed her to the gate. She took the pram and pushed it through the gateway. She tapped the brick pillars.

– Don't scrape the sides.

She tapped the sides of the pram.

– It is very valuable, said the mother.

– It was yours when you were a baby? Alina asked.

– No, said the mother. – We bought it.

– It is very nice.

– Just be careful with it, said the mother.

– Yes, said Alina. – I will be careful.

Every morning, she brought the baby for his walk. She pushed the pram down to the sea and walked along the path beside the sea wall. She walked for two hours, every morning. She had been ordered to do this. She had been told which route to take. She stopped at the wooden bridge, the bridge out to the strange sandy island, and she turned back. She did not see the mother or the father but, sometimes, she thought she was being watched. She never took a different route. She never let the pram scrape a wall or gate. She was drenched and cold; her hands felt frozen to the steel bar with which she pushed the pram, despite the gloves her own mother had sent to her from home. But, still, Alina loved the baby.

The little girls, his sisters, she was not so sure about. They were beautiful little girls. They were clever and lively and they played the piano together, side by side, with a confidence and sensitivity that greatly impressed Alina. The piano was in the tiled hall, close to the stained-glass windows of the large front door. The coloured sunlight of the late afternoon lit the two girls as they played. Their black hair became purple, dark red and the green of deep-forest leaves. Their fingers on the keys were red and yellow. Alina had not seen them play tennis – it was the middle of December – but the mother assured her that they were excellent players. They were polite and they ate with good manners and apologised when they did not eat all that was on their plates.

They were not twins. They had names, of course, and they had different ages. Ocean was ten years old and Saibhreas was almost nine. But Alina rarely – or, never – saw them apart. They played together; they slept together. They stood beside each other, always. From the first time Alina saw them, three weeks earlier, when she arrived at Dublin Airport, they were side by side.

The next morning, Alina's first working day, they came up to Alina's bedroom in the attic. It was dark outside. They were lit only by the light from the landing below, down the steep stairs. Their black hair could not be seen. Alina saw only their faces. They sat at the end of the bed, side by side, and watched Alina.

– Good morning, said Alina.

– Good morning, they said, together.

It was funny. The young ladies laughed. Alina did not know why she did not like them.

2

Every morning, Alina brought the baby for his walk. Always, she stopped at one of the shelters at the seafront. She took the baby, swaddled in cotton and Gortex, from his pram and held him on her lap. She looked at the changing sea and bounced him gently.

She spoke to him only in English. She had been instructed never to use her own language.

– You can teach the girls a few words of Polish, the mother told her.

– It might be useful. But I don't want Cillian confused.

The shelter had three walls, and a wooden bench. The walls had circular windows, like portholes. Alina held the baby and lifted him to one of these windows, so he could see through it. She did it again. He laughed. Alina could feel his excitement through the many layers of cloth. She lifted him high. His hat brushed the roof of the shelter.

– Intelligent boy!

It was the first time he had laughed. She lowered him back into his pram. She would not tell the mother, she decided. But, almost immediately, she changed her mind. She had the sudden feeling, the knowledge; it crept across her face. She was being watched.

She walked as far as the wooden bridge, and turned.

Every morning, Alina saw mothers, and other young women like herself. These women pushed modern, lighter baby-conveyances, four-wheeled and three-wheeled. Alina envied them. The pram felt heavy and the wind from the sea constantly bashed against its hood.

One thing, however, she liked about the pram. People smiled when they saw it.

– I haven't seen one of those in years, one woman said.

– God almighty, that takes me back, said another.

One morning, she pushed past a handsome man who sat on the sea wall eating a large sandwich. She kept pushing; she did not look back. She stopped at the old wooden bridge. She would never bring the pram onto the bridge. She looked at its frail wooden legs rising out of the sludge. The mutual contact, of old wood and old pram; they would all collapse into the ooze below. She could smell it – she could almost feel it, in her hair and mouth. She walked quickly back along the promenade.

The handsome man was still there. He held up a flask and a cup.

– Hot chocolate? he said. – I put aside for you.

He was a biochemist from Lithuania but he was working in Dublin for a builder, constructing an extension to a very large house on her street. They met every morning, in the shelter. Always, he brought the flask. Sometimes, she brought cake. She watched through the portholes as they kissed. She told him she was being watched. He touched her breast; his hand was inside her coat. She looked down at the baby. He smiled; he bucked. He started to cry. The pram rocked on its springs.

One morning in February, Alina heard her mobile phone as she was carefully bringing the pram down the granite steps of the house. She held the phone to her ear.

– Hello?

– Alina. It's O'Reilly.

O'Reilly was the mother. Everyone called her by her surname. She insisted upon this practice. It terrified her clients, she told Alina. It was intriguing; it was sexy.

– Hello, O'Reilly, said Alina.

– The girls are off school early today, said O'Reilly. – Twelve o'clock. I forgot to tell you.

– Fine, said Alina.

But it was not fine.

– I will be there at twelve o'clock, said Alina.

– Five to, said O'Reilly.

– Yes, said Alina.

– Talk to you, said O'Reilly.

– Your mother is not very nice, Alina told the baby, in English.

She could not now meet her biochemist. He did not own a mobile phone. She would miss her hot chocolate. She would miss his lips on her neck. She would not now feel his hands as she peeped through the porthole and watched for approaching joggers and buggy-pushing women.

She arrived at the gates of the girls' school at ten minutes to twelve. They were waiting there, side by side.

– But school ends at twelve o'clock, said Alina.

– A quarter to, said Ocean.

– We've been here *ages*, said Saibhreas.

– So, said Alina. – We will now go home.

– We want to go along the seafront, said Ocean.

– No, said Alina. – It is too windy today, I think.

– You were *late*, said Saibhreas.

– Very well, said Alina. – We go.

The biochemist waved his flask as she approached. Alina walked straight past him. She did not look at him. She did not look at the little girls as they strode past. She hoped he would be there tomorrow. She would explain her strange behaviour.

– That night, quite late, the mother came home. The girls came out of their bedroom.

– Guess what, O'Reilly, they said, together. – Alina has a boyfriend.

3

O'Reilly grabbed Alina's sleeve and pulled her into the kitchen. She shut the door with one of her heels. She grabbed a chair and made Alina sit. She stood impressively before Alina.

– So, she said. – Tell all.

Alina could not look at O'Reilly's face.

– It is, she said, – perhaps my private affair.

– Listen, babes, said O'Reilly. – Nothing is your private affair. Not while you're working here. Are you fucking this guy?

Alina felt herself burn. The crudity was like a slap across her face. She shook her head.

– Of course, said O'Reilly. – You're a good Catholic girl. It would be quaint, if I believed you.

O'Reilly put one foot on the chair beside Alina.

– I couldn't care less, she said. – Fuck away, girl. But with three provisos. Not while you're working. Not here, on the property. And not with Mister O'Reilly.

Shocked, appalled, close – she thought – to fainting, Alina looked up at O'Reilly. O'Reilly smiled down at her. Alina dropped her head and cried. O'Reilly smiled the more. She'd mistaken Alina's tears and gulps for gratitude. She patted Alina's head. She lifted Alina's blonde hair, held it, and let it drop.

Alina was going to murder the little girls. This she decided as she climbed the stair to her attic room. She closed the door. It had no lock. She sat on the bed, in the dark. She would poison them. She would drown them. She would put pillows on their faces, a pillow in each of her hands. She would lean down on the pillows until their struggles and kicking ceased. She picked up her own pillow. She put it to her face.

She would not, in actuality, kill the girls. She could not do such a thing – two such things. She would, however, frighten them. She would terrify them. She would plant nightmares that would lurk, prowl, rub their evil backs against the soft walls of their minds, all their lives, until they were two old ladies, lying side by side on their one big deathbed. She would – she knew the phrase – scare them shitless.

– Once upon a time, said Alina.

It was two days later. They sat in the playroom, in front of the bay window. The wind scratched the glass. They heard it also crying in the chimney. The baby lay asleep on Alina's lap. The little girls sat on the rug. They looked up at Alina.

– We're too old for *once upon a time*, said Ocean.

– Nobody is too old for *once upon a time*, said Alina.

The wind shrieked in the chimney. The girls edged closer to Alina's feet. Alina thought of her biochemist, out there mixing cement or cutting wood. She had not seen him since. She had pushed the pram past the shelter. Twice she had pushed; three times. He had not been there. She looked down at the girls. She resisted the urge to kick their little upturned faces. She smiled.

– Once upon a time, she said, again. – There was a very old and wicked lady. She lived in a dark forest.

– Where? said Ocean.

– In my country, said Alina.

– Is this just made up?

– Perhaps.

She stood up. It was a good time for an early interruption, she thought. She carried the baby to his pram, which was close to the door. She lowered him gently. He did not wake. She returned to her chair. She watched the girls watch her approach. She sat.

– From this dark forest the wicked lady emerged, every night. With her she brought a pram.

– Like Cillian's? said Saibhreas.

– Very like Cillian's, said Alina.

She looked at the pram.

– Exactly like Cillian's. Every night, the old lady pushed the pram to the village. Every night, she chose a baby. Every night, she stole the baby.

– From only one village?

– The dark forest was surrounded by villages. There were many babies to choose from. Every night, she pushed the pram back into the forest. It was a dark, dark shuddery place and nobody was brave enough to follow her. Not one soldier. Not one handsome young woodcutter. They all stopped at the edge of the forest. The wind in the branches made – their – flesh – creep. The branches stretched out and tried to tear their hearts from their chests.

The wind now shook the windows. A solitary can bounced down the street.

– Cool, said Ocean.

But the little girls moved in closer. They were now actually sitting on Alina's feet, one foot per girl.

– Every night, said Alina, – the wicked old lady came out of the forest. For many, many years.

– Did she take all the babies? asked Saibhreas.

– No, said Alina. – She did not.

Outside, a branch snapped, a car screeched.

– She took only one kind, said Alina.

– What kind? said Ocean.

– She took only – the girls.

4

– Why? Ocean asked.

– Why? Alina asked back.

– Why did the old lady take girls and not boys?

– They probably taste better, said Saibhreas.

– Yeah, Ocean agreed. – They'd taste nicer than boys, if they were cooked properly.

– And some girls are smaller, said Saibhreas. – So they'd fit in the oven.

– Unless the old lady had an Aga like ours, said Ocean. – Then boys would fit too.

Alina realised: she would have to work harder to scare these practical little girls.

– So, she said. – We return to the story.

The girls were again silent. They looked up at Alina. They waited for more frights.

– It is not to be thought, said Alina, – that the old lady simply *ate* the little girls.

– Cool.

– This was not so, said Alina.

– What did she do to them?

– You must be quiet, said Alina.

– Sorry, said both girls.

They were faultlessly polite.

Alina said nothing until she felt control of the story return to her. She could feel it: it was as if the little girls leaned forward and gently placed the story onto Alina's lap.

– So, she said. – To continue. There were none brave enough to follow the old lady into the dark forest. None of the mothers had a good night's sleep. They pinched themselves to stay awake. They lay on top of sharp stones. And the fathers slept standing up, at the doors of their houses, their axes in their hands, at the ready. And yet –

– She got past them, said Ocean. – I bet she did.

– Why didn't they have guns? said Saibhreas.

– Silence.

– Sorry.

– And yet, said Alina. – The old lady pushed the pram—

– Excuse me, Alina? said Saibhreas.

– Yes?

– You didn't tell us what she did with the babies.

– Besides eating them, said Ocean.

– You do not wish to hear this story?

– We do.

– And so, said Alina. – The old lady took all the baby girls. She carried every baby girl deep into the forest, in her pram. Until there were no more. Then she took the girls who were no longer babies.

Alina saw that Ocean was about to speak. But Saibhreas nudged her sister, warning her not to interrupt. Alina continued.

– She crept up to the girls in their beds and whispered a spell into their sleeping ears. The girls remained sleeping as she picked them up and placed them in the pram. She pushed the pram past the fathers who did not see her, past the mothers as they lay on stones. The wicked old lady took girls of all ages, up to the age of – ten.

Alina waited, as the little girls examined their arms and legs, wondering how the old lady had done this. She watched Ocean look at the pram. Above them, a crow perched on the chimneypot cawed down the chimney; its sharp beak seemed very close. The wind continued to shriek and groan.

– But, said Alina.

– She looked from girl to girl. Their mouths stayed closed. They were – Alina knew the phrase – putty in her hands.

– But, she said, again. – One day, a handsome woodcutter had an idea so brilliant, it lit his eyes like lamps at darkest midnight. This was the idea. Every woodcutter should cut a tree every day, starting at the edge of the forest. That way, the old witch's forest would soon be too small to remain her hiding place. Now, all the men in this part of my country were woodcutters. They all took up their axes and, day by day, cut down the trees.

– But, Alina, said Ocean. – Sorry for interrupting.

– Yes? said Alina.

– What would the woodcutters do afterwards, if they cut down all the trees?

– This did not concern them at that time, said Alina. – They cut, to save their daughters.

– Did the plan work?

– Yes, said Alina. – And no. I will tell.

She waited, then spoke.

– Every morning, and all day, the old lady heard the axes of the woodcutters. Every morning, the axes were a little louder, a little nearer. Soon, after many months, she could see the woodcutters through the remaining trees.

She looked down at Ocean.

– One night she left. She sneaked away, with her pram. So, yes, the plan worked. But—

Again, she waited. She looked across, at the pram.

– She simply moved to another place. She found new babies and new little girls, up to the age of – ten.

– Where? said Saibhreas.

– You have not guessed? said Alina.

She watched the little girls look at each other. Ocean began to speak.

– You forgot to tell us—

– I did not forget, said Alina. – You wish to know why she took the little girls.

– Yes, please, said Ocean.

– Their skin, said Alina.

She watched, as the goose-bumps rose on the arms and legs of the little girls in front of her.

5

It was dark outside, and dark too in the room. Alina stood up.

– But the story, said Ocean.

Alina went to the door and walked behind the pram. She pushed it slowly towards the girls. She let them see it grow out of the dark, like a whale rising from a black sea. She let them hear it creak and purr. She heard them shuffle backwards on their bottoms. Then she stopped. She stepped back to the door, and turned on the light.

She saw the girls squinting, looking at her from around the front of the pram.

– Tomorrow I will continue, said Alina.

They followed her into the kitchen. They stayed with her as she peeled the potatoes and carrots. They offered to help her. They washed and shook each lettuce leaf. They talked to fill the silence.

Alina left them in the kitchen, but they were right behind her. She went back to the sitting room, and stopped.

The pram had been moved. She had left it in the centre of the room, where the little girls had been sitting. But now it was at the window. The curtain was resting on the hood.

Alina heard the girls behind her.

– Did you move the pram? she asked.

– No, said Saibhreas.

– We've been with you all the time, said Ocean.

Alina walked over to the pram. She wasn't so very concerned about its mysterious change of position. In fact, she thought, it added to the drama of the interrupted story. The little girls lingered at the door. They would not enter the room.

Alina picked up the baby from the pram's warm bed. He still slept. O'Reilly would be annoyed.

– I pay you to keep him awake, she'd told Alina, once. – In this country, Alina, the babies sleep at night. Because the mummies have to get up in the morning to work, to pay the bloody childminders.

Alina walked out to the hall. She heard the car outside; she heard the change of gear. She saw the car lights push the colours from the stained-glass windows, across the ceiling. She felt the baby shift. She looked down, and saw him watch the coloured lights above him.

– Intelligent boy.

The engine stopped; the car lights died. Alina turned on the hall light. The little girls were right beside her.

– Your mother, I think, said Alina.

– Our dad, actually, said Ocean.

– How do you know this? Alina asked.

– Their Beemers, said Ocean. – Mum's Roadster has a quieter engine.

– It's the ultimate driving machine, said Saibhreas.

The lights were on, their daddy was home, and the little girls were no longer frightened. But Alina was satisfied. The lights could be turned off, and their fear could be turned back on – any time she wished to flick the switch.

She walked the next morning and thought about her story. She pushed the pram past the shelter and hoped to see her handsome biochemist. He was not there. She pushed into the wind and rain. Seawater jumped over the wall and drenched the promenade in front of her. She turned back; she could not go her usual, mandatory distance. She felt eyes stare – she felt their heat – watching her approach. But there was no one in front of her, and nothing. She was alone. She looked into the pram, but the baby slept. His eyes were firmly closed.

The little girls had their hair wrapped in towels when Alina continued her story that afternoon. They'd had showers when they came home from school, because they'd been so cold and wet.

Alina closed the curtains. She turned on only one small side-light.

The baby slept in the pram, beside Alina's chair.

– And so, said Alina.

She sat.

The little girls were at her feet, almost under the pram.

– Did the old witch come to Ireland? Ocean asked.

Alina nodded.

– To Dublin, she said.

– There are no forests in Dublin, Alina, said Saibhreas.

– There are many parks, said Alina.

– What park?

Alina held up her hands.

– I must continue.

– Sorry, Alina.

Alina measured the silence, then spoke.

– Soon, she said, – the squeak of the pram's wheels became a familiar and terrifying sound late at night as the old lady pushed it through the streets of this city. It was a very old pram, and rusty. And so it creaked and—

Beside them, the pram moved. It did not creak but it moved, very slightly.

The girls jumped.

Alina had not touched it.

The baby was waking. They heard a little cry.

Alina laughed.

– Strong boy, she said. – It was your brother.

Ocean stood up.

– Maybe O'Reilly's right, she said.

– Yes, said Saibhreas.

She crawled away from the pram.

– What did O'Reilly say? Alina asked.

– She said the pram was haunted.

Inside the pram, the baby began to howl.

6

Alina stared at the pram while, inside, the baby kicked and screeched.

– Aren't you going to pick him up? said Ocean.

– Of course, said Alina.

But, yet, she did not move. It was as if she'd woken up in a slightly different room. The angles weren't quite right. The baby's screech was wrong.

She stood up. She approached the rocking pram. The movement did her good. The room was just a room.

She looked into the pram. The baby was there, exactly as he should have been. He was angry, red, and rightly so. She had been silly; the little girls had frightened her.

She turned on the light and the pram was just a pram.

– The pram moved today, said Saibhreas.

She said this later, in the kitchen.

– I should hope so, said O'Reilly. – It's supposed to bloody move. I pay a Polish *cailín* to move it.

Alina blushed; her rage pushed at her skin. She hated this crude woman.

– It moved all by itself, said Ocean.

Alina stared down at her chicken. She felt something, under the table, brush against her leg. Mr O'Reilly's foot. He sat opposite Alina.

– Sorry, he said.

– Down, Fido, said O'Reilly.

She looked at Alina.

– Lock your door tonight, sweetie.

– I do not have a key, said Alina.

– Interesting, said O'Reilly. – What happened the pram?

– The baby cried, said Alina. – And so, the pram moved some centimetres.

– And why, asked O'Reilly, – did Cillian cry?

– O'Reilly? said Ocean.

– What?

– The pram moved before Cillian cried.

– Yes, said Saibhreas. – It's haunted, like you said.

Alina sat as the little girls told their mother about the wicked old lady and her pram full of kidnapped babies, and how the wicked old lady had pushed the pram all the way to Ireland.

– Enough, already, said O'Reilly.

She turned to Alina.

– That's some hardcore storytelling, Alina.

– She takes the skin off the babies, said Ocean.

– Who does? said O'Reilly. – Alina?

– No, said Saibhreas. – The old woman.

– My my, said O'Reilly. – And look at the fair Alina's skin. How red can red get?

Alina stared at the cold chicken on her plate. She felt the shock – O'Reilly's fingers on her cheek.

– Hot, said O'Reilly.

The little girls laughed.

– We'd better call a halt to the story, Alina, said O'Reilly. – It's getting under your skin.

The little girls laughed again.

The following morning, Alina pushed the pram along the promenade. She had not slept well. She had not slept at all. O'Reilly's fingers, Mr O'Reilly's foot – Alina had felt their presence all round her. She'd got up and torn a piece of paper from a notebook. She'd chewed the paper. Then she'd pushed the pulp into the keyhole of her bedroom door. She'd lain awake all night.

She walked. The wind was strong and pushed against the pram. It woke her up; it seemed to wash her skin. It was a warm wind. Gloves weren't necessary. But Alina wore her gloves.

The pram was haunted. O'Reilly had said so; she'd told her little daughters. Alina did not believe it. She knew her folklore. Prams did not haunt, and were never haunted. And yet, she did not wish to touch the pram. She did not want to see it move before her fingers reached it. She'd put on her gloves inside the house, before she'd lowered the baby into the pram. She did not want to touch it. Not even out here, in bright sunshine, away from walls and shadows.

The pram was not possessed. A dead rat could not bite, but Alina would wear gloves to pick one up. That was how it was with the pram. Today, it was a dead rat. Tomorrow, it would simply be a pram.

She took off one of her gloves. She stopped walking. The pram stayed still. Alina put her bare fingers on the handle. She waited. Nothing happened. She felt the wind rock the pram on its springs. But the pram did not move backwards or forwards.

She removed her other glove. She pushed the pram. She pushed it to the wooden bridge, and back. She would continue her story that afternoon, despite O'Reilly's command. She would plant the most appalling nightmares and leave the little imps in the hands of their foul mother.

And then she would leave.

She pushed the pram with her bare hands. But, all the time, and all the way, she felt she was being watched. She put the gloves back on. She was watched. She felt it – she *knew* it – on her face and neck, like damp fingers.

– One night, Alina said that afternoon, – the old lady left her lair in the park and made her way to a tree-lined street.

– Our street has trees, said Ocean.

Outside, the wind cracked a branch. The little girls moved closer to Alina.

7

Alina looked down at the little girls.

– The old lady crept along the tree-lined street, she said. – She hid behind the very expensive cars. The SUVs. This is what they are called?

The little girls nodded.

– And the Volvos, said Alina. – And – the Beemers.

Alina watched the little girls look at each other.

– She looked through windows where the velvet curtains had not yet been drawn.

Alina watched the girls look at the window. She had left the velvet curtains open.

She heard the gasp, and the scream.

– The curtains!

– I saw her!

Alina did not look. She leaned down and placed her hands beneath the little girls' chins.

– Through one such window, said Alina, – the old lady saw a bargain.

Alina held the chins. She forced the girls to look at her. She stretched her leg – she had earlier measured the distance from foot to pram – and raised her foot to the wheel.

– She saw *two* girls.

They heard the creak.

The little girls screamed. And so did Alina. She had not touched the wheel. The pram had moved before her foot had reached it.

Alina almost vomited. She felt the pancakes, the *nalesniki* she had earlier made and eaten, and the sour cream; she could taste them as they rushed up to her throat. Her eyes watered. She felt snails of cold sweat on her forehead. The little girls screamed. And Alina held their chins. She tightened her grip. She felt bone and shifting tongues. She could feel their screams in her hands. And the pram continued to move. Slowly, slowly, off the rug, across the wooden floor.

Alina held the faces.

– Two little girls, she said. – And, such was her wicked joy, she did not wait until they slept.

The pram crept on. It rolled nearer to the window. She heard the baby. She watched his waking rock the pram.

– The old lady found an open window, said Alina.

The baby screeched. And then other babies screeched. There was more than one baby in the pram.

The girls screamed, and urinated. And, still, Alina told her story.

– Through the window she slid. And through the house she sneaked.

The pram was at the window. The screeching shook the window glass.

– She found the girls quite easily.

The girls were squirming, trying to free their jaws from Alina's big fingers, and trying to escape from the wet rug beneath them. But Alina held them firm. She ignored their fingernails on her neck and cheeks.

– She had her sharp knife with her, said Alina. – She would cut the little girls. And she would take their skin, while their mother neglected them. Far, far away, in her Beemer.

But their mother wasn't far, far away in her Beemer. She was at the door, looking at her daughters and Alina.

– Hell-oh! she roared. – HELL-oh!

The pram stopped rocking. The little girls stopped screaming. And Alina stopped narrating.

O'Reilly stepped into the room. She turned on the light.

– She frightened us, said Ocean.

The girls escaped from Alina's grip. They shuffled backwards, off the rug.

– She hurt us, Mummy.

– We don't like her.

Alina took her hands down from her face. There was blood on her fingertips. She could feel the scratches, on her cheeks and neck.

She looked up.

The girls were gone; she could hear them on the stairs. She was alone with O'Reilly and the screaming baby. O'Reilly held the baby and made soft, soothing noises. She rocked the baby gently and walked in a small circle around the rug. The baby's screams soon lessened, and ceased. O'Reilly continued to make soft noises, and it was some time before Alina realised that, amid the kisses and whispers, O'Reilly was giving out to her.

– My fucking rug, she cooed. – Have you any idea how much it cost? There, there, good boy.

– I am sorry, said Alina.

– What the fuck were you doing, Alina?

Alina looked at the pram. It was against the wall, beside the window. It was not moving.

– The pram is haunted, said Alina.

– It's haunted because I said it's haunted, said O'Reilly. – I told the girls the bloody thing was haunted, to keep them away from the baby when he was born.

– But it *is* haunted, said Alina. – It has nothing to do with the lies you told your daughters.

– Excuse me?

– I saw it move, said Alina. – Here.

She stamped her foot. She stood up.

– Here, she said. – I saw. And I heard. More babies.

– Jesus, said O'Reilly. – The sooner you find a peasant or something to knock you up the better.

– I felt their eyes, said Alina.

– Enough, said O'Reilly.

– Many times, said Alina, – I have felt their eyes. I know now. There are babies in the pram.

– Look at me, Alina, said O'Reilly.

Alina looked.

– Are you listening? said O'Reilly.

– Yes, said Alina.

– You're sacked.

8

O'Reilly wondered if Alina had heard her. She was facing O'Reilly, but her eyes were huge and far away.

– Do you understand that, Alina?

– Yes.

– You're fired.

Alina nodded.

– As of now, said O'Reilly.

– Yes.

– You can stay the night, then off you fucking go.

– Yes.

– Stop saying yes, Alina, said O'Reilly.

But she wasn't looking at Alina now. She was searching for a phone number and balancing the baby on her shoulder as she walked over to the window and the pram.

– I'll have to stay home tomorrow, said O'Reilly. – So, fuck you, Alina, and life's complications.

She gently slid the baby from her shoulder and, her hands on his bum and little head, she lowered him into the cradle of the pram.

She heard the scream.

– No!

– Fuck off, Alina, said O'Reilly.

She didn't turn, or lift her face from the pram. She kissed the baby's forehead and loosely tucked the edges of his quilt beneath the mattress.

She stood up. She looked down at her son.

– There's only one baby in there, Alina.

She had the phone to her ear. She began to speak.

– Conor? she said. – It's O'Reilly. We have to cancel tomorrow's meeting. Yes. No. My Polish peasant. Yes; again. Yes. Yes. A fucking nightmare. You can? I'll suck your cock if you do. Cool. Talk to you.

O'Reilly brought the phone down from her ear at the same time that Alina brought the poker down on O'Reilly's head. The poker was decorative, and heavy. It had never been used, until now. The first blow was sufficient. O'Reilly collapsed with not much noise, and her blood joined the urine on the rug.

Mr O'Reilly was inserting his door-key into the lock when Alina opened the front door.

– Alina, he said. – Bringing Cillian for a stroll?

– Yes, she said.

– Excellent.

He helped her bring the pram down the granite steps.

– Is he well wrapped up in there? said Mr O'Reilly. – It's a horrible evening.

– Yes, said Alina.

– And yourself, he said. – Have you no coat?

He looked at her breasts, beneath her Skinni Fit T-shirt, and thought how much he'd like to see them when she returned after a good walk in the wind and rain.

Alina did not answer.

– I'll leave you to it, he said. – Where's O'Reilly?

– In the playroom, said Alina.

– Fine, said Mr O'Reilly. – See you when you get back.

Alina turned left, off her usual path, and brought the pram down a lane that ran behind the houses. It was dark there, and unpleasant. The ground wasn't properly paved or, if it was, the surface was lost under years of dead leaves, dumped rubbish and dog shit. But Alina stayed on the lane, away from streetlights and detection. She pushed straight into darkness and terror. She held her arms stiff, to keep the pram as far from her as possible. And, yet, she felt each shudder and jump, each one a screaming, shuddering baby.

At the end of the lane, another lane, behind the pub and Spar. Alina stayed in this lane, which brought her to another. And another. This last one was particularly dreadful. The ground was soft, and felt horribly warm at her ankles. She pushed hard, to the lane's end and fresh air. The sea was now in front of her. Alina couldn't hide.

She knew what she had to do.

But now she wasn't pushing. The wind shook the pram, filled the hood, and lifted it off the ground. She heard the cries – the pram landed on its wheels, just a few centimetres ahead, and continued on its course. Alina had to run behind it, pulling it back, as the infant ghosts, their murderers or demons – she did not know – perhaps their spirit parents, she did not know, as all of them tried to wrench the pram from her. She heard the wails, and under, through them all, she heard the cries of the baby, Cillian. Her adorable, intelligent Cillian. Now gone, murdered by the murdered infants.

She refused to feel the cold. She didn't pause to rub the rain from her eyes. She held onto the pram and its wailing evil, and she pulled and pushed the length of the promenade, a journey of two kilometres, to her goal, the wooden bridge, the bridge out to the strange island.

They found her in the sludge. She was standing up to her thighs in the ooze and seaweed. She was trying to push the pram still deeper into the mud. They found the baby – they found only one baby. The quilt had saved him. He lay on it, on top of the mud. The tide was out, but coming back. The water was starting to fill and swallow the quilt. They lifted the baby and the struggling woman onto the bridge. They left the pram in the rising water.

AN ATTACK OF HUNGER

Maeve Brennan

Mrs Derdon had the face of a woman who had a good deal to put up with. At this moment, she was in the kitchen, putting up with getting the tea ready for herself and her husband. Her husband's name was Hubert. She was putting up with setting out the two cups and the two plates and the two saucers and so on, two of everything. There was no need now to set the table for more than two people. The third place was empty, and the third face was missing. John, her son, had left the house and he would not be back, because he had vanished forever into the commonest crevasse in Irish family life – the priesthood. John had gone away to become a priest.

The thought that Mrs Derdon was not putting up with (because she had never faced it) was, Oh, if only Hubert had died, John would never have left me, never, never, never. He would never have left me alone. . . . But she was putting up with the secret presence of this thought in her spirit, where it lived hidden, nourishing itself on her energy and on her will and on her dwindling capacity for hope.

She had never made up her mind about anything. Decision was unknown to her. Her decisions, the decisions she made about the food she put on the table and about various matters about the house, were dictated by habit and by the amount of housekeeping money Hubert allowed her. Hubert was a frugal man. It was not that he meant to be unkind, but he was careful. He had calculated that the household could be run on such and such a sum, and that was the sum he produced every Friday morning. He always had it ready in his hand, counted out to the penny, when he came downstairs on his way to work. Every Friday morning she waited at the foot of the stairs and he handed her the money without a comment.

Before, when John was still at home, he would sometimes be there when Hubert gave her the money, and then the two of them, she and John, would exchange a look. On her part the look said, 'You see the way he treats me.' And John's look said, 'I see. I see.' They agreed that Hubert knew no better than to behave the way he behaved. This knowledge, that Hubert *knew no better*, formed the foundation and framework of the conspiracy between them that made their days so interesting and that gave a warm start to most of their conversations. They were always talking about Hubert. There was no need for Hubert to do anything unusual to get himself talked about – not that he ever did do anything unusual or out of the ordinary. All he had to do was go about in his habitual way, coming in after work and sitting down with the paper and then sitting down to his tea and going to bed and getting up in the morning and doing all the things he always did in his routine that never varied and that at the same time never became monotonous. There was something insistent about Hubert's daily procedure that called attention to itself, as though he was behaving as he did on purpose, and as though at any moment he might drop the charade and turn and show them the face they both suspected him of possessing, his true face, the face of a *villain*, the face of a man of violence, capable of saying and doing the most passionate and awful things, shocking things. He kept them in a constant state of suspense, and they were always exchanging looks when he was in the house, even when they only heard him walking about upstairs. But Hubert maintained his accustomed countenance, mild, amiable, complacent, burnished with his natural distrust of everyone and of every word anyone said, and held in firm focus by his consciousness of the worth of his own judgment.

Now, with John gone, there was no one for Mrs Derdon to exchange glances with. There was no one for her to look at, except Hubert, and Hubert could turn into a raving lunatic, frothing and cursing, and there would be no one to see him except herself. There was no one to look at her, and she felt that she had become invisible, and at the same time she felt that in her solitude she followed herself about the house all day, up and down stairs, and she could hardly bear to look in the mirror, because the face she saw there was not the one that was sympathetic to her but her own face, her own strong defenseless face, the face of one whose courage has long ago been petrified into mere endurance in the anguish of truly helpless self-pity. There was no hope for her. That is what she said to herself.

There was no hope for her inside the house. Her entire life was in the house. She only left it to do her shopping or to go to Mass. She went to the early Mass on Sundays (she and John had always gone together), and Hubert went to the late Mass by himself. It had been many years before John left since the three of them had gone for a walk together, and she and Hubert never went anywhere or visited anyone. He never brought anybody from the shop to his house, to spend an evening or to see the garden in the summertime or anything like that. From the time they were married, Hubert had shown that he distrusted her with money – he said she had no head for money – and as the years went by he had come to distrust her presence everywhere except in the house. In moments of nervousness – with the priests at John's school or at occasional gatherings they had attended in the early days of their marriage – Hubert had noticed that his wife turned into a different person. In the presence of strangers, she sometimes took to smiling. One minute she would produce a smile of trembling timidity, as though she had been told she would be beaten unless she looked pleasant, and then again, a minute later, there would be a grimace of absurd condescension on her face. And before anyone knew it, she would be standing or sitting in stony silence, without a word to say, causing everybody to look at her and wonder about her. And if she did speak, she would try to cover her country accent with a genteel enunciation, very precise and thin, that Hubert, from his observation of the world, knew to be vulgar. He felt it was better to leave her where she felt at ease, at home. Somehow she wasn't up to the mark. She wasn't able to learn how things were done or what to say. She had no self-confidence, and then, too, her feelings were very easily hurt. If you tried to tell her anything she took it as an insult. Hubert thought it was very hard for a man in his position to have to be ashamed of his wife, but there it was, he was ashamed of her. And he was sorry for her, because her failure was not her fault. She had been born the way she was. There was nothing to be done about it.

When Mrs Derdon turned away from the mirror that reflected her hopelessness, she saw the walls of her house, and its furniture, the pictures and chairs and the little rugs and ornaments, and the sight of all these things hurt her, because she had tried hard to keep the house as it had been when John left it, and the house was getting away from her and away from the way it had been when John lived in it, when she and John lived in it together. There seemed to be no way of controlling the change that was taking place in the house. Two of the cups from the good set had slipped out of her hands for no reason at all when she was taking them with the rest of the good china to wash, and now her arrangement of glass and china in the glass-fronted cupboard in the back sitting room looked incomplete. There was a big stain on one of the sofa cushions in the front sitting room and she did not know how it had got there. One of the children from the neighbouring houses threw a ball into the front garden and crippled a rose tree that had grown in safety for years there. She herself in a fit of despair removed a little pile of newspapers and magazines and pamphlets that John had left on his desk in his bedroom. She had not thrown them out, they were on the bottom shelf of the cupboard in the kitchen, but even if she carried them back up to his room they would not be exactly as he had left them, and they would never again look just as they had when he had last seen them. And she bitterly regretted pulling out the rusty little wad of newspaper that he had been accustomed to stuff underneath the door of his wardrobe to keep it tightly shut. She had thrown it into the fire and fitted a new bit of newspaper under the door. Nothing would ever be the same.

There were worn patches in the stair carpet that had appeared suddenly after all these years, and the wallpaper around the hall door had begun to peel badly and something would have to be done about it. Even the dust seemed to have found new places to settle, or to be settling in different places, and it seemed to her that in sweeping up the dust, day in and day out, all she was doing was sweeping up the time since John had left – more dust every day, more time every day – and she began to think that all she would do for the rest of her life was sweep up the time since John left. The dust got on her nerves. It made her feel sick to see the way it was there every day, new dust, but looking just as old and dirty as the old dust her mother used to be always sweeping up and throwing away, long ago in the country town where she had been born and brought up. As surely as the clock ticked and had to be wound up again, the dust made its way around the house, and it got on her hands. It got on her hands and on her wrists, and no matter how hard she scrubbed her nails, there always seemed to be some of it left there under her nails. She told herself that she had the hands of a servant. Hubert's hands were soft and neat, but hers were big and rough, as though she were a person who worked with her hands. She had often caught Hubert looking at her hands when she was dealing with the food on her plate and looking at her when she put food into her mouth. She always ate a lot of bread, and she thought he must sometimes wonder how she could eat so much bread or why she ate it so fast. She couldn't help it – she felt there was something shameful about eating so much of bread or of any food, but she wanted it and she ate it quickly and there were times when she felt her face getting red with defiance and longing when she reached for the loaf to cut another slice. One thing, she had stopped putting jam on the table since John left. She and John both loved jam, but Hubert had no taste for it at all. When John was at home, she used to make jam – raspberry, damson and gooseberry – but what they both liked best was the thick expensive jam that came in jars from England. It was best not to put the jar on the table. Hubert never questioned the expense, but he would sometimes take the jar in his hand and turn it around and read the label very slowly and then put the jar back again. Even if the jar was nearly full he would tip it and look into it. One time he had said, 'It's a good idea, having something to read on the table.' John had laughed out loud, and she had thought it heartless of him to laugh when he knew that his father was only looking for another way to make little of her.

Every day of the six months that had passed since John left to become a priest, Mrs Derdon realised that he was gone and that he was not coming back, and every day she thought she was only realising it for the first time. The realisation was alive and it possessed her completely and directed all her actions, one minute telling her to sit down and the next minute telling her to stand up immediately without delay and without reason – except that the power of the realisation was reason enough, because it directed her every minute now, and controlled her and kept her going and gave its own mysterious organisation to everything she did. If it had not been for this realisation, keeping at her all day, she would not have known what to do next and she would have done what she really wanted to do, which was to crawl in under the bed and put her face down on the floor and sleep. She kept wanting to lie down on the floor. The realisation that John was gone and would not be back took different shapes inside her, but it always stayed in the same place, just under her chest, in the centre, between her ribs. Sometimes it went away altogether and she felt empty, and then, at these moments, she would go and get herself something to eat, but almost always when she had the food before her, the realisation would come back again and she would feel sick at the thought of eating. At times the realisation would go away altogether, or seem to go away, and she would become terribly excited and run to the front windows knowing that John was coming home, that he was at this exact moment walking along the street carrying his suitcase, and that she would have to wait only a minute or so to get her first sight of him, coming around the corner from the main road. But of course he wasn't coming, and he wouldn't be coming, and the excitement inside her would flatten out and stupefy her with its weight, and her disappointment and humiliation at being made a fool of would be as cruel as though what she had felt had really been hope and not what it was, the delirium of loss.

Out of this recurrent delirium two daydreams had grown, long, peaceful, pleasant dreams, always expanding, always increasing in their progress and in their detail, alike in only two respects – in their soothing monotony and in their endings. Both dreams ended at the moment when John became her own again, only hers.

In the first dream, John came back. In this dream, she was watching for him at the front window, and when he turned the corner she went to open the front door for him, but then she wanted him to have his first glimpse of her framed in the window and she went back and stood in the window (holding the net curtain aside with her hand) until he saw her and smiled. When he got to the low gate that opened backwards into her tiny front garden, she hurried into the hall to open the front door wide so that he could walk straight in and put his suitcase down in the hall, to get rid of the weight of it – he had never been very strong. Then they would look at each other and she would say, 'I knew you'd be back, John.' Or she might put it this way: 'I knew you'd come back to me, John.' And he would say, 'You always knew what was best for me, Mother.' They would go down to the kitchen, where she would have the table set and ready, everything he liked on the table. He would eat something, and then he wouldn't be able to hold it in any longer, what was bothering him, and he would say, 'But Mother, didn't you mind when I went away? Didn't you miss me at all? You never said one word, not a word.' Those words would tell her what she wanted to know – that he had noticed her heroic silence, how she hadn't said a word when she realised he was going off and leaving her, how she had kept back all the reminders and reproaches that she had been longing to let loose at him, and that he understood how brave and unselfish she had been, letting him go off free as she had done. There would be no end to the amount they would have to say to each other, once that point in their reunion had been reached. They would drink an awful lot of tea. She would tell him that she had missed him terribly. She would say that she had been dead lonely, even crying with the need of him (she would remind him that his father wasn't much company), but that she had been only thinking of his own good, and only wanting the same thing that she had always wanted – what was best for him. And that she had never imagined not letting him go in peace, as long as his heart was set on it.

But it was all a dream. He wasn't coming back at all, and she bitterly regretted having let him go as easily as she had done. She had been so sure he would come back that she hadn't said a word, getting her sacrifice ready for him to admire. There were many things she could have said to him, the evening when he finally spoke to her, telling her that it was all settled and that his mind was made up and he was going. At that point, his mind wasn't made up at all. She could have stopped him with a word. She could have reminded him that he was an only child and that his duty was to his father and mother. And he had no faith at all in himself; it was only because of her prayers and encouragement that he had got through his examinations his last year in school. She had carried him all his life, and now he imagined he was going to be able to get along without her. And how did he think he was going to be able to get along in a house full of men – priests and students – all better ready for the priesthood than he was, and all better up on the world than he would ever be. They would look down on him. He would be very glad to get away out of that place and come back to her.

But he wasn't coming back, there was the realisation of that stirring in her again, and it would start giving her orders again, taking charge, and she would obey it, getting up and sitting down and walking here and there and never easy anywhere, because the only ease that could come to her would come if she could just get down on the floor and put her face in the corner and let her mind wander away into sleep, but into a different, roomy kind of sleep, very deep and distant, where there was no worry and where her mind would not be confined in dreams but could float and become vague and might even break free and sail off up like a child's balloon, taking her burden of memory with it.

There was not only nothing nice, there was nothing definite at all to remember, only a great many years that had passed along and were now finished, leaving only the remnants of themselves – herself, Hubert, the furniture; even the plants in the garden only seemed to hold their position in order to mark the shabbiness of time. All the things that she had collected together and arranged about the house could blow away, or fall into a pitiful heap, if it were not that the walls of the house were attached on both sides to the walls of the neighbouring houses. There was nothing in sight that rested her eyes and nothing in her mind except the realisation that John was gone, and the necessity of obeying the dictates of that realisation in order to continue, even for a little while longer, her flight from it. The realisation badgered her, and she had to obey it and at the same time pretend she didn't notice it. There was only one time of day when she ignored it, when it was weakest and she was strongest, when they first woke up in the morning, she and it, and it barely stirred, and what it told her then was that she should go back to sleep at once and not wake up at all. But she ignored it then, because it was a matter of pride with her to be up and dressed and downstairs before Hubert opened his eyes, and to have his breakfast ready and waiting for him and part of her housework done by the time he came down to the kitchen.

It was terrible having nobody to complain to; not that she had anything actual to complain about, but it was terrible having no one to talk to. John had always been a great confidant, and the Blessed Virgin had been a great consolation to Mrs Derdon all her life, the One she had always turned to for help and advice and understanding, but she could hardly turn to the Blessed Virgin now, when it was the Blessed

Virgin who had taken John away. It was not the Blessed Virgin herself
who had taken John away but his own devotion to the Blessed Virgin,
but it all amounted to the same thing in the end, and between the two
of them she felt she was left out and left behind.

John had always been a very holy little boy. He was always going
over his collection of holy pictures and sorting them out and looking
at the holy medals he had and strewing his little saints' relics all over
the house. He had a habit when he was small of wandering into the
kitchen with a holy picture in his hand and standing looking at it until
she asked him to tell her what he was thinking, and it was always some
holy thought, surprising in such a young child. Sometimes he would
prop a holy picture in front of his father's place at tea, prop it against
the sugar bowl or the milk jug so that his father would see it when he
was sitting down to the table. But Hubert put a stop to that one
evening by putting the holy picture – it was of St Sebastian being
tortured – on his bread and smoothing it with his knife as though it
were butter and then biting it. He tore off a corner of it, along with
some bread, and he sat there chewing it and smiling what he called his
happy-family-man smile. John cried, and Hubert pretended he didn't
know what he had done wrong, and she said, 'Hubert, I'm scandalised
at you.' Then she cried, too, because Hubert said, 'I'm fed up with the
two of you.'

The second dream she had of John was a very simple one. It was
more a vision than a daydream, and all that really happened in it was
that she saw his grave. In the second dream, he had not gone away at
all, he had died. It had not been his fault, after all. He had not wanted
to leave her. In the second dream she visited his grave every day, and
sat beside it for hours, and wore black, like a widow. When she cried,
everybody sympathised with her, because who has a better right to cry
than a woman who has lost her only son. Everyone marvelled at her
devotion when they saw her going to the grave every day, rain, hail,
sleet or snow, no matter how she felt, bringing flowers and leaves and
ferns according to the season of the year. She would mourn John
constantly, and even Hubert would hardly have the heart to reproach
her for her long face.

This evening, getting the tea for herself and Hubert, she was arranging
Christmas holly and ivy on John's grave when she heard Hubert's key

in the lock, and then the closing of the front door. Now Hubert would go into the back sitting room and light the fire there and sit beside it until she called him to tea. Sometimes she lighted the fire in the back sitting room and sat there herself. This afternoon she had hardly left the kitchen. They burned coal. They kept the coal and the firewood, together with her garden things, in a small wooden shed that was attached to the back of the house. Every day she carried in two scuttles of coal, one made of iron, for the kitchen stove, and one made of brass, for the sitting room. She sometimes wondered, when she lifted the coal, if Hubert had any idea how heavy it was. Now, crossing the kitchen to turn the gas from low to high under the kettle, she saw the brass scuttle standing alongside the stove, filled and ready. She had carried it in and then forgotten to carry it up to the sitting room. She was irritated with herself for forgetting to bring it up and leave it ready for him when he came in. It was a bad sign – to start to be forgetful, to start forgetting things that ought to be done. Well, she wouldn't give him the chance to come down and ask for it, or to watch her clamber with it up the three steps that led to the hall and the sitting room. He said his heart was bad and that that was why he couldn't do much of anything that would exert him. But it had been the same when he was forty and thirty and younger. He loved to be waited on.

She took the handle of the brass scuttle in both hands and carried it with difficulty across the kitchen and up the stairs and into the back sitting room. She found that Hubert had already put a match to the fire, which she had laid ready with paper and wood and a few bits of coal that she had dotted across the top of it. He was fanning the small blaze with his open newspaper, his evening paper. He turned when she came in, and the newspaper billowed towards the fire and then blazed up. Hubert dropped the newspaper in his fright. Mrs Derdon ran and got the poker and pushed the newspaper into the grate. Scraps of the blazing newspaper floated out and around the room. While she was stamping them out, Hubert raced off to the kitchen shouting, 'That's all right, that's all right. I'll get some water!' and then he came dashing in with the hot kettle that he had snatched off the stove and poured a stream of water all over the fireplace. The fire, already tamed, gave up at once and turned into black soup, which streamed out between the bars of the grate and down onto the tiles of the hearth, where it settled into puddles of various sizes and shapes.

Mrs Derdon sat down in a chair and began to cry helplessly. She hid her face behind her hands and then she pushed her hands into her hair and pushed her hair about and then she wrapped her arms about herself and rocked in grief. Disorder had finally prevailed against her, and there was nothing further she could do. She could kill herself over this room now and it would never look the same. This was the worst thing Hubert had ever done, and John had not been here to see it, and she would never be able to find the words to describe it to him. She glared at Hubert, who was watching her with dislike and alarm.

'Oh, what will I do!' she cried.

'Oh, for God's sake, pull yourself together,' Hubert cried. 'What ails you? No harm done.'

'What ails me?' she cried. 'It's what ails *you* coming in here and setting fire to the grate with nothing in it but paper. You couldn't come down to the kitchen and ask me for the coal. Oh, no, not you. You'll wait till it's brought up to you and burn down the house in the meantime.'

'You shut up!' Hubert shouted. 'Do you hear me? Shut up before I say something you won't want to hear.'

'First you drive my son out of the house and then you try to burn the place down around my ears, around my *ears!*' Mrs Derdon screamed.

'I suppose I should have tried to burn the place down while he was still in it!' Hubert shouted. 'It was you gave me a fright, clumping in here with your Mother of Mercy face and banging the coal down on the floor so that I dropped the paper. It was you did it, with your spite and your bad temper.'

She sat forward in her chair and spoke, but Hubert could not catch her words through the storm of hatred that blinded, deafened and choked her, and that shook her so that when she leaned forward to fling her accusations more heavily towards him, she tumbled out of her chair and onto her hands and knees on the floor. She dragged herself back up into the chair as though she were dragging herself up onto a rock out of the sea, and then she sent Hubert a look of terrified appeal that vanished at once under a witless, imploring, craven smile.

Hubert saw the smile and knew that she was silenced. 'Well, now you've made a proper fool of yourself,' he cried, 'falling and flopping all over the room and crying over a few spots on the linoleum!

Come on now and cheer up and stop making a show of yourself over nothing.'

'Over nothing is it!' she cried. 'If John was here, he'd tell you. John would stand up for me. John knew how hard I worked. Working and slaving to keep the place nice and you call it nothing. But what do you care! You never cared about me and you never cared about him and you ended up driving him out of the house.' She stopped because Hubert had leaned back in his chair and was smiling at her.

'I'm going to tell you something, Rose,' said Hubert. 'You won't like it, but I think it's time you learned. Do you know who really drove John out of the house?'

Mrs Derdon said nothing.

'Answer me,' said Hubert.

'I thought you did,' Mrs Derdon said.

'You thought what it suited you to think,' Hubert said. 'No, I didn't drive John out. We never got along, but that was because you made it your business to see that we didn't get along. You drove him out yourself,' Hubert said. 'It was to get away from you. That was all he wanted. You wouldn't even let him go to school by himself. He couldn't go on the tram by himself like the other boys until the priests told you to leave him alone. And when he went to work, you were down there at lunchtime half the time, weren't you? He got so that he was ashamed to be seen with you. A month before he left, he told me he was leaving, but he didn't tell you till the very last minute, because he knew you'd find some way to stop him, and he was bound and determined to go. How do you like that? Tell me, how do you like that little piece of information? He told me first.'

'If he got ashamed of me he got it from you,' Rose said.

'Oh, of course you'd have to say that,' said Hubert. 'Of course you can't face facts. But I've had to face facts. He was sick of you and I'm sick of you, sick of your long face and your moans and sighs – I wish you'd get out of the room, I wish you'd go, go on, go away. I don't want any tea. All I want is not to have to look at you any more this evening. Will you go?'

'Oh, I will,' Mrs Derdon said. 'I'll go. Indeed I will. Only to get away from you, that's all I ask.'

She hurried out into the hall. She felt very free. She felt very independent. In that untrammelled moment she surveyed herself in the hall mirror as she adjusted her hat and stuck her two mother-of-pearl hatpins through her thick, light brown hair. For the first time for many years she saw the colour of her own eyes. They were a clouded green, and as she stared at them she saw that they were filling up with tears.

Giving the hatpins a final push, buttoning her coat, taking her key to the front door out of her handbag and throwing it on the hall table, she saw that she was in terrible danger. She was in danger of hurling herself back into the room and throwing herself into the chair alongside Hubert and begging him to forgive her and to comfort her. She listened fearfully for the sound of her own running footsteps and for the sound of his voice, but there was only silence in the house, no sound at all. She had been in danger, but she had not given way, she had not moved. She turned off the light in the hall and also the light that shone over the front door, to show that she expected no welcome back, because she was not coming back, and she left the house. She was astonished; she felt an indulgent astonishment at her former anguish and helplessness and at the importance she had attached to the house and all its little furnishings, when all the time all she had ever really wanted was to run away as far as she could go. It had taken the awful things Hubert had said to make her see the true facts of the case. He had hunted her out of her own house. He must have been mad for a moment there, to say such things. His face had been very red. He had never been so angry before. But he had ordered her out. She had always felt responsible for the house. She had always thought he needed her there to take care of him. There were a lot of little things she did for him – waiting on him and seeing that things were as he liked them to be. He would miss her. But nobody could ever blame her for going, not after tonight. Nobody could ever accuse her of running away from her duty. And she could not blame herself, after what he had said to her, after the terrible things he had said. It showed the sort of man he was, that he would make up things like that. She would never give him away, she would never let out a word of what he had said, even to John. She would never tell anybody. She would try to forget it herself, but it was going to be difficult to forget a shock like that.

She reached the corner of her own street and began to hurry along Sandford Road. She began to consider what she was about to do. She would have to tell Father Carey that Hubert had driven her out of her home for no reason. She would tell him that she was afraid to go back there. What she had in mind was to borrow enough money from Father Carey to pay her way to where John was. She was sure that when the priest heard her story he would give her the money. She didn't know him well, she had only had the one talk with him, when John went away, but she had often attended his Mass and she was sure he would not refuse her. Once she saw John again and talked with him, she would be on sure ground. She would find some kind of work, maybe even in the seminary. Sewing, cooking, minding children, even ordinary housework, she would do anything, and when you came to think of it, there were a lot of things she could do. She had always wanted to be a nurse, when she was young. There might be some work to be found in a hospital. She would expect very little in the way of pay, only enough to keep body and soul together. She would do her work, she would go to Mass, she would pray, and that is all she would ask in exchange for the chance of seeing John once in a while. She would become friendly with all of John's friends. They would come to her with their troubles, and she would be the one who would know best how to talk to them. The priests in charge would wonder how they had ever got along without her. She was surprised that all this had not occurred to her before, and then she remembered that she could never have left the house if Hubert had not thrown her out. Now nobody could attach blame to her. She had done the only thing she could do. Some day she hoped Hubert would be ashamed of himself, but by then it would be too late. It was too late now. As long as she lived she would not be able to forget what he had said, or to remember exactly what it was he had said, only that it was the sort of thing people in their right minds didn't think of.

She was hurrying along Sandford Road in the direction of Eglinton Road, which led to Donnybrook and the church where John had been baptised and where they had all always gone to Mass. Sandford Road was always very busy, a main road out from town. On her side, on the side of the road where she was walking, the noisy trams went by her on their way out from town. The trams were nearly empty; the depot was not far away. The corner of the street where she lived was one of the last stops out from town. On the other side of Sandford Road, the trams passed on their way into town and they, too, were nearly empty. It was dark, except for the light from the street lamps and the occasional dim glare of light from the trams as they passed. It was the time of evening when nearly everybody was at home. A few men passed her, getting home from offices, and a few young girls. Boys and girls whirled by her on bicycles, not in crowds, as they would have been half an hour or an hour earlier, but in ones and twos. It had rained during the afternoon and the air was damp and cold, with a vigorous wind that she was grateful for because it seemed to wash her stiff face. The wind felt clean.

She crossed Sandford Road and stood on the corner where Eglinton Road runs in to Sandford Road. Eglinton Road was very wide, with big stone houses set back from the road and high up with stone steps in front of them. It was a residential road, quite well-to-do. There was no one on Eglinton Road, as far as she could see, and the way looked far and dark that she had to walk. She thought she had better sit down for a minute and collect her thoughts before she saw the priest. She wanted to tell him enough to convince him, but she did not want to tell him too much. She wanted to speak to him clearly and sensibly, so that he would respect her and give her the money. She wanted him to give her the money, but she wanted him to continue to regard her as an upright, dependable woman who had been driven to do what she had done. A few paces from the corner there was a wooden bench set alongside one of the heavy, big-branched trees that marked the length of Eglinton Road. This tree, the one nearest the bench, was so old and secure that some of its root lay coiled and twisted about it above the ground, making a rocky pediment on which John had often climbed when he was small, finding his way around the tree with his small hands against the trunk while she watched him from this bench. Although it could hardly have been the same bench. That was a long time ago.

She sat down and began to try to select and arrange the words that would best describe her plight to Father Carey and win his sympathy. There was what she had to tell him, about Hubert, and what she had to ask him for, the money, and her reason for having to ask for the money, to get to John. She started her appeal to the priest one way, and then she started it another way. She put in more and more details to make her story more persuasive, and then she took out some of the details. She couldn't make up her mind whether to end by asking for the money or to work the money in as she went along. The more she fumbled with the words, the more she became convinced that her story was lame and sounded suspicious. She hadn't the ability to describe the scene that had just taken place between her and Hubert. A person would have had to be there, to have heard it, to believe it, and if a person had been there the scene would not have occurred. She was going to go to Father Carey and make a show of herself, that was plain. He would never believe her. He would think she was making it all up, or that she was making an excuse of some little incident to spite her husband and get to her son. In either case, he would disapprove. He would tell her to go back to her husband. He would say, 'Mrs Derdon, you must return home at once. And you must on no account go near your son. If you interrupt your son's studies now, you may endanger his vocation.' She could hear the priest saying the same words over and over again, and she couldn't hear him saying anything else. It was no use. He would never give her the money. She would have to find the money somewhere else, and there was no other place to go. But it would be useless to go to Father Carey. Worse than useless, even. He might get out of his car and take her back to Hubert and make her go into the house. He might side with Hubert against her. It was more than likely that he would.

If John had happened along Eglinton Road at that moment he would have seen on his mother's face the fierce, cruel expression that they had both always thought belonged on his father's face. She looked capable of anything. She looked capable of murder, but she was only suffering what murderers suffer before they strike. But she would never strike. She was afraid. She thought it was pride that held her hand, but it was only fear. Fear and longing struggled for supremacy in her soul, but it was not their struggle against one another and against her that troubled her – it was her lifelong denial of herself, bolstered and fed as it was by fear. She longed to be near to someone, but there was no one who wanted her. She was sure of that. Nobody wanted her; it was her only certainty. It was bad that people turned their backs on her, but what was worse, worst of all, was that she saw no reason why they should not turn their backs on her. She was not surprised at the way her life had gone. She sat bewildered by her own judgement against herself, and unaware of it.

She felt cold. It was foolish to stay out in the air this time of year, this time of night. She put her hands inside the sleeves of her coat. She did not want to move just yet. She kept thinking that something wonderful might happen, and that if she stayed patiently where she was, somehow or another she would be able to get to where John was. If she fainted from the cold and from exposure, an ambulance would have to come and take her to the hospital, and if she was in there, sick in the hospital, surely they would see that there was great necessity for John to come home again.

She must have come this way, around this corner, thousands of times, and she looked curiously about, because she had almost never been here at night before. She looked at Sandford Road, where trams and cars and bicycles and people moved steadily, passing one another, and she gazed down Eglinton Road at all the lighted houses, as far as she could see. She seemed to be saluting what she looked at, but she was no longer thinking of where she was. She was thinking of the place where John was, and of the town where she had been brought up, and of the hospital that was not going to admit her, and she was seeing the future that had once lain before her, full of light, reflecting heaven, that was now opaque and blank like fear and reflected nothing.

She got up and started walking. When she got to the corner of her street she saw that the light over the front door was lighted, and the light in the hall was lighted, too, and all the lights in the front sitting room were on. As she unlatched the gate, the front door opened and Hubert peered out. He opened the door wide and she walked in past him and began taking off her hat and coat. He closed the door and followed her down to the kitchen.

'Rose, listen to me a minute,' Hubert said. 'I'm awful sorry about what I said to you. I don't know what got into me. I had no right to say what I said.'

'It doesn't matter,' she said.

'Oh, it does matter,' he said. 'Forgive and forget.'

'I'll forgive you because that's what John would want me to do. John would never want me to hold a grudge, and that's the reason I'll forgive you. But I didn't come back for his sake. I came back because it's my duty to stay here and keep your house.'

She was trying to keep her dignity, but her voice trembled and she was wearing the craven smile, but Hubert could not see that, because she was standing at the stove with her back to him, waiting for the kettle to boil.

'Have it your own way,' he said. 'Maybe some day your precious John'll have his own parish and you can go and keep house for him. Then you'll have him all to yourself. All to yourself. Maybe then you'll be satisfied.'

'The tea is ready now,' she said.

They had their tea in silence, and when he was finished Hubert left the kitchen and she heard him go along the hall and into the front sitting room. That meant he must have lighted a fire for himself there. She would have two grates to clean in the morning, and the back sitting room to do, if she could do it. She would not look at it until morning. The damage would all be very clear then. She poured herself another cup of tea. It was warm in the kitchen, and there was no hurry about clearing up. She didn't mind the thought of tomorrow as much as she might have. She kept going back to Hubert's remark about her keeping house for John. There was more in that remark than met the eye. Sometimes people said more than they meant to say. She wondered if Hubert had realised what he was saying. He had probably meant it for a sneer at John, at the idea that John would ever be given a parish. But why should John not be given a parish? It was very likely that he would get one, sooner or later. Of course it might be a long time, but she could wait. Her family was long-lived on her mother's side. If anything happened to Hubert, she could sell this house, keeping only enough of the furniture and other things to make John's new home look familiar to him. She would make a new cover for the armchair he always liked, and a new cover for the cushion that had the mysterious stain on it. She would manage his house for him. The first few days would be strange, but after that they would settle down as though they had never been apart. She would become known in his parish as a very holy woman, and everyone would look up to her. His vocation would be her vocation. Everybody would say what a devoted mother she was, an example to all. All the ladies would consider it a privilege to have tea with her, and she would invite some of them. She would wear only black. John and she would have a great deal to say to one another, there would be no end to their conversations. She saw quite clearly now that all this was going to happen. It might be thirty years before John got a parish, but then again it might not take anything like as long as that. Whenever it happened, she would be ready. She would always be ready to go to his side, whenever he needed her. All she had to do was wait. There was no doubt that what she foresaw would happen, and when the day came she would pack up, sell out and go straight to John, and after that it would be roses for the two of them all the way, roses, roses all the way.

SUMMER VOICES

John Banville

. . . Shalt thou hope. His truth shall compass thee with a shield. Thou shalt not be afraid of the terror of the night, of the arrow that flies in the day, of the business that walks in the dark, of invasion or of the noonday devil.

The old voice droned on, and the boy wondered at the words. He looked through the window at the countryside, the fields floating in the summer heat. On Hallowe'en people must stay indoors for fear of the devils that fly in the darkness. Once he had heard them crying, those dark spirits, and she said it was only the wind. But to think of the wind in the black trees out on the marsh was almost as bad as imagining devils. And late that night from the window of his bedroom he saw huge shadows of leaves dancing on the side of the house, and the circle of light from the street lamp shivering where it fell on the road.

– Are you going to ask her?

– What?

The little girl frowned at him and leaned close to his ear, her curls falling about her face. She whispered:

– Ssh, will you. Are you going to ask her can we go? He said seven days and the tide will be up in an hour. Go on and ask her.

He nodded.

– In a minute.

She stuck out her tongue at him. Through his crossed legs he touched his fists on the cool tiles of the floor. The old woman in the chair before him licked her thumb and turned a page of the black missal. The thin paper crackled and the ribbons stirred where they hung from the torn spine.

– I will deliver him and glorify him. I will fill him with length of days and I will show him my salvation.

She raised her eyes from the page and glared at them over the metal rims of her spectacles. Crossly she said:

– What are you two whispering about there?

– Tantey, can we go for a swim? the little girl cried and jumped to her feet. The old woman smiled and shook her head.

– O it's a swim is it? You'd rather be off swimming now than listening to the words of God.

– Ah but it's a lovely day, Tantey. Can we go, can we?

– I suppose so. But mind now and be careful. And you're not to stay out late.

She closed the missal and kissed reverently the tattered binding. Groaning, she pulled herself up from her chair and hobbled to the door. There she paused and turned, and said to the boy who still sat on the floor with his legs crossed:

– Mind what I say now. Be back here early.

When she was gone the girl went and sat in the armchair, and with her shoulders bent she mimicked the old woman, intoning:

– Achone achone the Lord and all his angels are coming to damn us all to hell.

– Ah stop that, said the boy.

– Nor you needn't be afeared of the devil in the day. Achone achone O.

– I told you to stop it.

– All right. All right. Don't be always bossing me around.

She made a face at him and tramped from the room, saying over her shoulder:

– I'm going to get the bikes and if you're not out before I count ten I'm going on my own.

The boy did not move. Sunlight fell through the tiny window above the stove. The radiance of the summer afternoon wove shadows about him. Beyond the window a dead tree stood like a crazy old naked man, a blackbird hopping among its twisted branches. The boy stood up and went into what had once been the farmyard – the barn and the sties had long since crumbled. After the dimness of the kitchen the light here burned his eyes. He moved across to stand under the elm tree and listen to the leaves. Out over the green fields the heat lay heavy, pale blue and shimmering. In the sky a bird circled slowly. He lifted his head and gazed into the thickness of the leaves. Light glinted gold through the branches. He stood motionless, his arms hanging at his sides, listening, and slowly, from the far fields, the strange cry floated to his ears, a needle of sound that pierced the stillness. He held his breath. The voice hung poised a moment in the upper airs, a single liquid note, then slowly faded back into the fields, and died away, leaving the silence deeper than before.

– Are you coming or are you just going to stand there all day?

He turned. The girl stood between the two ancient bicycles, a saddle held in each of her small hands.

– I'm coming, he grunted.

They mounted and rode slowly down to the gate, where he halted while the girl swung carelessly out into the road. When he was sure of safety he pedalled furiously after her.

– You'll get killed some day, he said when he was beside her again.

The girl turned up her nose and shook her hair in the warm wind.

– You're an awful scaredy cat, she said contemptuously.

– I just don't want to get run over, that's all.

– Hah.

She trod on the pedals and glided away from him. He watched her as she sailed along, her bony knees rising and falling. She took her hands from the handlebars and waved them in the air.

– You'll fall off, he shouted.

She glanced over her shoulder at him and pulled her hair above her head, and the long gold tresses coiled about her pale arms. Her teeth glinted as she laughed.

Free now, they slowed their pace and leisurely sailed over the road, tyres whispering in the soft tar. The fields trembled on either side of them. Sometimes the girl sang in her high-pitched, shaky voice, and the notes carried back to him, strangely muted by the wide fields, a distant, piping song. Tall shoots of vicious grass waving from the ditches scratched their legs. The boy watched the land as it moved slowly past him, the sweltering meadows, the motionless trees, and high up on the hill the cool deep shadows under Wild Wood.

– Listen, the girl said, allowing him to overtake her. Do you think they'll let us see him?

– I don't know.

– Jimmy would. He'd let me see him all right. But there's bound to be others.

She brooded, gazing at her feet circling under her.

– How do you know they'll find him? the boy asked.

– Jimmy said so.

– Jimmy.

– You shut up. You don't know anything about him.

– He's dirty, the boy said sullenly.

– You never saw him.

– I did.

– Well he's not dirty. And anyway I don't care. I'm in love with him, so there.

– He's dirty and he's old and he's mad, too.

– I don't care. I love him. I'd love him to kiss me.

She closed her eyes and puckered her lips at the sky. Suddenly she turned and pushed the boy violently, so that he almost lost his balance. She watched him try to control the wobbling wheels, and she screamed with laughter. Then she sailed ahead of him once again, crying:

– You're only jealous, you are.

The girl disappeared around a bend in the road, and he stepped down from the machine. He plodded scowling up the first steep slope of Slane Hill.

When he came round the bend he found the girl standing beside her bicycle waiting for him, her hands at her mouth.

– Listen, she said, and grasped his arm. There's somebody up there.

At the top of the hill a dark figure was huddled in the ditch at the side of the road.

– It's only a man, the boy said.

– I don't like the look of him.

– You're afraid.

– I am not. I just don't like the look of him.

– Not so brave now, the boy sneered.

– All right then, smartie. Come on.

They began the climb. Sweat gathered at the corners of their eyes and on their lips. Under their hands the rubber of the grips on the

handlebars grew moist and sticky. Flies came and buzzed about them.
They lowered their heads and pushed the awkward black machines to
the crest of the hill. Below them now was the sea, warm and blue and
glittering with flakes of silver light. A cool breeze came up over the
sandy fields, carrying a faint bitterness of salt against their mouths. A
stirring beside them in the ditch. A hoarse voice. Panic stabbed them.
They leaped into the saddles and careered off down the hill, while
behind them a ragged, strangely uncertain figure stood dark against
the sky, querulously calling.

The air whistled by their ears as they raced along the pitted road.
The sea was coming to meet them, the dunes rose up green and gold,
sea salt cutting their nostrils, the sun whirling like a rimless spoked
wheel of gold, sea and dunes rushing, then abruptly the road ended,
their tyres sank in the sand and they toppled from the saddles.

For a while they lay panting, and listened to the sea whispering
gently on the shore. Then the girl raised her head and looked back up
the hill.

– He's gone, she whispered hoarsely.

The boy sat up and rubbed his knee.

– I hurt myself.

– I said he's gone.

– Who is?

– The fellow up on the hill. He's gone.

The boy shaded his eyes and gazed back along the road. He pursed
his lips and murmured vaguely:

– O yes.

She caught his wrist in her bony fingers.

– Did you hear what he was shouting? Did you hear what he
called you?

– Me?

– He was shouting at you. He called you mister.

– Did he?

– Didn't you hear him?

He did not answer, but stood up and brushed the sand from his
faded cord trousers.

– Come on, he said, and grasping her hand he pulled her to her feet.
The tide is up. We'll leave the bikes here.

He walked away from her, limping slightly. She stared after him for a moment and then began to follow. She scowled at his back and cried:

– You're a right fool!

– Come on.

Through a gap in the dunes they passed down to the beach. The sea was quiet, a bowl of calm blue waters held in the arms of the horseshoe bay. Lines of sea-wrack scored the beach, evidence of the changing limits of the tide. They walked slowly towards the pier, a grey finger of stone accusing the ocean.

– I'd love a swim, the little girl said.

– Why didn't you bring your togs?

– I think I'll go in in my skin.

– You will not.

– If I met some fellow swimming underwater wouldn't he get a great shock?

Giggling, she tucked the hem of her dress into her knickers and waded into the sea. She splashed about, drenching herself. Her cries winged out over the water like small swift birds. The boy watched her, then he turned away and moved on again.

– Wait for me, she cried, and came thrashing out of the sea.

At the end of the pier a bent old man was sitting on a bollard, his back turned towards them. The girl ran ahead and began to dance excitedly around him. The boy came up and stopped behind the old man. He put his hands into his pockets and stared out to sea with studied indifference, softly whistling. A distant sail trembled on the horizon.

– And did your auntie let you go? the old man was asking of the girl, mocking her. He had a low, hoarse voice, and he spoke slowly, as though to hide an impediment.

– She did, the girl said, and laughed slyly. It was such a grand day.

– Aye, it's a great day.

He turned his head and considered the boy a moment.

– And who's this young fellow?

– That's my brother.

– Aye now? he said blankly.

He turned back to the sea, grinding his gums. The boy shifted from one foot to the other. For a while there was silence but for the faint crackling of the seaweed over on the beach. The old man spat noisily and said:

– Well, they've took him out anyway.

The girl's eyes flashed. She looked at her brother and winked.

– Did they? she said casually. Today, eh?

– Aye. Fished him out today. Didn't I tell them? Aye.

– What did they do with him, Jimmy? I suppose they took him away long ago.

– Not at all, said the old man. Sure it's no more than half an hour since he come in. Ah no. He's still down there.

He waved an arm towards the beach at his back.

– Did they just leave him there? asked the girl in surprise.

– Aye. They're gone off to get something to shift him in.

– I see.

She bit her lip, and leaned close to the old man's ear and whispered. He listened a moment, then turned and stared at her from one yellowed eye.

– What? What? You don't want to see a thing like that. Do you? What?

– We do. That's why we came. Isn't it?

She rammed her elbow into the boy's ribs.

– O yes, he said quickly. That's why we came.

The old man stared from one to the other, shook his head, then got to his feet, saying:

– Come on then, before your men come back. Begod, you're the strange ones then. Hah. Aren't you the strange ones? Heh heh.

They walked back along the pier, the girl rushing excitedly between the old man and the boy, urging them to hurry. When they reached the sand the old man led them down behind the sea wall. At the edge of the waves a bundle covered in an old piece of canvas lay in the shade of the pier. The girl rushed forward and knelt beside it in the sand. The old man cried:

– Wait there now, young one. Don't touch anything there.

The three of them stood in silence and gazed down at the object where it lay in the violet shade. Out on the rocks a seabird screeched. The old man leaned down and pulled away the canvas. The boy turned away his face, but not before he had glimpsed the creature, the twisted body, the ruined face, the soft, pale swollen flesh like the flesh of a rotted fish. The girl knelt and stared, her mouth open. She whispered:

– There he is, then.

– Aye, the old man muttered. That's what the sea will do to you. The sea and the rocks. And the fish too.

The boy stood with his back to them, looking at his hands. And then a shout came from far up the beach.

– Hi! Get them children away from there! Get out of it, you old fool!

The boy looked up along the sand. Figures were running towards them, waving their fists. The old man muttered a curse and hobbled away with surprising speed over the dunes. The girl leaped to her feet and was away beside the waves, her bare feet slapping the sand and raising splashes that flashed in the sun like sparks. The boy stood motionless, and listened to her wild laughter that floated back to him on the salt air. He knelt in the sand and looked down at the strange creature lying there. He spoke a few words quietly, a message, then with care he gently replaced the canvas shroud. Then he ran away up the beach after his sister, who was already out of sight.

Some time later he found her, sitting under a thorn tree in the fields behind the beach. She was rubbing the damp sand from her feet with a handful of grass. When she saw him she sniffed derisively and said:

– O, it's you.

He lay down in the warm grass at her side, panting. Bees hummed about him.

– Did they catch you? she asked.

– No.

– That's a wonder. I thought you were going to stand there all day.

The boy said nothing, and she went on:

– Jimmy was here a minute ago. He said I was a right little bitch getting him into trouble. He's worried as anything. That fellow's not a bit mad. Anyway, he's gone now. I don't care.

She looked down at him. He was chewing a blade of grass and staring into thorns above him. She poked him with her toe.

– Are you listening to me?

– No.

He stood up, and said:

– We'll have to go home. Tantey will be worried.

– Ah, sugar on Tantey.

They found their bicycles and started home through the glimmering evening. Clouds of midges rode with them. The tiny flies found a way into their hair and under their clothes. The girl cursed them and waved her hands about her head. The boy rode on without a word, his head bent.

The old woman was indeed angry with them.

– I warned you before you went, she said, and glared at them from her chair beside the stove. I warned you. Well now you can just hop it off to bed for yourselves. Go on.

– But what about our supper, Tantey?

– You'll have no supper tonight. Get on now.

– I'm tired, anyway, the girl said carelessly when they were climbing the stairs.

By the window on the first landing the boy stopped and looked out over the countryside down to the sea. The sun was setting blood-red over the bay. He stood and watched it until it fell into the sea. When it was long gone he heard the girl's voice calling plaintively from above.

– *Where are you? Where are you?*

He climbed to her room and stood at the end of the bed, looking down at her.

– I have a pain, she said, as she twisted fitfully among the rumpled sheets, her legs thrown wide, her hand clutching her stomach. He leaned his hands on the metal bedpost and watched her. As she twisted and turned she glanced at him now and then through half-closed eyes. After a moment he looked away from her, and with his lips pursed he considered the ceiling.

– Do you want to know something? he asked.

– What? O my stomach.

– You know that fellow today? The one that shouted at us on the hill? Do you know who he was?

She was quiet now. She lay on her back and stared at him, her eyes glittering.

– No. Who was he?

– He was the other fellow. The one that got drowned. That was him.

He turned to go and she leaped forward and clutched his hand.

– Don't leave me, she begged, her eyes wide. I'm frightened. You can sleep here. Look, here, you can sleep here with me. Please.

He took his hand from hers and went to the door.

– All right, the girl cried. Go on, then. I don't want you. You didn't need to be coaxed last night. Did you, mister? Ha ha. Mister.

He left the room and closed the door quietly behind him. Strange shapes before him in the shadows of the stairs. For a while he walked about the house, treading carefully on the ancient boards. All was quiet but for the small sounds of his sister's weeping. On the top landing a black square thing lay precariously balanced on the banister. Tantey's missal. As he passed he casually pushed it over the edge. The heavy book tumbled down the stairs, its pages fluttering.

He went into the bathroom and locked the door. On the handbasin he knelt and pushed open the small window of frosted glass set high in the wall. Darkness was approaching. Black clouds, their edges touched with red, were gathering out over the sea, and shadows were lowering on the ugly waters. A cold damp breath touched his face. In the distance a long peal of thunder rumbled. He closed the window and climbed down from the basin. He scrubbed his hands and dried them carefully, finger by finger. For a moment he was still, listening. No sounds. Then he went and stood before the mirror and gazed into it at his face for a long time.

SUMMER NIGHT

Elizabeth Bowen

As the sun set its light slowly melted the landscape, till everything was
made of fire and glass. Released from the glare of noon, the haycocks
now seemed to float on the aftergrass: their freshness penetrated the
air. In the not far distance hills with woods up their flanks lay in light
like hills in another world – it would be a pleasure of heaven to stand
up there, where no foot ever seemed to have trodden, on the spaces
between the woods soft as powder dusted over with gold. Against
those hills, the burning red rambler roses in cottage gardens along the
roadside looked earthy – they were too near the eye.

The road was in Ireland. The light, the air from the distance, the air
of evening rushed transversely through the open sides of the car. The
rims of the hood flapped, the hood's metal frame rattled as the tourer,
in great bounds of speed, held the road's darkening magnetic centre
streak. The big shabby family car was empty but for its small driver –
its emptiness seemed to levitate it – on its back seat a coat slithered
about, and a dressing-case bumped against the seat. The driver did not
relax her excited touch on the wheel: now and then while she drove she
turned one wrist over, to bring the watch worn on it into view, and she
gave the mileage marked on the yellow signposts a flying, jealous, half-
inadvertent look. She was driving parallel with the sunset: the sun
slowly went down on her right hand.

The hills flowed round till they lay ahead. Where the road bent for
its upward course through the pass she pulled up and lighted a
cigarette. With a snatch she untwisted her turban; she shook her hair

free and threw the scarf behind her into the back seat. The draught of the pass combed her hair into coarse strands as the car hummed up in second gear. Behind one brilliantly outlined crest the sun had now quite gone; on the steeps of bracken in the electric shadow, each frond stood out and climbing goats turned their heads. The car came up on a lorry, to hang on its tail, impatient, checked by turns of the road. At the first stretch the driver smote her palm on the horn and shot past and shot on ahead again.

The small woman drove with her chin up. Her existence was in her hands on the wheel and in the sole of the foot in which she felt through the sandal, the throbbing pressure of the accelerator. Her face, enlarged by blown-back hair, was as overbearingly blank as the face of a figure-head; her black eyebrows were ruled level, and her eyes, pupils dilated, did little more than reflect the slow burn of daylight along horizons, the luminous shades of the half-dark.

Clear of the pass, approaching the county town, the road widened and straightened between stone walls and burnished, showering beech. The walls broke up into gateways and hoardings and the suburbs began. People in modern building estate gardens let the car in a hurry through their unseeing look. The raised footpaths had margins of grass. White and grey rows of cottages under the pavement level let woodsmoke over their half-doors: women and old men sat outside the doors on boxes, looking down at their knees; here and there a bird sprang in a cage tacked to a wall. Children chasing balls over the roadway shot whooping right and left of the car. The refreshed town, unfolding streets to its centre, at this hour slowly heightened, cooled; streets and stones threw off a grey-pink glare, sultry lasting ghost of the high noon. In this dayless glare the girls in bright dresses, strolling, looked like colour photography.

Dark behind all the windows: not a light yet. The in-going perspective looked meaning, noble and wide. But everybody was elsewhere – the polished street was empty but cars packed both the kerbs under the trees. What was going on? The big tourer dribbled, slipped with animal nervousness between the static, locked cars each side of its way. The driver peered left and right with her face narrow, glanced from her wrist-watch to the clock in the tower, sucked her lip, manoeuvred for somewhere to pull in. The AA sign of the hotel hung out from under a balcony, over the steps. She edged in to where it said *Do Not Park*.

At the end of the hotel hall one electric light from the bar shone through a high-up panel: its yellow sifted on to the dusty desk and a moth could be seen on the glass pane. At the door end came in street daylight, to fall weakly on prints on the oiled walls, on the magenta announcement strip of a cinema, on the mahogany bench near the receptionist's office, on the hatstand with two forgotten hats. The woman who had come breathlessly up the steps felt in her face a wall of indifference. The impetuous click of her heeled sandals on the linoleum brought no one to the receptionist's desk, and the drone of two talkers in the bar behind the glass panel seemed, like the light, to be blotted up, word by word. The little woman attacked the desk with her knuckles. 'Is there nobody there – I say? Is there nobody *there*?'

'I am, I am. Wait now,' said the hotel woman, who came impassively through the door from the bar. She reached up a hand and fumbled the desk light on, and by this, with unwondering negligence, studied the customer – the childish, blown little woman with wing-like eyebrows and eyes still unfocused after the long road. The hotel woman, bust on the desk, looked down slowly at the bare legs, the crumple-hemmed linen coat. 'Can I do anything for you?' she said, when she had done.

'I want the telephone – want to put through a call!'

'You can of course,' said the unmoved hotel woman. 'Why not?' she added after consideration, handing across the keys of the telephone cabinet. The little woman made a slide for the cabinet: with her mouth to the mouthpiece, like a conspirator, she was urgently putting her number through. She came out then and ordered herself a drink.

'Is it long distance?'

'Mm-mm . . . What's on here? What are all those cars?'

'Oh, this evening's the dog racing.'

'Is it?'

'Yes, it's the dog racing. We'd a crowd in here, but they're all gone on now.'

'I wondered who they were,' said the little woman, her eyes on the cabinet, sipping at her drink.

'Yes, they're at the dog racing. There's a wonderful crowd. But I wouldn't care for it,' said the hotel woman, fastidiously puckering up her forehead. 'I went the one time, but it didn't fascinate me.'

The other forgot to answer. She turned away with her drink, sat down, put the glass beside her on the mahogany bench and began to chafe the calves of her bare legs as though they were stiff or cold. A man clasping sheets of unfurled newspaper pushed his way with his elbow through the door from the bar. 'What it says here,' he said, shaking the paper with both hands 'is identically what I've been telling you.'

'That proves nothing,' said the hotel woman. 'However, let it out of your hand.' She drew the sheets of the paper from him and began to fold them into a wad. Her eyes moved like beetles over a top line. 'That's an awful battle . . .'

'What battle?' exclaimed the little woman, stopping rubbing her legs but not looking up.

'An awful air battle. Destroying each other,' the woman added, with a stern and yet voluptuous sigh. 'Listen, would you like to wait in the lounge?'

'She'd be better there,' put in the man who had brought the paper. 'Better accommodation.' His eyes watered slightly in the electric light. The little woman, sitting upright abruptly, looked defiantly, as though for the first time, at the two watching her from the desk. 'Mr Donovan has great opinions,' said the hotel woman. 'Will you move yourself out of here?' she asked Mr Donovan. 'This is very confined – *There's* your call, now!'

But the stranger had packed herself into the telephone box like a conjuror's lady preparing to disappear. '*Hullo?*' she was saying 'Hullo! I want to speak to—'

'—You are,' the other voice cut in. 'All right? Anything wrong?'

Her face flushed all over. 'You sound nearer already! I've got to C—.' The easy calm voice said: 'Then you're coming along well.'

'Glad, are you?' she said, in a quiver.

'Don't take it too fast,' he said. 'It's a treacherous light. Be easy, there's a good girl.'

'You're a fine impatient man.' His end of the line was silent. She went on: 'I might stay here and go to the dog racing.'

'Oh, is that tonight?' He went on to say equably (having stopped, as she saw it, and shaken the ash off the tip of his cigarette), 'No, I shouldn't do that.'

'Darling . . .'

'Emma . . . How is the Major?'

'He's all right.' she said, rather defensively.

'I see,' he said. 'Everything quite OK?'

'In an hour, I'll be . . . where you live.'

'First gate on the left. Don't kill yourself, there's a good girl. Nothing's worth that. Remember we've got the night. By the way, where are you talking?'

'From the hotel.' She nursed the receiver up close to her face and made a sound into it. Cutting that off she said: 'Well, I'll hang up. I just . . .'

'Right,' he said – and hung up.

Robinson, having hung up the receiver, walked back from the hall to the living room where his two guests were. He still wore a smile. The deaf woman at the table by the window was pouring herself out another cup of tea. 'That will be very cold!' Robinson shouted – but she only replaced the cosy with a mysterious smile. 'Let her be,' said her brother. 'Let her alone!'

The room in this uphill house was still light: through the open window came in a smell of stocks from the flower beds in the lawn. The only darkness lay in a belt of beech trees at the other side of the main road. From the grate, from the coal of an unlit fire came the fume of a cigarette burning itself out. Robinson still could not help smiling: he reclaimed his glass from the mantelpiece and slumped back with it into his leather armchair in one of his loose, heavy, good-natured attitudes. But Justin Cavey, in the armchair opposite, still looked crucified at having the talk torn. 'Beastly,' he said, 'you've a beastly telephone.' Though he was in Robinson's house for the first time, his sense of attraction to people was marked, early, by just this intransigence and this fretfulness.

'It is and it's not,' said Robinson. That was that. 'Where had we got to?' he amiably asked.

The deaf woman, turning round from the window, gave the two men, or gave the air between them, a penetrating smile. Her brother, with a sort of lurch at his pocket, pulled out a new packet of cigarettes: ignoring Robinson's held-out cigarette case he frowned and split the cellophane with his thumbnail. But, as though his sister had put a hand on his shoulder, his tension could be almost seen to relax. The impersonal, patient look of the thinker appeared in his eyes, behind the spectacles. Justin was a city man, a black-coat, down here (where his

sister lived) on holiday. Other summer holidays before this he had
travelled in France, Germany, Italy: he disliked the chaotic 'scenery' of
his own land. He was down here with Queenie this summer only
because of the war, which had locked him in: duty seemed to him
better than failed pleasure. His father had been a doctor in this place;
now his sister lived on in two rooms in the square – for fear Justin
should not be comfortable she had taken a room for him at the hotel.
His holiday with his sister, his holiday in this underwater, weedy
region of memory, his holiday on which, almost every day, he had to
pass the doors of their old home, threatened Justin with a pressure he
could not bear. He had to share with Queenie, as he shared the dolls'
house meals cooked on the oil stove behind her sitting-room screen, the
solitary and almost fairylike world created by her deafness. Her
deafness broke down his only defence, talk. He was exposed to the
odd, immune, plumbing looks she was for ever passing over his face.
He could not deflect the tilted blue of her eyes. The things she said out
of nowhere, things with no surface context, were never quite off the
mark. She was not all solicitude; she loved to be teasing him.

In her middle-age Queenie was very pretty: her pointed face had the
colouring of an imperceptibly fading pink-and-white sweet pea. This
hot summer her artless dresses, with their little lace collars, were
mottled over with flowers, mauve and blue. Up the glaring main street
she carried a *poult-de-soie* parasol. Her rather dark first-floor rooms
faced north, over the square with its grass and lime trees: the crests of
great mountains showed above the opposite facades. She would slip in
and out on her own errands, as calm as a cat, and Justin, waiting for
her at one of her windows, would see her cross the square in the noon
sunshine with hands laced over her forehead into a sort of porch. The
little town, though strung on a through road, was an outpost under the
mountains: in its quick-talking, bitter society she enjoyed, to a degree
that surprised Justin, her privileged place. She was woman enough to
like to take the man Justin round with her and display him; they went
out to afternoon or to evening tea, and in those drawing rooms of
tinted lace and intently-staring family photographs, among octagonal
tables and painted cushions, Queenie, with her cotton gloves in her lap,
well knew how to contribute, while Justin talked, her airy, brilliant,
secretive smiling and looking on. For his part, he was man enough to
respond to being shown off – besides, he was eased by these breaks in

their tête-à-tête. Above all, he was glad, for these hours or two of chatter, not to have to face the screen of his own mind, on which the distortion of every one of his images, the war-broken towers of Europe, constantly stood. The immolation of what had been his own intensely had been made, he could only feel, without any choice of his. In the heart of the neutral Irishman indirect suffering pulled like a crooked knife. So he acquiesced to, and devoured, society: among the doctors, the solicitors, the auctioneers, the bank people of this little town he renewed old acquaintanceships and developed new. He was content to bloom, for this settled number of weeks – so unlike was this to his monkish life in the city – in a sort of tenebrous popularity. He attempted to check his solitary arrogance. His celibacy and his studentish manner could still, although he was past forty, make him acceptable as a young man. In the mornings he read late in his hotel bed; he got up to take his solitary walks; he returned to flick at his black shoes with Queenie's duster and set off with Queenie on their tea-table rounds. They had been introduced to Robinson, factory manager, in the hall of the house of the secretary of the tennis club.

Robinson did not frequent drawing rooms. He had come here only three years ago, and had at first been taken to be a bachelor – he was a married man living apart from his wife. The resentment occasioned by this discovery had been aggravated by Robinson's not noticing it: he worked at very high pressure in his factory office, and in his off times his high-powered car was to be seen streaking too gaily out of town. When he was met, his imperturbable male personality stood out to the women unpleasingly, and stood out most of all in that married society in which women aspire to break the male in a man. Husbands slipped him in for a drink when they were alone, or shut themselves up with him in the dining room. Justin had already sighted him in the hotel bar. When Robinson showed up, late, at the tennis club, his manner with women was easy and teasing, but abstract and perfectly automatic. From this had probably come the legend that he liked women 'only in one way'. From the first time Justin encountered Robinson, he had felt a sort of anxious, disturbed attraction to the big, fair, smiling, offhand, cold-minded man. He felt impelled by Robinson's unmoved physical presence into all sorts of aberrations of talk and mind; he committed, like someone waving an anxious flag, all sorts of absurdities, as though this type of creature had been a woman;

his talk became exaggeratedly cerebral, and he became prone, like a perverse person in love, to expose all his own piques, crotchets and weaknesses. One night in the hotel bar with Robinson he had talked until he burst into tears. Robinson had on him the touch of some foreign sun. The acquaintanceship – it could not be called more – was no more than an accident of this narrowed summer. For Justin it had taken the place of travel. The two men were so far off each other's beat that in a city they would certainly not have met.

Asked to drop in some evening or any evening, the Caveys had tonight taken Robinson at his word. Tonight, the night of the first visit, Justin's high, rather bleak forehead had flushed from the moment he rang the bell. With Queenie behind his shoulder, in muslin, he had flinched confronting the housekeeper. Queenie, like the rest of the town ladies, had done no more till now than go by Robinson's gate.

For her part, Queenie showed herself happy to penetrate into what she had called 'the china house'. On its knoll over the main road, just outside the town, Bellevue did look like china up on a mantelpiece – it was a compact, stucco house with mouldings, recently painted a light blue. From the lawn set with pampas and crescent-shaped flower beds the hum of Robinson's motor mower passed in summer over the sleepy town. And when winter denuded the trees round them the polished windows, glass porch and empty conservatory sent out, on mornings of frosty sunshine, a rather mischievous and uncaring flash. The almost sensuous cleanness of his dwelling was reproduced in the person of Robinson – about his ears, jaw, collar and close clipped nails. The approach the Caveys had walked up showed the broad, decided tyre-prints of his car.

'Where had we got to?' Robinson said again.

'I was saying we should have to find a new form.'

'Of course you were,' agreed Robinson. 'That was it.' He nodded over the top of Justin's head.

'A new form for thinking and feeling . . .'

'But one thinks what one happens to think, or feels what one happens to feel. That is as just so happens – I should have thought. One either does or one doesn't?'

'One doesn't!' cried Justin. 'That's what I've been getting at. For some time we have neither thought nor felt. Our faculties have slowed down without our knowing – they had stopped without our knowing!

We know now. Now that there's enough death to challenge being alive we're facing it that, anyhow, we don't live. We're confronted by the impossibility *of* living – unless we can break through to something else. There's been a stop in our senses and in our faculties that's made everything round us so much dead matter – and dead matter we couldn't even displace. We can no longer express ourselves: what we say doesn't even approximate to reality; it only approximates to what's been said. I say, this war's an awful illumination; it's destroyed our dark; we have to see where we are. Immobilised, God help us, and each so far apart that we can't even try to signal each other. And our currency's worthless – our "ideas", so on, so on. We've got to mint a new one. We've got to break through to the new form – it needs genius. We're precipitated, this moment, between genius and death. I tell you, we must have genius to live at all.'

'I am certainly dished, then,' said Robinson. He got up and looked for Justin's empty glass and took it to the sideboard where the decanters were.

'We have it!' cried Justin, smiting the arm of his chair. 'I salute your genius, Robinson, but I mistrust my own.'

'That's very nice of you,' said Robinson. 'I agree with you that this war makes one think. I was in the last, but I don't remember thinking: I suppose possibly one had no time. Of course, these days in business one comes up against this war the whole way through. And to tell you the truth,' said Robinson, turning round, 'I do like my off times to *be* my off times, because with this and then that they are precious few. So I don't really think as much as I might – though I see how one might always begin. You don't think thinking gets one a bit rattled?'

'I don't think!' said Justin violently.

'Well, you should know,' said Robinson, looking at his thumbnail. 'I should have thought you did. From the way you talk.'

'I couldn't think if I wanted: I've lost my motivation. I taste the dust in the street and I smell the limes in the square and I beat round inside this beastly shell of the past among images that all the more torment me as they lose any sense that they had. As for feeling—'

'You don't think you find it a bit slow here? Mind you, I haven't a word against this place but it's not a place I'd choose for an off time—'

'My dear Robinson,' Justin said, in a mincing, school-masterish tone, 'you seem blind to our exquisite sociabilities.'

'Pack of old cats,' said Robinson amiably.

'You suggest I should get away for a bit of fun?'

'Well, I did mean that.'

'I find my own fun,' said Justin, 'I'm torn, here, by every single pang of annihilation. But that's what I look for; that's what I want completed; that's the whole of what I want to embrace. On the far side of the nothing – my new form. Scrap "me"; scrap my wretched identity and you'll bring to the open some bud of life. I *not* "I" – I'd be the world . . . You're right: what you would call thinking does get me rattled. I only what you call think to excite myself. Take myself away, and I'd *think*. I might see; I might feel purely; I might even love—'

'Fine,' agreed Robinson, not quite easy. He paused and seemed to regard what Justin had just said – at the same time, he threw a glance of perceptible calculation at the electric clock on the mantelpiece. Justin halted and said: 'You give me too much to drink.'

'You feel this war may improve us?' said Robinson.

'What's love like?' Justin said suddenly.

Robinson paused for just less than a second in the act of lighting a cigarette. He uttered a shortish, temporising and, for him, unnaturally loud laugh.

Queenie felt the vibration and turned round, withdrawing her arm from the windowsill. She had been looking intently, between the clumps of pampas, down the lawn to the road: cyclists and walkers on their way into town kept passing Robinson's open gate. Across the road, above the demesne wall, the dark beeches let through glitters of sky, and the colour and scent of the mown lawn and the flowers seemed, by some increase of evening, lifted up to the senses as though a new current flowed underneath. Queenie saw with joy in her own mind what she could not from her place in the window see – the blue china house, with all its reflecting windows, perched on its knoll in the brilliant, fading air. They are too rare – visions of where we are.

When the shock of the laugh made her turn round, she still saw day in Robinson's picture frames and on the chromium fingers of the clock. She looked at Robinson's head, dropped back after the laugh on the leather scroll of his chair: her eyes went from him to Justin. 'Did you two not hit it off?'

Robinson laughed again, this time much more naturally: he emitted a sound like that from inside a furnace in which something is being consumed. Letting his head fall sideways towards Queenie, he seemed to invite her into his mood. 'The way things come out is sometimes funny,' he said to Justin, 'if you know what I mean.'

'No, I don't,' Justin said stonily.

'I bet your sister does.'

'You didn't know what I meant. Anything I may have said about your genius I do absolutely retract.'

'Look here, I'm sorry,' Robinson said, 'I probably took you up all wrong.'

'On the contrary: the mistake was mine.'

'You know, it's funny about your sister: I never can realise she can't hear. She seems so much one of the party. Would she be fond of children?'

'You mean, why did she not marry?'

'Good God, no – I only had an idea . . .'

Justin went on: 'There was some fellow once, but I never heard more of him. You'd have to be very oncoming, I daresay, to make any way with a deaf girl.'

'No, I meant my children,' said Robinson. He had got up, and he took from his mantelpiece two of the photographs in silver frames. With these he walked down the room to Queenie, who received them with her usual eagerness and immediately turned with them to the light. Justin saw his sister's profile bent forward in study and saw Robinson standing above her leaning against the window frame. When Robinson met an upward look from Queenie he nodded and touched himself on the chest. 'I can see that – aren't they very like you?' she said. He pointed to one picture then held up ten fingers, then to the other and held up eight. 'The fair little fellow's more like you, the bold one. The dark one has more the look of a girl – but he will grow up manly, I daresay . . .' With this she went back to the photographs: she did not seem anxious to give them up, and Robinson made no movement to take them from her – with Queenie the act of looking was always reflective and slow. To Justin the two silhouettes against the window looked wedded and welded by the dark. 'They are both against me,' Justin thought. 'She does not hear with her ears, he does not hear with his mind. No wonder they can communicate.'

'It's a wonder,' she said, 'that you have no little girl.'

Robinson went back for another photograph – but, standing still with a doubtful look at Queenie, he passed his hand, as though sadly expunging something, backwards and forwards across the glass. 'She's quite right; we did have a girl,' he said. 'But I don't know how to tell her the kid's dead.'

Sixty miles away, the Major was making his last round through the orchards before shutting up the house. By this time the bronze-green orchard dusk was intense; the clumped curves of the fruit were hardly to be distinguished among the leaves. The brilliance of evening, in which he had watched Emma driving away, was now gone from the sky. Now and then in the grass his foot knocked a dropped apple – he would sigh, stoop rather stiffly, pick up the apple, examine it with the pad of his thumb for bruises and slip it, tenderly as though it had been an egg, into a baggy pocket of his tweed coat. This was not a good apple year. There was something standardised, uncomplaining about the Major's movements – you saw a tall, unmilitary-looking man with a stoop and a thinnish, drooping moustache. He often wore a slight frown, of doubt or preoccupation. This frown had intensified in the last months.

As he approached the house he heard the wireless talking, and saw one lamp at the distant end of the drawing room where his aunt sat. At once, the picture broke up – she started, switched off the wireless and ran down the room to the window. You might have thought the room had burst into flames. 'Quick!' she cried. 'Oh, gracious, quick! – I believe it's the telephone.'

The telephone was at the other side of the house – before he got there he heard the bell ringing. He put his hands in his pockets to keep the apples from bumping as he legged it rapidly down the corridor. When he unhooked on his wife's voice he could not help saying haggardly: 'You all right?'

'Of course. I just thought I'd say goodnight.'

'That was nice of you,' he said, puzzled. 'How is the car running?'

'Like a bird,' she said in a singing voice. 'How are you all?'

'Well, I was just coming in; Aunt Fran's in the drawing room listening to something on the wireless, and I made the children turn in half an hour ago.'

'You'll go up to them?'

'Yes, I was just going.' For a moment they both paused on the line, then he said: 'Where have you got to now?'

'I'm at T— now, at the hotel in the square.'

'At T—? Aren't you taking it rather fast?'

'It's a lovely night; it's an empty road.'

'Don't be too hard on the car, she—'

'Oh, I know,' she said, in the singing voice again. 'At C— I did try to stop, but there was a terrible crowd there: dog racing. So I came on. Darling . . .?'

'Yes?'

'It's a lovely night, isn't it?'

'Yes, I was really quite sorry to come in. I shall shut up the house now, then go up to the children; then I expect I'll have a word or two with Aunt Fran.'

'I see. Well, I'd better be pushing on.'

'They'll be sitting up for you, won't they?'

'Surely,' said Emma quickly.

'Thank you for ringing up, dear: it was thoughtful of you.'

'I was thinking about you.'

He did not seem to hear this. 'Well, take care of yourself. Have a nice time.'

'Goodnight,' she said. But the Major had hung up.

In the drawing room Aunt Fran had not gone back to the wireless. Beside the evening fire lit for her age, she sat rigid, face turned to the door, plucking round and round the rings on her left hand. She wore a foulard dress, net jabot and boned-up collar, of the type ladies wear to dine in private hotels. In the lamplight her waxy features appeared blurred, even effaced. The drawing room held a crowd of chintz-covered chairs, inlaid tables and wool-worked stools; very little in it was antique, but nothing was strikingly up-to-date. There were cabinets of not rare china, and more blue-and-white plates, in metal clamps, hung in lines up the walls between watercolours. A vase of pink roses arranged by the governess already dropped petals on the piano. In one corner stood a harp with two broken strings – when a door slammed or one made a sudden movement this harp gave out a faint vibration or twang. The silence for miles around this obscure country house seemed to gather inside the folds of the curtains and to dilute the indoor air like a mist. This room Emma liked too little to touch already felt the touch of decay; it threw lifeless reflections into the two mirrors – the walls were green. Aunt Fran's body was stranded here like some object on the bed of a pool that has run dry. The magazine that she had been looking at had slipped from her lap to the black fur rug.

As her nephew appeared in the drawing-room door Aunt Fran fixed him urgently with her eyes. '*Nothing wrong*?'

'No, no – that was Emma.'

'What's happened?'

'Nothing. She rang up to say goodnight.'

'But she had said goodnight,' said Aunt Fran in her troubled way. 'She said goodnight to us when she was in the car. You remember, it was nearly night when she left. It seemed late to be starting to go so far. She had the whole afternoon, but she kept putting off, putting off. She seemed to me undecided up to the very last.'

The Major turned his back on his aunt and began to unload his pockets, carefully placing the apples, two by two, in a row along the chiffonier. 'Still, it's nice for her having this trip,' he said.

'There was a time in the afternoon,' said Aunt Fran, 'when I thought she was going to change her mind. However, she's there now – did you say?'

'Almost,' he said, 'not quite. Will you be all right if I go and shut up the house? And I said I would look in on the girls.'

'Suppose the telephone rings?'

'I don't think it will, again. The exchange will be closing, for one thing.'

'This afternoon,' said Aunt Fran, 'it rang four times.'

She heard him going from room to room, unfolding and barring the heavy shutters and barring and chaining the front door. She could begin to feel calmer now that the house was a fortress against the wakeful night. 'Hi!' she called, 'don't forget the window in here' – looking back over her shoulder into the muslin curtains that seemed to crepitate with dark air. So he came back, with his flat, unexpectant step. I'm not cold,' she said, 'but I don't like dark coming in.'

He shuttered the window. 'I'll be down in a minute.'

'Then we might sit together?'

'Yes, Aunt Fran: certainly.'

*

The children, who had been talking, dropped their voices when they heard their father's step on the stairs. Their two beds creaked as they straightened themselves and lay silent, in social, expectant attitudes. Their room smelled of toothpaste; the white presses blotted slowly into the white walls. The window was open, the blind up, so in here darkness was incomplete – obscured, the sepia picture of the Good Shepherd hung over the mantelpiece. 'It's all right,' they said, 'we are quite awake.' So the Major came round and halted between the two beds. 'Sit on mine,' said Di nonchalantly. 'It's my turn to have a person tonight.'

'Why did Mother ring up?' said Vivie, scrambling up on her pillow. 'Now how on earth did *you* know?'

'We knew by your voice – we couldn't hear what you said. We were only at the top of the stairs. Why did she?'

'To tell me to tell you to be good.'

'She's said that,' said Vivie, impatient. 'What did she say truly?'

'Just goodnight.'

'Oh. Is she there?'

'Where?'

'Where she said she was going to.'

'Not quite – nearly.'

'Goodness!' Di said; 'it seems years since she went.' The two children lay cryptic and still. Then Di went on: 'Do you know what Aunt Fran said because Mother went away without any stockings?'

'No,' said the Major, 'and never mind.'

'Oh, *I* don't mind,' Di said, 'I just heard.' 'And I heard,' said Vivie: she could be felt opening her eyes wide, and the Major could just see, on the pillow, an implacable miniature of his wife's face. Di went on: 'She's so frightened something will happen.'

'Aunt Fran is?'

'She's always frightened of that.'

'She is very fond of us all.'

'Oh,' burst out Vivie, 'but Mother likes things to happen. She was whistling all the time she was packing up. Can't *we* have a treat tomorrow?'

'Mother'll be back tomorrow.'

'But *can't* we have a treat?'

'We'll see; we'll ask Mother,' the Major said.

'Oh yes, but suppose she didn't come back?'

'Look, it's high time you two went to sleep.'

'We can't: we've got all sorts of ideas . . . *You* say something Daddy. Tell us something. Invent.'

'Say what?' said the Major.

'Oh goodness,' Vivie said, '*something*. What do you say to Mother?'

He went downstairs to Aunt Fran with their dissatisfied kisses stamped on his cheek. When he had gone Di fanned herself with the top of her sheet. 'What makes him so disappointed, do you know?'

'I know, he thinks about the war.'

But it was Di who, after the one question, unlocked all over and dropped plumb asleep. It was Vivie who, turning over and over, watched in the sky behind the cross of the window the tingling particles of the white dark, who heard the moth between the two window-sashes, who fancied she heard apples drop in the grass. One arbitrary line only divided this child from the animal: all her senses stood up, wanting to run the night. She swung her legs out of bed and pressed the soles of her feet on the cool floor. She got right up and stepped out of her nightdress and set out to walk the house in her skin. From each room she went into the human order seemed to have lapsed – discovered by sudden light, the chairs and tables seemed set round for a mouse's party on a gigantic scale. She stood for some time outside the drawing-room door and heard the unliving voices of the Major and aunt. She looked through the ajar door to the kitchen and saw a picked bone and a teapot upon the table and a maid lumped mute in a man's arms. She attempted the front door, but did not dare to touch the chain: she could not get out of the house. She returned to the schoolroom, drawing her brows together, and straddled the rocking horse they had not ridden for years. The furious bumping of the rockers woke the canaries under their cover: they set up a wiry springing in their cage. She dismounted, got out the box of chalks and began to tattoo her chest, belly and thighs with stars and snakes, red, yellow and blue. Then, taking the box of chalks with her, she went to her mother's room for a look in the long glass – in front of this she attempted to tattoo her behind. After this she bent right down and squinted, upside down between her legs, at the bedroom – the electric light over the dressing table poured into the vacantly upturned mirror and on to Emma's left-behind silver things. The anarchy she felt all through the house tonight made her, when she had danced in front of the long glass, climb up to dance on the big bed. The springs bounced her higher and higher; chalk-dust flew from her body on to the fleece of the blankets, on to the two cold pillows that she was trampling out of their place. The bed-castors lunged, under her springing, over the threadbare pink bridal carpet of Emma's room.

Attacked by the castors, the chandelier in the drawing room tinkled sharply over Aunt Fran's head.

She at once raised her eyes to the ceiling. 'Something has got in,' she said calmly – and, rising, made for the drawing-room door. By reflex, the Major rose to stop her: he sighed and put his weak whisky down. 'Never mind,' he said, 'Aunt Fran. It's probably nothing. I'll go.'

Whereupon, his Aunt Fran wheeled round on him with her elbows up like a bird's wings. Her wax features sprang into stony prominence. 'It's never me, never me, never me! Whatever *I* see, whatever I hear it's "nothing", though the house might fall down. You keep everything back from me. No one speaks the truth to me but the man on the wireless. Always things being said on the telephone, always things being moved about, always Emma off at the end of the house singing, always the children hiding away. I am never told, never told, never told. I get the one answer, "nothing". I am expected to wait here. No one comes near the drawing room. I am never allowed to go and see!'

'If that's how you feel,' he said, 'do certainly go.' He thought: it's all right, I locked the house.

So it was Aunt Fran's face, with the forehead lowered, that came by inches round Emma's door. She appeared to present her forehead as a sort of a buffer, obliquely looked from below it, did not speak. Her glance, arriving gradually at its object, took in the child and the whole room. Vivie paused on the bed, transfixed, breathless, her legs apart. Her heart thumped; her ears drummed; her cheeks burned. To break up the canny and comprehensive silence she said loudly: 'I am all over snakes.'

'So this is what . . .' Aunt Fran said. 'So this is what . . .'

'I'll get off this bed, if you don't like.'

'The bed you were born in,' said Aunt Fran.

Vivie did not know what to do; she jumped off the bed saying, 'No one told me not to.'

'Do you not know what is wicked?' said Aunt Fran – but with no more than estranged curiosity. She approached and began to try to straighten the bed, her unused hands making useless passes over the surface, brushing chalk-dust deeper into the fleece. All of a sudden, Vivie appeared to feel some majestic effluence from her aunt's person: she lagged round the bed to look at the stooping, set face, at the mouth held in a curve like a dead smile, at the veins in the downcast eyelids and the backs of the hands. Aunt Fran did not hurry her ceremonial fumbling; she seemed to exalt the moment that was so fully hers. She picked a pillow up by its frill and placed it high on the bolster.

'That's Mother's pillow,' said Vivie.

'Did you say your prayers tonight?'

'Oh, *yes*.'

'They didn't defend you. Better say them again. Kneel down and say to Our Lord—'

'In my skin?'

Aunt Fran looked directly at, then away from, Vivie's body, as though for the first time. She drew the eiderdown from the foot of the bed and made a half-blind sweep at Vivie with it, saying: 'Wrap up, wrap up.' 'Oh, they'll come off – my snakes!' said Vivie, backing away. But Aunt Fran, as though the child were on fire, put into motion an extraordinary strength – she rolled, pressed and pounded Vivie up in the eiderdown until only the prisoner's dark eyes, so like her mother's, were left free to move wildly outside the great sausage, of padded taffeta, pink.

Aunt Fran, embracing the sausage firmly, repeated: 'Now say to Our Lord—'

Shutting the door of her own bedroom, Aunt Fran felt her heart beat. The violence of the stranger within her ribs made her sit down on the ottoman – meanwhile, her little clock on the mantelpiece loudly and, it seemed to her, slowly ticked. Her window was shut, but the pressure of night silence made itself felt behind the blind, on the glass.

Round the room, on ledges and brackets, stood the fetishes she travelled through life with. They were mementoes – photos in little warped frames, musty, round straw boxes, china kittens, palm crosses, the three Japanese monkeys, *bambini*, a Lincoln Imp, a merry-thought pen-wiper, an ivory spinning-wheel from Cologne. From these objects the original virtue had by now almost evaporated. These gifts' givers, known on her lonely journey, were by now faint as their photographs:

she no longer knew, now, where anyone was. All the more, her nature clung to these objects that moved with her slowly towards the dark.

Her room, the room of a person tolerated, by now gave off the familiar smell of herself – the smell of the old. A little book wedged the mirror at the angle she liked. When she was into her ripplecloth dressing gown she brushed and plaited her hair and took out her teeth. She wound her clock and, with hand still trembling a little, lighted her own candle on the commode, then switched off her nephew's electric light. The room contracted round the crocus of flame as she knelt down slowly beside her bed – but while she said the Lord's Prayer she could not help listening, wondering what kept the Major so long downstairs. She never felt free to pray till she had heard the last door shut, till she could relax her watch on the house. She never could pray until they were *all* prostrate – loaned for at least some hours to innocence, sealed by the darkness over their lids.

Tonight she could not attempt to lift up her heart. She could, however, abase herself, and she abased herself for them all. The evil of the moment down in the drawing room, the moment when she had cried, 'It is never me!' clung like a smell to her, so closely that she had been eager to get her clothes off, and did not like, even now, to put her hands to her face.

Who shall be their judge? Not I.

The blood of the world is poisoned, feels Aunt Fran, with her forehead over the eiderdown. Not a pure drop comes out at any prick – yes, even the heroes shed black blood. The solitary watcher retreats step by step from his post – who shall stem the black tide coming in? There are no more children: the children are born knowing. The shadow rises up the cathedral tower, up the side of the pure hill. There is not even the past: our memories share with us the infected zone; not a memory does not lead up to this. Each moment is everywhere, it holds the war in its crystal; there is no elsewhere, no other place. Not a benediction falls on this apart house of the Major; the enemy is within it, creeping about. Each heart here falls to the enemy.

So this is what goes on . . .

Emma flying away – and not saying why, or where. And to wrap the burning child up did not put out the fire. You cannot look at the sky without seeing the shadow, the men destroying each other. What is the matter tonight – is there a battle? This is a threatened night.

Aunt Fran sags on her elbows; her knees push desperately in the woolly rug. She cannot even repent; she is capable of no act; she is undone. She gets up and eats a biscuit, and looks at the little painting of Mont Blanc on the little easel beside her clock. She still does not hear the Major come up to bed.

Queenie understood that the third child, the girl, was dead: she gave back the photograph rather quickly, as though unbearable sadness emanated from it. Justin, however, came down the room and looked at the photograph over Robinson's shoulder – at the rather vulgar, frank, blonde little face. He found it hard to believe that a child of Robinson's should have chosen the part of death. He then went back to the table and picked up, with a jerky effrontery, the photographs of the two little boys. 'Do they never come here?' he said. 'You have plenty of room for them.'

'I daresay they will; I mean to fix up something. Just now they're at Greystones,' Robinson said – he then looked quite openly at the clock.

'With their mother?' Justin said, in a harsh impertinent voice.

'Yes, with my wife.'

'So you keep up the two establishments?'

Even Robinson glanced at Justin with some surprise. 'If you call it that,' he said indifferently. 'I rather landed myself with this place, really – as a matter of fact, when I moved in it looked as though things might work out differently. First I stopped where you are, at the hotel, but I do like to have a place of my own. One feels freer, for one thing.'

'There's a lot in that,' said Justin, with an oblique smile. 'Our local ladies think you keep a Bluebeard's castle up here.'

'What, corpses?' Robinson said, surprised.

'Oh yes, they think you're the devil.'

'Who, me?' replied Robinson, busy replacing photographs on the mantelpiece. 'That's really very funny: I'd no idea. I suppose they may think I've been pretty slack – but I'm no good at teafights, as a matter of fact. But I can't see what else can be eating them. What ought I to do, then? Throw a party here? I will if your sister'll come and pour out tea – but I don't think I've really got enough chairs . . . I hope,' he added, looking at Queenie, '*she* doesn't think it's not all above board here?'

'You're forgetting again: she misses the talk, poor girl.'

'She doesn't look very worried.'

'I daresay she's seldom been happier. She's built up quite a romance about this house. She has a world to herself – I could envy her.'

Robinson contrived to give the impression that he did not wish to have Queenie discussed – partly because he owned her, he understood her, partly because he wished to discuss nothing: it really was time for his guests to go. Though he was back again in his armchair, regard for time appeared in his attitude. Justin could not fail to connect this with the telephone and the smile that had not completely died. It became clear, staringly clear, that throughout the evening his host had been no more than marking time. This made Justin say 'Yes,' (in a loud, pertinacious voice) 'this evening's been quite an event for us. Your house has more than its legend, Robinson; it has really remarkable character. However, all good things—' Stiff with anger, he stood up.

'Must you?' said Robinson, rising. 'I'm so sorry.'

Lighting-up time, fixed by Nature, had passed. The deaf woman, from her place in the window, had been watching lights of cars bend over the hill. Turning with the main road, that had passed the foot of the mountains, each car now drove a shaft of extreme brilliance through the dark below Robinson's pampas grass. Slipping, dropping with a rush past the gate, illuminating the dust on the opposite wall, car after car vanished after its light – there was suddenly quite a gust of them, as though the mountain country, before sleeping, had stood up and shaken them from its folds. The release of movement excited Queenie – that and the beat of light's wings on her face. She turned round very reluctantly as Justin approached and began to make signs to her.

'Why, does Mr Robinson want us to go?' she said.

'That's the last thing I want!' shouted Robinson.

('She can't hear you.')

'Christ . . .' said Robinson, rattled. He turned the lights on – the three, each with a different face of despair, looked at each other across the exposed room, across the tea tray on the circular table and the superb leather backs of the chairs. 'My brother thinks we've kept you too long,' she said – and as a lady she looked a little shaken, for the first time unsure of herself. Robinson would not for worlds have had this happen; he strode over and took and nursed her elbow, which tensed then relaxed gently inside the muslin sleeve. He saw, outdoors, his window cast on the pampas, saw the whole appearance of shattered night. She looked for reassurance into his face, and he saw the delicate lines in hers.

'And look how late it's got, Mr Robinson!'

'It's not that,' he said in his naturally low voice, 'But—'

A car pulled up at the gate. Alarmed by the lit window it cut its lights off and could be felt to crouch there, attentive, docile, cautious, waiting to turn in. 'Your friend is arriving,' Justin said.

On that last lap of her drive, the eighteen miles of flat road along the base of the mountains, the last tingling phase of darkness had settled down. Grassy sharpness passed from the mountains' outline, the patches of firs, the gleam of watery ditch. The west sky had gradually drunk its yellow and the ridged heights that towered over her right hand became immobile cataracts, sensed not seen. Animals rising out of the ditches turned to Emma's headlamps green lamp-eyes. She felt the shudder of night, the contracting bodies of things. The quick air sang in her ears; she drove very fast. At the crossroads above Robinson's town she pulled round in a wide swerve: she saw the lemon lights of the town strung along under the black trees, the pavements and the pale, humble houses below her in a faint, mysterious glare as she slipped down the funnel of hill to Robinson's gate. (The first white gate on the left, you cannot miss it, he'd said.) From the road she peered up the lawn and saw, between pampas-tufts, three people upright in his lit room. So she pulled up and switched her lights and her engine off and sat crouching in her crouching car in the dark – night began to creep up her bare legs. Now the glass porch sprang into prominence like a lantern – she saw people stiffly saying goodbye. Down the drive came a man and woman almost in flight; not addressing each other, not looking back – putting the back of a fist to her mouth quickly Emma checked the uprush of an uncertain laugh. She marked a lag in the steps – turning their heads quickly the man and woman looked with involuntary straightness into the car, while her eyes were glued to their silhouettes. The two turned down to the town and she turned in at the gate.

Farouche, with her tentative little swagger and childish, pleading air of delinquency, Emma came to a halt in Robinson's living room. He had pulled down the blind. She kept recoiling and blinking and drawing her fingers over her eyes, till Robinson turned off the top light. 'Is that that?' there was only the reading lamp.

She rested her shoulder below his and grappled their enlaced fingers closer together as though trying to draw calmness from him. Standing against him, close up under his height, she held her head up and began to look round the room. 'You're whistling something,' she said, after a moment or two.

'I only mean, take your time.'

'Why, am I nervous?' she said.

'Darling, you're like a bat in out of the night. I told you not to come along too fast.'

'I see now, I came too early,' she said. 'Why didn't you tell me you had a party? Who were they? What were they doing here?'

'Oh, they're just people in this place. He's a bit screwy and she's deaf, but I like them, as a matter of fact.'

'They're mackintoshy sort of people,' she said. 'But I always thought you lived all alone . . . Is there anyone else in the house now?'

'Not a mouse,' said Robinson, without change of expression. My housekeeper's gone off for the night.'

'I see,' said Emma. 'Will you give me a drink?'

She sat down where Justin had just been sitting, and, bending forward with a tremulous frown, began to brush ash from her arm of the chair. You could feel the whole of her hesitate. Robinson, without hesitation, came and sat easily on the arm of the chair from which she had brushed the ash. 'It's sometimes funny,' he said, 'when people drop in like that. "My God," I thought when I saw them, "what an evening to choose." ' He slipped his hand down between the brown velvet cushion and Emma's spine, then spread the broad of his hand against the small of her back. Looking kindly down at her closed eyelids he went on: 'However, it all went off all right. Oh, and there's one thing I'd like to tell you – that chap called me a genius.'

'How would he know?' said Emma, opening her eyes.

'We never got that clear. I was rather out of my depth. His sister was deaf . . .' here Robinson paused, bent down and passed his lips absently over Emma's forehead. 'Or did I tell you that?'

'Yes, you told me that . . . Is it true that this house is blue?'

'You'll see tomorrow.'

'There'll hardly be time, darling; I shall hardly see this house in the daylight. I must go on to – where I'm supposed to be.'

'At any rate, I'm glad that was all OK. They're not on the telephone, where you're going?'

'No, it's all right; they're not on the telephone . . . *You'll* have to think of something that went wrong with my car.'

'That will keep,' said Robinson. 'Here you are.'

'Yes, here I am.' She added: 'The night was lovely,' speaking more sadly than she knew. Yes, here she was, being settled down to as calmly as he might settle down to a meal. Her naïvety as a lover . . . She could not have said, for instance, how much the authoritative male room – the electric clock, the sideboard, the unlit grate, the cold of the leather chairs – put, at every moment when he did not touch her, a gulf between her and him. She turned her head to the window. 'I smell flowers.'

'Yes, I've got three flower beds.'

'Darling, for a minute could we go out?'

She moved from his touch and picked up Queenie's tea tray and asked if she could put it somewhere else. Holding the tray (and given countenance by it) she halted in front of the photographs. 'Oh . . .' she said. 'Yes. Why?' 'I wish in a way you hadn't got any children.' 'I don't see why I shouldn't have: you have.'

'Yes, I . . . But Vivie and Di are not so much *like* children—'

'If they're like you,' he said, 'those two will be having a high old time, with the cat away—'

'Oh darling, I'm not the cat.'

In the kitchen (to put the tray down) she looked round: it shone with tiling and chromium and there seemed to be switches in every place. 'What a whole lot of gadgets you have,' she said. 'Look at all those electric . . .' 'Yes I like them.' 'They must cost a lot of money. My kitchen's all over blacklead and smoke and hooks. My cook would hate a kitchen like this.'

'I always forget that you have a cook.' He picked up an electric torch and they went out. Going along the side of the house, Robinson played a mouse of light on the wall. 'Look, really blue.' But she only looked absently. 'Yes – but have I been wrong to come?' He led her off the gravel on to the lawn, till they reached the edge of a bed of stocks. Then he firmly said: 'That's for you to say, my dear girl.'

'I know it's hardly a question – I hardly know you, do I?'

'We'll be getting to know each other,' said Robinson.

After a minute she let go of his hand and knelt down abruptly beside the flowers: she made movements like scooping the scent up and laving her face in it – he, meanwhile, lighted a cigarette and stood looking down. 'I'm glad you like my garden,' he said. 'You feel like getting fond of the place?'

'You say you forget that I have a cook.'

'Look, sweet, if you can't get that off your mind you'd better get in your car and go straight home . . . But you will.'

'Aunt Fran's so old, too old; it's not nice. And the Major keeps thinking about the war. And the children don't think I am good; I regret that.'

'You have got a nerve,' he said, 'but I love that. You're with me. Aren't you with me? – Come out of that flower bed.'

They walked to the brow of the lawn; the soft feather-plumes of the pampas rose up a little over her head as she stood by him overlooking the road. She shivered. 'What are all those trees?' 'The demesne – I know they burnt down the castle years ago. The demesne's great for couples.' 'What's in there?' 'Nothing, I don't think; just the ruin, a lake . . .'

'I wish—'

'Now, what?'

'I wish we had more time.'

'Yes: we don't want to stay out all night.'

So taught, she smothered the last of her little wishes for consolation. Her shyness of further words between them became extreme; she was becoming frightened of Robinson's stern, experienced delicacy on the subject of love. Her adventure became the quiet practice with him. The adventure (even, the pilgrimage) died at its root, in the childish part of her mind. When he had headed her off the cytherean terrain – the leaf-drowned castle ruin, the lake – she thought for a minute he had broken her heart, and she knew now he had broken her fairy tale. He seemed content – having lit a new cigarette – to wait about in his garden for a few minutes longer: not poetry but a sort of tactile wisdom came from the firmness, lawn, under their feet. The white gateposts, the boles of beeches above the dust-whitened wall were just seen in reflected light from the town. There was no moon, but dry, tense, translucent darkness: no dew fell.

*

Justin went with his sister to her door in the square. Quickly, and in their necessary silence, they crossed the grass under the limes. Here a dark window reflected one of the few lamps, there a shadow crossed a lit blind, and voices of people moving under the trees made a reverberation in the box of the square. Queenie let herself in; Justin heard the heavy front door drag shut slowly across the mat. She had not expected him to come in, and he did not know if she shared his feeling of dissonance, or if she recoiled from shock, or if she were shocked at all. Quitting the square at once, he took the direct way to his hotel in the main street. He went in at the side door, past the bar in which he so often encountered Robinson.

In his small, harsh room he looked first at his bed. He looked, as though out of a pit of sickness, at his stack of books on the mantelpiece. He writhed his head round sharply, threw off his coat and began to unknot his tie. Meanwhile he beat round, in the hot light, for some crack of outlet from his constriction. It was at his dressing table, for he had no other, that he began and ended his letter to Robinson: the mirror screwed to the dressing table constituted a witness to this task – whenever his look charged up it met his own reared head, the flush heightening on the bridge of the nose and forehead, the neck from which, as though for an execution, the collar had been taken away.

My dear Robinson: Our departure from your house (Bellevue, I think?) tonight was so awkwardly late, and at the last so hurried, that I had inadequate time in which to thank you for your hospitality to my sister and to myself. That we exacted this hospitality does not make its merit, on your part, less. Given the inconvenience we so clearly caused you, your forbearance with us was past praise. So much so that (as you may be glad to hear) my sister does not appear to realise how very greatly we were *de trop*. In my own case – which is just – the same cannot be said. I am conscious that, in spite of her disability, she did at least prove a less wearisome guest than I.

My speculations and queries must, to your mind, equally seem absurd. This evening's fiasco has been definitive: I think it better our acquaintance should close. You will find it in line with my usual awkwardness that I should choose to state this decision of mine at all. Your indifference to the matter I cannot doubt. My own lack of indifference must make its last weak exhibition in this letter – in which, if you have fine enough nostrils (which I doubt) every sentence will almost certainly stink. In attempting to know you I have attempted to enter, and to comport myself in, what might be called an area under your jurisdiction. If my inefficacies appeared to you ludicrous, my curiosities (as in one special instance tonight) appeared more – revolting. I could gauge (even before the postscript outside your gate) how profoundly I had offended you. Had we either of us been gentlemen, the incident might have passed off with less harm.

My attempts to know you I have disposed of already. My wish that you should know me has been, from the first, ill found. You showed yourself party to it in no sense, and the trick I played on myself I need not discuss. I acted and spoke (with regard to you) upon assumptions you were not prepared to warrant. You cannot fail to misunderstand what I mean when I say that a year ago this might not have happened to me. But – the assumptions on which I acted, Robinson, are becoming more general in a driven world than you yet (or may ever) know. The extremity to which we are each driven must be the warrant for what we do and say.

My extraordinary divagation towards you might be said to be, I suppose, an accident of this summer. But there are no accidents. I have the fine (yes) fine mind's love of the fine plume, and I meet no fine plumes down my own narrow street. Also, in this place (birthplace) you interposed your solidity between me and what might have been the full effects of an exacerbating return. In fact, you had come to constitute for me a very genuine holiday. As things are, my five remaining days here will have to be seen out. I shall hope not to meet you, but must fear much of the trap-like size of this town. (You need not, as I mean to, avoid the hotel bar.) Should I, however, fail to avoid you, I shall again, I suppose, have to owe much, owe any face I keep, to your never-failing imperviousness. Understand that it will be against my wish that I re-open this one-sided account.

I wish you goodnight. Delicacy does not deter me from adding that I feel my good wish to be superfluous. I imagine that, incapable of being haunted, you are incapable of being added to.

Tomorrow (I understand) you will feel fine, but you will not know any more about love. If the being outside your gate came with a question, it is possible that she should have come to me. If I had even seen her she might not go on rending my heart. As it is, as you are, I perhaps denounce you as much on her behalf as my own. Not trying to understand, you at least cannot misunderstand the mood and hour in which I write. As regards my sister, please do not discontinue what has been your even kindness to her: she might be perplexed. She has nothing to fear, I think.

Accept, my dear Robinson (without irony) my kind regards,

J. C.

Justin, trembling, smote a stamp on this letter. Going down as he was, in the hall he unhooked his mackintosh and put it over his shirt. It was well past midnight; the street, empty, lay in dusty reaches under the few lamps. Between the shutters his step raised an echo; the cold of the mountains had come down; two cats in his path unclinched and shot off into the dark. On his way to the letterbox he was walking towards Bellevue; on his way back he still heard the drunken woman sobbing against the telegraph pole. The box would not be cleared till tomorrow noon.

Queenie forgot Justin till next day. The house in which her rooms were was so familiar that she went upstairs without a pause in the dark. Crossing her sitting room she smelled oil from the cooker behind the screen: she went through an arch to the cubicle where she slept. She was happy. Inside her sphere of silence that not a word clouded, the spectacle of the evening at Bellevue reigned. Contemplative, wishless, almost without an 'I', she unhooked her muslin dress at the wrists and waist, stepped from the dress and began to take down her hair. Still in the dark, with a dreaming sureness of habit, she dropped hairpins into the heart-shaped tray.

This was the night she knew she would find again. It had stayed living under a film of time. On just such a summer night, once only, she had walked with a lover in the demesne. His hand, like Robinson's, had been on her elbow, but she had guided him, not he her, because she had better eyes in the dark. They had gone down walks already deadened with moss, under the weight of July trees; they had felt the then fresh aghast ruin totter above them; there was a moonless sky. Beside the lake they sat down, and while her hand brushed the ferns in the cracks of the stone seat emanations of kindness passed from him to her. The subtle deaf girl had made the transposition of this nothing or everything into an everything – the delicate deaf girl that the man could not speak to and was afraid to touch. She who, then so deeply contented, kept in her senses each frond and breath of that night, never saw him again and had soon forgotten his face. That had been twenty years ago, till tonight when it was now. Tonight it was Robinson who, guided by Queenie down leaf tunnels, took the place on the stone seat by the lake.

The rusted gates of the castle were at the end of the square. Queenie, in her bed facing the window, lay with her face turned sideways, smiling, one hand lightly against her cheek.

MUSIC AT ANNAHULLION

Eugene McCabe

She put her bike in the shed and filled a basket of turf. Curtains still pulled across Teddy's window. Some morning the gable'd fall, and he'd wake sudden. Course you had to pretend to Liam Annahullion was very special. 'See the depth of them walls' . . . 'Look at that door; they don't use timber like that now' . . . and 'Feel that staircase, solid, made to last.' Bit of a dose the way he went on; sure what was it only a mud and stone lofted cottage, half thatched, half slated, with a leaning chimney and a cracked gable.

'The finest view in Ireland,' Liam said a hundred times a year. High to the north by Carn Rock it was fine in spring and summer, very fine, but all you ever saw from this door in winter was the hammered out barrels on the hayshed, the rutted lane and a bottom of rushes so high you'd be hard put at times to find the five cows. Liam went on about 'the orchard' at the front put down by their grandfather Matt Grue: a few scabby trees in the ground hoked useless by sows, a half acre of a midden, but you couldn't say that to his face.

One night Teddy said, 'Carried away auld cod: it's because he owns it.'

'Shush,' Annie said, pointing upstairs.

'A rotten stable, it'll fall before we're much older.'

'We grew up here, Teddy.'

'Signs on it we'll all die here. They'll plant it with trees when we're gone.'

'It's home.'

'Aye.'

Teddy talked like that when he came in late. He drank too much. His fingers were tarry black from fags, the eyes burned out of his head. Even so you could look into his eyes, you could have a laugh with Teddy. She called up the stairs as she closed the kitchen door.

'Teddy, it's half-eleven.'

'Right.'

He gave a brattle of a cough and then five minutes later shouted down: 'Is there a shirt?'

'Where it's always.'

'It's not.'

'Look again.'

She listened.

'Get it? In the low drawer?'

'It was under a sheet.'

'But you've got it?'

'I got it.'

'Thanks very much,' Annie said to herself. She hooked a griddle over the glow of sods to warm a few wheaten scones. She could maybe mention it quiet like, give it time to sink. He might rise to it after a while maybe, or again he might know what she was up to and say nothing. He was always low over winter, got it tight to pay Liam the three quid a week for board and keep. In the summer he had cash to spare, on hire through the country with a 1946 Petrol Ferguson, cutting meadows, moulding spuds, buckraking, drawing corn shigs to the thrasher. Sometimes he was gone a week.

'Knows all the bad weemen in the country,' Liam once said. 'Got a lot to answer for, that bucko.'

Teddy came down and sat at the north window under an empty birdcage, his elbows on the oilcloth. A tall stooped frame. He ate very little very slowly, put her in mind often of some great grey bird; a bite, a look out the window, another bite. 'You were up at Reilly's?'

'We'd no butter.'

'Who was there?'

'George McAloon.'

'Wee blind George?'

'He's not that blind.'

Teddy lit a cigarette and looked out. He could see Liam stepping from ridge to ridge in the sloping haggard. The field had earthy welts running angle ways, like the ribs in a man's chest, hadn't felt the plough since the Famine or before.

'Anyone else?'

'Only Petey Mulligan the shopboy. He kep' sayin' "Jasus" every minute to see poor George nod and bless himself, and then he winked at me, much as to say "Mad frigger, but we're wise" ... too old-fashioned by half.'

Teddy was quiet for a minute and then said: 'Religion puts people mad.'

'No religion puts them madder.'

He thought about this. He hadn't confessed for near forty years, lay in bed of a Sunday with rubbishy papers Liam wouldn't use to light fires. Sometimes they had bitter arguments about religion and the clergy. Liam and Annie never missed Mass.

'It's a big question,' Teddy said.

Annie filled a tin basin from the kettle.

'I saw a piana at Foster's.'

'Aye?'

'In the long shed at the back of the garden.'

'What's it doin' there?'

'They've put a lot of stuff out.'

'What kind?'

'Horsetedder, cart wheels, pig troughs, beehives, auld churns, a grass harrow, stuff like that.'

'Useless?'

'Less or more.'

'Over from the auction.'

'Must be.'

'Odd place to leave a piana.'

'The very thing I thought.'

After a moment she said, 'It looks very good, shiny with two brass candlesticks, like the one in the photo.'

'Auld I'd say?'

'Must be.'

'The guts of fifty years.'

'And maybe fifty along with that.'

Teddy went to the door and looked out. Annie said to his back,

'Pity to see a thing like that going to rack and loss.'

'If it's worth money,' Teddy said, 'some fly boy goin' the road'll cob it . . . maybe it's got no insides or it's rusted or seized up some way, must be something wrong with it or it would have gone in the auction.'

'If it come out of Foster's it's good, and it could come at handy money.'

Teddy looked round at her. 'Who'd want it?'

Annie shrugged.

'You want it, Annie?'

'A nice thing, a piana.'

'Everyone wants things.'

Teddy looked through stark apple trees towards the wet rushy bottom and the swollen river; rain again today.

'Who'd play it?'

'A body can pick out tunes with one finger, the odd visitor maybe, and you could put flowers on top of it, light candles at special times.'

Teddy was picking at his teeth with a tarry thumb: 'When one of us dies Annie?'

'Christmas, Easter, times like that.'

He went on picking his teeth with the tarry thumb.

'It's a bit daft, Annie.'

'Is it?'

There was a silence and Teddy looked round; when he saw her face he said, 'Don't go by me, but it's a dud I'd swear.'

'I'd say you're right.'

He took his cap from the top of the wireless.

'I'll see if there's letters.'

'Tell Liam there's tay.'

Annie saw him cross the yard, a scarecrow of a man, arms hung below his knees. Teddy wouldn't bother anyway. A Scotch collie bitch circled round him, yapping and bellycrawling. Guinea hens flapped to the roof of a piggery. She could see Liam blinding potholes in the rutted lane. Even in winter scutch grass clung to the middle ridge. Teddy stopped for a word; hadn't much to say to each other that pair, more like cold neighbours than brothers. Teddy went on down the road. Two years back Liam had put the post box on an ash tree near the gate . . . 'to keep Elliot the Postman away from about the place.'

'What's wrong with him?' Teddy had asked.

'Bad auld article,' Liam said.

'What way?'

'Handles weemen, or tries to, in near every house he goes to, anyway he's black Protestant.'

Teddy let on he didn't understand. 'Handles weemen? What weemen?'

Liam got redder.

'He'll not put a foot about this place.'

Annie thought about Joe Elliot, a rumpledy wee fellow, with a bate-in face, doggy eyes and a squeaky voice. No woman in her right mind could let him next or near her without a fit of the giggles, but there was no arguing with Liam. He was proud and very private. Four or five signs about the farm forbade this and that. A 'Land Poisoned' sign had been kept up though there hadn't been sheep about Annahullion for twenty years. When stray hounds crossed the farm Liam fired at them. Every year in the *Anglo-Celt* he put a notice prohibiting anyone from shooting or hunting.

'Jasus,' Teddy said, 'thirty wet sour acres and maybe a dozen starved snipe, who's he stopping? Who'd want to hunt or shoot about here? There's nothin' only us.'

Near the bridge there was a notice 'Fishing Strictly Forbidden'. The river was ten feet wide, the notice nailed to an alder in a scrub of stunted blackthorn that grew three yards out from the riverbank. When the water was low barbed wire under the bridge trapped the odd carcass of dog and badger; sometimes you could see pram wheels, bicycle frames, tins and bottles. Liam once hooked a pike on a nightline. She had cooked it in milk. It tasted strong, oily. Teddy wouldn't touch it:

'I'd as lief ate sick scaldcrows, them auld river pike ates rats and all kinds of rubbish.'

Annie found it hard to stomach her portion. She fed the leftovers to the cat. Teddy swore later he saw the cat puke. Liam was dour for days. She heard him crossing the yard now and began pouring his tea; he blessed himself as he came across the floor, pulling off the cap.

'Half-eleven I'd say?'

'Nearer twelve,' Annie said.

Liam nodded and sucked at his tea.

'You could say midday.'

'Next or near, you could say that.'

Liam shook his head. Every day or so they had this exchange about Teddy.

'I'm never done tryin' to tell him,' Annie said. 'I get sick hearin' myself.'

'It's a pity of any man, he couldn't be tould often enough or strong enough.'

'True for you,' Annie said, and thought how neither of them ever dared a word, let alone hint. Teddy was his own man, paid steady for his room, helped about the yard or farm when he felt like it. Liam sucked his teeth. They were big and a bad fit, put you in mind of a horse scobing into a sour apple. He was squatter than Teddy, sturdier, slate-coloured eyes and tight reddish skin. He smiled seldom and no one had ever heard him laugh. Sometimes Annie heard him laugh alone about the yard and fields.

'Same as the Uncle Eddie,' Liam said, 'lazy and pagan and you know how he ended. In a bog-hole . . . drunk . . . drownded.'

Crabbed this morning, better leave it till evening. 'Teddy said you remarked a piana at Foster's.'

Oh God, Annie thought, and said, 'I saw it from the road.'

Liam ate another scone before he said, 'Scrap.'

'I'd say.'

'Whole place was red out at the sale. Piana must have been lyin' about in a pig house or some of them auld rotten lofts.'

'That's what Teddy said, a dud.'

'He's right about that anyway.'

And that's that, Annie thought. Soon they'd all be pensioned, maybe then she could buy the odd thing. It was put up to her to run the house on the milk cheque. It could be a very small one in winter. She made up by crocheting, anything but approach Liam. All afternoon she thought of the piano. In the end she found herself crying as she kneaded bread. 'Yerra God,' she thought, 'I'm goin' astray in the head . . . an auld scrap piana, an' not a body in the house fit to play, and here I am all snivels over the head of it.' She blew her nose and put it out of her mind.

It was dark when Teddy got back. He smelled of whiskey and fags and his eyes looked bright. Liam didn't look up from the *Anglo-Celt*.

'Your dinner's all dried up,' Annie said.

'No odds,' Teddy said.

Liam switched on the wireless for the news. They all listened. When it was over Teddy said: 'I saw your piana, I made a dale for it.'

'Ah you're coddin, Teddy!'

'It's out of tune.'

'That's aisy fixed.'

'Woodworm in the back.'

'You can cure that too.'

'There's a pedal off.'

'What odds.'

From the way Liam held the paper she could tell he was cut. God's sake couldn't he let on for once in his life, his way of showing he kept the deeds. Teddy winked.

'Who sould it?' Liam asked.

'Wright, the auctioneer. It was forgot at the sale, hid under a heap of bags in the coach house.'

'Cute boy, Wright.'

'He's all that.'

'How much?'

'Two notes, he give it away.'

'You paid him?'

'He's paid.'

'That's all right,' Liam said and went out.

They heard him rattling buckets in the boiler house.

'Pass no remarks,' Teddy said. 'If you want a thing, get it. What's he bought here all his years but two ton weight of the *Anglo-Celt*, one second-hand birdcage that no bird ever sang in and a dose of holy pictures.'

'Horrid good of you, Teddy,' Annie said.

'Ah!'

'No, it was,' Annie said. 'If you'd waited to chaw it over with Liam you'd be that sick hearin' about it you'd as lief burn it as have it.'

'Liam's a cautious man.'

Next day Teddy took the tractor out and went off about three o'clock. Annie lit a fire in the parlour. It led off the kitchen at the end of the staircase. It was a long, narrow room smelling of turpentine, damp and coats of polish on the parquetry lino. The white-painted boards, ceiling and wainscoting was yellow and spotty. Like the kitchen, it had two windows at either end, a black horsehair chaise longue in one, a small table with a red chenille cover and potplant in the other. Two stiff armchairs faced the painted slate fireplace. On the mantelshelf there was a clock stopped since 1929, a china dog and a cracked Infant of Prague. Annie looked at the photograph over the shelf: Teddy with a hoop, Liam wearing a cap and buttoned britches. Her mother had on a rucked blouse, a long skirt with pintucks at the bottom, high boots and gloves, and that was her with a blind doll on her mother's knee. Their father stood behind looking sideways. At the bottom of the photograph 'McEniff, Photographer, Dublin Road, Monaghan 1914' . . . some fair day long ago, no memory of it now. The rough-faced man and the soft young woman buried. She was now twenty years older than her mother was then, and she thought now how her mother in her last sickness had kept raving: 'The childer, the childer, where are my childer?' She remembered saying, 'This is me; Annie, one of your childer.' Her mother had looked at her steady for a minute, then shook her head. Course she was old, dying of old age.

It was dark when they sat down to tea and Liam said, 'Long as he's not drunk . . . and lyin' in some ditch under the piana. That would be a square snippet for the *Celt*.'

'He'll be all right,' Annie said.

No noise for an hour but wind in the chimney, the hiss of thornlogs through turf and the crackle of Liam's paper. She began to worry. Supposing he did cross a ditch, get buried or worse over the head of it. Then she heard the tractor, and went to the door. A single light was pulsing on the bonnet of the old Ferguson as it came into the yard. Teddy reversed to the front door and let the buck-rake gently to the ground. He untied the ropes and put the tractor away. Annie tested the keyboard in the dark windy yard. There was an odd note dumb. Guinea hens cackled and the collie bitch barked. Liam was watching from the door.

'What's wrong with them?'

'Damp,' Annie said. 'Nothing a good fire won't mend.' It was heavy, the castors seized or rusted.

'Like a coffin full of rocks,' Liam said.

'Time enough,' Teddy said. 'No hurry.'

They had a lot of bother getting it into the kitchen, Liam wouldn't let Annie help.

'Stand back woman, we're well fit.'

It seemed very big in the kitchen. Teddy sat down and lit a cigarette. Annie took down the Tilley lamp and went round the piano. Made from that thin shaved timber; damp had unstuck some of it. That could be fixed. The keys had gone yellow but the candlesticks were very nice and the music stand was carved. God, it was lovely. She lifted the top lid and looked down into the frame. She could see something . . . a newspaper? She pulled it out, faded and flittered by mice. Liam came over.

'That's an auld one.' Teddy said from the hearth.

'The 7th November, 1936,' Liam read.

'The weight of forty years,' Annie said.

From where he was sitting Teddy could read an ad:

WHAT

LIES

AHEAD

FOR

YOU

Why not make the future certain?

'What's in it?'

Liam had put on his glasses . . . 'A Cavan man hung himself in an outhouse.'

'Aye?'

'Last thing he said to his wife was "Will I go to Matt Smith's or get the spade shafted?" . . . and the wife said "Damn the hair I care but the childer have wet feet . . . don't come back without boots."'

Liam looked up. 'Then he hung himself.'

'God help her.' Annie said. 'Women have a hard life.'

'God help *him*,' Liam said.

'Safer lave God out of it,' Teddy said.

'I must have bought that paper and read that maybe ten times . . . and it's all gone . . . forgot . . . Do *you* mind it, Annie?'

'No.'

'You, Ted?'

'It's like a lot of things you read, you couldn't mind them all.'

Liam put the paper aside. 'Better get this thing out of the way.'

He went to the parlour door, looked at it and looked at the piano. The two last steps of the staircase jutted across the parlour door. It was made from two heavy planks, each step dowelled into place. The whole frame was clamped to the wall with four iron arms. 'None of your fibby boxed in jobs,' Liam often said. 'That's solid, made to last.' He went to the dresser, got a ruler, measured, folded the ruler and said: 'Won't fit.'

'It'll be got in some way,' Annie said.

'How?'

'Let's try and we'll know.'

'If it doesn't fit, it doesn't fit. Damn thing's too big.'

Teddy took the rule and measured.

'We might jiggle it in,' he said, 'it's worth a try.'

'Won't fit,' Liam said.

Annie made tea and watched for an hour, measuring, lifting, forcing, levering, straining, Liam getting angrier and redder.

'For Christ's sake, don't pull agin me.'

'Where are you goin' now, up the friggin' stairs?'

'What in the name of Jasus are you at now?'

Finally he shouted, 'Have you no wit at all, the bloody thing's too big, the door's too small, the staircase is in the way, it won't fit or less you rip down them stairs.'

Annie tried not to listen. Teddy kept his voice low, but he was vexed and lit one fag off the other.

'Maybe we could strip her down,' he said, 'and lift in the insides, build her up again in the room.'

'Maybe we could toss the sidewall of the house,' Liam said, 'and drag her through, that's the only way.'

They said nothing for a while and then Annie said, 'I suppose it'll have to go out again?'

'Where else?' Liam said.

They got it out the door again and half lifted, half dragged it to the turf shed. Two castors broke off. The thrumming and jumble of notes set the guinea hens clucking and flapping in the apple trees.

Liam went to bed early. Teddy sat at the hearth with Annie and drank more tea.

'It's only a couple of quid, Annie.'

'No odds,' she said.

He looked at her. He felt a bit of an eejit; maybe she did too.

'What odds what people say.'

'I don't give tuppence what people say . . . never wanted a thing so bad, dunno why, and to have it in the house.'

'If you're that strong for a piana, we'll get one, the same brass candlesticks, one that fits.'

'No.'

Teddy looked at her again. If she'd come out straight and say what was in her head; women never did. They never knew rightly what was in their heads.

'Two quid is nothing, Annie.'

'I told you, it's not the money.'

Teddy sat a while at the fire.

'I'll go up.'

He paused halfway up the stairs. 'It's only scrap, Annie, means nothing.'

'I know.'

Annie dreamed that night that Liam had hung himself in the turf shed. Teddy cut him down and they laid him out in the parlour. She looked at the awful face on the piano, and then the face of the little boy in the photograph, and knelt. She felt her heart was breaking, she wanted to pray but all she could do was cry. 'What are you cryin' for, Annie?' Teddy was standing in the parlour door. 'Everything . . . all of us . . . I wish to God we were never born.'

When she woke up it was dark. She lit a candle and prayed for a while. It was almost light again when she fell asleep. That morning she covered the piano with plastic fertiliser bags. The guinea hens roosted on it all winter. Near dark one evening in February she saw a sick rat squeeze in where the pedal had broken off. By April varnish was peeling off the side. One wet day in July Teddy unscrewed the brass candlesticks. On and off she dreamed about it, strange dreams that made her unhappy. It was winter again and one evening she said, 'I'm sick to death lookin' at that thing in the turf shed. For God's sake get shut of it.'

She watched Teddy smash it with an axe. In ten minutes the rusted steel frame lay in the hen mess of the yard like the carcass of a skinned animal. Teddy slipped the buck-rake under it and drew it out of the yard. From under the empty birdcage Liam watched through the kitchen window. 'No wit, that man,' he said. 'Always bought foolish. His uncle Eddie was identical.'

NAMING THE NAMES

Anne Devlin

Abyssinia, Alma, Bosnia, Balaclava, Belgrade, Bombay.

It was late summer – August, like the summer of the fire. He hadn't rung for three weeks.

I walked down the Falls towards the reconverted cinema: THE LARGEST SECOND-HAND BOOKSHOP IN THE WORLD, the billboard read. Of course it wasn't. What we did have was a vast collection of historical manuscripts, myths and legends, political pamphlets, and we ran an exchange service for readers of crime, western and paperback romances. By far the most popular section for which Chrissie was responsible, since the local library had been petrol-bombed.

It was late when I arrived, the dossers from the St Vincent de Paul hostel had already gone in to check the morning papers. I passed them sitting on the steps every working day: Isabella wore black fishnet tights and a small hat with a half veil, and long black gloves even on the warmest day and eyed me from the feet up; Eileen, who was dumpy and smelt of meths and talcum powder, looked at everyone with the sad eyes of a cow. Tom was the thin wiry one, he would nod, and Harry, who was large and grey like his overcoat, and usually had a stubble, cleared his throat and spat before he spoke. Chrissie once told me when I started working there that both of the men were in love with Isabella and that was why Eileen always looked so sad. And usually too Mrs O'Hare from Spinner Street would still be cleaning the brass handles and finger plates and waiting like the others for the papers, so that she could read the horoscopes before they got to the racing pages. On this particular day, however, the brasses had been cleaned and the steps were empty. I tried to remember what it had been like as a cinema, but couldn't. I only remember a film I'd seen there once, in black and white: *A Town like Alice*.

Sharleen McCabe was unpacking the contents of a shopping bag on to the counter. Chrissie was there with a cigarette in one hand flicking the ash into the cap of her Yves St Laurent perfume spray and shaking her head.

She looked up as I passed: 'Miss Macken isn't in yet, so if you hurry you'll be all right.'

She was very tanned – because she took her holidays early – and her pink lipstick matched her dress. Sharleen was gazing at her in admiration.

'Well?'

'I want three murders for my granny.'

I left my coat in the office and hurried back to the counter as Miss Macken arrived. I had carefully avoided looking at the office phone, but I remember thinking: I wonder if he'll ring today?

Miss Macken swept past: 'Good morning, ladies.'

'Bang goes my chance of another fag before break,' Chrissie said.

'I thought she was seeing a customer this morning.'

Sharleen was standing at the desk reading the dust-covers of a pile of books, and rejecting each in turn:

'There's only one here she hasn't read.'

'How do you know?'

'Because her eyes is bad, I read them to her,' Sharleen said.

'Well, there's not much point in me looking if you're the only one who knows what she's read.'

'You said children weren't allowed in there!' she said, pointing to the auditorium.

'I've just given you permission,' Chrissie said.

Sharleen started off at a run.

'Popular fiction's on the stage,' Chrissie called after her. 'Children! When was that wee girl ever a child!'

'Finnula, the Irish section's like a holocaust! Would you like to do something about it. And would you please deal with these orders.'

'Yes, Miss Macken.'

'Christine, someone's just offered us a consignment of Mills and

Boon. Would you check with the public library that they haven't been stolen.'

'Righto,' sighed Chrissie.

It could have been any other day.

Senior: *Orangeism in Britain and Ireland*; Sibbett: *Orangeism in Ireland and Throughout the Empire*. Ironic. That's what he was looking for the first time he came in. It started with an enquiry for two volumes of Sibbett. Being the Irish specialist, I knew every book in the section. I hadn't seen it. I looked at the name and address again to make sure. And then I asked him to call. I said I thought I knew where I could get it and invited him to come and see the rest of our collection. A few days later, a young man, tall, fair, with very fine dark eyes, as if they'd been underlined with a grey pencil, appeared. He wasn't what I expected. He said it was the first time he'd been on the Falls Road. I took him round the section and he bought a great many things from us. He was surprised that such a valuable collection of Irish historical manuscripts was housed in a rundown cinema and he said he was glad he'd called. He told me that he was a historian writing a thesis on Gladstone and the Home Rule Bills, and that he lived in Belfast in the summer but was at Oxford University. He also left with me an extensive booklist and I promised to try to get the other books he wanted. He gave me his phone number, so that I could ring him and tell him when something he was looking for came in. It was Sibbett he was most anxious about. An antiquarian bookseller I knew of sent me the book two weeks later, in July. So I rang him and arranged to meet him with it at a café in town near the City Hall.

He was overjoyed and couldn't thank me enough, he said. And so it started. He told me that his father was a judge and that he lived with another student at Oxford called Susan. I told him that I lived with my grandmother until she died. And I also told him about my boyfriend Jack. So there didn't seem to be any danger.

We met twice a week in the café after that day; he explained something of his thesis to me: that the Protestant opposition to Gladstone and Home Rule was a rational one because Protestant industry at the time – shipbuilding and linen – was dependent on British markets. He told me how his grandfather had been an Ulster Volunteer. I told him of my granny's stories of the Black and Tans, and of how she once met de Valera on a Dublin train while he was on the run disguised as an old woman. He laughed and said my grandmother had a great imagination. He was fascinated that I knew so much history; he said he'd never heard of Parnell until he went to Oxford. And he pronounced *Parnell* with a silent *n*, so that it sounded strange.

By the end of the month, the café owner knew us by sight, and the time came on one particular evening he arrived before me, and was sitting surrounded by books and papers, when the owner remarked, as the bell inside the door rang:

'Ah. Here's your young lady now.'

We blushed alarmingly. But it articulated the possibility I had constantly been pushing to the back of my mind. And I knew I felt a sharp and secret thrill in that statement.

A few hours later, I stood on tiptoe to kiss him as I left for the bus – nothing odd about that. I often kissed him on the side of the face as I left. This time however I deliberately kissed his mouth, and somehow, the kiss went on and on; he didn't let me go. When I stepped back on my heels again I was reeling, and he had to catch me with his arm. I stood there staring at him on the pavement. I stammered 'goodbye' and walked off hurriedly towards the bus stop. He stood on the street looking after me – and I knew without turning round that he was smiling.

'Sharleen. *Murder in the Cathedral* is not exactly a murder story,' Chrissie was saying wearily.

'Well, why's it called that, then?'

'It's a play about' – Chrissie hesitated – 'martyrdom!'

'Oh.'

'This is just too, too grisly,' Chrissie said, examining the covers. 'Do they always have to be murders? Would you not like a nice love story?'

'She doesn't like love stories,' Sharleen said stubbornly. 'She only likes murders.'

At that moment Miss Macken reappeared: 'You two girls can go for tea now – what is that smell?'

'I can't smell anything,' Chrissie said.

'That's because you're wearing too much scent,' Miss Macken said. She was moving perfunctorily to the biography shelving, and it wasn't until I followed her that I became aware of a very strong smell of methylated spirits. Harry was tucked behind a newspaper drinking himself silly. He appeared to be quite alone.

'Outside! Outside immediately!' Miss Macken roared. 'Or I shall have you forcibly removed.'

He rose up before us like a wounded bear whose sleep we had disturbed, and stood shaking his fist at her, and cursing all of us, Isabella included, he ran out.

'What's wrong with him?'

'Rejection. Isabella ran off with Tom this morning, and didn't tell him where she was going. He's only drowning his sorrows,' Chrissie said. 'Apparently they had a big win yesterday. Eileen told him they'd run off to get married. But they've only gone to Bangor for the day.'

'How do you know this?'

'Eileen told Mrs O'Hare and she told me.'

'What kind of supervision is it when you two let that man drink in here with that child wandering around?' Miss Macken said, coming back from seeing Harry off the premises.

We both apologised and went up for tea.

There was little on the Falls Road that Mrs O'Hare didn't know about. As she made her way up and down the road in the mornings on her way to work she would call in and out of the shops, the library, the hospital, until a whole range of people I had never met would enter my life in our tea room by eleven o'clock. I knew that Mr Quincey, a Protestant, from the library, had met his second wife while burying his first at the City Cemetery one Saturday morning. I knew that Mr Downey, the gate-housekeeper at the hospital, had problems with his eldest daughter and didn't like her husband, and I was equally sure that thanks to Mrs O'Hare every detail of Chrissie's emotional entanglements were known by every ambulance driver at the Royal. As a result, I was very careful to say as little as possible in front of her. She didn't actually like me. It was Chrissie she bought buns for at tea time.

'Oh here! You'll never guess what Mrs McGlinchy at the bakery told me—' she was pouring tea into cups, but her eyes were on us. 'Wait till you hear—' she looked down in time to see the tea pouring over the sides of the cup. She put the teapot down heavily on the table and continued: 'Quincey's being transferred to Ballymacarrett when the library's reopened.'

'Och, you don't say?'

'It's the new boss at Central – that Englishwoman. It's after the bomb.'

'But sure that was when everybody'd gone home.'

'I know but it's security, you know! She doesn't want any more staff crossing the peace line at night. Not after that young – but wait till you hear – he won't go!'

'Good for him.'

'He says he's been on the Falls for forty years and if they transfer him now they might as well throw the keys of the library into the Republican Press Centre and the keys of the Royal Victoria Hospital in after them.'

'He's quite right. It's ghettoisation.'

'Yes, but it's inevitable,' I said.

'It's not inevitable, it's deliberate,' said Chrissie. 'It's exactly what the crowd want.'

'Who?'

'The Provos. They want a ghetto: the next thing they'll be issuing us with passes to come and go.'

'Security works both ways.'

'You're telling me.'

After that Chrissie left us to go down the yard to renew her suntan. Mrs O'Hare watched her from the window.

'She'd find the sun anywhere, that one.' She turned from the window. 'Don't take what she says too much to heart. She's Jewish, you know. She doesn't understand.'

I was glad when she went. She always felt a bit constrained with me. Because I didn't talk about my love life, as she called it, like Chrissie. But then I couldn't. I never really talked at all, to any of them.

The room overlooked the rooftops and backyards of West Belfast.

Gibson, Granville, Garnet, Grosvenor, Theodore, Cape, Kasmir.

Alone again, I found myself thinking about the last time I had seen Jack. It was a long time ago: he was sitting at the end of the table. When things are not going well my emotions start playing truant. I wasn't surprised when he said:

'I've got an invitation to go to the States for six months.'

I was buttering my toast at the time and didn't look up.

'I'm afraid I'm rather ambivalent about this relationship.'

I started battering the top of my eggshell with a spoon.

'Finn! Are you listening?'

I nodded and asked: 'When do you go?'

'Four weeks from now.'

I knew the American trip was coming up.

'Very well. I'll move out until you've gone.'

I finished breakfast and we spoke not another word until he dropped me at the steps of the bookshop.

'Finn, for God's sake! Get yourself a flat somewhere out of it! I don't imagine I'll be coming back.' He said: 'If you need any money, write to me.'

I slammed the car door. Jack was always extremely practical: if you killed someone he would inform the police, get you legal aid, make arrangements for moving the body, he'd even clear up the mess if there was any – but he would never, never ask you why you did it. I'd thrown milk all over him once, some of it went on the floors and walls, and then I ran out of the house. When I came back he'd changed his clothes and mopped up the floor. Another time I'd smashed all the dinner dishes against the kitchen wall and locked myself in the bathroom, when I came out he had swept up all the plates and asked me if I wanted a cup of tea. He was a very good journalist, I think, but somehow I never talked to him about anything important.

Because Mrs Cooper from Milan Street had been caught trying to walk out with sixteen stolen romances in a shopping bag and had thrown herself on the floor as if having a heart attack, saying: 'Oh holy Jay! Don't call the police. Oh holy Jay, my heart,' Chrissie forgot to tell me about the phone call until nearly twelve o'clock.

'Oh, a customer rang, he wanted to talk to you about a book he said he was after. Sibbett. That was it. You were still at tea.' She said, 'I told him we were open to nine tonight and that you'd be here all day.'

For three weeks he hadn't rung. I only had to pick up the phone and ring him as I'd done on other occasions. But this time I hoped he would contact me first.

'Is something wrong?' Chrissie said.

'I have to make a phone call.'

*

After that first kiss on the street, the next time we met I took him to the house, about ten minutes' walk from the park.

'When did you say your granny died?' he asked, looking with surprise around the room.

'Oh, ages ago. I'm not very good at dates.'

'Well, you don't appear to have changed much since. It's as if an old lady still lived here.'

He found the relics, the Sacred Heart pictures and the water font strange. 'You really ought to dust in here occasionally,' he said, laughing. 'What else do you do apart from work in the bookshop?'

'I read, watch television. Oh, and I see Jack,' I said quickly, so as not to alarm him.

'Good Lord. Would you look at that web; it looks like it's been there for donkeys!'

A large web attaching itself in the greater part to the geraniums in the window had spread across a pile of books and ended up clinging heavily to the lace curtains.

'Yes. I like spiders,' I said. 'My granny used to say that a spider's web was a good omen. It means we're safe from the soldiers!'

'It just means that you never open the curtains!' he said, laughing. Still wandering round the small room he asked, 'Who is that lady? Is she your grandmother?'

'No. That's the Countess Markievicz.'

'I suppose your granny met her on a train in disguise – as an old man.'

'No. But she did visit her in prison.'

He shook his head. 'The trouble with you—' he began, then suddenly he had a very kind look in his eyes. 'You're improbable. No one would ever believe me.' He stopped, and began again. 'Sometimes I think' – he tapped me on the nose – 'you live in a dream, Finn.'

And then he kissed me, and held me; he only complained that I was too quiet.

It was nine thirty when I left the building and shut it up for the night: Miss Macken had offered to drop me home as she was leaving, but I said I'd prefer to walk. There were no buses on the road after nine because a few nights before a group of youths had stoned a bus passing Divis Flats, and the bus driver was hurt. The whole day was a torment to me after that phone call and I wanted to think and walk.

When I got to the park I was so giddy that I didn't care whether he came or not. My stomach was in a knot – and I realised it was because I hadn't eaten all day. The summer was nearly over – I only knew that soon this too would be over. I had kept my feelings under control so well – I was always very good at that, contained, very contained – so well, that I thought if he even touched me I'd tell him – Oh run! Run for your life from me! At least I didn't tell him that I loved him or anything like that. Was it something to be glad about? And suddenly there were footsteps running behind me. I always listened for footsteps. I'd walked all through those streets at night but I had never been afraid until that moment.

I suddenly started to run when a voice called out:

'Finn! Wait!' It was his voice.

I stopped dead, and turned.

We stood by the grass verge.

'Why didn't you ring me?' I asked, listlessly, my head down in case he saw my eyes.

'Because I didn't think it was fair to you.'

'Fair?'

'Because, well—'

'Well?'

'I'm in England and you're here. It's not very satisfactory.'

'I see.'

'Look, there's something I should tell you. It's – Susan's been staying with us for the past three weeks.'

'I see.'

I couldn't possibly object since we were both supposed to have other lovers, there was no possibility of either of us complaining.

'But we could go to your place now if you like.'

I was weakening. He stooped to kiss me and the whole business began as it had started. He kissed me and I kissed him and it went on and on.

'I was just getting over you,' I said, standing up.

'I didn't know there was anything to get over. You're very good at saying nothing.'

And before I could stop myself I was saying: 'I think I've fallen in love with you.'

He dropped his head and hardly dared look at me – he looked so pained – and more than anything I regretted that statement.

'You never told me that before,' he said.

'I always felt constrained.'

He began very slowly: 'Look, there is something I have to say now. I'm getting married at the end of the summer.' And more quickly. 'But I can't give you up. I want to go on seeing you. Oh don't go! Please listen!'

It was very cold in the park. I had a piercing pain in my ear because of the wind. A tricolour hung at a jaunty angle from the top of the pensioner's bungalow, placed there by some lads. The army would take it down tomorrow in the morning. The swings, the trees and grass banks looked as thoroughly careworn as the surrounding streets.

Lincoln, Leeson, Marchioness and Mary, Slate, Sorella and Ward.

I used to name them in a skipping song.

The park had been my playplace as a child, I used to go there in the mornings and wait for someone to lead me across the road, to the first gate. Sometimes a passer-by would stop and take my hand, but most times the younger brother of the family who owned the bacon shop would cross with me.

'No road sense!' my grandmother used to say. 'None at all.'

In the afternoon he would come back for me. And I remember—

'Finn, are you listening? You mustn't stop talking to me, we could still be friends. I love being with you – Finn!'

I remember standing in the sawdust-filled shop waiting for him to finish his task – the smooth hiss of the slicing machine and the thin strips of bacon falling on the greaseproof paper.

I began to walk away.

'Finn. I do love you.' He said it for the first time.

I pulled up the collar of my coat and walked home without looking back.

It should have ended before I was so overcome with him I wept. And he said: 'What's wrong?' and took me and held me again.

It should have ended before he said: 'Your soul has just smiled in your eyes at me – I've never seen it there before.'

Before, it should have ended before. He was my last link with life and what a way to find him. I closed my eyes and tried to forget, all vision gone, only sound left: the night noises came.

The raucous laughter of late-night walkers; the huddle of tomcats on the backyard wall; someone somewhere is scraping a metal dustbin across a concrete yard; and far off in the distance a car screeches to a halt: a lone dog barks at an unseen presence, the night walkers pause in their walk past – the entry. Whose is the face at the empty window? – the shadows cast on the entry wall – the shape in the darkened doorway – the steps on the broken path – who pulled that curtain open quickly – and let it drop?

I woke with a start and the sound of brakes screeching in my ears – as if the screech had taken on a human voice and called my name in anguish. Finn! But when I listened, there was nothing. Only the sound of the night bells from St Paul's tolling in the distance.

I stayed awake until daybreak and with the light found some peace from dreams. At eight o'clock I went out. Every day of summer had been going on around me, seen and unseen, I had drifted through those days like one possessed.

Strange how quickly we are reassured by ordinariness: Isabella and Tom, Harry and Eileen, waiting on the steps. And Mrs O'Hare at the counter with her polishing cloth, and Miss Macken discussing her holiday plans with Chrissie. Externally, at least, it could have been the same as the day before, yesterday – the day before I left him in the park. But I saw it differently. I saw it in a haze, and it didn't seem to have anything to do with me.

'The body was discovered by bin-men early this morning,' Miss Macken said. 'He was dumped in an entry.'

'Oh, Finn, it's awful news,' said Chrissie, turning.

'It's the last straw as far as I am concerned,' Miss Macken said.

'Mr Downey said it's the one thing that turned him – he'll not be back to the Royal after this.'

'We knew him,' Chrissie said.

'Who?'

'That young man. The one who looked like a girl.'

'The police think he was coming from the Falls Road,' Miss Macken said.

'They said it was because he was a judge's son,' said Chrissie.

'The theory is,' said Miss Macken, 'that he was lured there by a woman. I expect they'll be coming to talk to us.'

'Aye, they're all over the road this morning,' said Mrs O'Hare.

At lunchtime they came.

'Miss McQuillen, I wonder?'

A noisy row between Isabella and Eileen distracted me – Eileen was insisting that Isabella owed her five pounds.

'Miss McQuillen, I wonder if you wouldn't mind answering a few questions?'

'How well did you know . . .'

'When did you last see him?'

'What time did you leave him?'

'What exactly did he say?'

'Have you any connection with . . .?'

Osman, Serbia, Sultan, Raglan, Bosnia, Belgrade, Rumania, Sebastopol.

The names roll off my tongue like a litany.

'Has that something to do with Gladstone's foreign policy?' he used to laugh and ask.

'No. Those are the streets of West Belfast.'

Alma, Omar, Conway and Dunlewey, Dunville, Lady and McDonnell.

Pray for us. (I used to say, just to please my grandmother.) Now and at the hour.

At three o'clock in the afternoon of the previous day, a man I knew came into the bookshop. I put the book he was selling on the counter in front of me and began to check the pages. It was so still you could hear the pages turn: 'I think I can get him to the park,' I said.

Eileen had Isabella by the hair and she stopped. The policeman who was writing – stopped.

Miss Macken was at the counter with Chrissie, she was frowning – she looked over at me, and stopped. Chrissie suddenly turned and looked in my direction. No one spoke. We walked through the door on to the street.

Still no one spoke.

Mrs O'Hare was coming along the road from the bread shop, she raised her hand to wave and then stopped.

Harry had just tumbled out of the bookies followed by Tom. They were laughing. And they stopped.

We passed the block where the babyclothes shop had been, and at the other end the undertaker's: everything from birth to death on that road. Once. But gone now – just stumps where the buildings used to be – stumps like tombstones.

'Jesus. That was a thump in the stomach if ever I felt one,' one policeman said to the other.

Already they were talking as if I didn't exist.

There were four or five people in the interview room.

A policewoman stood against the wall. The muscles in my face twitched. I put up my hand to stop it.

'Why did you pick him?'

'I didn't pick him. He was chosen. It was his father they were after. He's a judge.'

'They?'

'I, I recognised the address when he wrote to me. Then he walked in.'

'Who are the others? What are their names?'

'Abyssinia, Alma, Balaclava, Balkan.'

'How did you become involved?'

'It goes back a long way.'

'Miss McQuillen. You have a captive audience!'

'On the fourteenth of August 1969 I was escorting an English journalist through the Falls: his name was Jack McHenry.'

'How did you meet him?'

'I am coming to that. I met him on the previous night, the thirteenth; there was a meeting outside Divis Flats to protest about the police in the Bogside. The meeting took a petition to Springfield Road Police Station, But the police refused to open the door. Part of the crowd broke away and marched back down to Divis to Hastings Street Police Station and began throwing stones. There was trouble on the road all night because of roaming gangs. They stoned or petrol-bombed a car with two fire chiefs in it and burned down a Protestant showroom at the bottom of Conway Street. I actually tried to stop it happening. He was there, at Balaclava Street, when it happened. He stopped me and asked if I'd show him around the Falls. He felt uneasy, being an Englishman, and he didn't know his way around without a map. I said I'd be happy to.'

'Were you a member of an illegal organisation?'

'What organisation? There were half a dozen guns in the Falls in '69 and a lot of old men who couldn't even deliver the *United Irishman* on time. And the women's section had been disbanded during the previous year because there was nothing for them to do but run around after the men and make tea for the céilis. He asked me the same question that night, and I told him truthfully that I was not – then.

'On the evening of the fourteenth we walked up the Falls Road, it was early, we had been walking round all day, we were on our way back to his hotel – the Grand Central in Royal Avenue – he wanted to phone his editor and give an early report about events on the road. As we walked up the Falls from Divis towards Leeson Street, we passed a group of children in pyjamas going from Dover Street towards the flats. Further up the road at Conway Street a neighbour of ours was crossing the road to Balaclava Street with his children; he said he was taking them to Sultan Street Hall for the night. Everything seemed quiet. We walked on down Leeson Street and into town through the Grosvenor Road: the town centre was quiet too. He phoned his paper and then took me to dinner to a Chinese restaurant across the road from the hotel. I remember it because there was a false ceiling in the restaurant, like a sky with fake star constellations. We sat in a velvet alcove and there were roses on the table. After dinner we went to his hotel and went to bed. At five o'clock in the morning the phone rang. I thought it was an alarm call he'd placed. He slammed down the phone and jumped up and shouted at me: 'Get up quickly. All hell's broken loose in the Falls!'

'We walked quickly to the bottom of Castle Street and began to walk hurriedly up the road. At Divis Street I noticed that five or six shops around me had been destroyed by fire. At Divis Flats a group of men stood, it was light by this time. When they heard that Jack was a journalist they began telling him about the firing. It had been going on all night, they said, and several people were dead, including a child in the flats. They took him to see the bullet holes in the walls. The child was in a cot at the time. And the walls were thin. I left him there at Divis and hurried up the road to Conway Street. There was a large crowd there as well, my own people. I looked up the street to the top. There was another crowd at the junction of Ashmore Street – this crowd was from the Shankill – they were setting fire to a bar at the corner and looting it. Then some of the men began running down the street and breaking windows of the houses in Conway Street. They used brush handles. At the same time as the bar was burning, a number of the houses at the top of the street also caught fire in Conway Street. The crowd were throwing petrol bombs in after they broke the windows. I began to run up towards the fire. Several of the crowd also started running with me.

'Then I noticed for the first time, because my attention had been fixed on the burning houses, that two turreted police vehicles were moving slowly down the street on either side. Somebody shouted: "The gun turrets are pointed towards us!" And everybody ran back. I didn't. I was left standing in the middle of the street, when a police-man, standing in a doorway, called to me: "Get back! Get out of here before you get hurt."

'The vehicles were moving slowly down Conway Street towards the Falls Road with the crowd behind them, burning houses as they went. I ran into the top of Balaclava Street at the bottom of Conway Street where our crowd were. A man started shouting at the top of his voice: "They're going to fire. They're going to fire on us!"

'And our crowd ran off down the street again.

'A woman called to me from an upstairs window: "Get out of the mouth of the street." Something like that.'

'I shouted: "But the people! The people in the houses!"

'A man ran out and dragged me into a doorway. "They're empty!" he said. "They got out last night!" Then we both ran down to the bottom of Balaclava Street and turned the corner into Raglan Street. If he hadn't been holding me by the arm then that was the moment when I would have run back up towards the fires.'

'Why did you want to do that? Why did you want to run back into Conway Street?'

'My grandmother lived there – near the top. He took me to Sultan Street refugee centre. "She's looking for her granny," he told a girl with a St John Ambulance armband on. She was a form below me at school. My grandmother wasn't there. The girl told me not to worry because everyone had got out of Conway Street. But I didn't believe her. An ambulance from the Royal arrived to take some of the wounded to hospital. She put me in the ambulance as well. It was the only transport on the road other than police vehicles. "Go to the hospital and ask for her there," she said.

'It was eight o'clock in the morning when I found her sleeping in a quiet room at the Royal. The nurse said she was tired, suffering from shock and a few cuts from flying glass. I stayed with her most of the day. I don't remember that she spoke to me. And then about six I had a cup of tea and wandered on to the road up towards the park. Jack McHenry was there, writing it all down: "It's all over," he said. "The Army are here." We both looked down the Falls, there were several mills that I could see burning: the Spinning Mill and the Great Northern, and the British Army were marching in formation down the Falls Road. After that I turned and walked along the Grosvenor Road into town and spent the night with him at his hotel. There was nowhere else for me to go.'

I was suddenly very tired; more tired than on the day I sat in her room watching her sleep; more tired than on the day Jack left; infinitely more tired than I'd ever been in my life. I waited for someone else to speak. The room was warm and heavy and full of smoke. They waited. So I went on.

'Up until I met Jack McHenry I'd been screwing around like there was no tomorrow. I only went with him because there was no one else left. He stayed in Belfast because it was news. I never went back to school again. I had six O-levels and nothing else.'

'Is that when you got involved?'

'No, not immediately. My first reaction was to get the hell out of it. It wasn't until the summer of '71 that I found myself on the Falls Road again. I got a job in the new second-hand bookshop where I now work. Or did. One day a man came in looking for something: "Don't I know you?" he said. He had been a neighbour of ours at one time. "I carried your granny out of Conway Street." He told me that at about eleven o'clock on the night of August fourteenth, there were two families trapped at the top of Conway Street. One of them, a family of eight, was escorted out of their house by a policeman and this man. Bottles and stones were thrown at them from a crowd at the top of the street. The policeman was cut on the head as he took the children out. The other family, a woman, with her two teenage daughters, refused to leave her house because of her furniture. Eventually they were forced to run down the back entry into David Street to escape. It was she who told him that Mrs McQuillen was still in the house. He went back up the street on his own this time. Because the lights in our house were out he hadn't realised there was anyone there. He got scared at the size of the crowd ahead and was going to run back when he heard her call out: "Finn! Finn!" He carried her down Conway Street running all the way. He asked me how she was keeping these days. I told him that she had recently died. Her heart gave up. She always had a weak heart.

'A few weeks later Jack took me on holiday to Greece with him. I don't really think he wanted me to go with him, he took me out of guilt. I'd rather forced the situation on him. We were sitting at a harbour café one afternoon, he was very moody and I'd had a tantrum because I found out about his latest girlfriend. I got up and walked away from him along the harbour front. I remember passing a man reading a newspaper at another café table, a few hundred yards along the quay. I saw a headline that made me turn back.

'"The Army have introduced internment in Belfast," I said.

'We went home a few days later and I walked into a house in Andersonstown of a man I knew: 'Is there anything for me to do?' I said. And that was how I become involved.'

'And the man's name?'

'You already know his name. He was arrested by the Army at the beginning of the summer. I was coming up the street by the park at that time, when he jumped out of an Army Saracen and ran towards me. A soldier called out to him to stop, but he ran on. He was shot in the back. He was a well-known member of the Provisional IRA on the run. I was on my way to see him. His father was the man who carried my grand-mother out of Conway Street. He used to own a bacon shop.'

'Did Jack McHenry know of your involvement?'

'No. He didn't know what was happening to me. Eventually we drifted apart. He made me feel that in some way I had disappointed him.'

'What sort of operations were you involved in?'

'My first job was during internment. Someone would come into the shop, the paymaster, he gave me money to deliver once a week to the wives of the men interned. The women would then come into the shop to collect it. It meant that nobody called at their houses, which were being watched. These were the old Republicans. The real movement was reforming in Andersonstown.'

'And the names? The names of the people involved?'

'There are no names. Only places.'

'Perhaps you'll tell us the names later.'

When they left me alone in the room I began to remember a dream I'd had towards the end of the time I was living with Jack. I slept very badly then, I never knew whether I was asleep or awake. One night it seemed to me that I was sitting up in bed with him. I was smoking, he was writing something, when an old woman whom I didn't recognise came towards me with her hands outstretched. I was horrified; I didn't know where she came from or how she got into our bedroom. I tried to make Jack see her but he couldn't. She just kept coming towards me. I had my back against the headboard of the bed and tried to fight her off. She grasped my hand and kept pulling me from the bed. She had very strong hands, like a man's, and she pulled and pulled and I struggled to release my hands. I called out for help of every sort, from God, from Jack. But she would not let me go and I could not get my hands free. The struggle between us was so furious that it woke Jack. I realised then that I was dreaming. He put his hands on me to steady me: 'You're having a fit. You're having a fit!' he kept saying. I still had my eyes closed even though I knew I was awake. I asked him not to let me see him. Until it had passed. I began to be terribly afraid, and when I was sure it had passed, I had to ask him to take me to the toilet. He never asked any questions but did exactly what I asked. He took me by the hand and led me to the bathroom, where he waited with me. After that he took me back to bed again. As we passed the mirror on the bedroom door I asked him not to let me see it. The room was full of mirrors, he went round covering them all up. Then he got into bed and took my hand again.

'Now please don't let me go,' I said. 'Whatever happens don't let go of my hand.'

'I promise you. I won't,' he said.

But I knew that he was frightened.

I closed my eyes and the old woman came towards me again. It was my grandmother; she was walking. I didn't recognise her the first time because – she had been in a wheelchair all her life.

She reached out and caught my hands again and the struggle

between us began: she pulled and I held on. She pulled and I still held on.

'Come back!' Jack said. 'Wherever you are, come back!'

She pulled with great force.

'Let go of me!' I cried.

Jack let go of my hand.

The policewoman who had been standing silently against the wall all the time stepped forward quickly. When I woke I was lying on the floor. There were several people in the room, and a doctor.

'Are you sure you're fit to continue?'

'Yes.'

'What about the names?'

'My father and grandmother didn't speak for years: because he married my mother. I used to go and visit him. One night, as I was getting ready to go there, I must have been about seven or eight at the time, my grandmother said, "Get your father something for his birthday for me" – she handed me three shillings – "but you don't have to tell him it's from me. Get him something for his cough."

'At the end of Norfolk Street was a sweet shop. I bought a tin of barley sugar. The tin was tartan: red and blue and green and black. They wrapped it in a twist of brown paper. I gave it to my mother when I arrived. "It's for my Daddy for his birthday in the morning."

'"From whom?"

'"From me."

'"Can I look?"

'"Yes."

'She opened the paper: "Why it's beautiful," she said. I remember her excitement over it. "He'll be so pleased." She seemed very happy. I remember that. Because she was never very happy again. He died of consumption before his next birthday.'

'Why did you live with your grandmother?'

'Because our house was too small.'

'But the names? The names of the people in your organisation?'

'Conway, Cupar, David, Percy, Dover and Divis. Mary, Merrion, Milan, McDonnell, Osman, Raglan, Ross, Rumania, Serbia, Slate, Sorella, Sulktan, Theodore, Varna and Ward Street.'

When I finished they had gone out of the room again. Only the policewoman remained. It is not the people but the streets I name.

The door opened again.

'There's someone to see you,' they said.

Jack stood before me.

'In God's name, Finn. How and why?'

He wasn't supposed to ask that question. He shook his head and sighed: 'I nearly married you.'

Let's just say it was historical.

'I ask myself over and over what kind of woman are you, and I have to remind myself that I knew you, or thought I knew you, and that I loved you once.'

Once, once upon a time.

'Anything is better than what you did, Finn. Anything! A bomb in a pub I could understand – not forgive, just understand – because of the arbitrariness of it. But – you caused the death of someone you had grown to know!'

I could not save him. I could only give him time.

'You should never have let me go!' I said, for the first time in ten years.

He looked puzzled: 'But you weren't happy with me. You didn't seem very happy.'

He stood watching for a minute and said: 'Where are you, Finn? Where are you?'

The door closed. An endless vista of solitude before me, of sleeping and waking alone in the dark – in the corner a spider was spinning a new web. I watched him move from angle to angle. An endless confinement before me and all too soon a slow gnawing hunger inside for something – I watched him weave the angles of his world in the space of the corner.

Once more they came back for the names, and I began: 'Abyssinia Alma, Balaclava, Balkan, Belgrade, Bosnia,' naming the names: empty and broken and beaten places. I know no others.

Gone and going all the time.

Redevelopment. Nothing more dramatic than that; the planners are our bombers now. There is no heart in the Falls these days.

'But the names? The names of the people who murdered him? The others?'

'I know no others.'

The gradual and deliberate processes weave their way in the dark corners of all our rooms, and when the finger is pointed, the hand turned, the face at the end of the finger is my face, the hand at the end of the arm that points is my hand, and the only account I can give is this: that if I lived for ever I could not tell: I could only glimpse what fatal visions stir that web's dark pattern, I do not know their names. I only know for certain what my part was, that even on the eve, on such a day, I took him there.

SHAME

Keith Ridgway

This is the start of the story, I know. It is the clearness in my head that tells me. My eyes open slick as fish eyes and I see the world sharp and sudden and my mind is strong this morning. I can feel it. It's cold, but a good cold, on the skin only, no deeper, and I dress fast and steady.

The city is squat. There's a section of it pressed to my window, starting with the river and rising then, up the hill towards the Castle. There's a wetness in the morning, and the sun not working right, hidden in a low place somewhere, not touching us. On the hill by St Audon's there was a fire in the night, an orange glow with crackling that woke the child, who woke us, and we stood by the river and stared up at it for a while until the rain came. Now the fire has left a dirty smudge in the middle of the rooftops, a damp patch, with grey timber pointing out of it, shards and black splinters, and a thin smoke still rising, all the colour gone, as if the night has drained it from the day.

By the Custom House I can see two ships that have arrived since last night. They are regular, Liverpool boats, and there are barrel boys running to and from them now, and a bulging crate swinging on the crane a little too wildly, and there are shouts that come to me over the water. The big three-master is gone, though I had seen its shadows and the glow of its watch while we stood staring at the fire only hours since. There is another ship cutting towards the sea now, just passing the lotts.

There is a boat tied to the near bank that I've not seen before. It has a small cabin perched on it like an upturned box and it has a load of wood spilled along its length. There's an ugly man on the deck, drinking from a bottle, talking to my wife who stands with her foot on the hawser, the child at her side, him turned from the river and waving at me. He is five now and curly headed and clever as I am. He does not smile as he waves, but squints an eye at me like he knows something I don't and he's seeing me in a new light. I nod and move from the window and try to find some food.

I have dreamed of eavesdropping now for three nights. I have dreamed of overhearing the noise of the world spun out as a kind of song by a ghost. She was a ghost because I knew her face and the face I knew belonged to my mother. But she was not my mother. She was a ghost with my mother's face. She sang or moaned, I am not sure. She gave off the sound like a scent, a noisome, clicking, pungent wail, and it flowed around me as I hid by a tree in a sunlit field where a silent river winked at me. I choked, and fled, and woke then.

And the next night I listened to my wife, her voice clear and strong and unembarrassed, her words so strange to me that it was a long time before I understood them, understood their meaning, their tight plot. She was discussing my murder with an Englishman. Planning it, working it out. I heard the details that would ensure the rapid decay of my remains, the chemical requirements, what kind of blade, what kind of barrel, a place to place me, a quiet cellar, for three days. Then I would be soup, and they would feed me to the river. The Englishman chuckled, but my wife was businesslike and still, and I awoke as she turned her face and peered into the gloom towards me, and lifted the candle and hissed like a god.

Last night I dreamed of my son. He spoke in his own voice but his words were older, older than I, and though I tried I could not make out their meaning. It was English, of that I'm sure, for there were 'ifs' and 'ands' and 'buts' and once he said 'Mother' and once he said 'Father' and once he said 'fleece'. He sat on the quay, his legs dangling, and he spat once, and I awoke then, in fright, for as his spit arced towards me I knew where I was, that I was in the water.

She's left a pot of tea still hot for me, and dark strong by now as I like it. There's a loaf cut, and a slice of bacon, and I eat a little and drink the tea, hum, and check the pocket watch she keeps in the drawer. It's after eight already and I curse and pull on my boots with my mouth full of bread, and I take my coat and sling it over my shoulder and fill the mug with tea once more and take it out into the day, out to where my wife and son stand by the river.

'Are you late?'

'I am.'

'This man has wood to sell.'

He looks up at me and his head rises and falls slightly with the water.

'We're not buying wood. We have wood.'

I drain my mug and hand it to my wife, and turn and leave a silence behind me, and I can feel their two pairs of eyes on my back, and my son makes three. She has a liking for ugly men, and foreign men of any kind. She takes them to her bed while I am gone and she leaves the boy to wander the house and hear whatever he might, and see whatever he can. I know this to be true because of the strength with which I know it, and because of the evidence.

I walk along the river, quickly. It is not good to be late, even if there will be little enough to do when I get there. I am hailed by men who know me, and I nod at them and gesture, and call out a greeting sometimes, and it is by that means, as if being handed on from voice to voice, from face to face, that I make my way down to the house where the Englishman is kept. It is for him that I work, although I am paid by his employer, and it is to both of them that I appear to be answerable, which is not to my liking, for their relationship has of late been strained. The Englishman is frustrated at the delays, and he is anxious to begin, and he has had enough of plans and drawings and consultations and wishes to get the thing started. So he tries me for information, of which I have none, and is short with me when I can give him no answer. And on the other side, his employer, and mine, blames me for the strain, saying that I am not properly occupying the Englishman, which I feel is a nonsense – I am not employed as a playmate or companion or lady-in-waiting. My job is narrow and I like it that way, and I think that I will throw it all in if it continues in this manner for much longer.

I arrive near the quarter hour, to find that my alternate has left already. I am admitted by a manservant, who smiles at me and is affable and attempts to start a conversation about the night's fire. But I cannot linger, and I knock the door of the gentleman's study and am summoned in, a light sweat on my brow, brought on by my hurrying.

'Good morning Sir.'

He grunts and stays where he is, at his desk, writing. He is not genuine in his humours, putting them on and taking them off again like a coat, with a shrug of his shoulders and a flap of his arms. So this morning he is wearing his black mood, and he does not raise his eyes and he writes with a bad-tempered hand, and takes up muttering while I stand in front of him and stare at the top of his head. The room is cluttered with books and papers and plans, and instruments of measurement and calculation, and much more besides which I do not understand. I believe that he is unproven in his field, which I do not think bodes well for the project, about which I know little but that it involves building a new Custom House and a new bridge and that it is causing upset to a lot of people.

'Are you well sir?'

'No.'

He is a small-framed man, narrow hands, thin hair, his eyes are pulsing blue and he takes no notice of his appearance, sitting now this morning in a dirty high-collared shirt and wrapped in a blue robe as if straight from his bed. I cannot see his feet.

'You'll take this letter to Mr Beresford directly.'

I raise my eyebrows a little but he's not looking at me at all, he's busy folding and sealing and stamping, and my silence is not worth much to him.

'And you will wait for an answer.'

'I'll have the boy go Sir.'

He looks at me now.

'You'll go yourself.'

I frown at him, at his angry face. My frown is well shaped and says to him that there is nothing to be gained from snarling at me – I am not the cause of his irritation. Directly he sees it he changes his coat of black humour for a hair shirt, for a cloud grey heavy garment full of weariness and supplication.

'Forgive me, I do not mean to snap at you. But you can understand my frustrations, you can understand my position. It is difficult and tiresome and it does not have a pleasant effect. The letter will read more urgent if it is delivered by you.'

'My job is to stay with you Sir, until the evening.'

'I will not be alone.'

'Nevertheless Sir . . .'

He sighs and lets his head fall back a little. The room is lit from a window onto the garden, and I can see green leaves leaning on the glass, and I think again about the life I lead, and how it is contained within rooms, and takes place through words and directions, and I wonder whether it is a life at all, and whether it might not be just a dreamed thing, and that I might myself, in my essentials, be elsewhere. For what belongs here?

'I feel like a prisoner,' says the gentleman, and I want to smile but do not.

'Indeed Sir.'

'So you will not take the letter?'

'I will see to it that it is delivered, and that a reply is awaited, and I will ensure that the urgency is impressed upon Mr Beresford.'

He sighs again, and ducks his head now, and scratches it, and yawns.

'All right, all right. See to it.'

I take the letter from his hand, and he looks me miserably in the eye and says nothing, has nothing to say, and I want to test my notion and I glance at the window and the leaves on the glass and I look back at him and I start to say it but I am stopped by the part of myself which does not allow me to test anything.

'What's that?'

'Time Sir . . .'

'What of it?'

I am for a moment at a loss.

'Passes quickly,' I say, lowly, and I feel my cheeks run red, and feel the damp line still on my forehead, and I wish to be asleep so that I can wake.

He nods, or rather, he lowers his head and raises it again, like that.

'Indeed. Not it seems, Mr Beresford's time.'

'Yes Sir.'

He regards me as peculiar, as well he might, and I turn and leave him and I see to it that the letter is sent, and that a reply is received, and I walk in the garden and I count the leaves.

I have given the impression that my wife is not trustworthy, and this is not true. She does not take men to her bed when I am gone. She does not allow the child to wander freely while she does it. And yet, there is the evidence.

I understand the nature of things by the evidence that is presented to me concerning their substance and their place. Evidence is that which I see and hear which allows me to determine whether a thing is as it seems to be. I learned this subject from a man I knew in the Americas who had both curiosity and learning, and who, I think, died, in front of my eyes, as a result of a scuffle with an Indian knifeman in the country of Virginia. But he would have cautioned me to be unsure, as I do not have the evidence that he is for certain dead. He was wounded in the chest, and if he lived it would surprise me, knowing what I know of wounds like those, but what do I know about living and dying? Not enough. Never enough. Circumstances did not allow me to linger and to find out.

But of my wife, there is too much evidence. For I dream of her often, and I think of her more, and these dreams and these thoughts show me more than I know by other means, and I cannot, in truth, separate them out and judge one as weightier than the other. So that there is always doubt, and this doubt infects my life with her, and I know that there is no reason to it, but that does not disperse it.

I am no fool. I have seen men torn apart by jealousy, and rage at imagined slights. I am aware of those dangers. These are not things I take on. It is not jealousy that fills me. It is dreams that fill me. Thoughts. Evidence. I see her in the past and in the future, sometimes with me and sometimes not, sometimes alone and benign and faultless, sometimes rank and foul and eager for others. And I know that she does not dream these dreams. I know that she does not plot my death with Englishmen and barrels. I know that she has no plans other than the plans she should have, and that she has no desire to hurt me or to wrong me or to see me dead. But these things exist. I have seen them.

Where do they come from?

It is past midday and the reply from Mr Beresford has cheered my gentleman considerably. I have instructions to escort him in the evening to the site, and to allow him to survey and take measurements and so forth, though I must take my alternate with me, as well as three of Mr Beresford's own men, in convoy, for protection. This is good news for me. It will break the monotony of these days.

There is a caller at the house, a woman who will not give her name. She stands in the reception room and surveys the furniture and the paintings and is haughty and will have no truck with me, though she is not very moneyed or grand or impressive. It is the gentleman she wants to see.

I knock on his door and interrupt him at his soup, which he slurps as I tell him that there is a caller, a lady, who will not tell me her name, but who says she is expected. He is properly dressed now. I can see that already he has grouped together those items he needs for our expedition.

'No. I have no appointments. What does she look like?'

'She is a delicate lady Sir, dark-haired, pale-skinned.'

'Is she pretty?'

I hesitate. I do not find her handsome, but I wonder if he will.

'Well?'

'She is pleasant Sir.'

'That's no answer.'

I am silent. It is not my job to answer questions like that.

'Oh show her in then.'

I am not entirely easy with this. My instructions are to admit civilised callers and to report their visits, but there have been few, and none before who have not either been expected or known to me. When I summon her she gives me a small shake of her head which is intended to scold me for my foolishness. I lead her to his study, and follow her into the room, remaining at the door, behind the precise, cut out shape of her back. He stands, his soup things pushed to one side, and waits for her to speak. She glances behind herself, at me.

'Good day ma'am. How may I help you?'

'You are Mr Gandon?'

'Indeed,' he says, shrugging a little.

'I am Mrs Millington.'

His face changes. It opens wider, in surprise or shock, I do not know. For a moment he stares at her. And then he becomes solicitous, sympathy floods his features, as if the name has evidence hanging from it like ivy. He moves from behind his desk, walks towards her, all the time saying, 'Mrs Millington, my dear lady, I had no idea you were in Dublin, but of course, how do you do, how do you do, it is an honour . . .'

And he shoos me away with a flick of his wrist and an irritated look. I hesitate, but if he is content with her then it is none of my business who she is. I leave them, and the last sight I have of them both is like a painting, I view it like I would a painting, so clear is it, so fixed and certain. He stands slightly to her side, with her hands held in his, and his head is at an angle, inclined towards the window, and he smiles, but a sorrowful smile, as if he wishes to commiserate with her, to condole and to comfort. She stands with her head bowed, staring somewhere towards his chest, accepting his wishes, surrendering herself to his sympathy, giving up her shallow indifference for a shallow kind of grace. I do not like her.

Why do I say that it is the last sight I have of them? For I do not mean that it is the last sight I have of them for the moment, but for ever. This is how it presents itself to me. And yet this is unlikely to be the case, unless I die now and am removed from seeing this daily unfolding of my standard life, my routine life, my measured time.

I go to the kitchens and eat some bread and some cheese, and find a jug of claret and help myself to a glass. A maid flirts with me and I am silent in the face of it and she withdraws, a little sullen, her fingertips gone green from polishing. The kitchen is warm, and it has the look of an older place that has not changed in many years, and it puts me in mind of my boyhood, when I was quiet and still and scolded for it. We had dogs who nuzzled me and snapped at strangers, and they would take me sometimes, to strange parts of the city, to streets and lanes which were at odds with the rest of it, and I would want to return home but the dogs were always onward bound, seeking out cracks in the ground, holes in the walls, tears in the blanket of my little mind. I would think us lost, and be ready to bawl and ask a stranger to take care of me, when the dogs would turn a corner and we would be home, suddenly, as if we had never left it. With my mother or my father I knew where I lived. With the dogs I was never sure.

She has left without my knowing, after spending maybe an hour with him, or not much more. He is packing two bags now, with instruments and papers and notebooks, and he worries that I have not left enough time to make all the arrangements necessary, and will not listen when I tell him that all is in hand, that my alternate is on his way, that Mr Beresford's men are due at five, that he is not to concern himself with that side of things. Concern himself he does however, and from upstairs somewhere he produces a short sword in a black scabbard, and he confronts my amusement with hoods on his eyes and a grim look and words about chance and importance. It seems to me at first that he inflates the latter, but I am not sure after all, where all of this is leading.

He is impatient to be gone, but there is nothing else to be done – other than to wait for the hour to approach us. He sits with his bags at his feet, his sword hung from his waist, and glances at the sky in the window, and at his pocket watch. It will not rain. I wonder how he would use the sword, and try to draw him out about it, but he is not keen on conversation, preferring to hum and fret and make occasional notes in a moleskin book he keeps in his pocket, licking his pencil more than he needs to and leaving a black line on his lip.

I find him so ridiculous that he scares me somewhat. What is he doing here? I mean in this life, my life. In my city. What are his plans? He has about him an arrogance and surety of purpose which does not seem to fit here. He is come amongst us to alter things, and I cannot frame the alteration properly in my mind, cannot see its reach or its import. Maybe it is nothing.

It is close to five, and my alternate has arrived – I can hear him complaining to the staff about his rest being disturbed. He is a surly man, hard, well suited to looking after our charge during the night, but without much usefulness otherwise.

Our gentleman now wants to be on his way, and I have to persuade him repeatedly that we cannot meet Beresford's men en route, that there is too much chance in it, that we should follow our directions. But they are late, and he is restless, and my alternate grumbles incessantly, and the house is too warm, and my mind is unsettled here, it edges towards the reckless and the river, towards moving home along the dark water, towards leaving all of this for a different time. I want to be gone.

They arrive, three of them, loudly, and it is just as well, for it gives me a chance to be angry, and my anger fixes me, points me frontwise, along the line I'm on, and before long they are chastised and we are organised, one bag on my shoulder, one on that of my alternate and the three heavies around the gentleman like an arrowhead. It occurs to me that this will raise a few eyebrows, and that perhaps just the two of us, early in the morning, might have gone unnoticed – but it is too late now for that. We move down the steps of the house and into the street, and we set a decent pace east, parallel to the river, with my alternate wondering out loud why we do not take a coach, and the heavies casting glances at children, and our gentleman a touch embarrassed, but as excited as a boy, his legs skipping a little on the stones, his sword hung beneath his coat, the bulge of it front and back both comic and grotesque.

I do not know what we look like. I do not know who sees us. Six men in procession through the back streets, making our way to the thin parts of the city, taking the leaking lanes and the cobbled, straw strewn pathways, seeping out of the civilised world with all the waste and the wretched surplus, spilling out into the shallows, into the mud and the stagnant pools and the half swamps, into the sinking part of the island, the nearest to water, where we stand then, as if we have arrived at a centre, and we breathe deep and stand in a circle, and our feet are sudden wet, and our noses tight, and the gentleman amongst us claps his hands in fear and wonder, and exclaims, and I know not where he finds the words –

'By God it's worse than they told me, by God it is, what a wonderful worse it is.'

And indeed it is. It seems to me that in a thousand years of trying you could not build a solid thing here, nothing lasting or secure. This is madness. The river here is invisible, in that it is everywhere, we are standing in it, it is level, it washes my boots with its black mud. My alternate gapes at me. One of the heavies laughs. But our gentleman notices nothing. He is gesturing at me for the bag, and I hand it to him, and he looks for a place to set it down, and has to balance it in the end on a bramble bush bare of leaves, and he rummages and mutters, and mutters and squints, and comes up with a measuring stick of polished wood, and I know that he wants to find a solid surface under us, a layer or rock or some such, and I know by the smell of the place that he'll need a longer stick than that. But he fiddles with it then, and I think for a moment that he is trying to snap it, but I see then that the stick extends – that it has been folded in on itself, and now he unfolds it, and it becomes longer and longer until it is maybe five yards, and thin but solid.

Beresford's men stand together, and I think they probably have a flask to share amongst themselves. My alternate has found a small rock, and has sat himself down upon it, gingerly, holding the tails of his coat out of the dirt, and he pulls up his knees and crosses his arms on them, and lays his head upon his arms, and pays no more attention to anything. I retrieve the second bag from his side, and I go next to the gentleman, and when he looks at me I help him with the measuring stick, which we push down together, using a clever cross wood slotted to its end. He tells me to keep it straight, to watch his hands, to keep my own level with them. He stops a few times, and stands back and squints at the notches in the handle piece and at notches in the stick, and when he is satisfied that they are aligned, he allows us to continue. When we come to a halt, he makes a note in his pocketbook. Then he pulls the stick from the ground, making his hands and his coat muddy. He walks some distance, and we repeat the procedure. We do this four times, over a wide area, and he would do it more, but is concerned at what little light we have left and remarks that the whole site will need proper measuring in any case. The pushing is very hard. It makes us grunt and sweat. The heavies simply stare at us, silently, their flask out in the open now, one of them with a pipe lit.

Of all the instruments he uses, and of all the tasks he performs, the measuring stick is the only thing I understand.

He retrieves various devices from the bags, and either puts them to his eye, or lays them on the ground, and makes copious notes. He has me walk through the mud some five hundred yards away from the river, holding another polished stick in my hand, and he peers at me through some complicated instrument which reminds me of those sextants a ship's navigator might use to fix himself against the stars, or the sun, or whatever they do. He waves at me and shouts, and has me move this way and that, and I can see that this is to the great amusement of Mr Beresford's men. My alternate appears to be dozing.

At this distance from him, from my gentleman I mean, I can see him against the city, with the sun going down in the west, and the shadows creeping out across the pools and the weeds and the scattered rocks. He is small. His group is small. I can see the far bank only as low land and the occasional building, and in the distance I can see the hills with their bright peaks, and to my left I can see the widening of the water and the falling away of the land. It has been this way for centuries.

I am baffled by what I do. I cannot grasp it. Something in my chest hangs heavy, like a dead branch, and I cannot lift it. I am unable to explain myself. This place is empty, it has always been so, but I have seen the gentleman's drawings, I have seen his plans, and I know what he intends to do here, and I no longer know where I am, I no longer know what this place is, whether it is barren and useless or whether it is more real in his mind than it is now in the last of the day, with the sun ending at last, leaving at last, giving up its watch. Where does this place belong? When does it belong?

When the light is too little we gather up his things and wake my alternate and set off again across the marshy ground towards the first paths. The gentleman is happy, his face is glowing, his eyes are bright. He sees what we do not, he occupies the future like a child, his plans are everything. So he does not appear to notice that a small crowd follows us from the edge of the lotts, and that the heavies, a little rough now with the liquor, are shouldering him along briskly, while my alternate and I swing the bags and bring up the rear. There is a man amongst them whom I know, I do not recall his name, but he is a well known city man and popular, and I can hear him at the back, his voice loud, crying 'Shame,' the same word, over and over, as if it is sensible, as if there is no need to explain it, as if everyone who hears will understand what he means. His rabble of men and boys call it too, and throw stones and laugh, and we move quickly through the streets, pushing guilt ahead of us, pursued by an anger that has its root in the future, clinging to a sorrow that is always present now.

My wife has prepared a meal for me, and the child is still awake, and I do not talk about my day – I eat and say nothing and I watch them at play. I wish to live with them. I wish to stay here in my home, with my family, to be present when my life comes to its end, to be here amongst the things I know and almost understand. I will not work for Mr Beresford any longer. Tomorrow I will go to him and say that he must find another keeper for his plans.

I am tired but I am afraid of sleeping. I repeat to myself that I am to quit my position, in the hope that it will influence my dreams and that I will not once more spend my night eavesdropping on the future, or on other times that are neither the future nor the past, but cracked views of the time I occupy. I am tired of the chronologies that compete and intertwine and which clutter my mind like weeds.

My son plays with pebbles on a board. He moves them and lets them roll, and determines where they rest by the tilt and balance of the wood, moving his hands as if struggling with a great weight. I can see him deciding in his mind which way they will go, and I can see what he likes and does not like, and I can see that he likes to come close to dropping them, to let them run along the edge until it is almost too late, and then to save them with the smallest movement of his tiny hand. He is skilful at it. My wife sees me watching, and she smiles at me proudly, and I return her smile, and I think that we are happy here, by the river, the three of us.

I remember the woman who called, I remember the picture of her that I am left with, of her acceptance, her pride. It comes to me suddenly, unexpectedly, and I do not welcome it. There is too much evidence here, my head swims through it, and I wonder who she is, and I think of saying her name to my wife, but I do not want to tie one to the other, I do not want to mix the stories that flow here. I finish my food and I kiss my wife and my son and I go out of our home and I stand in the dark and watch the river.

I know that I am not being sensible, that I do not see things clearly, that my mind worries at loose threads, that I cannot find room enough for all that I see, all that I hear, all that I dream. I sit by the trough and look at the river, and I let my mind run on in the hope that it will tire itself, but it collects things, gathers them together, and the great mass that results is too big for me to contain, and I feel that I will burst, and that all the parts of me will be thrown to the river and there they will scatter and swim and that they will not – no matter how I desire it, no matter how I weigh them down – they will not drown. This is what I feel. That I will always swim the river. That I will always be there, separated out, made into essentials, never knowing my time, slipping through the water, hiding beneath the bridges, never knowing my time, always in the river, my skinless mind, swimming the river, trying to find a standard time, a set place, a dry bank, a stopped city, a place to emerge, a complete place, to emerge again.

My wife comes out to me. She holds my shoulders and kisses my hair. We stand together silent in the dark, and we can hear, without wanting to, without listening for it, we can hear the city breathe, and sigh, and breathe, and continue.

MEMORY AND DESIRE

Val Mulkerns

The television people seemed to like him and that was a new feeling he found exciting. Outside his own work circle he was not liked, on the whole, although he had a couple of lifelong friends he no longer cared for very much. The sort of people he would have wished to be accepted by found him arrogant, unfriendly, and not plain enough to be encouraged as an oddity. His wealth made him attractive only to the types he most despised. He was physically gross and clumsy with none of the social graces except laughter. Sometimes his jokes were good and communicable. More often they were obscure and left him laughing alone as though he were the last remaining inhabitant of an island.

Sometimes, indeed, he wondered if he spoke the same language as most other people, so frequently were they baffled if not positively repelled. He liked people generally, especially physically beautiful people who seemed to him magical as old gods. Sometimes he just looked at such people, not listening or pretending to listen to what they said, and then he saw the familiar expression of dislike and exclusion passing across their faces and he knew he had blundered again. Now for several weeks he had been among a closely knit group who actually seemed to find his company agreeable. When the invitation had first come he had been doubtful. He knew nothing about television and seldom watched it. But because his father's small glass-making business had blossomed under his hand and become an important element in the export market, the television people thought a programme could be made out of his success story, a then-and-now sort of

approach which seemed to him banal in the extreme. He had given his
eventual consent because time so often hung on his hands now that
expansion had progressed as far as was practicable and delegation had
left him with little to do except see his more lucrative contacts in
Europe and the United States a couple of times a year.

The only work he would actually have enjoyed doing these days
was supervising the first efforts of young glass-blowers. Two of the
present half-dozen were grandsons of his father's original men. At a
time when traditional crafts were dying out everywhere or falling into
strange (and probably passing) hands, this pleased him. He tried to
show signs of his approval while keeping the necessary distance right
from the boys' first day at work, but this was probably one of the few
places left in Ireland where country boys were shy and backward still,
and their embarrassment had been so obvious that nowadays he
confined himself to reports on them from the foreman. It had been
different in his father's time. The single cutter and the couple of
blowers had become personal friends of his father and mother, living
in the loft above the workshops (kept warm in winter by the kiln) and
eating with the family in the manner of medieval apprentice craftsmen.
During holidays from boarding school they had become his friends
too, gradually and naturally passing on their skills to him, and so
listening without resentment to the new ideas on design he had in due
course brought back with him from art school and from working spells
in Sweden. Gradually over the years of expansion after his father's
death he had grown away from the men. Now since the new factory
had been built in Cork he knew very few of them any more.

The odd thing about the television people was that right from the
beginning they had been unawed and called him Bernard, accepting
that he had things to learn about their business and that he would stay
with them in the same guest house, drink and live with them during the
shooting of the film, almost as though they were his family and he an
ordinary member of theirs. It had irritated and amused and baffled and
pleased him in rapid progression and now he even found it hard to
remember what his life had been like before he knew them or how his
days had been filled in. Their youth too had shocked him in the
beginning; they seemed like children at play with dangerous and
expensive toys. The director in particular (who was also the producer
and therefore responsible for the whole idea) had in addition to a good-

humoured boy's face an almost fatherly air of concern for his odd and not always biddable family. What was more remarkable, he could discipline them. The assistant cameraman who had got drunk and couldn't be wakened on the third day of shooting had not done it again. When Eithne, the production assistant, had come down to breakfast one morning with a streaming cold and a raised temperature, Martin had stuffed a handful of her notes into the pocket of his jeans and sent her back up to bed, weeping and protesting that she was perfectly all right and not even her mother would dare to treat her like that.

Martin was very good with uncooperative fishermen, and with the farmer on whose land the original workshop still hung over the sea. A nearby hilly field had recently been sown with oats, and the farmer began with the strongest objection to a jeep laden with gear coming anywhere near it. He had agreed to it during preliminary negotiations, but shooting had in fact been delayed (delayed until more money became available) and that field, the farmer said, was in a delicate condition now. If they'd only come at the right time – Martin it was who finally talked him around with a guarantee against loss which would probably land him in trouble back in Dublin. But Martin (the Marvellous Boy was Bernard's private label for him) would worry about that one when he came to it and he advised Bernard to do the same about his fear of appearing ridiculous in some sequences. Not even half the stuff they were shooting would eventually be used, Martin said, and anyhow he'd give Bernard a preview at the earliest possible moment. Bernard stopped worrying again. Most of the time he had the intoxicating illusion of drifting with a strong tide in the company of excellent seamen and a captain who seemed to know his business.

The actual process of remembering was occasionally painful, of course. His only brother Tom had been swept away by a spring tide while fishing down on the rocks one day after school, and at first Bernard hadn't believed any reference to it would be possible when the script finally came to be written. Martin had come back to it casually again and again however, and finally one day of sharp March winds and flying patches of blue sky he had stood with Bernard on the headland near the roofless house.

'Let me show you what I have in mind,' Martin said gently, the south Kerry accent soft as butter. 'It will be very impressionistic, what

I've in mind, a mere flash. A spin of sky and running tides, a moment. If you'd prefer, it won't need anything specific in the script. Just a reference to this friendly big brother mad about fishing, who knew about sea birds and seals and liked to be out by himself for hours on end. Maybe then, a single sentence about the nature of spring tides. The viewers generally won't know that spring tides have nothing to do with spring. You may say we're telling them about a successful glass industry, not about the sea, but the sea takes up a large part of your own early background and this piece is about you too. I'd write you a single sentence myself for your approval if you wouldn't mind – just to show you what I think would work – OK?'

' "These are pearls that were his eyes" – you could end like that, couldn't you?' Bernard heard himself sneering and almost at once regretted it. The director actually blushed and changed the subject. In a few seconds it was as if the moment had never happened, but it seemed to Bernard that a kind of bond had been perversely established.

Two days later a spring tide was running and he watched a few sequences being shot that might well be used for the passage he knew now he was going to write. He walked away from the crew when he found he could no longer watch the sort of sling from which the chief cameraman had been suspended above the cliffs to get some of the necessary angles. The whole thing could have been done better and more safely by helicopter but Martin had explained about the problems he had encountered after overrunning the budget for the last production. It wasn't of course that he wanted necessarily to make Bernard's backward look a cheaper affair; you often got a better end result (in his own experience) by using more ingenuity and less money: he thought he knew exactly how to do it. The somewhat unconvincing argument amused and didn't displease Bernard, who thought it more than likely that something less conventional might finally emerge. The last he saw of the crew was that crazy young man, clad as always when working in a cotton plaid shirt, suspending himself without benefit of the cameraman's sling to try to see exactly what the lens saw.

A fit of nervousness that had in it something of the paternal and something else not paternal at all made him walk the seven miles around to the next headland. He hadn't thought like a father for five years. For half of that isolated time he hadn't brought home casual male encounters either because nothing stable had ever emerged from them and more often than not he was put off by the jungle whiff of the predator and managed to change direction just in time. Now he tried to resist looking back at the pair of boys busy with their games which they apparently regarded as serious. The head cameraman was even younger than Martin. He had a fair freckled face and red hair so long that it would surely have been safer to tie it back in a girl's ponytail before swinging him out in that perilous contraption. Bernard turned his face again into the stiff wind and looked back at the receding insect wriggling above the foaming tide, man and technology welded together in the blasting sunlight. The weird shape drew back his eyes again and again until a rock they called the Billygoat's Missus cut it off and he was alone for (it seemed) the first time in several weeks.

For the first time as in a camera's framed eye he saw his own room at home. Tidy as a well-kept grave, it was full of spring light from the garden. There were daffodils on his desk. Spangles of light from the rocky pool outside danced on the Yeats canvas that took up most of one wall and struck sparks from the two early balloons which he treasured. Five poplars in a haze of young green marked the end of his garden. Beyond it, the sharp-breasted great Sugarloaf and eventually the sea. The room had been tidy for five years now. No maddening litter of dropped magazines, no hairpins, no shoes kicked off and left where they fell: left for the woman next morning to carry to the appropriate place in the appropriate room because she was born to pick up the litter of other people's lives, paid for it as the only work she knew. One night in a fit of disgust he had kicked into the corner a black leather clog, left dead centre on the dark carpet awaiting the exact moment to catch his shin. Uncontrolled fits of violence he despised. Recovering quickly he had placed the shoes side by side outside the door as though this were an old-fashioned hotel with a dutiful boots in residence. She had come in laughing later on, both clogs held up incredulously in her hand, laughing and laughing, tossing them finally up in the air to fall where they might before she left the room. As perhaps she had done last night and would do again tomorrow. Wherever she was.

A rising wind drove before it into the harbour a flock of black clouds that had appeared from nowhere, and when drops of rain the size of old pennies began to lash down he sought refuge in the hotel which had been small and unpretentious in its comfort when he was a child. His father's clients had often stayed here. He had sometimes been sent on messages to them with his brother. Now the place had several stars from an international guidebook and was famous both for its seafood and the prices that foreign gourmets were willing to pay for it.

He sat in the little bar full of old coastal maps and looked out at the sea; alone for the first time in two weeks he was no less content than in the casual company of the television people. Their young faces and their voices were still inside his head. As though on cue, Martin suddenly came through into the bar, also alone. The wind had made any more shooting too dangerous for today, he said, and the girls had gone off to wash their hair. He had his fishing gear in the boot, but he doubted if he'd do much good today.

'Have lunch with me, then, and eat some fish instead,' Bernard invited, and was amused to see a flash of pure pleasure light up the director's face. Beer and a sandwich usually kept them going until they all sat down together at the end of the day.

'This place has got so much above itself even since the last time I was down here that I expect to be asked my business as soon as I set foot inside the door,' Martin grinned.

'They wouldn't do that in late March,' Bernard assured him. 'Neither the swallows nor the tourists have arrived yet, so I fancy even people in your advanced state of sartorial decay would be encouraged.'

Martin took an imaginary clothes brush out of the jeans pocket (too tight to hold anything larger than a toothbrush) and began to remove stray hairs from that well-worn garment which had seaweedy stains in several places and looked slightly damp. The boy walked with a sort of spring, like a healthy cat, and there was no trace yet of the flab which his pint-drinking would eventually bring. He ate the bouillabaise and the fresh baked salmon which followed with the relish of a child brought out from boarding school for the day and determined to take full advantage of it. He praised the Alsace wine which was apparently new to him and Bernard decided that one of the great remaining pleasures of money was never to have to worry about the cost of anything one suddenly wanted to do. Bernard listened abstractedly to a little house politics over the coffee and then at the end of the first cognac he spoke one unwary line about buying all those bandy little boss men for a next birthday present for Martin should he wish it. The sea-reflecting blue eyes opposite him narrowed coldly for a moment before they closed in a bellow of laughter and the moment passed, like the rain outside. The sea was too uneasy, however, in the whipping wind to yield anything, but Bernard remembered one good story about his dead brother on a long-ago trip to Kinsale. Martin made a note in biro on the back of the wrist which held his fishing rod and Bernard knew it would be transferred to the mounting heaps of papers back at the hotel. More and more in the course of the programme he was being his own production assistant.

Mr O'Connor had carried in a mountain of turf for the fire and Eithne rather liked to listen to the rattle of the rain outside by way of contrast. Her hair was dry by now but spread all over the hearthrug and she swung it back in a tickling blanket over the recumbent John D who was still struggling with the *Irish Times* crossword.

'Give that over and sit up,' she said, fetching her eternal dice-throwing version of Scrabble which she had bought somewhere in Holland.

'I was just going to work out another angle for that last shot to put to Martin when he gets back.'

'Martin is probably half way to France by now on an ebbing tide. We'll find his pathetic little bits and pieces in the morning.'

'Stop that!' John D was superstitious as well as red-haired. He was nervous about things like that. 'All right, I'll give you three games and that's it.'

'Nice John D. Did you notice Bernard's face today when you were strung up over the cliff, by the way?'

'I had other things to worry about. Is "cadenza" allowed?'

'It's not English but I suppose it's in the OED like everything else – it's virtually been taken over, after all.'

'OK, it's allowed.' John D formed the word.

'But no *brio* or *allegro molto*,' Eithne warned.

'No *brio* or *allegro molto* – I haven't the makings of them anyhow. What sort of look did Bernard have on his unlovely mug?'

'A bit nervous for you, I think. I think that's why he walked away.'

'Arrogant bastard a lot of the time.' John D swept up the dice after totting his score. 'Are capitalists human? You should put that theme to Martin some time.'

'More a Neville sort of line, surely? But I think you're wrong. He's shy and he's only just stopped being uneasy with us.'

'Just in time to say goodbye then,' said John D with satisfaction. 'There's hardly a week in it, if the weather lifts a bit.'

'If,' Eithne said, scooping a single good score. It was her game, her thing, but the others always won. 'I think he's lonely, which only goes to show you money isn't everything.'

'You can be miserable in much more comfort though. He looks to me like a bod who'd have it off wherever he pleased with one sex or t'other, despite his ugly mug. He has the brazen confidence you only get from too much money.'

'I think you're wrong and the death of his brother is still bothering him after all these years. It's something I just have a hunch about. And then of course his wife walked out on him a few years ago. Prime bitch they say she was too. He came home one night and found not as much as a hair-clip left behind, and his baby gone too.'

' "Hunch" is not a permissable word all the same. Thirties slang,' said John D with finality. 'Why wouldn't she walk out on him when he's probably given to buggery?'

'It's much more permissable than "Cadenza". How about to hunch one's shoulders?'

'Go and ask Mr O'Connor if he has a dictionary then.'

'You go. My hair isn't dry yet.'

'Your hair is practically on fire, lady,' John D said, settling himself comfortably on the hearthrug again. A car crunched in the sandy drive outside and Eithne gave a long sigh.

'Thank God. I couldn't have borne the smell of good country roast beef much longer.'

'There'll be frogs' eyes to follow.'

'At worst there'll be stewed apples, at best apple pie. Doesn't your nose tell you anything except whether a pint's good or bad?'

In out of the rain and the early dusk, Bernard was touched all over again by the sight of two apparent children playing a game beside the fire. He came over very willingly to join them when Eithne called and Martin went upstairs to look over his notes before dinner. He would call Evelyn on his way down, he said.

Later they all went out in the pouring rain to the pub and listened while a couple of local Carusos rendered songs like 'Two

Sweethearts' – one with hair of shining gold, the other with hair of grey
– or the endless emigrant laments favoured by local taste. Whiskey
chasing several pints made John D a bit quarrelsome and he shouted
for a song from Bernard just to embarrass him. To everybody's surprise
Bernard was not embarrassed. He stood up, supported only by two
small Jamesons (the second of which he was still nursing) and gave the
company a soft-voiced but not untuneful version of 'Carrickfergus'
which was vociferously applauded by the locals and earned him
delighted approval from the team. Eithne thought they ought maybe
incorporate 'Carrickfergus' into the soundtrack, and John D wanted to
know why they couldn't all move up to Carrickfergus and let Bernard
do his party piece with his back against the castle walls. This
suggestion was received with the contempt it deserved but Bernard
wasn't discomfited.

That happened only when they got back to the guest house and he
heard Martin telling Mrs O'Connor that they would almost certainly
be finished shooting by the end of the week and would hardly stay
over the weekend. The sinking of the heart was like what came
long ago with the necessity of facing back to school after the long
summer holidays. He felt ashamed of his emotion and unsure how to
conceal it, so he went up early to his room. Normally they would
hang about for hours yet, reading the newspapers they hadn't had
time for during the day, swapping stories, doing crossword puzzles,
discussing the next day's work. Usually he didn't contribute much to
the conversation; like a silent member of a big family he was simply
there, part of what was going on, perfectly content to sit up as long
as they did.

Now there was something symbolic about hearing the murmur of
their voices downstairs. The script had still to be written and there
would be consultations in Dublin about it, hopefully with Martin, but
(give or take a few days from now) the thing was over. Next week they
would all be busy taking somebody else through his mental lumber-
room. The little family would reform itself around another fire, and it
would have nothing to do with him. And soon it would be April,
breeding lilacs out of the dead land, mixing memory and desire. Time
perhaps to go away; he had promised himself a few weeks in April. On
the other hand, why not stay on here?

He let down the small dormer window and looked out over the

water. This house echoed, in almost exact detail, that other, roofless, house; the murmur of voices, even, was like his sisters' voices before they settled down for the night, all together in the big back bedroom. His own small room above the harbour used to be shared with his brother. The rain had stopped now and there was almost no sound from the sea and he wasn't surprised when Martin came to his door to say the weather forecast had been very good for the south-west and they might get in a full day's shooting tomorrow.

'Come in and have a nightcap,' he invited, and Martin said he wouldn't stay long but happily didn't refuse the brandy when it was taken from the wardrobe.

'What will you do next?' Bernard asked, just for a moment unsure of how to begin.

'A bit of a break before I join Current Affairs for a short stint,' the boy smiled. 'Yours is the last programme in the present series. No more now until next season.'

'You mean you're going to take a holiday?' He strove to make his voice sound casual, although he was suddenly aware of the beating of his heart.

'Unless something untoward crops up, yes.'

'Why not join me in Greece, then, since that's where I'm heading next week or the week after? The place I have on Ios needs to be opened up after the winter and there's plenty of room, I assure you. Also two local women waiting to cook and clean for us.' Bernard saw the refusal before it came; it was only a question of how it would be framed, how lightly he would be let down.

'It's a tempting offer, and there's nothing I'd enjoy more, all things being equal. Never been further than Corfu as a matter of fact. But my wife has organised a resident babysitter for the two boys and we're off on a busman's holiday to Canada as soon as I'm free. Laura is Canadian you know. I met her when I was training in London with the BBC. When we get back, maybe you'd come over for supper with us some evening? Laura's an unpredictable cook, but you'll agree that doesn't matter too much when you meet her. Is it a deal?'

He drained the glass and got up off Bernard's bed with the same catspring which was noticeable also in the way he walked.

'It's a deal. Many thanks. And maybe you'll both join me some time in Greece?'

Martin made the appropriate noises and didn't go at once, but started talking about a painter called Richard Dadd who (somebody had told him) had probably given Yeats his Crazy Jane themes. He hadn't seen the paintings himself at the Tate but Bernard had, so this kept them going until the door closed behind him, and on his youth, and on the hollow promise of knowing him as one knew every line of one's own hand. There was a lot of the night left and, fortunately, a lot of the brandy too.

The weather behaved as the weathermen said it would and the rest of the shooting went without a hitch. During this couple of weeks the year had turned imperceptibly towards summer, primroses in the land-facing banks, sea-pinks along the cliffs and an air about the television people that Bernard had seen before and couldn't quite place. Only when he went with them for the final day's shooting did he pin it down; a fairgound the day after the circus. The television gear was more easily moved, of course; no long hours were needed for the pull-out. But the feeling was the same. They didn't believe him when he said he was staying on and they seemed shocked, which amused him, when he determinedly heaped presents on them the morning they were going: his Leica for Eithne who (incredibly) had never owned a camera of her own, a sheepskin jacket for John D because his own was in flitters from the rocks, a silver brandy flask (circa 1840), a cigarette lighter and a gold biro scattered apparently at random among the rest. The vulgarity of the largesse amused Bernard himself because such behaviour was not usual and he didn't entirely understand his impulse. But he understood perfectly why he gave Martin his signed first edition of *The Winding Stair*, a volume which for a year or more had lived in the right-hand door-pocket of his car for no better reason than that he liked to have it there. He had bought it somewhere along the quays in Cork.

> Fair and foul are near of kin
> And fair needs foul,' I cried,
> 'My friends are gone and that's a truth
> Nor grave nor bed denied
> Learned in bodily lowliness,
> And in the heart's pride.

A former owner had marked that with a small star in the margin, and Martin smiled slightly as he read it aloud in gratitude when the book fell open.

'I often have a disturbing feeling when I finish a job like this that I know—' he searched patiently for the words he wanted and his hesitation seemed to Bernard like comfort consciously-given for some loss he could understand. 'That I know almost enough to begin all over again. Properly.' He didn't smile at all when they shook hands so that the handgrip seemed warmer. 'Until soon, in Dublin,' were his last words, a rather childish farewell which would have left a pleasant glow behind if Bernard had not known by now that they would not meet again. The vanful of technology went on ahead of the boy's unreliable little red sports car, and watching from the drive of the guest house, Bernard had the feeling of the fairground again after the circus caravans have rolled away. It was peaceful, though, with the blue sea breathing quietly all around him and a few mares' tails of cloud slowly unravelling in the sky.

He was leaning over the wall considering how he would fill his remaining time when the guest house owner strolled by, indicating the blue boat which bobbed at the end of its mooring rope below them. 'You could take the aul' boat out fishing any day you had a fancy for it, Mr Golden. You're more than welcome to her any time though I wouldn't recommend today, mind you.'

'I'm much obliged to you, Stephen. I have all the gear I need in the boot of the car so I might do just that. But why not today?'

'She'll rise again from the south-west long before evening,' his host said positively. 'And she'll blow herself out if I'm not mistaken. 'Twould be a dangerous thing to go fishing out there today.'

'The weathermen last night didn't mention any gales blowing up.'

'The weathermen don't live around this Hook either,' O'Connor said drily. 'I've caught those same gentlemen out once or twice, and will again with the help of God.'

'You might be right at that, I suppose. But if I do go out, I'll only fish for a short while, I promise you.'

A pleasant man, Stephen O'Connor, a retired Civic Guard with an efficient wife to make a business out of the beautiful location of their house and her own hard work. Bernard remembered him vaguely from childhood, pedalling wet and fine around the coast roads, stopping here and there for a chat, missing nothing. It was he who had brought the news that Tom's body had been washed ashore somewhere near Kinsale. It was he who had in fact identified it. On remembering this Bernard toyed for a moment with the idea of having an actual conversation with this kindly man whose memories touched his own at one black juncture. The moment passed, however, and Stephen made a little more chat, lingering with natural courtesy just long enough for a guest to make up his mind whether or not further company would be welcome, and then he ambled contentedly in the direction of the greenhouse for the day's pottering. Old man, old man, if you never looked down again at a drowned face of my father's house it would be time enough for you. Forgive me, Stephen O'Connor.

The first warm sun of the year touched Bernard's eyes and he smiled, sitting up on the sea wall. No more Aprils, no more lilacs breeding out of the dead land, no more carnal awakenings. He felt peaceful, then a little surprised that the image behind his closed eyelids was not of his brother or of the young Martin or even of the caravans pulling out. It was the small wilful face of his daughter in the act of breaking away when one tried to hold her. He didn't know where she was, or even how she looked now, whether she still mirrored her mother in every gesture. He had a perfect right to know for the mere trouble of enforcing it. He hadn't done that, at first put off by the refusal of maintenance, by the eternal sound of the phone ringing in an empty flat and by two or three unanswered letters. He hadn't made a very energetic effort to keep in touch. As one year became two or three and now five, it had always seemed too late, but it would be untrue to pretend he greatly cared. It was just that, not being able to understand why the child's face should be so vivid in his mind, he was bothered by it as by some minor irritation, a door that slammed somewhere out of sight, a dripping tap. It wasn't until he was actually aboard the boat starting up the engine in a freshening breeze that he realised why he couldn't rid himself of his daughter's face today, of all days.

THE MAD LOMASNEYS

Frank O'Connor

Ned Lowry and Rita Lomasney had, one might say, been lovers from childhood. The first time they had met was when he was fourteen and she a year or two younger. It was on the North Mall on a Saturday afternoon, and she was sitting on a bench under the trees; a tall, bony string of a girl with a long, obstinate jaw. Ned was a studious young fellow in a blue and white college cap, thin, pale and spectacled. As he passed he looked at her owlishly and she gave him back an impudent stare. This upset him – he had no experience of girls – so he blushed and raised his cap. At that she seemed to relent.

'Hello,' she said experimentally.

'Good afternoon,' he replied with a pale smile.

'Where are you off to?' she asked.

'Oh, just up the dyke for a walk.'

'Sit down,' she said in a sharp voice, laying her hand on the bench beside her, and he did as he was told. It was a lovely summer evening, and the white quay walls and tall, crazy, claret-coloured tenements under a blue and white sky were reflected in the lazy water, which wrinkled only at the edges and seemed like a painted carpet.

'It's very pleasant here,' he said complacently

'Is it?' she asked with a truculence that startled him. 'I don't see anything very pleasant about it.'

'Oh, it's very nice and quiet,' he said in mild surprise as he raised his fair eyebrows and looked up and down the Mall at the old

Georgian houses and the nursemaids sitting under the trees. 'My name is Lowry,' he added politely.

'Oh, are ye the ones that have the jeweller's shop on the Parade?' she asked.

'That's right,' replied Ned with modest pride.

'We have a clock we got from ye,' she said. ' 'Tisn't much good of an old clock either,' she added with quiet malice.

'You should bring it back to the shop,' he said in considerable concern. 'It probably needs overhauling.'

'I'm going down the river in a boat with a couple of chaps,' she said, going off at a tangent. 'Will you come?'

'Couldn't,' he said with a smile.

'Why not?'

'I'm only left go up the dyke for a walk,' he said complacently. 'On Saturdays I go to Confession at St Peter and Paul's, then I go up the dyke and back the Western Road. Sometimes you see very good cricket matches. Do you like cricket?'

'A lot of old sissies pucking a ball!' she said shortly. 'I do not.'

'I like it,' he said firmly. 'I go up there every Saturday. Of course, I'm not supposed to talk to anyone,' he added with mild amusement at his own audacity.

'Why not?'

'My mother doesn't want me to.'

'Why doesn't she?'

'She comes of an awfully good family,' he answered mildly, and but for his gentle smile she might have thought he was deliberately insulting her. 'You see,' he went on gravely in his thin, pleasant voice, ticking things off on his fingers and then glancing at each finger individually as he ticked it off – a tidy sort of boy – 'there are three main branches of the Hourigan family: the Neddy Neds, the Neddy Jerrys and the Neddy Thomases. The Neddy Neds are the Hayfield Hourigans. They are the oldest branch. My mother is a Hayfield Hourigan, and she'd have been a rich woman only for her father backing a bill for a Neddy Jerry. He defaulted and ran away to Australia,' he concluded with a contemptuous sniff.

'Cripes!' said the girl. 'And had she to pay?'

'She had. But, of course,' he went on with as close as he ever seemed likely to get to a burst of real enthusiasm, 'my grandfather was a well-behaved man. When he was eating his dinner the boys from the National School in Bantry used to be brought up to watch him, he had such beautiful table manners. Once he caught my uncle eating cabbage with a knife and he struck him with a poker. They had to put four stitches in him after,' he added with a joyous chuckle.

'Cripes!' the girl said again. 'What did he do that for?'

'To teach him manners,' Ned said earnestly.

'He must have been dotty.'

'Oh, I wouldn't say so,' Ned exclaimed in mild surprise. Everything this girl said came as a shock to him. 'But that's why my mother won't let me mix with other children. On the other hand, we read a good deal. Are you fond of reading, Miss – I didn't catch the name.'

'You weren't told it,' she said, showing her claws. 'But if you want to know, it's Rita Lomasney.'

'Do you read much, Miss Lomasney?'

'I couldn't be bothered.'

'I read all sorts of books,' he said enthusiastically. 'And as well as that, I'm learning the violin from Miss Maude on the Parade. Of course, it's very difficult, because it's all classical music.'

'What's classical music?' she asked with sudden interest.

'*Maritana* is classical music,' he replied eagerly. He was a bit of a puzzle to Rita. She had never before met anyone with such a passion for handing out instruction. 'Were you at *Maritana* in the opera house, Miss Lomasney?'

'I was never there at all,' she said curtly.

'And *Alice Where Art Thou* is classical music,' he added. 'It's harder than plain music. You see,' he went on, composing signs in the air, 'it has signs on it like this, and when you see the signs, you know it's after turning into a different tune, though it has the same name. Irish music is all the same tune and that's why my mother won't let us learn it.'

'Were you ever at the opera in Paris?' she asked suddenly.

'No,' said Ned. 'I was never in Paris. Why?'

'That's where you should go,' she said with airy enthusiasm. 'You couldn't hear any operas here. The staircase alone is bigger than the whole opera house here.'

It seemed as if they were in for a really informative conversation when two fellows came down Wyse's Hill. Rita got up to meet them. Lowry looked up at them and then rose too, lifting his cap politely.

'Well, good afternoon,' he said cheerfully. 'I enjoyed the talk. I hope we meet again.'

'Some other Saturday,' said Rita.

'Oh, good evening, old man,' one of the two fellows said in an affected drawl, pretending to raise a top hat. 'Do come and see us soon again.'

'Shut up, Foster!' Rita said sharply. 'I'll give you a puck in the gob.'

'Oh, by the way,' Ned said, coming back to hand her a number of the *Gem* which he took from his coat pocket, 'you might like to look at this. It's not bad.'

'Thanks, I'd love to,' she said insincerely, and he smiled and touched his cap again. Then with a polite and almost deferential air he went up to Foster. 'Did you say something?' he asked.

Foster looked as astonished as if a kitten had suddenly got on its hind legs and challenged him to fight.

'I did not,' he said, and backed away.

'I'm glad,' Ned said, almost purring. 'I was afraid you might be looking for trouble.'

It came as a surprise to Rita as well. Whatever opinion she might have formed of Ned Lowry, fighting was about the last thing she would have associated him with.

The Lomasneys lived in a house on Sunday's Well, a small house with a long, sloping garden and a fine view of the river and city. Harry Lomasney, the builder, was a small man who wore grey tweed suits and soft collars several sizes too big for him. He had a ravaged brick-red face with keen blue eyes, and a sandy, straggling moustache with one side going up and the other down, and his workmen said you could tell his humour by the side he pulled. He was nicknamed 'Hasty Harry'. 'Great God!' he fumed when his wife was having her first baby. 'Nine months over a little job like that! I'd do it in three weeks if I could only get started.' His wife was tall and matronly and very pious, but her piety never got much in her way. A woman who had survived Hasty would have survived anything. Their eldest daughter, Kitty, was loud-voiced and gay and had been expelled from school for writing indecent letters to a boy. She had copied the letters out of a French novel but she failed to tell the nuns that. Nellie was placider and took more after her mother; besides, she didn't read French novels.

Rita was the exception among the girls. There seemed to be no softness in her. She never had a favourite saint or a favourite nun; she said it was soppy. For the same reason she never had flirtations. Her friendship with Ned Lowry was the closest she ever got to that, and though Ned came regularly to the house, and the pair of them went to the pictures together, her sisters would have found it hard to say whether she cared any more for him than she did for any of her girl acquaintances. There was something in her they didn't understand, something tongue-tied, twisted and unhappy. She had a curious raw, almost timid smile as though she felt people desired no better sport than hurting her. At home she was reserved, watchful, almost mocking. She could listen for hours to her mother and sisters without once opening her mouth, and then suddenly mystify them by dropping a well-aimed jaw-breaker – about classical music, for instance – before relapsing into a sulky silence; as though she had merely drawn back the veil for a moment on depths in herself which she would not permit them to explore.

After taking her degree, she got a job in a convent school in a provincial town in the west of Ireland. She and Ned corresponded and he even went to see her there. He reported at home that she seemed quite happy.

But this didn't last. A few months later the Lomasney family were at supper one evening when they heard a car stop, the gate squeaked, and steps came up the long path to the front door. Then came the sound of a bell and a cheerful voice from the hall.

'Hullo, Paschal, I suppose ye weren't expecting me?'

"Tis never Rita!' said her mother, meaning that it was but that it shouldn't be.

'As true as God, that one is after getting into trouble,' Kitty said prophetically.

The door opened and Rita slouched in, a long, stringy girl with a dark, glowing face. She kissed her father and mother lightly.

'Hullo,' she said. 'How's tricks?'

'What happened you?' her mother asked, rising.

'Nothing,' replied Rita, an octave up the scale. 'I just got the sack.'

'The sack?' said her father, beginning to pull the wrong side of his moustache. 'What did you get the sack for?'

'Give me a chance to get something to eat first, can't you?' Rita said laughingly. She took off her hat and smiled at herself in the mirror over the mantelpiece. It was a curious smile as though she were amused by the spectacle of what she saw. Then she smoothed back her thick black hair. 'I told Paschal to bring in whatever was going. I'm on the train since ten. The heating was off as usual. I'm frizzled.'

'A wonder you wouldn't send us a wire,' said Mrs Lomasney as Rita sat down and grabbed some bread and butter.

'Hadn't the tin,' replied Rita.

'Can't you tell us what happened?' Kitty asked brightly.

'I told you. You'll hear more in due course. Reverend Mother is bound to write and tell ye how I lost my character.'

'But what did you do, child?' her mother asked placidly. Her mother had been through all this before, with Hasty and Kitty, and she knew God was very good and nothing much ever happened.

'Fellow that wanted to marry me,' said Rita. 'He was in his last year at college, and his mother didn't like me, so she got Reverend Mother to give me the push.'

'And what has it to do with Reverend Mother?' Nellie asked indignantly. 'What business is it of hers?'

'That's what I say,' said Rita.

But Kitty looked suspiciously at her. Rita wasn't natural; there was something wild about her, and this was her first real love affair. Kitty just couldn't believe that Rita had gone about it the same as anyone else.

'Still, I must say you worked pretty fast,' she said.

'You'd have to in that place,' said Rita. 'There was only one possible man in the whole village and he was the bank clerk. We called him 'The One'. I wasn't there a week when the nuns ticked me off for riding on the pillion of his motorbike.'

'And did you?' asked Kitty.

'I never got the chance, girl. They did it to every teacher on principle to give her the idea that she was well watched. I only met Tony Donoghue a fortnight ago – home after a breakdown.'

'Well, well, well!' her mother exclaimed without rancour. 'No wonder his poor mother was upset. A boy that's not left college yet! Couldn't ye wait till he was qualified anyway?'

'Not very well,' said Rita. 'He's going to be a priest.'

Kitty sat back with a superior grin. Of course, Rita could do nothing like anyone else. If it wasn't a priest it would have been a Negro, and Rita would have made theatre of it in precisely the same deliberate way.

'A what?' asked her father, springing to his feet.

'All right, don't blame me!' Rita said hastily. 'It wasn't my fault. He told me he didn't want to be a priest. It was his mother was driving him into it. That's why he had the breakdown.'

'Let me out of this,' said her father, 'before I—'

'Go on!' Rita said with tender mockery (she was very fond of her father). 'Before you what?'

'Before I wish I was a priest myself,' he snarled. 'I wouldn't be saddled with a family like I am.'

He stumped out of the room, and the girls laughed. The idea of their father as a priest appealed to them almost as much as the idea of him as a mother. Hasty had a knack of stating his grievances in such a way that they inevitably produced laughter. But Mrs Lomasney did not laugh.

'Reverend Mother was perfectly right,' she said severely. 'As if it wasn't hard enough on the poor boys without girls like you throwing temptation in their way. I think you behaved very badly, Rita.'

'All right, if you say so,' Rita said shortly with a boyish shrug of her shoulders, and refused to answer any more questions.

After her supper she went to bed, and her mother and sisters sat on in the front room discussing the scandal. Someone rang and Nellie opened the door.

'Hullo, Ned,' she said. 'I suppose you came up to congratulate us on the good news?'

'Hullo,' Ned said, smiling with his mouth primly shut. With a sort of automatic movement he took off his coat and hat and hung them on the rack. Then he emptied the pockets with the same thoroughness. He hadn't changed much. He was thin and pale, spectacled and clever, with the same precise and tranquil manner, 'like an old Persian cat,' as Nellie said. He read too many books. In the last year or two something seemed to have happened him. He didn't go to Mass any longer. Not going to Mass struck all the Lomasneys as too damn clever. 'What good news?' he added, having avoided any unnecessary precipitation.

'You didn't know who was here?'

'No,' he replied, raising his brows mildly.

'Rita!'

'Oh!' The same tone. It was part of his cleverness not to be surprised at anything.

'She's after getting the sack for trying to run off with a priest,' said Nellie.

If Nellie thought that would shake him she was mistaken. He merely tossed his head with a silent chuckle and went in, adjusting his pince-nez. For a fellow who was supposed to be in love with her since they were kids, he behaved in a very peculiar manner. He put his hands in his trouser pockets and stood on the hearth with his legs well apart.

'Isn't it awful, Ned?' Mrs Lomasney asked in her deep voice.

'Is it?' Ned purred, smiling.

'With a priest?' cried Nellie.

'Now, he wasn't a priest, Nellie,' said Mrs Lomasney reprovingly. ''Tis bad enough as it is without making it any worse.'

'Suppose you tell me what happened,' suggested Ned.

'But we don't know, Ned,' cried Mrs Lomasney. 'You know what that one is like in one of her sulky fits. Maybe she'll tell you. She's up in bed.'

'I'll try,' said Ned.

Still with his hands in his pockets, he rolled after Mrs Lomasney up the thickly carpeted stairs to Rita's little bedroom on top of the house. She left him on the landing and he paused for a moment to look out over the river and the lighted city behind it. Rita, wearing a pink dressing-jacket, was lying with one arm under her head. By the bed was a table with a packet of cigarettes she had been using as an ashtray. He smiled and shook his head reprovingly at her.

'Hullo, Ned,' she cried, reaching him a bare arm. 'Give us a kiss. I'm quite kissable now.'

He didn't need to be told that. He was astonished at the change in her. Her whole bony, boyish face seemed to have gone mawkish and soft and to be lit up from inside. He sat on an armchair by the bed, carefully pulling up the bottoms of his trousers, then put his hands in his trouser pockets again and sat back with crossed legs and shoulders slightly hunched.

'I suppose they're all in a floosther downstairs?' Rita asked with amusement.

'They seem a little excited,' said Ned with bowed head cocked a little sideways, looking like a wise old bird.

'Wait till they hear the details and they'll have something to be excited about,' said Rita grimly.

'Why?' he asked mildly. 'Are there details?'

'Masses of them,' said Rita. 'Honest to God, Ned, I used to laugh at the glamour girls in the convent. I never knew you could get like that about a fellow. It's like something busting inside you. Cripes, I'm as soppy as a kid!'

'And what's the fellow like?' Ned asked curiously.

'Tony Donoghue? His mother had a shop in the Main Street. He's decent enough, I suppose. I don't know. He kissed me one night coming home. I was furious. I cut the blooming socks off him. Next evening he came round to apologise. I never got up or asked him to sit down or anything. I suppose I was still mad with him. He said he never slept a wink. "Didn't you?" said I. "It didn't trouble me much." Bloody lies, of course. "I did it because I was fond of you," says he. "Is that what you told the last one too?" said I. Then he got into a wax too. Said I was calling him a liar. "And aren't you?" said I. Then I waited for him to hit me, but, begor, he didn't, and I ended up sitting on his knee. Talk about the Babes in the Wood! First time he ever had a girl on his knee, he said, and you know how much of it I did.'

They heard a step on the stairs and Mrs Lomasney smiled benevolently at them both round the door.

'I suppose 'tis tea Ned is having?' she asked in her deep voice.

'No, I'm having the tea,' said Rita. 'Ned says he'd sooner a drop of the hard tack.'

'Oh, isn't that a great change, Ned?' cried Mrs Lomasney.

''Tis the shock,' Rita explained lightly, throwing him a cigarette. 'He didn't think I was that sort of girl.'

'He mustn't know much about girls,' said Mrs Lomasney.

'He's learning now,' said Rita.

When Paschal brought up the tray, Rita poured out tea for Ned and whiskey for herself. He made no comment. Things like that were a commonplace in the Lomasney household.

'Anyway,' she went on, 'he told his old one he wanted to chuck the Church and marry me. There was ructions, of course. The people in the shop at the other side of the street had a son a priest. She wanted to be as good as them. So away with her up to Reverend Mother, and Reverend Mother sends for me. Did I want to destroy the young man's life and he on the threshold of a great calling? I told her 'twas they wanted to destroy him. I asked her what sort of priest Tony would make. Oh, 'twas a marvellous sacrifice, and after it he'd be twice the man. Honest to God, Ned, the way that woman went on, you'd think she was talking about doctoring an old tomcat. I told her that was all she knew about Tony, and she said they knew him since he was an altar boy in the convent. "Did he ever tell you how he used to slough the convent orchard and sell the apples in town?" says I. So then she dropped the Holy Willie stuff and told me his ma was after getting into debt to put him in for the priesthood, and if he chucked it, he'd never be able to get a job at home to pay it back. Three hundred quid! Wouldn't they kill you with style?'

'And what did you do then?' asked Ned with amusement.

'I went to see his mother.'

'You didn't!'

'I did. I thought I might work it with the personal touch.'

'You don't seem to have been very successful.'

'I'd as soon try the personal touch on a traction engine, Ned. That woman was too tough for me altogether. I told her I wanted to marry Tony. "I'm sorry," she said; "you can't." "What's to stop me?" said I. "He's gone too far," says she. "If he was gone farther it wouldn't worry me," says I. I told her then what Reverend Mother said about her being three hundred pounds in debt and offered to pay it back to her if she let him marry me.'

'And had you the three hundred?' Ned asked in surprise.

'Ah, where would I get three hundred?' she replied ruefully. 'And she knew it too, the old jade! She didn't believe a word I said. After that I saw Tony. He was crying; said he didn't want to break his mother's heart. As true as God, Ned, that woman had as much heart as a traction engine.'

'Well, you seem to have done it in style,' Ned said approvingly as he put away his teacup.

'That wasn't the half of it. When I heard the difficulties his mother was making, I offered to live with him instead.'

'Live with him?' asked Ned. Even he was startled.

'Well, go away on holidays with him. Lots of girls do it. I know they do. And, God Almighty, isn't it only natural?'

'And what did he say to that?' asked Ned curiously.

'He was scared stiff.'

'He would be,' said Ned, wrinkling up his nose and giving his superior little sniff as he took out a packet of cigarettes.

'Oh, it's all very well for you,' Rita cried, bridling up. 'You may think you're a great fellow, all because you read Tolstoy and don't go to Mass, but you'd be just as scared if a girl offered to go to bed with you.'

'Try me,' Ned said sedately as he lit her cigarette for her, but somehow the notion of suggesting such a thing to Ned only made her laugh.

He stayed till quite late, and when he went downstairs the girls and Mrs Lomasney fell on him and dragged him into the sitting room.

'Well, doctor,' said Mrs Lomasney, 'how's the patient?'

'Oh, I think the patient is coming round nicely,' said Ned.

'But would you ever believe it, Ned?' she cried. 'A girl that wouldn't look at the side of the road a fellow was at, unless 'twas to go robbing orchards with him. You'll have another drop of whiskey?'

'I won't.'

'And is that all you're going to tell us?' asked Mrs Lomasney.

'Oh, you'll hear it all from herself.'

'We won't.'

'I dare say not,' he said with a hearty chuckle, and went for his coat.

'Wisha, Ned,' said Mrs Lomasney, 'what'll your mother say when she hears it?'

'"All *quite* mad,"' said Ned, sticking his nose in the air and giving an exaggerated version of what Mrs Lomasney called 'his Hayfield sniff'.

'The dear knows, I think she's right,' she said with resignation, helping him with his coat. 'I hope your mother doesn't notice the smell of whiskey from your breath,' she added dryly, just to show him that she couldn't be taken in, and then stood at the door, looking up and down, as she waited for him to wave from the gate.

'Ah,' she sighed as she closed the door behind her, 'with the help of God it might be all for the best.'

'If you think he's going to marry her, I can tell you now he's not,' said Kitty. 'I'd like to see myself trying it on Bill O'Donnell. He'd have my sacred life. That fellow only enjoys it.'

'Ah, God is good,' her mother said cheerfully, kicking a mat into place. 'Some men might like that.'

Inside a week Kitty and Nellie were sick to death of the sight of Rita round the house. She was bad enough at the best of times, but now she just brooded and mooned and snapped the head off you. In the afternoons she strolled down the dyke and into Ned's little shop, where she sat on the counter, swinging her legs and smoking, while Ned leaned against the side of the window, tinkering at the insides of a watch with some delicate instrument. Nothing seemed to rattle him. When he had finished work, he changed his coat and they went out to tea. He sat at the back of the teashop in a corner, pulled up the legs of his trousers, and took out a packet of cigarettes and a box of matches, which he placed on the table before them with a look that almost commanded them to stay there and not get lost. His face was pale and clear and bright, like an evening sky when the last light has drained from it.

'Anything wrong?' he asked one evening when she was moodier than usual.

'Just fed up,' she said, thrusting out her jaw.

'What is it?' he asked gently. 'Still fretting?'

'Ah, no. I can get over that. It's Kitty and Nellie. They're bitches, Ned; proper bitches. And all because I don't wear my heart on my sleeve. If one of them got a knock from a fellow she'd take two aspirins and go to bed with the other one. They'd have a lovely talk – can't you imagine? "And was it then he said he loved you?" I can't do that sort of stuff. And it's all because they're not sincere, Ned. They couldn't be sincere.'

'Remember, they have a long start on you,' Ned said smiling.

'Is that it?' she asked without interest. 'They think I'm batty. Do you?'

'I've no doubt that Mrs Donoghue, if that's her name, thought something of the sort,' replied Ned with a tight-lipped smile.

'And wasn't she right?' asked Rita with sudden candour. 'Suppose she'd agreed to take the three hundred quid, wouldn't I be in a nice pickle? I wake in a sweat whenever I think of it. I'm just a blooming chancer, Ned. Where would I get three hundred quid?'

'Oh, I dare say someone would have lent it to you,' he said with a shrug.

'They would like fun. Would you?'

'Probably,' he said gravely after a moment's thought.

'Are you serious?' she whispered earnestly.

'Quite.'

'Cripes,' she gasped, 'you must be very fond of me.'

'It looks like it,' said Ned, and this time he laughed with real heartiness, a boy's laugh of sheer delight at the mystification he was causing her. It was characteristic of Rita that she should count their friendship of years as nothing, but his offer of three hundred pounds in cash as significant.

'Would you marry me?' she asked frowningly. 'I'm not proposing to you, only asking,' she added hastily.

'Certainly,' he said, spreading out his hands. 'Whenever you like.'

'Honest to God?'

'Cut my throat.'

'And why didn't you ask me before I went down to that kip? I'd have married you then like a shot. Was it the way you weren't keen on me then?'

'No,' he replied matter-of-factly, drawing himself together like an old clock preparing to strike. 'I think I've been keen on you as long as I know you.'

'It's easily seen you're a Neddy Ned,' she said with amusement. 'I go after mine with a scalping knife.'

'I stalk mine,' said Ned.

'Cripes, Ned,' she said with real regret, 'I wish you'd told me sooner. I couldn't marry you now.'

'No?'

'No. It wouldn't be fair to you.'

'Isn't that my look-out?'

'It's my look-out now.' She glanced around the restaurant to make sure no one was listening and then went on in a dry voice, leaning one elbow on the table. 'I suppose you'll think this is all cod, but it's not. Honest to God, I think you're the finest bloody man I ever met – even though you do think you're an atheist or something,' she added maliciously with a characteristic Lomasney flourish in the cause of Faith and Fatherland. 'There's no one in the world I have more respect for. I think I'd nearly cut my throat if I did something you really disapproved of – I don't mean telling lies or going on a skite,' she added hastily, to prevent misunderstandings. 'They're only gas. Something that really shocked you is what I mean. I think if I was tempted to do anything like that I'd ask myself: "What would that fellow Lowry think of me now?"'

'Well,' Ned said in an extraordinary quiet voice, squelching the butt of his cigarette on his plate, 'that sounds to me like a very good beginning.'

'It is not, Ned,' she said sadly, shaking her head. 'That's why I say it's my look-out. You couldn't understand it unless it happened to yourself; unless you fell in love with a girl the way I fell in love with Tony. Tony is a scut, and a cowardly scut, but I was cracked about him. If he came in here now and said: "Come on, girl, we're going to Killarney for the weekend," I'd go out and buy a nightdress and toothbrush and be off with him. And I wouldn't give a damn what you or anybody thought. I might chuck myself in the lake afterwards, but I'd go. Christ, Ned,' she exclaimed, flushing and looking as though she might burst into tears, 'he couldn't come into a room but I went all mushy inside. That's what the real thing is like.'

'Well,' Ned said sedately, apparently not in the least put out – in fact, looking rather pleased with himself, Rita thought – 'I'm in no hurry. In case you get tired of scalping them, the offer will still be open.'

'Thanks, Ned,' she said absent-mindedly, as though she weren't listening.

While he paid the bill, she stood in the porch, doing her face in the big mirror that flanked it, and paying no attention to the crowds, coming homeward through streets where the shop windows were already lit. As he emerged from the shop she turned on him suddenly.

'About that matter, Ned,' she said, 'will you ask me again, or do I have to ask you?'

Ned just refrained from laughing outright. 'As you like,' he replied with quiet amusement. 'Suppose I repeat the proposal every six months.'

'That would be the hell of a long time to wait if I changed my mind,' she said with a thoughtful scowl. 'All right,' she said, taking his arm. 'I know you well enough to ask you. If you don't want me by that time, you can always say so. I won't mind.'

Ned's proposal came as a considerable comfort to Rita. It bolstered up her self-esteem, which was always in danger of collapse. She might be ugly and uneducated and a bit of a chancer, but the best man in Cork

– the best in Ireland, she sometimes thought – wanted to marry her, even after she had been let down by another man. That was a queer one for her enemies! So while her sisters made fun of her, Rita considered the situation, waiting for the best possible moment to let them know she had been proposed to and could marry before either of them if it suited her. Since her childhood Rita had never given anything away without extracting the last ounce of theatrical effect from it. She would tell her sisters, but not before she could make them sick with the news.

That was a pity, for it left Rita unaware that Ned, whom she respected, was far from being the only one who liked her. For instance, there was Justin Sullivan, the lawyer, who had once been by way of being engaged to Nellie. He hadn't become engaged to her, because she was as slippery as an eel, and her fancy finally lit on a solicitor called Fahy whom Justin despised with his whole heart and soul as a lightheaded, butterfly sort of man. But Justin continued to visit the house as a friend of the girls. There happened to be no other house that suited him half as well, and besides he knew that sooner or later Nellie would make a mess of her life with Fahy, and his services would be required.

Justin, in other words, was a sticker. He was a good deal older than Rita, a tall, burly man with a broad face, a brow that was rising from baldness as well as brains, and a slow, watchful ironic air. Like many lawyers, he tended to conduct conversation as though the person he was speaking to were a hostile witness who had either to be coaxed into an admission of perjury or bullied into one of mental deficiency. When Justin began, Fahy simply clutched his head and retired to sit on the stairs. 'Can't anyone shut that fellow up?' he would moan with a martyred air. Nobody could. The girls shot their little darts at him, but he only brushed them aside. Ned Lowry was the only one who could even stand up to him, and when the pair of them argued about religion, the room became a desert. Justin, of course, was a pillar of orthodoxy. 'Imagine for a moment,' he would declaim in a throaty rounded voice that turned easily to pomposity, 'that I am Pope.' 'Easiest thing in the world, Justin,' Kitty assured him. He drank whiskey like water, and the more he drank, the more massive and logical and orthodoxly Catholic he became.

At the same time, under his truculent air he was exceedingly gentle, patient and understanding, and disliked the ragging of Rita by her sisters.

'Tell me, Nellie,' he asked one night in his lazy, amiable way, 'do you talk like that to Rita because you like it, or because you think it's good for her?'

'How soft you have it!' Nellie cried. 'We have to live with her. You haven't.'

'That may be my misfortune, Nellie,' said Justin with a broad smile.

'Is that a proposal, Justin?' asked Kitty shrewdly.

'Scarcely, Kitty,' said Justin. 'You're not what I might call a good jury.'

'Better be careful or you'll have her dropping in on your mother, Justin,' Kitty said maliciously.

'Thanks, Kitty,' Rita said with a flash of cold fury.

'I hope my mother would have sufficient sense to realise it was an honour, Kitty,' Justin said severely.

When he rose to go, Rita accompanied him to the hall.

'Thanks for the moral support, Justin,' she said in a low voice, and then threw her overcoat over her shoulders to go as far as the gate with him. When he opened the door they both stood and gazed about them. It was a moonlit night; the garden, patterned in black and silver, sloped to the quiet roadway, where the gas lamps burned with a dim green light, and in the farther walls gateways shaded by black trees led to flights of steps or to steep-sloping avenues which led to moonlit houses on the river's edge.

'God, isn't it lovely?' Rita said in a hushed voice.

'Oh, by the way, Rita,' he said, slipping his arm through hers, 'that was a proposal.'

'Janey Mack, they're falling,' she said, giving his arm a squeeze.

'What are falling?'

'Proposals.'

'Why? Had you others?'

'I had one anyway.'

'And did you accept it?'

'No,' Rita said doubtfully. 'Not quite. At least, I don't think I did.'

'You might consider this one,' Justin said with unusual humility. 'You know, of course, that I was very fond of Nellie. At one time I was very fond of her indeed. You don't mind that, I hope. It's all over and done with now, and there are no regrets on either side.'

'No, Justin, of course I don't mind. If I felt like marrying you I wouldn't give it a second thought. But I was very much in love with Tony too, and that's not all over and done with yet.'

'I know that, Rita,' he said gently. 'I know exactly what you feel. We've all been through it.' If he had left it at that everything might have been all right, but Justin was a lawyer, which meant that he liked to keep things absolutely shipshape. 'But that won't last forever. In a month or two you'll be over it, and then you'll wonder what you saw in that fellow.'

'I don't think so, Justin,' she said with a crooked little smile, not altogether displeased to be able to enlighten him on the utter hopelessness of her position. 'I think it will take a great deal longer than that.'

'Well, say six months, even,' Justin went on, prepared to yield a point to the defence. 'All I ask is that in one month or six, whenever you've got over your regrets for this – this amiable young man' (momentarily his voice took on its familiar ironic ring), 'you'll give me a thought. I'm old enough not to make any more mistakes. I know I'm fond of you, and I feel pretty sure I could make a success of my end of it.'

'What you really mean,' said Rita, keeping her temper with the greatest difficulty, 'is that I wasn't in love with Tony at all. Isn't that it?'

'Not quite,' Justin said judiciously. Even if he'd had a serenade as well as the moonlight and the girl, it couldn't have kept him from correcting what he considered to be a false deduction. 'I've no doubt you were very much attracted by this – this clerical Adonis; this Mr Whatever-his-name-is, or that at any rate you thought you were, which in practice comes to the same thing, but I also know that that sort of thing, though it's painful enough while it lasts, doesn't last very long.'

'You mean yours didn't, Justin,' Rita said tartly.

'I mean mine or anybody else's,' Justin said pompously. 'Because love – the only sort of thing you can really call love – is something that comes with experience. You're probably too young yet to know what the real thing is.'

As Rita had only recently told Ned that he didn't yet know what the real thing was, she found this rather hard to stomach.

'How old would you say you'd have to be?' she asked viciously. 'Thirty-five?'

'You'll know soon enough – when it hits you,' said Justin.

'Honest to God, Justin,' she said, withdrawing her arm and looking at him with suppressed fury, 'I think you're the thickest man I ever met.'

'Goodnight, my dear,' said Justin with perfect good humour, and he raised his cap and took the few steps to the gate at a run.

Rita stood gazing after him with folded arms. At the age of eighteen to be told that there is anything you don't know about love is like a knife in your heart.

Kitty and Nellie grew so tired of her moodiness that they persuaded her mother that the best way of distracting her mind was to find her another job. A new environment was also supposed to be good for her complaint, so Mrs Lomasney wrote to her sister who was a nun in England, and the sister found her work in a convent there. Rita let on to pay no attention, though she let Ned see something of her resentment.

'But why England?' he asked wonderingly.

'Why not?' replied Rita challengingly.

'Wouldn't any place nearer do you?'

'I suppose I wouldn't be far enough away from them.'

'But why not make up your own mind?'

'I'll probably do that too,' she said with a short laugh. 'I'd like to see what's in theirs first though.'

On Friday she was to leave for England, and on Wednesday the girls gave a farewell party. This, too, Rita affected to take no great interest in. Wednesday was the half-holiday, and it rained steadily all day. The girls' friends all turned up. Most were men: Bill O'Donnell of the bank, who was engaged to Kitty; Fahy, the solicitor, who was Justin's successful rival for Nellie; Justin himself, who simply could not be kept out of the house by anything short of an injunction; Ned Lowry, and a few others. Hasty soon retired with his wife to the dining room to read the evening paper. He said all his daughters' young men looked exactly alike and he never knew which of them he was talking to.

Bill O'Donnell was acting as barman. He was a big man, bigger even that Justin, with a battered boxer's face and a Negro smile, which seemed to well up from depths of good humour with life rather than from any immediate contact with others. He carried on loud conversations with everyone he poured out drink for, and his voice overrode every intervening tête-à-tête, and challenged even the piano, on which Nellie was vamping music-hall songs.

'Who's this one for, Rita?' he asked. 'A bottle of Bass for Paddy. Ah, the stout man! Remember the New Year's Day in Bandon, Paddy? Remember how you had to carry me up to the bank in evening dress and jack me up between the two wings of the desk? Kitty, did I ever tell you about that night in Bandon?'

'Once a week for the past five years, Bill,' said Kitty philosophically.

'Nellie,' said Rita, 'I think it's time for Bill to sing his song. "Let Me like a Soldier Fall", Bill!'

'My one little song!' Bill said with a roar of laughter. 'My one and only song, but I sing it grand. Don't I, Nellie? Don't I sing it fine?'

'Fine!' agreed Nellie, looking up at his big, beaming moonface shining at her over the piano. 'As the man said to my mother, "Finest bloody soprano I ever heard."'

'He did not, Nellie,' Bill said sadly. 'You're making that up . . . Silence please!' he shouted joyously, clapping his hands. 'Ladies and gentlemen, I must apologise. I ought to sing something like Tosti's "Goodbye", but the fact is, ladies and gentlemen, that I don't know Tosti's "Good-bye".'

'Recite it, Bill,' said Justin amiably.

'I don't know the words of it either, Justin,' said Bill. 'In fact, I'm not sure if there's any such song, but if there is, I ought to sing it.'

'Why, Bill?' Rita asked innocently. She was wearing a long black dress that threw up the unusual brightness of her dark, bony face. She looked happier than she had looked for months. All the evening it was as though she were laughing to herself.

'Because 'twould be only right, Rita,' said Bill with great melancholy, putting his arm about her and drawing her closer to him. 'You know I'm very fond of you, don't you, Rita?'

'And I'm mad about you, Bill,' said Rita candidly.

'I know that, Rita,' he said mournfully, pulling at his collar as though to give himself air. 'I only wish you weren't going, Rita. This place isn't the same without you. Kitty won't mind my saying that,' he added with a nervous glance at Kitty, who was flirting with Justin on the sofa.

'Are you going to sing your blooming old song or not?' Nellie asked impatiently, running her fingers over the keys.

'I'm going to sing now in one minute, Nellie,' Bill said ecstatically, stroking Rita fondly under the chin. 'I only want Rita to know the way we'll miss her.'

'Damn it, Bill,' Rita said, snuggling up to him with her dark head on his chest, 'if you go on like that I won't go at all. Tell me, would you really prefer me not to go?'

'I would prefer you not to go, Rita,' he replied, stroking her cheeks and eyes. 'You're too good for the fellows over there.'

'Oh, go on doing that,' she said hastily, as he dropped his hand. 'It's gorgeous, and you're making Kitty mad jealous.'

'Kitty isn't jealous,' Bill said fondly. 'Kitty is a lovely girl and you're a lovely girl. I hate to see you go, Rita.'

'That settles it, Bill,' she said, pulling herself free of him with a determined air. 'I simply couldn't cause you all that suffering. As you put it that way, I won't go.'

'Won't you, just?' said Kitty with a grin.

'Now, don't worry your head about it anymore, Bill,' said Rita briskly. 'It's all off.'

Justin, who had been quietly consuming large whiskeys, looked round lazily.

'Perhaps I ought to have mentioned,' he boomed, 'that the young lady has just done me the honour of proposing to me and I've accepted her.'

Ned Lowry, who had been enjoying the scene between Bill and Rita, looked at him for a moment in surprise.

'Bravo! Bravo!' cried Bill, clapping his hands with childish delight. 'A marriage has been arranged and all the rest of it – what? I must give you a kiss, Rita. Justin, you don't mind if I give Rita a kiss?'

'Not at all, not at all,' replied Justin with a lordly wave of his hand. 'Anything that's mine is yours, old man.'

'You're not serious, Justin, are you?' Kitty asked incredulously.

'Oh, I'm serious all right,' said Justin. 'I'm not quite certain whether your sister is. Are you, Rita?'

'What?' Rita asked as though she hadn't heard.

'Serious,' repeated Justin.

'Why?' asked Rita. 'Trying to give me the push already?'

'We're much obliged for the information,' Nellie said ironically as she rose from the piano. 'Now, maybe you'd oblige us further and tell us does Father know.'

'Hardly,' said Rita coolly. 'It was only settled this evening.'

'Well, maybe 'twill do with some more settling by the time Father is done with you,' Nellie said furiously. 'The impudence of you! How dare you! Go in at once and tell him.'

'Keep your hair on, girl,' Rita advised with cool malice and then went jauntily out of the room. Kitty and Nellie began to squabble viciously with Justin. They were convinced that the whole scene had been arranged by Rita to make them look ridiculous, and in this they weren't very far out. Justin sat back and began to enjoy the sport. Then Ned Lowry struck a match and lit another cigarette, and something about the slow, careful way in which he did it drew everyone's attention. Just because he was not the sort to make a fuss, people realised from his strained look that his mind was very far away. The squabble stopped as quickly as it had begun and a feeling of awkwardness ensued. Ned was too old a friend of the family for the girls not to feel that way about him.

Rita returned, laughing.

'Well?' asked Nellie.

'Consent refused,' growled Rita, bowing her head and pulling the wrong side of an imaginary mustache.

'What did I say?' exclaimed Nellie, but without rancour.

'You don't think it makes any difference?' Rita asked drily.

'I wouldn't be too sure of that,' said Nellie. 'What else did he say?'

'Oh, he hadn't a notion who I was talking about,' Rita said lightly. '"Justin who?"' she mimicked. '"How the hell do you think I can remember all the young scuts ye bring to the house?"'

'Was he mad?' asked Kitty with amusement.

'Hopping.'

'He didn't call us scuts?' asked Bill in a wounded tone.

'Oh, begor, that was the very word he used, Bill,' said Rita.

'Did you tell him he was very fond of me the day I gave him the tip for Golden Boy at the Park Races?' asked Justin.

'I did,' said Rita. 'I said you were the stout block of a fellow with the brown hair that he said had the fine intelligence, and he said he never gave a damn about intelligence. He wanted me to marry the thin fellow with the specs. "Only bloody gentleman that comes to the house."'

'Is it Ned?' cried Nellie.

'Who else?' said Rita. 'I asked him why he didn't tell me that before and he nearly ate the head off me. "Jesus Christ, girl, don't I feed ye and clothe ye? Isn't that enough without having to coort for ye as well? Next thing, ye'll be asking me to have a few babies for ye." Anyway, Ned,' she added with a crooked, almost malicious smile, 'you can always say you were Pa's favorite.'

Once more the attention was directed to Ned. He put his cigarette down with care and sprang up with a broad smile, holding out his hand.

'I wish you all the luck in the world, Justin,' he said.

'I know that well, Ned,' boomed Justin, catching Ned's hand in his own two. 'And I'd feel the same if it was you.'

'And you too, Miss Lomasney,' Ned said gaily.

'Thanks, Mr Lowry,' she replied with the same crooked smile.

Justin and Rita got married, and Ned, like all the Hayfield Hourigans, behaved in a decorous and sensible manner. He didn't take to drink or break the crockery or do any of the things people are expected to do under the circumstances. He gave them a very expensive clock as a wedding present, went once or twice to visit them and permitted Justin to try and convert him, and took Rita to the pictures when Justin was away from home. At the same time he began to walk out with an assistant in Halpin's; a gentle, humorous girl with a great mass of jet-black hair, a snub nose and a long, pointed melancholy face. You saw them everywhere together.

He also went regularly to Sunday's Well to see the old couple and Nellie, who wasn't yet married. One evening when he called, Mr and Mrs Lomasney were at the chapel, but Rita was there, Justin being again away. It was months since she and Ned had met; she was having a baby and very near her time; and it made her self-conscious and rude. She said it made her feel like a yacht that had been turned into a cargo boat. Three or four times she said things to Ned which would have maddened anyone else, but he took them in his usual way, without resentment.

'And how's little Miss Bitch?' she asked insolently.

'Little Miss who?' he asked mildly.

'Miss – how the hell can I remember the names of all your dolls? The Spanish-looking one who sells the knickers at Halpin's.'

'Oh, she's very well, thanks,' Ned said primly.

'What you might call a prudent marriage,' Rita went on, all on edge.

'How's that, Rita?'

'You'll have the ring and the trousseau at cost price.'

'How interested you are in her!' Nellie said suspiciously.

'I don't give a damn about her,' said Rita with a shrug. 'Would Señorita What's-her-name ever let you stand godfather to my footballer, Ned?'

'Why not?' Ned asked mildly. 'I'd be delighted, of course.'

'You have the devil's own neck to ask him after the way you treated him,' said Nellie. Nellie was interested; she knew Rita and knew that she was in one of her emotional states, and was determined on finding out what it meant. Ordinarily Rita, who also knew her sister, would have delighted in thwarting her, but now it was as though she wanted an audience.

'How did I treat him?' she asked with amusement.

'Codding him along like that for years, and then marrying a man that was twice your age.'

'Well, how did he expect me to know?'

Ned rose and took out a packet of cigarettes. Like Nellie he knew that Rita had deliberately staged the scene and was on the point of telling him something. She was leaning very far back in her chair and laughed up at him while she took a cigarette and waited for him to light it.

'Come on, Rita,' he said encouragingly. 'As you've said so much you might as well tell us the rest.'

'What else is there to tell?'

'What you had against me.'

'Who said I had anything against you? Didn't I distinctly tell you when you asked me to marry you that I didn't love you? Maybe you thought I didn't mean it.'

He paused for a moment and then raised his brows.

'I did,' he said quietly.

She laughed.

'The conceit of that fellow!' she said to Nellie, and then with a change of tone: 'I had nothing against you, Ned. This was the one I had the needle in. Herself and Kitty were forcing me into it.'

'Well, the impudence of you!' cried Nellie.

'Isn't it true for me?' Rita said sharply. 'Weren't you both trying to get me out of the house?'

'We weren't,' Nellie replied hotly, 'and anyway that has nothing to do with it. It was no reason why you couldn't have married Ned if you wanted to.'

'I didn't want to. I didn't want to marry anyone.'

'And what changed your mind?'

'Nothing changed my mind. I didn't care about anyone, only Tony, but I didn't want to go to that damn place, and I had no alternative. I had to marry one of you, so I made up my mind that I'd marry the first of you that called.'

'You must have been mad,' Nellie said indignantly.

'I felt it. I sat at the window the whole afternoon, looking at the rain. Remember that day, Ned?'

He nodded.

'The rain had a lot to do with it. I think I half hoped you'd come first. Justin came instead – an old aunt of his was sick and he came for supper. I saw him at the gate and he waved to me with his old brolly. I ran downstairs to open the door for him. "Justin," I said, grabbing him by the coat, "if you still want to marry me, I'm ready." He gave me a dirty look – you know Justin! "Young woman," he said, "there's a time and place for everything." And away with him up to the lavatory. Talk about romantic engagements! Damn the old kiss did I get off him, even!'

'I declare to God!' said Nellie in stupefaction.

'I know,' Rita cried, laughing again over her own irresponsibility. 'Cripes, when I knew what I was after doing I nearly dropped dead.'

'Oh, so you came to your senses?' Nellie asked ironically.

'What do you think? That's the trouble with Justin; he's always right. That fellow knew I wouldn't be married a week before I didn't give a snap of my fingers for Tony. And me thinking my life was over and that was that or the river! God, the idiots we make of ourselves over men!'

'And I suppose 'twas then you found out you'd married the wrong man?' Nellie asked.

'Who said I married the wrong man?' Rita asked hotly.

'I thought that was what you were telling us,' Nellie said innocently.

'You get things all wrong, Nellie,' Rita replied shortly. 'You jump to conclusions too much. If I did marry the wrong man I wouldn't be likely to tell you – or Ned Lowry either.'

She looked mockingly at Ned, but her look belied her. It was plain enough now why she wanted Nellie as an audience. It kept her from admitting more than she had to admit, from saying things which, once said, might make her own life impossible. Ned rose and flicked his cigarette ash into the fire. Then he stood with his back to it, his hands behind his back, his feet spread out on the hearth.

'You mean if I'd come earlier you'd have married me?' he asked quietly.

'If you'd come earlier, I'd probably be asking Justin to stand godfather to your brat,' said Rita. 'And how do you know but Justin would be walking out the señorita, Ned?'

'Then maybe you wouldn't be quite so interested whether he was or not,' said Nellie, but she didn't say it maliciously. It was now only too plain what Rita meant, and Nellie was sorry for her.

Ned turned and lashed his cigarette savagely into the fire. Rita looked up at him mockingly.

'Go on!' she taunted him. 'Say it, blast you!'

'I couldn't,' he said bitterly.

A month later he married the señorita.

WALKING AWAY

Philip Ó Ceallaigh

Her telephone number remained in the pocket of his funeral trousers for over two weeks. He had not forgotten about it, but he had no particular interest in it either. It was late autumn and the days were getting shorter. The city, people, trees – all these were slowing and turning inwards upon themselves.

The branches dropped their leaves and the people, now wearing the hats and coats that had long hung in wardrobes, boarded buses and tramcars less lightly than before. Listening to their speech, watching them in the streets, he felt he was looking at people who spoke and moved but did not know why and did not care. During this interval he found it hard to be with them in confined spaces. In buses and trams he became agitated and hated every face he saw. He felt much better on the long walk from his office through the cold dark streets to his apartment, observing them from a distance. His route took him past the high walls of the Jewish cemetery, and every evening he noted the handwritten sign on the door requesting a groundsman. And each time he saw the notice he thought it would be good to do such work, to do something at that point with his hands, with the earth, in the garden of the dead Jews. And across the road from the cemetery, through the brightly lit plate-glass windows of the supermarket, he saw people moving down aisles, like sleepwalkers, placing coloured cans and packets in trolleys.

He arrived home that particular evening, the one when he had decided it was time again to do something. He swept the floor and washed some dishes. He ate a sandwich and poured himself a drink then stood by his window with the glass in his hand, looking at the lights of the city. There were streetlights and the lights of moving vehicles, and the bright patchwork of lighted windows from apartment blocks. Towards the centre, perhaps two kilometres away, a flashing giant green and red sign was advertising Beck's beer. Cranes against the horizon were paper cut-outs. The skyline of the city was being altered. Tall new office buildings were going up. Money was being put to work. The city appeared to be getting younger as he got older.

Looking out the window, he recalled how she had stuck close by him on the way to the graveyard, talking rapidly. It jarred with him at the time not only because her way of speaking lacked solemnity, but because the words themselves bore no relation to anything around them, or anything that had happened, as her left breast nudged his arm repeatedly. He finished his drink, still looking at the city. She was no longer quite so young. But nor was he, and some time had passed since he had been with a woman, and the invitation was a simple one. He thought of her hips, which were becoming heavy. But that was fine too. He felt like holding something solid and imperfect, pulling himself back to earth from those sleepwalking days.

And so, that evening, weeks after the funeral, he picked up the phone and called her. She sounded pleased to hear from him and invited him directly to her home. Though it was not so early, he felt like moving slowly, and did not order a taxi. He took a bus to the inter- section with the tramlines, then waited in the cold for a tram. After fifteen minutes two trams came at the same time, both the same number, and not the number that he needed. He waited longer and his feet became cold and then, when he doubted any more trams would come, he took a taxi.

He read the numbers on the gates and when he reached hers he entered the dark garden and approached the house and rang the bell. It was an old house, but well renovated. She opened the door to him, smiling, and he stepped inside. As she took his coat, he apologised for being late and she laughed and said it did not matter. She spoke rapidly, the way he remembered, with that same enthusiasm for speech that had seemed misplaced to him that day, walking in the procession. She could not hear herself as he heard her. This distance between them told him that it would not be complicated. She was not a person he would grow attached to.

They passed from the hall into a small well-heated living room, with a sofa facing a television with the sound turned down, and this room led into a superfluous larger room with antique furniture. It looked unlived in, as if she had only recently taken up residence at the home of a much older person.

They stayed in the smaller room and she invited him to sit down on an oddly angled wooden chair with a long straight narrow back, like an exhibit from an art museum, some kind of play on the idea of a chair. It forced a posture that was not quite natural. He got up and moved to the sofa, beside her. He opened the bottle of wine he had brought and they drank in front of the silent television, which showed a made-for-TV movie. The scenes were lit with such clarity that the objects looked unreal. She took care of the talking.

She had money. She was good at making it, but it was also clear that she had grown up with it, and a solid sense of her own worth. When she travelled she stayed in the best hotels. After she had drunk a glass of wine she told him that when she was younger she had written a novel, and she got up and went to a cabinet and retrieved a box. She sat down again and opened the box and showed him. He leafed through the words, the many thousands of words, and nodded, and could think of nothing to say about it. He put the pages back in the box for her and she replaced the lid. Then she showed him an old newspaper in which two of her poems had been published. They might have been good, but he could not tell because the words required analysis of some kind, or engaging in feelings in which he had no interest. But already she was talking about how she had once gone around with a group of Gypsies and walked barefoot in the streets, asking strangers for coins. She had been good at it. She had not needed the money, but had wanted to experience that side of life. She had done amateur theatre also. Once she had sold vegetables in the market and she showed him a photograph of herself at the stall, dressed as a peasant. Again, it was a part that she was trying. But she had been a very good vegetable seller also. Mostly she spoke, and he nodded. She had opened herself to him. He would have liked to participate, to open himself in return, but he was unable. He had a feeling that there was nothing there to show. He did not believe in any of the things he might have pointed to.

She began to talk about the circumstances in which they had met, and he found he could not talk about that either, though it was the only subject there was. Since the event he had been frozen and felt that if the right words could be found he could unlock himself from the state in which he was trapped, in those weeks when winter was closing in. But he could find no words. The closest he had come was a moment, standing in the street, when he caught sight of two young cats, playing in the shrubbery, fighting, inhabiting their bodies entirely, without thought. That is what it is about, he thought. To live like that. That is what life means. And he felt his own ageing body, slowing, stiffening, and burdened with thought and sadness. He would think about the cats from time to time, and this was as close as he came to clarity.

When the bottle was emptied – she had drunk only the one glass – he made his awkward move. It was reciprocated, and they went to the bedroom.

In the dark, without their clothes, it did not matter who she was or what age she was or what she looked like, and he forgot himself too, which was what he wanted. He forgot about yesterday, and tomorrow. They became everybody else, and nobody. They moved like shadows in the strange room and it became urgent and important. Then it was over, and they slept.

In the morning, before it was fully light, he rose quietly and began to dress, but she awoke and insisted on making coffee. He drank it with her in the semi-darkness, quickly, to preclude unnecessary talk. He wished to be away, swiftly, and not return.

As he put the drained cup on the saucer, she asked him to stay for another little while, but he did not see why he should, now that he was feeling something strong, and his mind beginning to awaken.

Nearly there, he thought, as he felt the weight of his coat about his shoulders, while she stood close beside him, as if wishing to hold him back a little longer. He patted his pocket for his wallet, kissed her goodbye and stepped outside the door. It closed behind him with a definite click. It was a satisfying sound. The air outside was cool in the first moments as he walked away and he breathed it in deeply, gratefully. The garden was crisp with early-morning frost. Perhaps a snowfall was only weeks away. It was possible. The noise from beyond her gate told him the city was gearing up for another day. He was one step ahead already. It was good to be moving, walking away.

The day they had met, walking in the procession, she had talked about a temple in Thailand, some place like that, one of her sightseeing tours, saying, It makes you think, you know, such places, about what it all means, about what lies beyond. And he did not contradict her, and might even have nodded, as if in agreement with that phrase, *what lies beyond*. But he was in fact thinking, What foolishness, to speak of beyond, when we hardly know what we have here, on this earth, right before our eyes. This is what he thought, as they went to the graveyard to bury his friend, who had been a rare man, good and generous, and had been open to the future, or so the world had imagined. There was no way to utter what had happened in words that would not be hollow. And, as the woman beside him brushed her flesh against his, he could not help but reckon he was in with a chance.

A simple solution to a complex problem, that was how someone had defined it, he remembered, feeling the beauty of walking away, past the garden, and towards the awakening city streets.

VILLA MARTA

Clare Boylan

The sun rose gently over Villa Marta like a little half-baked madeleine but by nine o'clock it was a giant lobster, squeezing the pretty pension in its red claws. Honeysuckle and rose tumbled over the walls of the villa. The petals fattened and were forced apart. Dismembered blossom dangled in the probing heat. Sally and Rose stumbled down to the patio and ate their hard rolls called bocadillos, and drank bowls of scummy coffee, feeling faintly sick because of the heat and the coffee. The tables on the terrace had been arranged under a filigree of vine and splashes of sun came through, burning them in patches. Behind a cascade of leaves which made a dividing curtain, a group of Swedish boys watched them with pale, intelligent eyes. 'You come out with us,' they hissed solemnly through the vines; 'you come fucky-fuckies.'

They stretched out beside the pool and talked about food and records and sex appeal and sex. Already they had learned a thing or two. Sally had discovered, from a survey in *Time* magazine, that smoking added fifty per cent more sex appeal to a girl. They wondered if you were hopelessly, truly in love, would you know because you would even think a man's thing was nice-looking. This was a mystery and also a risk because if such a love did not exist and you spent your life waiting for it, you would be on the shelf, an old maid and hairy.

Built into their contempt for old maids was the knowledge that marriage meant an end to office life and it was so pleasant to lie by the pool, barely disturbed by the prowling vigil of the Swedish boys and the sun rolling over them in bales of heat, that both were intent on a domestic resolution.

It was merely a question of finding the right man or finding the right feelings for some sort of man. When they spoke of their married lives, Sally detailed a red sofa and Japanese paper lanterns. Rose was going to have a television in the bedroom.

Sometimes they fetched a guitar and went and sat among the cacti and sang; 'Sally free and easy, that should be her name – took a sailor's loving for a nursery game.'

In the afternoons, they went for a walk around the streets of Palma. Sally wore a dress of turquoise frills. Rose's frock was white linen. It was the era of the minis but they turned up the hems several times over so that the twitch of their buttocks showed a glimpse of flower-patterned panty. Men followed them up and down the hot, narrow lanes. 'See how they look at you!' Sally shuddered. 'Their eyes go down and up as if they can look right inside you.'

'Why would they want to do that?' Rose said.

In fact she was very aware of their pursuers, of the tense silence in the street behind them as if the air itself was choked with excitement – the stalking whisper of plimsolled feet on cobbles – the hot, shocked breath on the back of the neck. One day one of them captured her as she rounded a corner, caught her by the waist with a hand as brown as a glove and gazed into her face with puzzled eyes and then he kissed her. She slapped his face and ran on giggling to catch up with her friend but all day little fingers of excitement crept up and twisted inside her.

In the evenings they grew despondent for the heat of the day made them lethargic and they did not enjoy the foreign food. 'Drunk-man's-vomit-on-a-Saturday-night,' Sally would sigh, spooning through a thick yellow bean soup.

After dinner there began a long ritual of preparation, of painting eyes and nails, of pinning little flowers and jewelled clips in their hair before going out dancing. They did not bother much with washing because they had dipped in the pool during the day and the showers at the Villa Marta were violent and boiling, but they sprayed recklessly with L'Air du Temps.

The dances were not, actually, fun. The boys were young and eager but their desire was not skilfully mounted. They yapped and scrabbled like puppies. They did not know how to make sex without touching so that it hung in heavy droplets on the air. They did not know how to make fire from sticks.

One day on the beach they met a group of Americans, schoolgirls from a convent in Valencia, tall and beautiful although they were only fifteen. They had come to the island for a holiday and the girls pitied them because they still seemed bound by school regulations, crunching the white-hot sand in leather shoes that were the colour of dried blood. The shoes were only taken off when they went into the water and tried to drown one of their companions. The girls joined in splashing the victim who was blonde and tanned and identical in appearance to the others, until they realised that she was terrified and in genuine danger of drowning. 'Stop!' Sally commanded nervously. 'She's afraid!'

'She's a creep,' one of the pretty girls said.

'Why?' Rose pulled the sodden beauty from the floor of the ocean.

'*She* hasn't got oxblood loafers.'

A few days later the Americans came running along the beach, their heavy golden hair bouncing, their feet like aubergines in the shiny purple shoes. 'Hey!' they called out to Rose and Sally who were bathing grittily in the sand. 'There's sailors.'

An American ship had docked in Palma. The girls watched silently as the sailors were strewn along the quay, wonderful in uniforms that were crisp as money. They whistled at the girls and the girls ran after them, their knees shivering on the sweet seductive note. 'Come on, honey,' one boy called to them. 'Where d'you wanna go? You wanna go to a bullfight?' 'Sure!' the American girls agreed, and their leather shoes squeaked and their rumps muscled prettily under little shorts as they ran to catch up.

Sally and Rose had been hoping for something more attractive than a bullfight. Given the opportunity they might have pressed for lunch in one of the glass-fronted restaurants in Palma, where lobsters and pineapples were displayed in the window; but the Americans moved in a tide, scrambling for a bus, juggling with coins, and they had to run or get left behind.

Following the example of the giant schoolgirls, they pressed themselves down beside the loose forms of two of the young men. 'I'm Will,' the boy beside Sally said, showing wonderful teeth and something small and grey and lumpy like a tiny sheep, which was endlessly ground between them. 'I'm Bob,' Rose's sailor said and laughed to show that names were not to be taken seriously.

The bullring smelled like a cardboard box that had got damp and been left to dry in the sun. It was constructed as a circus with benches arranged in circles on different levels and all of those spaces were crammed with human beings who were waiting for a death. They were pungent with heat and the tension of expectation. This dire harmony wrought a huge hot communal breath which had a little echo in the men who had followed the girls through the lanes of Palma, but here the fear was not exciting and pleasant. Sally and Rose did not believe in death. They sat clammy with dismay, waiting for the animals to be saved.

No matter that it was an honourable sport, that the dead bulls' meat fed the island's orphans; they were unimpressed by the series of little fancy men who pranced around the bewildered animals which lurched and pawed at bubbles of their own blood that bulged brilliantly and then shrank back shabbily into the sand.

How many orphans could so small an island support, Rose wondered, as one animal died and then two? She saw the orphans as the left luggage of tourists who had stayed too long in the lanes. She sympathised with this; she too had wanted, in an awful way, to go back alone, without Sally. Her only dismay was for the huge animals crumbling down one by one with hot dribbles and their sides all lacquered red by a pile of little sticks jammed in like knitting needles stuck in a ball of wool.

'He's dead!' Sally accused Will. A third animal folded up its slender legs and rolled in the sticky sawdust.

'Sure is, honey,' Will said eagerly and squeezed her fingers. He seemed radiantly happy. 'Say, can I come on back to your hotel?'

Sally gave Rose a careful look. Rose's sailor, Bob, was watching Will for a clue.

Rose thought it wouldn't matter much what happened to Sally since Sally's period was late following some home-based encounter. She calculated some basis on which to make it worthwhile for herself. 'We're late for our dinner,' she said. 'We'd have to have a hamburger.'

'Sure thing,' Bob said amiably.

The girls ate with the speed and concentration of thieving dogs.

Their pocket money did not run to delicacies. The sailors treated them to banana splits and the girls thought they should have ordered prawn cocktails and steaks since these men were so rich and so foolish with their money.

On their way back to the hotel after supper they were wreathed in virtue. It was thick around them, like scent over the honeysuckle. Both of them felt like sacrificial virgins although they were not, actually, virgins. In the terms of the understanding, they were going to lie down beside Will and Bob and let them do, within reason, what they wanted. They walked together, no longer feeling a need to be sociable. The sailors were playful in their wake.

When they got to the hotel they let the men into their room and sat with cold invitation on either bed. The sailors took cigarettes from their pockets and asked if there was anything to drink. Rose grudgingly brought a bottle of Bacardi from the wardrobe. 'I gotta girl like you at home,' Bob said. He rubbed her hand and drew up a linty patch on her burnt skin.

He kissed her then and she could feel his dry lips stretched in a smile even as they sought her mouth. He was the most amiable man she had ever met. She had no notion how to treat or be treated by a man as an equal. Sexual excitement grew out of fear or power. She could only regard him with contempt. 'You like to see my girl?' he said. He brought out his wallet and withdrew some coloured snapshots of a girl with a rounded face and baby curls.

Will had pictures too. Chapters of American life were spread out on the woven bedspreads and soon the girls were lulled into yawns by the multitude of brothers and sisters, moms and dads, *dawgs* and faithful girlfriends. The sailors spoke of the lives they would have, the houses and children. They had joined the navy to see the world but it seemed that their ship was in a bottle. Soon they would settle down, have families, mow the grass at weekends. The lives ahead of them were as familiar and wholesome as family serials on the television.

Catching Sally's eye, which was hard under the watering of boredom, Rose suddenly suffered an enlightenment. It was herself that she saw in the balding Polaroids – at the barbecue, at the bake sale – squinting into the faded glare of the sky. She was looking at her future.

She gathered in her mind from the assorted periods of films she had seen, a white convertible with a rug and a radio on the back seat, a beach house with a verandah, an orchestra playing round the pool in the moonlight. All Americans had television in the bedroom.

'Bob, put your arms around me,' she said. She swept the photographs into a neat pile and put them prissily face down. Bob's arms fell on her languidly. She drew them back and arranged them with efficiency, one on a breast and one on a hard, brown leg. He gave her a swift look of query but she closed her eyes to avoid it and offered him her open mouth. 'You're as ripe as a little berry. You sure are,' Bob sighed, and for once his smile faded and languor forsook him. He began kissing her in a heavy rhythmic way and his hands pursued the same rhythm on her spine, on her breasts, on her thighs. Rose had a moment of pure panic. She could not think. Her good shrewd plotting mind had deserted her. Clothes, body, common sense seemed to be slipping away and she was fading into his grasp, the touch of his tongue and fingertips.

She opened her eyes to gaze at him and saw his goodness in the chestnut sweep of his eyebrows and his hair. 'I love you,' was the first thought to return to her head. She reached out to touch his hair.

Bob felt her stillness. He opened his eyes. He found himself staring into blue eyes that were huge with something he saw as fear. He pushed her away harshly. 'Now don't you go around doing that sort of thing with all the guys,' he said. 'You're a nice girl.'

Rose did not know what to do. Bob shook his head and stood up. He fetched his cigarettes from the dressing table. He tapped the pack on his palm to release one, but he hit it with such violence that all the cigarettes were bent. He lit one anyway and went to the window, opening the shutters and leaning out to sigh long and deeply. Rose, watching the indifferently entwined bodies on the other bed, felt very close to tears.

'Jesus Christmas!' Bob let out a whoop. 'Would you look at that pool!'

In a second, Will had leaped from the disarrayed Sally and joined his friend, his buddy, at the window.

'Holy shit!' Will said with reverence.

'Mind your mouth.' Bob cuffed him good-humouredly. 'Last man in is a holy shit.'

The Villa Marta was constructed on a single storey so the young men were able to let themselves out the window with a soft thump on the cactussy lawn. They breathed muffled swear-words as the cacti grazed their ankles and then ran to the pool, tearing off their beautiful uniforms as they went.

The girls stood at the window watching them playing like small boys in the water. They splashed each other and pulled at one another's shorts. Will jumped from the water, waving his friend's underpants. 'Hey, come back here,' Bob yelled. 'I got a bare ass.'

'Don't worry,' his friend hollered back. 'It's a small thing.'

Bob scrambled from the pool and they tussled on the edge of the prickly lawn. With a cold pang Rose noted that his body was beautiful, every part of it, golden and beautiful. She beat on the shutters savagely with her knuckles. 'You out there! You better go now,' she said.

'Sure thing!' the sailors laughed with soft amusement as they pulled on their clothes.

They came to the window to kiss the girls goodnight and then leaped at the flower-covered wall to scramble on to the street.

'Bob,' Rose howled out softly. Bob dropped back lightly to the ground. He came back to where she was huddled at the window. 'What's up, honey?'

'Don't you have a pool at home?' she said. She was troubled by the way he had reacted to the pool at the Villa Marta. All Americans had swimming pools.

'What kind of a question is that?' Bob said. 'We don't have no pool. We live in the hills. We gotta few cows and hens and sheep. We gotta few acres but we ain't got no pool.'

He ran off again but before making his effortless jump at the wall he paused and cried out, 'Wait for me!' and she thought of his chestnut hair and the wild sweetness of his touch and said yes, she would wait, but then she saw the bleak snowfall of blossoms from the wall and she realised that he had been calling out to his buddy. He was gone.

She ran from the room and out into the dark, polish-smelling hall of the villa. As she stood trying to compose herself, the front door opened and two of the Swedish boys entered. They were immaculately attired in evening dress and carried half-filled bottles of whiskey but both seemed as sober as Mormons.

'Good evening,' one said.

'You like to fuck sailors?' the other enquired respectfully. He had watched the visitors emerging from the wall.

Rose hurled herself at him, slapping his face with both hands in a fury. He delivered his bottle for safekeeping to his friend and calmly trapped her hands with his. 'You act like the little wolf' – he spoke with detachment – 'but you are really the grandmother in disguise.'

He let her go and she fled through the carved entrance, tearing along the street, down one alley, through the next. She emerged into a long, tree-lined street and there were the sailors. She stood and watched them until the young men had disappeared and only the hipswing of their little buttocks was picked out by the moon, like ghostly butterflies in their tight white pants.

'Creeps,' she cried after them.

LILACS

Mary Lavin

'That dunghill isn't doing anyone any harm, and it's not going out of where it is as long as I'm in this house,' Phelim Mulloy said to his wife Ros, but he threw an angry look at his elder daughter Kate who was standing by the kitchen window with her back turned to them both.

'Oh Phelim,' Ros said softly. 'If only it could be moved somewhere else besides under the window of the room where we eat our bit of food.'

'Didn't you just say a minute ago people can smell it from the other end of the town? If that's the case I don't see what would be the good in shifting it from one side of the yard to the other.'

Kate could stand no more. 'What I don't see is the need in us dealing in dung at all!'

'There you are! What did I tell you!' Phelim said, 'I knew all along that was what was in the back of your minds, both of you! And the one inside there too,' he added, nodding his head at the closed door of one of the rooms off the kitchen. 'All you want, the three of you, is to get rid of the dung altogether. Why on earth can't women speak out – and say what they mean. That's a thing always puzzled me.'

'Leave Stacy out of this, Phelim,' said Ros, but she spoke quietly. 'Stacy has one of her headaches.'

'I know she has,' said Phelim. 'And I know something else. I know I'm supposed to think it's the smell of the dung gave it to her. Isn't that so?'

'Ah Phelim, that's not what I meant at all. I only thought you might wake her with your shouting. She could be asleep.'

'Asleep is it? It's a real miracle any of you can get a wink of sleep, day or night, with the smell of that poor harmless heap of dung out there, that's bringing good money to this house week after week.' He had lowered his voice, but when he turned and looked at Kate it rose again without his noticing. 'It paid for your education at a fancy boarding school – and for your sister's too. It paid for your notions of learning to play the piano, and the violin, both of which instruments are rotting away inside in the parlour and not a squeak of a tune ever I heard out of the one or the other of them since the day they came into the house.'

'We may as well spare our breath, Mother,' Kate said. 'He won't give in, now or ever. That's my belief.'

'That's the truest word that's ever come out of your mouth,' Phelim said to her, and stomping across the kitchen he opened the door that led into the yard and went out, leaving the door wide open. Immediately the faint odour of stale manure that hung in the air was enriched by a smell from a load of hot steaming manure that had just been tipped into a huge dunghill from a farm cart that was the first of a line of carts waiting their turn to unload. Ros sighed and went to close the door, but Kate got ahead of her and banged it shut, before going back to the window and taking up her stand there. After a nervous glance at the door of the bedroom that her daughters shared, Ros, too, went over to the window and both women stared out.

An empty cart was clattering out of the yard and Phelim was leading in another from which, as it went over the spudstone of the gate, a clod or two of dung fell out on the cobbles. The dunghill was nearly filled, and liquid from it was running down the sides of the trough to form pools through which Phelim waded unconcernedly as he forked back the stuff on top to make room for more.

'That's the last load,' Ros said.

'For this week, you mean,' Kate said. 'Your trouble is you're too soft with him, Mother. You'll have to be harder on him. You'll have to keep at him night and day. That is to say if you care anything at all about me and Stacy.'

'Ah Kate. Can't you see there's no use? Can't you see he's set in his ways?'

'All I can see is the way we're being disgraced,' Kate said angrily. 'Last night, at the concert in the Parish Hall, just before the curtain went up I heard the wife of that man who bought the bakehouse telling the person beside her that they couldn't open a window since they came here with a queer smell that was coming from somewhere, and asking the other person if she knew what it would be. I nearly died of shame, Mother. I really did. I couldn't catch what answer she got, but after the first item was over, and I could glance back, I saw it was Mamie Murtagh she was sitting beside. And you can guess what that one would be likely to have said! My whole pleasure in the evening was spoiled.'

'You take things too much to heart, Kate,' Ros said sadly. 'There's Stacy inside there, and it's my belief she wouldn't mind us dealing in dung at all if it wasn't for the smell of it. Only the other day she was remarking that if he'd even clear a small space under the windows we might plant something there that would smell nice. "Just think, Mother," she said. "Just think if it was a smell of lilac that was coming in to us every time we opened a door or a window."'

'Don't talk to me about Stacy,' Kate said crossly. 'She has lilac on the brain, if you ask me. She never stops talking about it. What did she ever do to try and improve our situation?'

'Ah now Kate, as you know, Stacy is very timid.'

'All the more reason Father would listen to her, if she'd speak to him. He may not let on to it, but he'd do anything for her.'

Ros nodded.

'All the same she'd never speak to him. Stacy would never have the heart to cross anyone.'

'She wouldn't need to say much. Didn't you hear him, today, saying he supposed it was the smell of the dung was giving her her headaches? You let that pass, but I wouldn't – only I know he won't take any more from me, although it's me has to listen to her moaning and groaning from the minute the first cart rattles into the yard. How is it that it's always on a Wednesday she has a headache? And it's been the same since the first Wednesday we came home from the convent.' With that last thrust Kate ran into the bedroom and came out with a raincoat. 'I'm going out for a walk,' she said, 'and I won't come back until the smell of that stuff has died down a bit. You can tell my father that, too, if he's looking for me.'

'Wait a minute, Kate. Was Stacy asleep?' Ros asked.

'I don't know and I don't care. She was lying with her face pressed to the wall, like always.'

When Kate went out, Ros took down the tea caddy from the dresser and put a few pinches of tea from it into an earthenware pot on the hob of the big open fire. Then, tilting the kettle that hung from a crane over the flames, she wet the tea, and pouring out a cup she carried it over to the window and set it to cool on the sill while she went on watching Phelim.

He was a hard man when you went against him, she thought, a man who'd never let himself be thwarted. He was always the same. That being so, there wasn't much sense in nagging him, she thought, but Kate would never be made see that. Kate was stubborn too.

The last of the carts had gone, and after shutting the gate Phelim had taken a yard brush and was sweeping up the dung that had been spilled. When he'd made a heap of it, he got a shovel and gathered it up and flung it up on the dunghill. But whether he did it to tidy the yard or not to waste the dung, Ros didn't know. The loose bits of dung he'd flung up on the top of the trough had dried out, and the bits of straw that were stuck to it had dried out too. They gleamed bright and yellow in a ray of watery sunlight that had suddenly shone forth.

Now that Kate was gone, Ros began to feel less bitter against Phelim. Like herself, he was getting old. She was sorry they had upset him. And while she was looking at him, he laid the yard brush against the wall of one of the sheds and put his hand to his back. He'd been doing that a lot lately. She didn't like to see him doing it. She went across to the door and opened it.

'There's hot tea in the pot on the hob, Phelim,' she called out. 'Come in and have a cup.' Then seeing he was coming, she went over and gently opened the bedroom door. 'Stacy, would you be able for a cup of tea?' she asked, leaning in over the big feather bed.

Stacy sat up at once.

'What did he say? Is it going to be moved?' she asked eagerly.

'Ssh, Stacy,' Ros whispered, and then as Stacy heard her father's steps in the kitchen she looked startled.

'Did he hear me?' she asked anxiously.

'No,' said Ros, and she went over and drew the curtains to let in the daylight. 'How is your poor head, Stacy?'

Stacy leaned towards Ros so she could be heard when she whispered. 'Did you have a word with him, Mother?'

'Yes,' said Ros.

'Did he agree?' Stacy whispered.

'No.'

Stacy closed her eyes. 'I hope he wasn't upset?' she said.

Ros stroked her daughter's limp hair. 'Don't you worry anyway, Stacy,' she said. 'He'll get over it. He's been outside sweeping the yard and I think maybe he has forgotten we raised the matter at all. Anyway, Kate has gone for a walk and I called him in for a cup of tea. Are you sure you won't let me bring you in a nice hot cup to sip here in the bed?'

'I think I'd prefer to get up and have it outside, as long as you're really sure Father is not upset.'

Ros drew a strand of Stacy's hair back from her damp forehead. 'You're a good girl, Stacy, a good, kind creature,' she said. 'You may feel better when you're on your feet. I can promise you there will be no more arguing for the time being anyway. I'm sorry I crossed him at all.'

It was to Stacy Ros turned, a few weeks later, when Phelim was taken bad in the middle of the night with a sharp pain in the small of his back that the women weren't able to ease, and after the doctor came and stayed with him until the early hours of the morning, the doctor didn't seem able to do much either. Before Phelim could be got to hospital, he died.

'Oh, Stacy, Stacy,' Ros cried, throwing herself into her younger daughter's arms. 'Why did I cross him over that old dunghill?'

'Don't fret, Mother,' Stacy begged. 'I never heard you cross him over anything else as long as I can remember. You were always good and kind to him, calling him in out of the yard every other minute for a cup of tea. Morning, noon and night I'd hear your voice, and the mornings the carts came with the dung you'd call him in oftener than ever. I used to hear you when I'd be lying inside with one of my headaches.'

Ros was not to be so easily consoled.

'What thanks is due to a woman for giving a man a cup of hot tea on a bitter cold day? He was the best man ever lived. Oh why did I cross him?'

'Ah Mother, it wasn't only on cold days you were good to him but on summer days too – on every and all kind of days. Isn't that so, Kate?' Stacy said, appealing to Kate.

'You did everything you could to please him, Mother,' Kate said, but seeing this made no impression on her mother she turned to Stacy. 'That's more than could be said about him,' she muttered.

But Ros heard her.

'Say no more, you,' she said. 'You were the one was always at me to torment him. Oh why did I listen to you? Why did I cross him?'

'Because you were in the right. That's why!' Kate said.

'Was I?' Ros said.

Phelim was laid out in the parlour, and all through the night Ros and her daughters sat up in the room with the corpse. The neighbours that came to the house stayed up all night too, but they sat in the kitchen, and kept the fire going and made tea from time to time. Kate and Stacy stared sadly at their dead father stretched out in his shroud, and they mourned him as the man they had known all their lives, a heavy man with a red face whom they had seldom seen out of his big rubber boots caked with muck.

Ros mourned that Phelim too. But she mourned many another Phelim besides. She mourned the Phelim who, up to a little while before, never put a coat on him going out in the raw, cold air, nor covered his head even in the rain. Of course his hair was as thick as thatch! But most of all, she mourned the Phelim whose hair had not yet grown coarse but was soft and smooth as silk, like it was the time he led her in off the road and up a little lane near the chapel one Sunday when he was walking her home from Mass. That was the time when he used to call her by the old name. When, she wondered, when did he stop calling her Rose? Or was it herself gave herself the new name? Perhaps it was someone else altogether, someone outside the family? Just a neighbour maybe? No matter! Ros was a good name anyway, wherever it came from. It was a good name and a suitable name for an old woman. It would have been only foolishness to go on calling her Rose after she faded and dried up like an old twig. Ros looked down at her bony hands and her tears fell on them. But they were tears for Phelim. 'Rose,' he said that day in the lane. 'Rose, I've been thinking about ways to make money. And do you know what I found out? There's a pile of money to be made out of dung.' Rose thought he was joking. 'It's true,' he said. 'The people in the town – especially women – would give any money for a bagful of it for their gardens. And only a few miles out from the town there are farmers going mad to get rid of it, with it piling up day after day and cluttering up their farmyards until they can hardly get in and out their own doors! Now, I was thinking, if I got hold of a horse and cart and went out and brought back a few loads of that dung, and if my father would let me store it for a while in our yard, I could maybe sell it to the people in the town.'

'Like the doctor's wife,' Rose said, knowing the doctor's wife was mad about roses. The doctor's wife had been seen going out into the street with a shovel to bring back a shovelful of horse manure.

'That's right. People like her! And after a while the farmers might deliver the loads to me. I might even pay them a few shillings a load, if I was getting a good price for it. Then if I made as much money as I think I might, maybe soon I'd be able to get a place of my own where I'd have room to store enough to make it a worthwhile business.' To Rose it seemed an odd sort of way to make money, but Phelim was only eighteen then and probably he wanted to have a few pounds in his pocket while he was waiting for something better. 'I'm going to ask my father about the storage today,' he said, 'and in the afternoon I'm going to get hold of a cart and go out the country and see how I get on.'

'Is that so?' Rose said, for want of knowing what else to say.

'It is,' said Phelim. 'And do you know the place I have in mind to buy if I make enough money? I'd buy that place we often looked at, you and me when we were out walking, that place on the outskirts of the town, with a big yard and two big sheds that only need a bit of fixing, to be ideal for my purposes.'

'I think so,' Rose said. 'Isn't there an old cottage there all smothered with ivy?'

'That's the very place. Do you remember we peeped in the windows one day last summer. There's no one living there.'

'No wonder,' Rose said.

'Listen to me. Rose. After I'd done up the sheds,' Phelim said, 'I could fix up the cottage too, and make a nice job of it. That's another thing I wanted to ask you, Rose. How would you like to live in that cottage – after I'd done it up, I mean – with me, I mean?' he added when he saw he'd startled her. 'Well Rose, what have you to say to that?'

She bent her head to hide her blushes, and looked down at her small thin-soled shoes that she only wore on a Sunday. Rose didn't know what to say.

'Well?' said Phelim.

'There's a very dirty smell off dung,' she said at last in a whisper.

'It only smells strong when it's fresh,' Phelim said. 'And maybe you could plant flowers to take away the smell?'

She kept looking down at her shoes.

'They'd have to be flowers with a strong scent out of them!' she said – but already she was thinking of how strongly sweet rocket and mignonette perfumed the air of an evening after rain.

'You could plant all the flowers you liked, you'd have nothing else to do the day long,' he said. How innocent he was, for all that he was thinking of making big money, and taking a wife. She looked up at him. His skin was as fair and smooth as her own. He was the best looking fellow for miles around. Girls far prettier than her would have been glad to be led up a lane by him, just for a bit of a lark, let alone a proposal – a proposal of marriage. 'Well, Rose?' he said, and now there were blushes coming and going in his cheeks too, blotching his face the way the wind blotches a lake when there's a storm coming. And she knew him well enough, even in those days, to be sure he wouldn't stand for anyone putting between him and what he was bent on doing. 'You must know, Rose Magarry, that there's a lot in the way people look at a thing. When I was a young lad, driving along the country roads in my father's trap, I used to love looking down at the gold rings of dung dried out by the sun, as they flashed past underneath the horses' hooves.'

Rose felt like laughing, but she knew he was deadly serious. He wasn't like anybody else in the world she'd ever known. Who else would say a thing like that? It was like poetry. The sun was spilling down on them and in the hedges little pink dog roses were swaying in a soft breeze.

'All right, so,' she said. 'I will.'

'You will? Oh, Rose! Kiss me so!' he said.

'Not here, Phelim!' she cried. People were still coming out of the chapel yard and some of them were looking up the lane.

'Rose Magarry, if you're going to marry me, you must face up to people and never be ashamed of anything I do,' he said, and when she still hung back he put out his hand and tilted up her chin. 'If you don't kiss me right here and now, Rose, I'll have no more to do with you.'

She kissed him then.

And now, at his wake, the candle flames were wavering around his coffin the way the dog roses wavered that day in the summer breeze.

Ros shed tears for those little dog roses. She shed tears for the roses in her own cheeks in those days. And she shed tears for the soft young kissing lips of Phelim. Her tears fell quietly, but it seemed to Kate and Stacy that, like rain in windless weather, they would never cease.

When the white light of morning came at last, the neighbours got up and went home to do a few chores of their own and be ready for the funeral. Kate and Stacy got ready too, and made Ros ready. Ros didn't look much different in black from what she always looked. Neither did Stacy. But Kate looked well in black. It toned down her high colour.

After the funeral Kate led her mother home. Stacy had already been taken home by neighbours, because she fainted when the coffin was being lowered into the ground. She was lying down when they came home. The women who brought Stacy home and one or two other women who had stayed behind after the coffin was carried out, to put the furniture back in place, gave a meal to the family, but these women made sure to leave as soon as possible to let the Mulloys get used to their loss. When the women had gone Stacy got up and came out to join Ros and Kate. A strong smell of guttered-out candles hung in the air and a faint scent of lilies lingered on too.

'Oh Kate! Smell!' Stacy cried, drawing in as deep a breath as her thin chest allowed.

'For Heaven's sake, don't talk about smells or you'll have our mother wailing again and going on about having crossed him over the dunghill,' Kate said in a sharp whisper.

But Ros didn't need any reminders to make her wail.

'Oh Phelim, Phelim, why did I cross you?' she wailed. 'Wasn't I the bad old woman to go against you over a heap of dung that, if I looked at things rightly, wasn't bad at all after it dried out a bit. It was mostly only yellow straw.'

'Take no heed of her,' Kate counselled Stacy. 'Go inside you with our new hats and coats, and hang them up in our room with a sheet draped over them. Black nap is a caution for collecting dust.' To Ros she spoke kindly, but firmly. 'You've got to give over this moaning, Mother,' she said. 'You're only tormenting yourself. Why wouldn't you let him see how we felt about the dung?'

Ros stopped moaning long enough to look sadly out the window.

'It was out of the dung he made his first few shillings,' she said.

'That may be! But how long ago was that? He made plenty of money other ways as time went on. There was no need in keeping on the dung and humiliating us. He only did it out of obstinacy.' As Stacy came back after hanging up their black clothes, Kate appealed to her. 'Isn't that so, Stacy?'

Stacy drew another thin breath.

'It doesn't smell too bad today, does it?' she said. 'I suppose the scent of the flowers drove it out.'

'Well, the house won't always be filled with lilies,' Kate said irritably. 'In any case, Stacy, it's not the smell concerns me. What concerns me is the way people look at us when they hear how our money is made.'

Ros stopped moaning again for another minute. 'It's no cause for shame. It's honest dealing, and that's more than can be said for the dealings of others in this town. You shouldn't heed people's talk, Kate.'

'Well, I like that!' she said. 'May I ask what you know, Mother, about how people talk. Certain kinds of people, I mean. Good class people! It's easily seen you were never away at boarding school like Stacy and me, or else you'd know what it feels like to have to admit our money was made out of horse manure and cow dung!'

'I don't see what great call there was on you to tell them!' Ros said.

'Stacy! Stacy! Did you hear that?' Kate cried.

Stacy put her hand to her head. She was getting confused. There was some truth in what Kate had said, and she felt obliged to side with her, but first she ran over and threw herself down at her mother's knees.

'We didn't tell them at first. Mother,' she said, hoping to make Ros feel better. 'We told them our father dealt in fertiliser, but one of the girls looked up the word in a dictionary and found out it was only a fancy name for manure.'

It was astonishing to Kate and Stacy how Ros took that. She not only stopped wailing but she began to laugh.

'Your father would have been amused to hear that,' she said.

'Well, it wasn't funny for us,' Kate said.

Ros stopped laughing, but the trace of a small black smile remained on her face.

'It wasn't everyone had your father's sense of humour,' she said.

'It wasn't everyone had his obstinacy either!' Kate said.

'You're right there, Kate,' Ros said simply. 'Isn't that why I feel so bad? When we knew how stubborn he was, weren't we the stupid women to be always trying to best him? We only succeeded in making him miserable.'

Kate and Stacy looked at each other.

'How about another cup of tea, Mother? I'll bring it over here to you beside the fire,' Stacy said, and although her mother made no reply she made the tea and brought over a cup. Ros took the cup but handed back the saucer.

'Leave that back on the table,' she said, and holding the cup in her two hands she went over to the window, although the light was fading fast.

'It only smells bad on hot muggy days,' she said.

Kate gave a loud sniff. 'Don't forget summer is coming,' she said.

For a moment it seemed Ros had not heard, then she gave a sigh.

'It is and it isn't,' she said. 'I often think that in the January of the year it's as true to say we have put the summer behind us as it is to say it's ahead!' Then she glanced at a calendar on the wall. 'Is tomorrow Wednesday?' she asked, and an anxious expression overcame the sorrowful look on her face. Wednesday was the day the farmers delivered the dung.

'Mother! You don't think the farmers will be unmannerly enough to come banging on the gate tomorrow, and us after having a death in the family?' Kate said in a shocked voice.

'Death never interfered with business yet, as far as I know,' Ros said coldly. 'And the farmers are kind folk. I saw a lot of them at the funeral. They might think it all the more reason to come. Knowing my man is taken from me.'

'Mother!' This time Kate was more than shocked, she was outraged. 'You're not thinking, by any chance, of keeping on dealing with them – of keeping on dealing in dung?'

Ros looked her daughter straight in the face.

'I'm thinking of one thing and one thing only,' she said. 'I'm thinking of your father and him young one day, and the next day, you might say, him stretched on the bed inside with the neighbours washing him for his burial.' Then she began to moan again.

'If you keep this up you'll be laid alongside him one of these days,' Kate said.

'Leave me be!' Ros said. 'I'm not doing any harm to myself by thinking about him. I like thinking about him.'

'He lived to a good age, Mother. Don't forget that,' Kate said.

'I suppose that's what you'll be saying about me one of these days,' Ros said, but she didn't seem as upset as she had been. She turned to Stacy. 'It seems only like yesterday, Stacy, that I was sitting up beside him on the cart, right behind the horse's tail, with my white blouse on me and my gold chain that he gave me bouncing about on my front, and us both watching the road flashing past under the horse's hooves, bright with gold rings of dung.'

Kate raised her eyebrows. But Stacy gave a sob. And that night, when she and Kate were in bed, just before she faced in to the wall, Stacy gave another sob.

'Oh Kate, it's not a good sign when people begin to go back over the past, is it?'

'Are you speaking about Mother?'

'I am. And did you see how bad she looked when you brought her home from the grave?'

'I did,' said Kate. 'It may be true what I said to her. If she isn't careful we may be laying her alongside poor Father before long.'

'Oh Kate. How could you say such a thing?' Stacy burst into tears. 'Oh Kate. Oh Kate, why did we make her cross Father about the dunghill? I know how she feels. I keep reproaching myself for all the hard things I used to think about him when I'd be lying here in bed with one of my headaches.'

'Well, you certainly never came out with them!' Kate said. 'You left it to me to say them for you! Not that I'm going to reproach myself about anything! There was no need in him keeping that dunghill. He only did it out of pig-headedness. And now, if you'll only let me, I'm going to sleep.'

Kate was just dropping off when Stacy leant up on her elbow.

'You don't really think they will come in the morning, do you Kate – the carts I mean – like our mother said?'

'Of course not,' Kate said.

'But if they do?'

'Oh go to sleep Stacy, for Heaven's sake. There's no need facing things until they happen. And stop fidgeting! You're twitching the blankets off me. Move over.'

Stacy faced back to the wall and lay still. She didn't think she'd be able to sleep, but when she did, it seemed as if she'd only been asleep one minute when she woke to find the night had ended. The hard, white light of day was pressing on her eyelids. It's a new day for them, she thought, but not for their poor father. Father laid away in the cold clay. Stacy shivered and drew up her feet that were touching the icy iron rail at the foot of the bed. It must have been the cold wakened her. Opening her eyes she saw, through a chink between the curtains, that the crinkled edges of the big corrugated sheds glittered with frost. If only – she thought – if only it was summer. She longed for the time when warm winds would go daffing through the trees, and when in the gardens to which they delivered fertiliser, the tight hard beads of lilac buds would soon loop out into soft pear-shaped bosoms of blossoms. And then, gentle as those thoughts, another thought came into Stacy's mind, and she wondered whether their father, sleeping under the close, green sods, might mind now if they got rid of the dunghill. Indeed it seemed the dunghill was as good as gone, now that Father himself was gone. Curling up in the warm blankets, Stacy was preparing to sleep again when there was a loud knocking on the yard-gates and the sound of a horse shaking its harness. She raised her head off the pillow, and as she did, she heard the gate in the yard slap back against the wall and there was a rattle of iron-shod wheels travelling in across the cobbles.

'Kate! Kate!' she screamed, shaking her. 'I thought Father was leading in a load of manure.'

'Oh shut up, Stacy. You're dreaming – or else raving,' Kate muttered from the depths of the blankets that she had pulled closer around her. But suddenly she sat up. And then, to Stacy's astonishment, she threw back the bedclothes altogether, right across the footrail of the bed, and ran across the floor and pressed her face to the window pane. 'I might have known this would happen!' she cried. 'For all her lamenting and wailing, she knows what she's doing. Come and look!' Out in the yard Ros was leading in the first of the carts, and calling out to the drivers of the other carts waiting their turn to come in. She was not wearing her black clothes, but her ordinary everyday coat, the colour of the earth and the earth's decaying refuse. In the raw cold air, the manure in the cart she was leading was still giving off, unevenly, the fog of its hot breath.

'Get dressed, Stacy. We'll go down together!' Kate ordered, and grabbed her clothes and dressed.

When they were both dressed, with Kate leading, the sisters went into the kitchen. The yard door was open and a powerful stench was making its way inside. The last cart was by then unloaded, and Ros soon came back into the kitchen and began to warm her hands by the big fire already roaring up the chimney. She had left the door open but Kate went over and banged it shut.

'Well?' said Ros.

'Well?' Kate said after her, only louder.

Stacy sat down at once and began to cry. The other two women took no notice of her, as they faced each other across the kitchen.

'Say whatever it is you have to say, Kate,' Ros said.

'You know what I have to say,' said Kate.

'Don't say it so! Save your breath!' Ros said, and she went as if to go out into the yard again, but Stacy got up and ran and put her arms around her.

'Mother, you always agreed with us! You always said it would be nice if—'

Ros put up a hand and silenced her.

'Listen to me, both of you,' she said. 'I had no right agreeing with anyone but your father,' she said. 'It was to him I gave my word. It was him I had a right to stand behind. He always said there was no shame in making money any way it could be made, as long as it was made honestly. And another thing he said was that money was money, whether it was in gold coins or in dung. And that was true for him. Did you, either of you, hear what the priest said yesterday in the cemetery? "God help all poor widows." That's what he said. And he set me thinking. Did it never occur to you that it might not be easy for us, three women with no man about the place, to keep going, to put food on the table and keep a fire on the hearth, to say nothing at all about finery and fal-lals.'

'That last remark is meant for me, I suppose,' Kate said, but the frown that came on her face seemed to come more from worry than anger. 'By the way, Mother,' she said. 'You never told us whether you had a word with the solicitor when he came with his condolences? Did you by any chance find out how Father's affairs stood?'

'I did,' Ros said. But that was all she said as she went out into the yard again and took up the yard brush. She had left the door open but Stacy ran over and closed it gently.

'She's twice as stubborn as ever Father was,' Kate said. 'There's going to be no change around here as long as she's alive.'

Stacy's face clouded. 'All the same, Kate, she's sure to let us clear a small corner and put in a few shrubs and things?' she said timidly.

'Lilacs, I suppose!' Kate said, with an unmistakable sneer, which however Stacy did not see.

'Think of the scent of them coming in the window,' she said.

'Stacy, you are a fool!' Kate cried. 'At least I can see that our mother has more important things on her mind than lilac bushes. I wonder what information she got from Jasper Kane? I thought her very secretive. I would have thought he'd have had a word with me, as the eldest daughter.'

'Oh, Kate.' Stacy's eyes filled with tears again. 'I never thought about it before, but when poor Mother' – she hesitated, then after a gulp she went on – 'when poor Mother goes to join Father, you and I will be all alone in the world with no one to look after us.'

'Stop whimpering, Stacy,' Kate said sharply. 'We've got to start living our own lives, sooner or later.' Going over to a small ornamental mirror on the wall over the fireplace, she looked into it and patted her hair. Stacy stared at her in surprise, because unless you stood well back from it you could only see the tip of your nose in that little mirror. But Kate was not looking at herself. She was looking out into the yard, which was reflected in the mirror, in which she could see their mother going around sweeping up stray bits of straw and dirt to bring them over and throw them on top of the dunghill. Then Kate turned around. 'We don't need to worry too much about that woman. She'll hardly follow Father for many a long day! That woman is as strong as a tree.'

But Ros was not cut out to be a widow. If Phelim had been taken from her before the dog roses had faded in the hedges that first summer of their lives together, she could hardly have mourned him more bitterly than she did when an old woman, tossing and turning sleeplessly in their big brass bed.

Kate and Stacy did their best to ease her work in the house. But there was one thing Kate was determined they would not do, and that was give any help on the Wednesday mornings when the farm carts arrived with their load. Nor would they help her to bag it for the townspeople, although as Phelim had long ago foreseen, the townspeople were often glad enough to bag it for themselves, or wheel it away in barrowfuls. On Wednesday morning when the rapping came at the gates at dawn, Kate and Stacy stayed in bed and did not get up, but Stacy was wide awake and lay listening to the noises outside. And sometimes she scrambled out of bed across Kate and went to the window.

'Kate?' Stacy would say almost every day.

'What?'

'Perhaps I ought to step out to the kitchen and see the fire is kept up. She'll be very cold when she comes in.'

'You'll do nothing of the kind, I hope! We must stick to our agreement. Get back into bed.'

'She has only her old coat on her and it's very thin, Kate.'

Before answering her, Kate might raise herself up on one elbow and hump the blankets up with her so that when she sank back they were pegged down.

'By all the noise she's making out there I'd say she'd keep up her circulation no matter if she was in nothing but her shift.'

'That work is too heavy for her, Kate. She shouldn't be doing it at all.'

'And who is to blame for that? Get back to bed, like I told you, and don't let her see you're looking out. She'd like nothing better than that.'

'But she's not looking this way Kate. She couldn't see me.'

'That's what you think! Let me tell you, that woman has eyes in the back of her head.' Stacy giggled nervously at that. It was what their mother herself used to tell them when they were small.

Then suddenly she stopped giggling and ran back and threw herself across the foot of the bed and began to sob.

After moving her feet to one side, Kate listened for a few seconds to the sobbing. Then she humped up her other shoulder and pegged the blankets under her on the other side.

'What ails you now?' she asked then.

'Oh Kate, you made me think of when we were children, and she used to stand up so tall and straight and with her gold chain and locket bobbing about on her chest.' Stacy gave another sob. 'Now she's so thin and bent the chain is dangling down to her waist.'

Kate sat up with a start. 'She's not wearing that chain and locket now, out in the yard, is she? Gold is worth a lot more now than it was when Father bought her that.'

Stacy went over to the window and looked out again. 'No, she's not wearing it.'

'I should hope not!' Kate said. 'I saw it on her at the funeral but I forgot about it afterwards in the commotion.'

'She took it off when we came back,' Stacy said. 'She put it away in Father's black box and locked the box.'

'Well, that's one good thing she did anyway,' Kate said. 'She oughtn't to wear it at all.'

'Oh Kate!' Stacy looked at her.

'What?' Kate asked, staring back.

Stacy didn't know what she wanted to say. She couldn't put it into words. She had always thought Kate and herself were alike, that they had the same way of looking at things, but lately she was not so sure of this. They were both getting older, of course, and some people were not as even-tempered as others. Not that she thought herself a paragon, but being so prone to headaches she had to let a lot of things pass that she didn't agree with – like a thing Kate said recently about the time when they were away at school. Their mother had asked how many years ago it was, and while Stacy was trying to count up the years, Kate answered at once.

'Only a few years ago,' she said. That wasn't true but perhaps it only seemed like that to Kate.

Gradually, as time passed, Stacy too, like Kate, used to put the blankets over her head so as not to hear the knocking at the gate, and the rattle of the cart wheels, or at least to deaden the noise of it. She just lay thinking. Kate had once asked her what went through her head when she'd be lying saying nothing.

'This and that,' she'd said. She really didn't think about anything in particular. Sometimes she'd imagine what it would be like if they cleared a small space in the yard and planted things. She knew of course that if they put in a lilac bush it would be small for a long time and would not bear flowers for ages. It would be mostly leaves, and leaves only, for years, or so she'd read somewhere. Yet she always imagined it would be a fully grown lilac they'd have outside the window. Once she imagined something absolutely ridiculous. She was lying half awake and half asleep, and she thought they had transplanted a large full grown lilac, a lilac that had more flowers than leaves, something you never see. And then, as she was half-dozing, the tree got so big and strong its roots pushed under the wall and pushed up through the floorboards – bending the nails and sending splinters of wood flying in all directions. And its branches were so laden down with blossom, so weighted down, that one big pointed bosom of bloom almost touched her face. But suddenly the branch broke with a crack and Stacy was wide awake again. Then the sound that woke her came again, only now she knew what it was – a knocking on the gate outside, only louder than usual, and after it came a voice calling out. She gave Kate a shake.

'Do you hear that, Kate? Mother must have slept it out.'

'Let's hope she did,' Kate said. 'It might teach her a lesson – it might make her see she's not as fit and able as she thinks.'

'But what about the farmers?'

'Who cares about them,' Kate said. '*I* don't! Do you?' When the knocking came again a third time, and a fourth time, Stacy shook Kate again.

'Kate! I wouldn't mind going down and opening the gate,' she said.

'You? In your nightdress?' Kate needed to say no more. Stacy cowered down under the blankets in her shame. All of a sudden she sat up again.

'There wouldn't be anything wrong with Mother, would there?' she cried. This time, without heeding Kate, Stacy climbed out over her to get to the floor. 'I won't go out to the yard, I promise, I'll just go and wake Mother,' she cried. She ran out of the room.

'Come back and shut that door,' Kate called after her. Stacy mustn't have heard. 'Stacy! Come back and shut this door,' Kate shouted.

Stacy still didn't come back.

'Stacy!' Kate yelled. 'Stacy?'

Then she sat up.

'Is there something wrong?' she asked. Getting no answer now either, she got up herself.

Stacy was in their mother's room, lying in a heap on the floor. As Kate said afterwards, she hardly needed to look to know their mother was dead, because Stacy always flopped down in a faint the moment she came up against something unpleasant. And the next day, in the cemetery, when the prayers were over and the gravediggers took up their shovels, Stacy passed out again and had to be brought home by two of the neighbours, leaving Kate to stand and listen to the stones and the clay rumbling down on the coffin.

'You're a nice one, Stacy! Leaving me to stand listening to that awful sound.'

'But I heard it, Kate,' Stacy protested. 'I did! Then my head began to reel, and I got confused. The next thing I knew I was on the ground looking up at the blue sky and thinking the noise was the sound of the horses going clipclap along the road.' Kate stared at her.

'Are you mad? What horses?'

'Oh Kate, don't you remember? The horses Mother was always talking about. She was always telling us how, when she and Father were young, she used to sit beside him on a plank across the cart and watch the road flashing by under the horses' hooves, glittering with bright gold rings of dung?'

Kate, however, wasn't listening.

'That reminds me. Isn't tomorrow Wednesday?' she said. 'Which of us is going to get up and let in the farm carts?' When Stacy stared vacantly, Kate stamped her foot. 'Don't look so stupid, Stacy! They came the day after Father was buried, why wouldn't they come tomorrow? Mother herself said it was their way of showing – showing that as far as they were concerned the death wouldn't make any difference.'

'Oh Kate. How do you think they'll take it when you tell them—'

'Tell them what? Really Stacy, you *are* a fool. Tomorrow is no day to tell them anything. We'll have to take it easy – wait and see how we stand, before we talk about making changes.'

Kate was so capable. Stacy was filled with admiration for her. She would not have minded in the least getting up to open the gate, but she never would be able to face a discussion of the future. Kate was able for everything, and realising this, Stacy permitted herself a small feeling of excitement at the thought of them making their own plans and standing on their own two feet.

'I'll get up and light the fire and bring you a cup of tea in bed before you have to get up, Kate,' she said.

Kate shrugged her shoulders. 'If I know you, Stacy, you'll have one of your headaches,' Kate said.

Stacy said nothing. She was resolved to get up, headache or no headache. On the quiet she set an old alarm clock she found in the kitchen. But the alarm bell was broken, and the first thing Stacy heard next morning was the rapping on the gate. When she went to scramble out, to her surprise Kate was already gone from the room. And when Stacy threw her clothes on and ran out to the kitchen, the fire was roaring up the chimney, and a cup with a trace of sugar and tea leaves in the bottom of it was on the windowsill. The teapot was on the hob but it had been made a long time and it was cold. She made herself another pot and took it over to sip it by the window, looking out.

Kate was in the yard, directing the carts and laughing and talking with the men. Kate certainly had a way with her and no mistake. When it would come to telling the farmers that they needn't deliver any more dung, they wouldn't be offended.

One big tall farmer, with red hair and whiskers, was the last to leave, and he and Kate stood talking at the gate so long Stacy wondered if, after all, Kate mightn't be discussing their future dealings with him. She hoped she wouldn't catch cold. She put a few more sods of turf on the fire.

'Do you want to set the chimney on fire?' Kate asked when she came in. Stacy didn't let herself get upset though. Kate was carrying all the responsibility now, and it was bound to make her edgy.

'I saw you talking to one of the men,' said she. 'I was wondering if perhaps you were giving him a hint of our plans and sounding him out?'

'I was sounding him out all right,' Kate said, and she smiled. 'You see, Stacy. I've been thinking that we might come up with a new plan. You mightn't like it at first, but you may come round when I make you see it in the right light. Sit down and I'll tell you.' Stacy sat down. Kate stayed standing. 'I've been looking into the ledgers, and I would never have believed there was so much money coming in from the dung. So, I've been thinking that, instead of getting rid of it, we ought to try and take in more, twice or three times more, and make twice or three times as much money. No! No! Sit down again, Stacy. Hear me out. My plan would be that we'd move out of here, and use this cottage for storage

– the sheds are not big enough. We could move into a more suitable house, larger and with a garden maybe—'

When Stacy said nothing Kate looked sharply at her. It wouldn't have surprised her if Stacy had flopped off in another faint, but she was only sitting dumbly looking into the fire. 'It's only a suggestion,' Kate said, feeling her way more carefully. 'You never heed anything, Stacy, but when I go out for my walks I take note of things I see – and there's a plot of ground for sale out a bit the road, but not too far from here all the same, and it's for sale – I've made enquiries. Now if we were to try and buy that it wouldn't cost much to build a bungalow. I've made enquiries about the cost of that too, and it seems—'

But Stacy had found her tongue. 'I don't want to move out of here, Kate,' she cried. 'This is where we were born, where my mother and father—' She began to cry. 'Oh Kate! I never want to leave here. Never! Never!'

Kate could hardly speak with fury.

'Stay here so!' she said. 'But don't expect me to stay with you. I'm getting out of here at the first chance I get to go. And let me tell you something else. That dunghill isn't stirring out of where it is until I've a decent dowry out of it. Cry away now to your heart's content for all I care.' Going over to their bedroom Kate went in and banged the door behind her.

Stacy stopped crying and stared at the closed door. Her head had begun to throb and she would have liked to lie down, but after the early hour Kate had risen she had probably gone back to bed. No. Kate was up and moving about the room. There was great activity going on. Stacy felt so much better. She knew Kate. Kate had never been one to say she was sorry for anything she said or did, but that need not mean she didn't feel sorry. She was giving their room a good turn-out? Perhaps this was her way of working off her annoyance and at the same time show she was sorry for losing her temper. Stacy sat back, thinking her thoughts, and waited for Kate to come out. She didn't have long to wait. In about five minutes the knob of the bedroom door rattled. 'Open this door for me, Stacy! My arms are full. I can't turn the handle,' Kate called and Stacy was glad to see she sounded in excellent form, and as if all was forgotten. For the second time in twenty-four hours Stacy felt a small surge of excitement, as Kate came out her arms piled sky high with dresses and hats and a couple of cardboard boxes, covered with wallpaper, in which they kept their gloves and handkerchiefs. It was to be a real spring cleaning! They hadn't done one in years. She hadn't noticed it before but the wallpaper on the boxes was yellowed with age and the flowery pattern faded. They might paste on new wallpaper? And seeing that Kate, naturally, had only her own things she went to run and get hers, but first she ran back to clear a space on the table so Kate could put her things down.

But Kate was heading across the kitchen to their mother's room.

'There's no sense in having a room idle, is there?' she said, disappearing into it. 'I'm moving in here.'

There was no further mention of the dunghill that day, nor indeed that week. Stacy felt a bit lonely at first in the room they had shared since childhood. But it had its advantages. It had been a bit stuffy sleeping on the inside. And she didn't have so many headaches, but that could possibly be attributed to Kate's suggestion that she ignore them.

Every Wednesday Kate was up at the crack of dawn to let the carts unload. As their father had also foreseen, they were now paying the farmers for the manure, but only a small sum, because they were still glad to get rid of it. And the townspeople on the other hand were paying five times more. Kate had made no bones about raising her prices. The only time there was a reference to the future was when Kate announced that she didn't like keeping cash in the house, and that she was going to start banking some of their takings. The rest could be put as usual in the black box, which was almost the only thing that had never been taken out of their mother's room. A lot of other things were thrown out.

Kate and Stacy got on as well as ever, it seemed to Stacy, but there were often long stretches of silence in the house because Kate was never as talkative as their mother. After nightfall they often sat by a dying fire, only waiting for it to go out, before getting up and going to bed. All things considered, Kate was right to have moved into the other room, and Stacy began to enjoy having a room of her own. She had salvaged a few of her mother's things that Kate had thrown out and she liked looking at them. If Kate knew she never said anything. Kate never came into their room anymore.

Then one evening when Con O'Toole – the big whiskery farmer with whom Kate had been talking the first day she took over the running of things – when Con started dropping in to see how they were getting on, Stacy was particularly glad to have a room of her own. She liked Con. She really did. But the smell of his pipe brought on her headaches again. The smell of his tobacco never quite left the house, and it even pursued her in through the keyhole after she had left him and Kate together, because of course it was Kate Con came to see.

'Can you stand the smell of his pipe?' she asked Kate one morning. 'It's worse than the smell of the dung!' She only said it by way of a joke, but Kate, who had taken out the black box and was going through the papers in it, a thing she did regularly now, shut the lid of the box and frowned.

'I thought we agreed on saying fertiliser instead of that word you just used.'

'Oh but that was long ago, when we were in boarding school,' Stacy stammered.

'I beg your pardon! It was agreed we'd be more particular about how we referred to our business when we were in the company of other people – or at least that was my understanding! Take Con O'Toole, for instance. He may deliver dung here but he never gives it that name – at least not in front of me. The house he lives in may be thatched and have a mud wall, but that's because his old mother is alive and he can't get her to agree to knocking it down and building a new house, which of course they can afford – I was astonished at the amount of land he owns. Come, Stacy, you must understand that I am not urging him to make any changes. So please don't mention this conversation to him. I'll tell him myself when I judge the time to be right. Then I'll make him see the need for building a new house. He needn't knock the old one either. He can leave the old woman in it for what time is left her. But as I say, I'll bide my time. I might even wait until after we are married.'

That was the first Stacy heard of Kate's intended marriage, but after that first reference there was talk of nothing else, right up to the fine blowy morning when Kate was hoisted up into Con O'Toole's new motor car, in a peacock blue outfit, with their mother's gold chain bumping up and down on her bosom.

Stacy was almost squeezed to death in the doorway as the guests all stood there to wave goodbye to the happy couple. There had been far more guests than either she or Kate had bargained on because the O'Tooles had so many relations, and they all brought their children, and – to boot – Kate's old mother-in-law brought along a few of her own cronies as well. But there was enough food, and plenty of port wine.

It was a fine wedding. And Stacy didn't mind the mess that was made of the house. Such a mess! Crumbs scattered over the carpet in the parlour and driven into it by people's feet! Bottle tops all over the kitchen floor! Port wine and lemonade stains soaked into the tablecloth! It was going to take time to get the place to rights again. Stacy was almost looking forward to getting it to rights again because she had decided to make a few changes in the arrangement of the furniture – small changes, only involving chairs and ornaments. But she intended attacking it that evening after the guests left. However, when the bridal couple drove off with a hiss of steam rising out of the radiator of the car, the guests flocked back into the house and didn't go until there wasn't a morsel left to eat, or a single drop left to refill the decanters. One thing did upset Stacy and that was when she saw the way the beautiful wedding cake on which the icing had been as hard and white as plaster had been attacked by someone who didn't know how to cut a cake. The cake had been laid waste, and the children that hadn't already fallen asleep on the sofas were stuffing themselves with the last crumbs. Stacy herself hadn't as much as a taste of that cake, and she'd intended keeping at least one tier aside for some future time. Ah well. It was nice to think everyone had had a good time, she thought, as she closed the door on the last of the O'Tooles, who had greatly outnumbered their own friends. Jasper Kane, their father's solicitor, had been their principal guest. He had not in fact left yet, but he was getting ready to leave.

'It will be very lonely for you now, Miss Stacy,' he said. 'You ought to get some person in to keep you company – at least for the nights.'

It was very kind of him to be so concerned. Stacy expressed her gratitude freely, and reassured him that she was quite looking forward to being, as it were, her own mistress. She felt obliged to add, hastily, that she'd miss Kate, although to be strictly truthful, she didn't think she'd miss her as much as she would have thought before Con O'Toole had put in his appearance.

'Well, well. I'm glad to hear you say that, Miss Stacy,' Jasper Kane said, as he prepared to leave. 'I expect you'll drop in to my office at your convenience. I understand your sister took care of the business, but I'm sure you'll be just as competent when you get the hang of things.' Then for a staid man like him, he got almost playful. 'I'll be very curious to see what changes you'll make,' he said, and she saw his eye fall on a red plush sofa that Kate had bought after Con started calling, and which Stacy thought was hideous. She gave him a conspiratorial smile. But she didn't want him to think she wasn't serious.

'I intend to make changes outside as well, Mr Kane,' she said, gravely. 'And the very first thing I'm going to do is plant a few lilac trees.'

Jasper Kane looked surprised.

'Oh? Where?' he asked, and although it was dark outside, he went to the window and tried to see out.

'Where else but where the dunghill has always been,' Stacy said, and just to hear herself speaking with such authority made her almost lightheaded.

Jasper Kane remained staring out into the darkness. Then he turned around and asked a simple question.

'But what will you live on, Miss Stacy?'

MELES VULGARIS

Patrick Boyle

'What are you reading, darling?'

Her voice was muffled by the turtleneck sweater out of which she was struggling.

He pulled the bedclothes further up his chest, adjusted the pillow and turned a page.

'Come again?'

'There wasn't a cheep' – her chin emerged – 'out of you' – the sweater was peeled from her rolled back ears – 'all evening. It must be' – a last effort and she was free – 'a powerful book.'

'Uh-huh.'

She pitched the sweater on to a chair seat, shook out her wiry black hair and examined herself critically in the mirror.

'Sitting hunched up over an old book since tea-time,' she told the frowning sun-tanned reflection, 'without a word to say for yourself.' Eyes – sloe-black, deep set, heavy-lidded – gazed back at her appraisingly. 'You know, darling, it's lonely all day in the house by yourself.' With tentative fingertips, she smoothed out the crow's feet. 'No one to talk to till you're home for the weekends.' Her gaze slid over the tiny frightening folds and wrinkles of the neck and sought comfort in the firm brown flesh of arms and shoulders. The mirrored face smiled ruefully. 'It's a wonder I don't start talking to myself.'

'Uh-huh.' With finger and thumb, he rasped gently the lifted ready-to-be-turned leaf.

She swung round.

'I believe you weren't listening to a word I said.'

'Sorry, honey. I wasn't paying attention.'

She reached out a hand. Curious.

'What's it about, anyway?'

He handed her the book.

'*The Badger.*' She leafed the pages rapidly. 'It looks like some sort of a textbook.'

'So it is.'

Frowning, she studied the stylised animal on the jacket.

'Why the sudden interest in badgers?' she asked.

'I saw it' – he nodded towards the book – 'displayed in a book shop window.'

'But what on earth induced you to buy it?'

'A sudden impulse. It reminded me of that holiday we had in the Blue Stack Mountains. When we saw the badger fight.'

Her face lit up.

'But that was years ago.'

He rolled over on his side, tucked the bedclothes in round his shoulders and burrowed into the pillow.

'Oh,' he mumbled, 'I remember it – remember it right well.'

He yawned.

'The book tells you how the little fellows tick.'

The common badger – meles vulgaris – a genus of burrowing carnivores, is found in hilly or wooded districts in almost every part of the country. More common in the West than in the East.

Sunday morning after Mass. Around the church gate the usual crowd of men standing about in groups, talking football, greyhounds, hangovers, weather. From the outskirts Micky Hogan beckoning. Moving away from the crowd before he spoke.

'Are you for the match the day?'

'I don't know. Why?'

'They're drawing a badger up at Johnny John's.'

'D'you tell me! What dogs have they got? Mind you, it's not everyone will chance getting his dog mauled or maybe killed by a brock.'

'Hawker Downey is bringing along that treacherous whelp of a Kerry Blue of his. A right mauling might put manners on it.'

'Any other?'

'They have another Kerry Blue lined up. A good one.'

'Whose?'

'The curate's. The boys are going to whip it when he's gone to the match.'

'Och, go to God. There'll be the queer rumpus when he finds out.'

'The dog'll be at the gate to meet him when he gets back from the game. It might be a wee scratch or two the worse for the trip but sure the silly brute is always in trouble. You should take the car and we'll head into the Blue Stacks. It'll be right gas.'

'How did they catch the badger?'

'D'you mind the Johnny Johns complaining about the fox slaughtering their fowl?'

'Aye.'

'Well, they found pad marks yesterday morning outside the hen house. The tracks led to a badger's earth not a stone's throw from the house. The nest was dug up, the sow and the three cubs killed and Mister Brock himself is for the high jump this afternoon.'

The badger is a member of the order Carnivora and has large teeth but, contrary to popular belief, it does not prey on poultry and young lambs. It feeds on insects, small mammals, molluses and earthworms, supplemented by vegetable material such as fruit, nuts and grass.

Still riffling the pages of the book, she stared blindly at the unfamiliar photographs. Tenderness welled up inside her, tearing at throat and eyes. Perhaps he too was thinking of their first holiday together after they were married. When he had taken the firm's car and they had driven into the foothills of Croaghgorm to his Aunt Ellen's tiny farmhouse. There was no money to go any place else. But who cared? They had spent three weeks there, coddled and fussed over by Aunt Ellen.

They had moved round together in a daze. Drunk with love. Shouting their crazy enchantment at the echoing hills. Bound together with such hunger for each other that the warmth left the blazing summer sun if they moved apart.

For those three weeks they had only one body between them – a parched thirsty body that soaked up happiness like a sponge. It was on the last day of that unforgettable holiday that they brought Micky with them to the badger fight in the Blue Stacks.

The baiting had already started when the car bumped and slithered up the last stretch of track and into Johnny John's yard. A crowd of mountain men stood around watching Hawker Downey – a fussy wee know-all – trying to coax, drag, push his stupid gulpin of a dog into an overturned barrel. Each time he got the Kerry Blue's forequarters inside the barrel, the dog would wriggle free, dashing around among the onlookers, wagging its stumpy tail.

The crowd hooted and jeered.

'Put your shoulder to him, Downey.'

'Take away the cowardly cur.'

'Give the curate's dog a trial.'

'Crawl into the barrel yourself, Hawker.'

Downey was nettled. He got the dog by the scruff of the neck and the skin of the rump and fairly hurled it into the barrel.

'Sic him, Garry!' he urged. 'Sic the brock!'

Never did dog react quicker. It bounced back out of the barrel, shot between Downey's splayed legs and never cried halt till it reached the safety of the dunghill, where it ploutered about in the soggy muck, wagging a doubtful, disillusioned tail. Whistles, threats, curses wouldn't shift it.

There was nothing for it but to try out the curate's dog. Much against his will Micky Hogan, who sometimes exercised the dog for Father Bradley, was prevailed on to handle it.

'I'll gamble the curate will blame me for this day's work, if he gets to hear of it. So keep your traps shut. All of you,' he said.

The Kerry Blue trotted at his heels to the barrel mouth. He patted its flank.

'In you go, champ,' he said.

The dog moved in willingly enough. For as long as it took Micky to straighten up, take a cigarette butt from behind his ear and light it, the dog stayed stiff-legged, tail quivering, before it backed out slowly. Once clear of the barrel it stopped, shaking its head violently.

Micky grabbed it. Examined the muzzle.

'Not a scratch,' he announced. 'There's only one remedy for this disease. The toe of me boot.'

'You may give over, Hogan,' a querulous voice called. It was the old fellow himself. Johnny John. He was standing at the kitchen door, watching the proceedings with a sardonic smile. 'I told the young fellows to get fox-terriers. But of course they knew better. Those dogs you've got aren't worth a curse. They'll never face the barrel.'

'For why?'

'The smell of the brock has them stomached.'

One of the characteristics of the badger is the possession of musk- or stink-glands. These anal glands are used as a result of fear or excitement. The recognition of danger will stimulate secretion and trigger off the defence mechanism.

A hand ruffled his hair.

'Unhook me, will you, honey.'

Reaching up a hand towards the voice, he pawed the air blindly.

'Come on, lazybones,' she urged. 'I can't get this wretched thing off.'

His eyes opened to black bra straps biting into sun-browned skin. As he fumbled with the hooks, buried deep in flesh, she chattered on:

'How's that for a tan? I was the whole week stretched out on the lawn. Sun-bathing. We get so little sun it would be a shame not to make the most of this hot spell. God knows, it's hard enough to get a decent tan up. Olive oil helps, of course. But then you must be careful not to fall asleep or you'll get fried. Properly fried.'

The loosened bra fell away. With outstretched arms she spun around.

'Becoming, isn't it?'

The brown body appeared to be encompassed by a monstrous pair of white plastic goggles out of which glared two angry bulging bloodshot eyes.

His flesh crept with embarrassment.

'Most exotic,' he said.

She flushed with pleasure.

'You really think so?'

He yawned wide and loud.

'Sure.'

His head dropped back on the pillow.

It was decided to let the dogs attack in the open where the rank smell would be dispersed. The crowd scattered back from the barrel. The two dogs were leashed.

One of the young Johnny Johns gripped the bottom of the barrel. Tilted it. Slowly. To knee level. Scrabbling noises. Higher still. More scrabbling noises. Up to hip level. Silence.

'He's lodged, boy,' called Johnny John. 'You may shake him out of it.'

The young fellow shook the barrel. Cautiously. Nothing happened. Harder this time. Still no result.

'You'll get no windfalls that way,' someone shouted.

'Slew the barrel round, Peter,' the old man ordered.

A murmur of appreciation went round.

'Sound man.'

'The old dog for the hard road.'

'It takes yourself Johnny.'

Slowly Peter swung the barrel on its base. The crowd began to close in. The old man moved out from the porch. One of the dogs whimpered.

At the quarter turn the badger came slithering out, still clawing wildly for purchase.

It crouched, facing its tormentors, the grey-black hair on its body bristling like a hedgehog, its black and white head flat to the ground. Although it remained motionless, its whole body, from snout to stumpy tail seethed with controlled energy.

This fierce smothered tension dominated the crowd with a threatening fist. No one moved. Peter still held up the tilted barrel. Hogan's smoked down butt scorched the palm of his hand unheeded. Halted in mid-stride Johnny John waited, ash-plant poised.

Again a dog whimpered.

The crouching badger leaped forward. It picked no gap in the ranks of its enemies. It hurled itself at them and they broke before it. Shouting and cursing: shouldering, elbowing, pushing each other, in their anxiety to get out of the path of this savage creature running amuck; they backed away.

Through this opening dashed the badger. Ahead lay freedom. A length of laneway, a thick hedge, a familiar track reeking with the smell of its kind, the safety – somewhere – of an unravaged set.

There was one enemy left. Johnny John.

Wily and tough as the brock itself, he had moved out towards the yard gate and now, with stamping feet and flailing ash-plant, he headed the badger back towards the closed and bolted outhouses.

Baffled, uncertain, the badger slowed down, scuttling along with a lurching, waddling gait. The length of the outhouses it ran, seeking shelter – scurrying, hesitating, scurrying again – like a business man hunting for a seat in a crowded train.

The feet of the badger are plantigrade: the animal walks on the flat of its feet, including the heel, in contrast to the Ungulates, which walk on their toes.

He clung doggedly to his share of the bedclothes as she plunged into bed, wriggling and threshing around, till she was coiled up under the glow of the bed light, an open magazine held between pillow and bedclothes.

The glossy leaves crackled imposingly as she flicked them over, seeing not mink-coated figures, luscious dishes of food, enormous luxury automobiles, but grim, hungry, plush-covered hills.

'Why don't we go back there again?' she said. 'Sometime.'

'Where?' His voice was muffled by the pillow.

'Croaghgorm.'

The bed springs creaked as he shifted peevishly.

'What would we be going there for? Aunt Ellen's dead.'

'We could stay some place else. A farmhouse in the hills.'

Again he shifted. Rolling over on his back. To the ceiling he spoke – patiently, reasonably, wearily.

'Look, Sheila. In a cottage in Croaghorm you would last exactly one night. No hot water. No foam rubber mattress. No thick pile carpets. No radiogram. Above all nothing to do. Except you tramp the mountains, helping them to herd sheep.'

Her heart contracted as she felt the spring of the moss under her bare feet, the cool squelch of mud oozing between her toes.

'Or sit in the house all day blinded by a smoking turf fire.'

She drew in her breath, sniffing the acrid, heady, wholly delicious fragrance of burning turf: watched with sleepy eyes the flames die down as the brown ash formed; heard the tired sigh as the burnt out sods collapsed.

'Not forgetting the peaceful night's rest you'll have with sheepdogs barking, cattle bawling and roosters crowing their heads off at daybreak.'

She rolled over facing him.

'We must go, dear. Some time. If it's only for the day.'

'All right. All right.'

He pulled the bedclothes over his head.

The badger disappeared into the opening between two outhouses.

'He's got away.'

'Why didn't you mill him, Johnny?'

'Loose the dogs.'

The old man pranced about in the gap, waving the stick.

'He picked the baiting-pitch himself,' he said, as the crowd gathered in the opening. 'And a better choice he couldn't have made if he'd searched all Ireland.'

It was a cul-de-sac. The gable ends of two outhouses – one of concrete, the other galvanised iron – a few yards apart, linked by a man-high stone wall.

Around these confines the badger sniffed, scratching the ground here and there with a tentative forepaw. Where the zinc shed met the wall, it started digging.

By the time the decision had been reached to send in Hawker's dog first, the badger had rooted out a hole large enough to warrant the use of its hind paws. With these it scattered back the uprooted clay into an ever-rising parapet. When the Kerry Blue came charging in, the badger wheeled around, keeping to the shelter of its burrow, to face its assailant, teeth bared in a silent snarl.

It crouched motionless but for the grinning muzzle that swung from side to side parrying the probing onslaughts of the dog. This swaying exotically-striped head, slender, graceful, compact with fierce vigilance seemed to repudiate the huddled body, craven, lumpish, dingy, belonging surely to a different and inferior species.

The dog pounced. It grabbed the badger at the back of the head where the long grey body-hairs begin. Secure from the snapping jaws by this shrewd grip, it whipped up the striped head, shook it violently and slammed it back to the ground. It pinned down the badger's head, pressing it into the loose clay whilst it gnawed and grunted, grunted and gnawed, shifting its grip deeper and deeper through the thick hair, as if it sought to sink its teeth into solid flesh.

Always it was thwarted. Choked by the mass of coarse wiry hair, it was forced to loosen its hold, gulping in a quick mouthful of air before it pounced again.

The badger crouched supine, muzzle buried in the clay. Waiting.

At last the gasping dog released its hold. For one vulnerable second it loomed over its enemy, its slavering jaws content to threaten. In that second the badger struck.

The striped head reared up. Snapping jaws closed on a dangling ear. A yelp. Frenzied scuffling as the growling dog sought to free itself. A wild howl. The badger, still gripping the torn ear, had lashed out with one of its forefeet, raking the dog's muzzle – once, twice – with its long gouging claws before the poor brute broke free. Bleeding from lacerated ear and jowl, it backed away yapping.

Johnny John struck the ground with his stick.

'You may take the cowardly brute to hell out of that,' he said. 'A Kerry Blue's no use to fight once it starts giving tongue.'

Downey grabbed his dog and lugged it away. The badger went back to its burrowing. Micky Hogan started to unleash the second dog, now trembling and straining at the lead.

'You mightn't bother your barney, Hogan,' said Johnny John. 'That dog'll never best a brock. Didn't I tell it was a soople, snapping animal you wanted. Not a big lazy get the like of thon, that'll fall asleep on the grip.'

Micky looked up.

'I'm surprised at you, Johnny,' he said. 'Have you no respect for the cloth?' He stooped over the dog. 'Go in there, Father Fergus, and show this anti-clerical gentleman how you handle a heretic.' He released the dog. 'Off you go, chum.'

The dog advanced cautiously. Every few paces it paused, straddle-legged, watchful, snarling muzzle out-thrust, its gaze fastened on the badger, now faced round awaiting its attacker. It advanced to within arm's length of the striped muzzle before it came to a halt, crouched on stiffened forefeet. It growled softly, continuously – a growl so far back in its throat that it sounded like a harmless gentle purr.

The badger held its ground, beady eyes bright, alert, muzzle cocked, lips drawn back in its soundless snarl.

The two animals crouched, locked into stasis by the hate and fear that glared back at them from alien eyes. So long did they remain poised that a shout went up when the tension was broken at last by the pouncing dog.

'He's nailed him!'

'Good on you, Fergus!'

'Hold tight to him!'

Johnny John said quietly:

'There'll be trouble when he loosens yon grip.'

The dog had gripped the badger by the snout and was tugging it from its burrow into open ground. The badger, with splayed feet, resisted. It was of no avail. Heaving and jerking, the Kerry Blue drew the badger inch by struggling inch over the clay parapet until it had the thirty-pound carcass out on level ground. At this moment the dog's hindfeet lost their purchase on the moiled ground.

The sudden skid loosened the hold of the dog's jaws. It was the badger's chance. Teeth crunched. A yelp of pain from the dog. The badger's clumsy body came to life – squirming, wriggling, jerking. At last it was free. Snout torn and bleeding. One eye damaged. Dragged from its sheltering burrow. But free.

It began to sidle towards the uprooted trench. The dog blocked its path, menacing the badger with bared and bloody teeth.

'The brock has relieved the poor bugger of half his bucking tongue,' someone said in an awe-stricken voice.

'What did I tell you?' said Johnny John.

This time there was no preliminary sparring. The dog closed in at once, only manoeuvring so that his attack came from the badger's rear, safe from the deadly teeth and claws. Like a boxer using his reach, the dog took advantage of longer legs and greater agility. It leapt around the badger, darting out and in, feinting to charge until it lured its enemy into position. Then it pounced.

Sometimes it succeeded in straddling the badger, flattening it on the ground, where it could tear and maul the defenceless animal's head. But not for long. The badger would break free, roll over on its back and rip with lethal claws the dog's unprotected belly.

Slow, ungainly, its heavy stumpy-legged body unsuited to swift exchanges, the badger was content to remain on the defensive. But always it was dangerous. Let the Kerry Blue fail to duck away quick

enough after releasing its grip and another gash was added to its
scored and bleeding body.

Except for the scuffle of paws on the trampled clay, the panting of
the dog as it sparred for an opening, an occasional grunt from either
animal, the struggle was fought out with quiet decorum. Indeed for
long stretches there was complete silence as the two animals lay locked
together, jerking spasmodically as the dog strove to deepen its grip or
the badger to free itself.

If both had not been so mired and bloody – the badger's slender
elegant head being so plastered with blood and clay that the parti-
coloured striping could no longer be discerned – they could have been
tricking together harmlessly. Or dozing in the sun. Or even coupling.

It was evident that the strain of continual attack was wearying the
dog. Its movements were now clumsy, sluggish: its lithe evasions
slowing down. At last the inevitable happened.

The Kerry Blue came charging in obliquely. Swerved to escape the
grinning expectant muzzle. A moment of teetering indecision. A shout
from the crowd.

'The brock has got him!'

'It'll tear the throat out of him!'

'Maybe we should separate them, lads?'

'Throw Downey's craven cur in on top of them.'

Hawker called:

'Will I let Garry have another go at him, Johnny?'

The old man squirted a jet of tobacco juice towards the straining
dog. Said he:

'Damn the differ it'll make. The brock is the boss. He'll beat the two
of them.'

Hawker loosed the dog.

'Sic him!' he said. 'Sic the bastard!'

The dog went in, running low to the ground, watching its comrade
back away, dragging after it the badger, in a frantic effort to break the
throttling hold. Ignoring threats, jeers and pleadings, it waited its
opportunity. An unexpected jerk put the badger's legs sprawling. The
wary dog pounced, grabbing the badger by a hind leg. Tugging at its
hold, it swung the badger off the ground till it dangled belly up, its
teeth still sunk in its enemy's throat.

Before the badger could right itself, the dog slammed the helpless body down on its back and, shifting its hold, bit deeply into the tender flesh of the groin.

So swiftly did the badger release its grip and lash out with scourging claws at the already lacerated muzzle of its new assailant that the agonised yapping of both dogs – the throttled and the mauled – broke out simultaneously. Still yapping, they fled to either side of the enclosure where they wheeled round, barking and growling. They were in poor shape. Bloody. Mangled. Shivering with fright.

'That burrowing bastard has made a slaughterhouse job of them,' said Micky Hogan.

Johnny John spat, a quick explosive spurt. He said:

'Didn't I warn you the brock would master the pair of them? Better if you call in your wretched curs before he drives them ahead of him into the village.'

The badger had limped back into the scooped out trench. It commenced digging again. With its forepaws only. Soon its claws could be heard rasping on the cement foundation of the shed. It stopped. Changed position and burrowed again till once more stopped by the cement. Twice more it tried, before it started on the galvanised iron. Inserting a paw under the bottom of the sheeting, it commenced to tear at it, tearing and tugging until at last it managed to secure a purchase for its jaws.

'In the name of God,' someone said, with a nervous laugh, 'does it mean to pull the building over its head like Samson?'

The badger was worrying at the metal sheeting – tugging, snapping, gnawing – its body coiling and uncoiling, as it strove to chew or tear its way to freedom.

'You'd think it was crunching biscuits,' one of the young Johnny Johns said. 'With jaws the like of yon, it'd chaw itself out of Sing Sing.'

The badger has extremely powerful jaws. A peculiar feature of the lower jaw is that it locks in a transverse elongated socket in such a complete manner that it will not dislocate: if it comes away at all the skull will be fractured.

An elbow jogged him.

'Are you asleep?'

'Eugh! . . . Eh? . . . Aye!' A long sighing breath. Part moan, part fretful wail.

'Come off it, Brer Fox. You're codding nobody. Lying awake brooding on the silly old badgers you were reading about all evening.'

She ran a teasing finger down the bones of his spine.

'Wha's-a-matter? Wh-dja-want?'

'Oh, nothing. I thought you were asleep.'

'Darling, I've had a long, hard day. I'm jaded out. Beat to the ropes. Let's go to sleep, what d'you say?'

He clutched the bedclothes. Huddled down lower in the bed. Breathed loudly, steadily, through his nose.

The men were debating the fate of the badger.

'Destroy the brute. That's the only thing to be done.'

'Look at the shape it's left the dogs.'

'What'll the curate say when he sees the cut of Fergus?'

'Small odds about those whining hoors,' said Johnny John. 'Didn't the brock lather the daylights out of the pair of them? We'd be poor sports to slaughter it after that.'

'Let it go,' he urged.

'So that it can raid more hen houses?'

'Or spread ruin round the district with its burrowing?'

'Aye! Or maybye start attacking the young lambs?'

Johnny John was overborne.

'All right,' he said. 'Fetch out a mattock.'

It was decided that Clarke, the village butcher, would dispatch the badger. Mattock at the ready, he moved in towards the gnawing animal. A few paces from the burrow he halted as the badger swung round to face him. Three cautious steps brought him within striking distance of the snarling muzzle. He hefted the mattock. Balanced it carefully, judging his target. Brought the blade smashing down square on the badger's poll, driving its head deep into the clay. A neat professional stroke.

The butcher stood over the motionless body, leaning on the shaft of the mattock. He was about to turn away, satisfied with a job well done, when the badger stirred. Raised its bloodied muzzle from the clay. Struggled erect.

Again Clarke chopped the heavy-bladed weapon down on the badger's skull, crushing the mangled head to the ground. Slowly, painfully, the snarling muzzle was raised in defiance.

Twice more the butcher swung down the mattock before Johnny
John's shouts penetrated his shocked bewilderment.

'In God's name, give over, Butcher. You'll never do away with the
brute that way.'

The old man rushed into the enclosure.

'Gimme that tool, man,' he said, grabbing the mattock. 'You'll take
the edge off the blade. D'you not know that a brock's skull will stand
up to a charge of buckshot?'

*A feature of the badger is the extraordinary growth of the interparietal ridge
of bone on the dorsal surface of the skull in the mid line. This ridge is half an
inch deep in places and serves to protect the main surface of the skull from
blows delivered directly from above, though its prime purpose is for the
attachment of the powerful jaw muscles.*

'Tell me,' she murmured, her breath fanning his ear, 'what attraction a
badger has got that the rest of us lack?'

She had rolled over, cuddling herself against his back.

'Can't you let a fellow sleep?' He edged away unobtrusively.

'What has it got?' she insisted, snuggling closer.

'It's got courage. Courage. Tenacity. Fortitude.'

'Where do the rest of us come in?' Her hand burrowed into the
jacket of his pyjamas. 'Wouldn't we all act the same way with our back
to the wall? Courage and ferocity!' She sniffed. 'There's more to it than
that. Surely?' Her fingers drummed an urgent message on his chest.
'You'd never ask someone to take second place to a stupid old badger.'
A warm leg slid over his own. 'Would you, darling?'

'Sheila . . . please!'

He shook himself free. Reached up and switched off the light. Fists
clenched, eyes squeezed shut – he lay, trying to ignore the reproach in
her rigid outstretched body. When at last her breathing had steadied to
the rhythm of sleep, he tugged the bedclothes back over himself,
relaxed and opened his eyes to the dark.

Queer, he thought, how she had got to the core of things. Unwit-
tingly. For surely, without tenacity, courage and ferocity were futile.

*The courage of the badger is legendary. A shy, inoffensive animal, with no
natural enemies, it will yet, if cornered, exhibit a ferocity noteworthy in a*

creature of such small dimensions. It is utterly fearless. Whether bird, beast or reptile: the forces of nature or the savagery of man – nothing can daunt it.

Johnny John was standing an arm's length from the badger.

'There's only one way to kill a brock,' he said, over his shoulder.

He raised the mattock. 'A clout on the muzzle.'

He swung down the blade.

At the same instant the badger charged. The squelch of the blade on the animal's back and the cry of dismay from the old man came together.

'So help me God,' he wailed. 'I didn't mean to do it.'

He dropped the mattock. With horror-stricken gaze he watched the badger. Hindquarters flattened to the ground, grinning muzzle still lifted in challenge, it continued towards him, dragging its helpless body forward on stubborn forepaws.

'A wee tap on the nose. As God is my judge, that's what I tried to do,' Johnny John pleaded.

'Come away out of that, Da, or it'll maybe maul you,' one of the boys called out.

The mattock lay across the badger's path. An insurmountable barrier to the crippled beast. Feebly it pawed at the heavy implement striving to push or pull it aside. Without success. At last, the infuriated animal sank its teeth in the wooden shaft, lifting the handle clear of the ground. Unable to drag itself further forward, it lay stretched out, eyes glaring madly ahead, clenched jaws holding aloft the murderous weapon. The matted, filthy, bloodstained animal had already the ugly anonymous appearance of death.

The old man was near to tears. In his distress he shuffled a few steps to either side, beating the fist of one hand into the palm of the other.

'Where's my stick?' he muttered. 'Where the hell's my stick?'

He shook his fist at the watching crowd.

'It's all your fault, you ignorant pack of hallions. Didn't I pray and plead with you to let the brock go? Now look what you've done.'

He moved back towards them, changing direction aimlessly, his gaze scanning the ground.

'Where did I drop my stick? It must be someplace hereabouts.'

He looked up.

'Let none of you ever boast of this day's work. It was pure butchery, that's what it was. A cowardly bit of blackguardism. There's more spunk in the brock than in the whole bloody issue of you.'

He halted.

'Will some of you find me stick . . . or some other implement . . .' He looked back over his shoulder, as though fearful of being overheard. 'Till I put an end to its . . . Oh, Mother of God!'

The badger had released its grip on the mattock. It rolled over on its back. Screaming.

It kept screaming – a loud sustained yell of defiance that not even the onslaught of death could subdue to a whimper: that ceased abruptly only with the slack-jaw and the glazing eye.

There are many conflicting theories regarding the significance of the badger's peculiar yell. Some naturalists believe it to have sexual origins: others that it has some connection with the death or funeral rites of this strange animal. All are agreed on the blood-curdling quality of the cry.

Lying wide-eyed and sleepless, he tried to close his ears to the appalling sound. It was no use. The voice of the dying badger refused to be silenced.

For all these years it had resounded in his memory with the urgency of a trumpet call – the wild defiant shout of an animal ringed about with enemies. He had thought to cast himself in this heroic mould. To be a maverick. Forever in the ranks of the embattled minority. Instead there had been a slow erosion of ideals, a cowardly retreat from one decent belief after another until at last he found himself in the ranks of the majority. The ring of craven curs that hemmed in and crushed the unruly, those few who dared cry: *'Non serviam!'*

The badger cry was now a pitiful sound. A shrill squeal of protest. The rage tinged with terror: the defiance with despair. The cry of something crushed, defeated, abandoned.

Desolation – a grey waste of futility and failure – engulfed him. His skin crawled. His limbs cringed in revulsion at the extent of his betrayal. Shivering, he eased over towards the warmth beside him. At once the rhythm of her breathing changed. She was awake. Had been all along. Lying there. Listening. Waiting to smother him with forgiveness. To hell with that for a caper. There was no absolution needed in this case.

The springs creaked as he shifted back, dragging the bedclothes with him. It would be the price of her if she got her death of cold. The answer to her prayer. He coiled himself up, tucking in round his neck the bedclothes stretched between them.

Hardly was he settled down for sleep than the tranquil breathing became intolerable. He could envisage the patient, anguished, uncomplaining eyes of a holy picture staring into the darkness. Nursing its bitter wounds. God knows, you'd find it hard not to pity her.

He turned towards her.

'Sheila,' he whispered.

Once more the tiny catch in her breathing.

Gently he stroked the tense stubborn body, feeling it yield to his touch. She rolled over. Facing him.

'What's wrong?' she murmured.

Disconcerted, he stammered:

'Are . . . are . . . are you awake?'

She snuggled closer.

Feebly he grappled with her questing hand, warm and sticky with sweat. Lips fastened on his. Murmured:

'You *do* . . . want me . . . don't you?'

She buried her face in his neck.

'Grrr!' she growled happily. 'It's good to know I'm still on the wanted list.'

Acting out the familiar prologue, he held her in his arms, seeing only a mangled body mired and misshaped, bloodied muzzle grinning senselessly at a senseless sky: hearing only the scream of agony that death alone could arrest.

A feeling of loneliness swept over him. A bitter hopeless loneliness that he knew to be surrender. The sin of Judas. The ultimate and unforgivable catastrophe.

He shivered.

'Darling!' Hoarse, breathless, she clutched at him with avid, furious bands. 'Oh, darling! Darling!'

THE TROUT

Seán Ó Faoláin

One of the first places Julia always ran to when they arrived in G——
was The Dark Walk. It is a laurel walk, very old; almost gone wild, a
lofty midnight tunnel of smooth, sinewy branches. Underfoot the
tough brown leaves are never dry enough to crackle: there is always a
suggestion of damp and cool trickle.

She raced right into it. For the first few yards she always had the
memory of the sun behind her, then she felt the dusk closing swiftly
down on her so that she screamed with pleasure and raced on to reach
the light at the far end; and it was always just a little too long in coming
so that she emerged gasping, clasping her hands, laughing, drinking
in the sun. When she was filled with the heat and glare she would turn
and consider the ordeal again.

This year she had the extra joy of showing it to her small brother,
and of terrifying him as well as herself. And for him the fear lasted
longer because his legs were so short and she had gone out at the far
end while he was still screaming and racing.

When they had done this many times they came back to the house
to tell everybody that they had done it. He boasted. She mocked. They
squabbled.

'Cry babby!'

'You were afraid yourself, so there!'

'I won't take you any more.'

'You're a big pig.'

'I hate you.'

Tears were threatening so somebody said, 'Did you see the well?' She opened her eyes at that and held up her long lovely neck suspiciously and decided to be incredulous. She was twelve and at that age little girls are beginning to suspect most stories: they have already found out too many, from Santa Claus to the Stork. How could there be a well! In The Dark Walk? That she had visited year after year? Haughtily she said, 'Nonsense.'

But she went back, pretending to be going somewhere else, and she found a hole scooped in the rock at the side of the walk, choked with damp leaves, so shrouded by ferns that she only uncovered it after much searching. At the back of this little cavern there was about a quart of water. In the water she suddenly perceived a panting trout. She rushed for Stephen and dragged him to see, and they were both so excited that they were no longer afraid of the darkness as they hunched down and peered in at the fish panting in his tiny prison, his silver stomach going up and down like an engine.

Nobody knew how the trout got there. Even old Martin in the kitchen-garden laughed and refused to believe that it was there, or pretended not to believe, until she forced him to come down and see. Kneeling and pushing back his tattered old cap he peered in.

'Be cripes, you're right. How the divil in hell did that fella get there?'

She stared at him suspiciously.

'You knew?' she accused; but he said, 'The divil a know'; and reached down to lift it out. Convinced she hauled him back. If she had found it then it was her trout.

Her mother suggested that a bird had carried the spawn. Her father thought that in the winter a small streamlet might have carried it down there as a baby, and it had been safe until the summer came and the water began to dry up. She said, 'I see,' and went back to look again and consider the matter in private. Her brother remained behind, wanting to hear the whole story of the trout, not really interested in the actual trout but much interested in the story which his mummy began to make up for him on the lines of, 'So one day Daddy Trout and Mammy Trout . . . ' When he retailed it to her she said, 'Pooh.'

It troubled her that the trout was always in the same position; he had no room to turn; all the time the silver belly went up and down; otherwise he was motionless. She wondered what he ate and in between visits to Joey Pony, and the boat and a bathe to get cool, she thought of his hunger. She brought him down bits of dough; once she brought him a worm. He ignored the food. He just went on panting. Hunched over him she thought how, all the winter, while she was at school he had been in there. All the winter, in The Dark Walk, all day, all night, floating around alone. She drew the leaf of her hat down around her ears and chin and stared. She was still thinking of it as she lay in bed.

It was late June, the longest days of the year. The sun had sat still for a week, burning up the world. Although it was after ten o'clock it was still bright and still hot. She lay on her back under a single sheet, with her long legs spread, trying to keep cool. She could see the D of the moon through the fir-tree – they slept on the ground floor. Before they went to bed her mummy had told Stephen the story of the trout again, and she, in her bed, had resolutely presented her back to them and read her book. But she had kept one ear cocked.

'And so, in the end, this naughty fish who would not stay at home got bigger and bigger and bigger, and the water got smaller and smaller . . .'

Passionately she had whirled and cried, 'Mummy, don't make it a horrible old moral story!' Her mummy had brought in a Fairy Godmother, then, who sent lots of rain, and filled the well, and a stream poured out and the trout floated away down to the river below. Staring at the moon she knew that there are no such things as Fairy Godmothers and that the trout, down in The Dark Walk, was panting like an engine. She heard somebody unwind a fishing-reel. Would the *beasts* fish him out!

She sat up. Stephen was a hot lump of sleep, lazy thing. The Dark Walk would be full of little scraps of moon. She leaped up and looked out of the window, and somehow it was not so lightsome now that she saw the dim mountains far away and the black firs against the breathing land and heard a dog say, bark-bark. Quietly she lifted the ewer of water, and climbed out the window and scuttled along the cool but cruel gravel down to the maw of the tunnel. Her pyjamas were very short so that when she splashed water it wet her ankles. She peered into the tunnel. Something alive rustled inside there. She raced in, and up and down she raced, and flurried, and cried aloud, 'Oh, gosh, I can't find it,' and then at last she did. Kneeling down in the damp she put her hand into the slimy hole. When the body lashed they were both mad with fright. But she gripped him and shoved him into the ewer and raced, with her teeth ground, out to the other end of the tunnel and down the steep paths to the river's edge.

All the time she could feel him lashing his tail against the side of the ewer. She was afraid he would jump right out. The gravel cut into her soles until she came to the cool ooze of the river's bank where the moon-mice on the water crept into her feet. She poured out watching until he plopped. For a second he was visible in the water. She hoped he was not dizzy. Then all she saw was the glimmer of the moon in the silent-flowing river, the dark firs, the dim mountains, and the radiant pointed face laughing down at her out of the empty sky.

She scuttled up the hill, in the window, plonked down the ewer, and flew through the air like a bird into bed. The dog said bark-bark. She heard the fishing-reel whirring. She hugged herself and giggled. Like a river of joy her holiday spread before her.

In the morning Stephen rushed to her, shouting that 'he' was gone, and asking 'where' and 'how'. Lifting her nose in the air she said superciliously, 'Fairy Godmother, I suppose?' and strolled away patting the palms of her hands.

NIGHT IN TUNISIA

Neil Jordan

That year they took the green house again. She was there again, older than him and a lot more venal. He saw her on the white chairs that faced the tennis-court and again in the burrows behind the tennis court and again still down on the fifteenth hole where the golf course met the mouth of the Boyne. It was twilight each time he saw her and the peculiar light seemed to suspend her for an infinity, a suspended infinite silence, full of years somehow. She must have been seventeen now that he was fourteen. She was fatter, something of an exhausted woman about her and still something of the girl whom adults called mindless. It was as if a cigarette between her fingers had burnt towards the tip without her noticing. He heard people talking about her even on her first day there, he learnt that underneath her frayed blouse her wrists were marked. She was a girl about whom they would talk anyway since she lived with a father who drank, who was away for long stretches in England. Since she lived in a green corrugated-iron house. Not even a house, a chalet really, like the ones the townspeople built to house summer visitors. But she lived in it all the year round.

They took a green house too that summer, also made of corrugated iron. They took it for two months this time, since his father was playing what he said would be his last stint, since there was no more place for brassmen like him in the world of three-chord showbands. And this time the two small bedrooms were divided differently, his sister taking the small one, since she had to dress on her own now, himself and his father sharing the larger one where two years ago his sister and he had slept. Every night his father took the tenor sax and left for Mosney to play with sixteen others for older couples who remembered what the big bands of the forties sounded like. And he was left alone with his sister who talked less and less as her breasts grew bigger. With the alto saxaphone which his father said he could learn when he forgot his fascination for three-chord ditties. With the guitar which he played a lot, as if in spite against the alto saxaphone. And with the broken-keyed piano which he played occasionally.

When it rained on the iron roof the house sang and he was reminded of a green tin drum he used to hand when he was younger. It was as if he was inside it.

He wandered round the first three days, his sister formal and correct beside him. There was one road made of tarmac, running through all the corrugated houses towards the tennis court. It was covered always with drifts of sand, which billowed while they walked. They passed her once, on the same side, like an exotic and dishevelled bird, her long yellow cardigan coming down to her knees, covering her dress, if she wore any. He stopped as she passed and turned to face her. Her feet kept billowing up the sand, her eyes didn't see him, they were puffy and covered in black pencil. He felt hurt. He remembered an afternoon three years ago when they had lain on the golf links, the heat, the nakedness that didn't know itself, the grass on their three backs.

'Why don't you stop her?' he asked his sister.

'Because', she answered. 'Because, because'.

He became obsessed with twilights. Between the hour after tea when his father left and the hour long after dark when his father came home he would wait for them, observe them, he would taste them as he would a sacrament. The tincture of the light fading, the blue that seemed to be sucked into a thin line beyond the sea into what the maths books called infinity, the darkness falling like a stone. He would look at the long shadows of the burrows on the strand and the long shadows of the posts that held the sagging tennis nets on the tarmac courts. He would watch his sister walking down the road under the eyes of boys that were a little older than him. And since he hung around at twilight and well into the dark he came to stand with them, on the greens behind the clubhouse, their cigarette-tips and their laughter punctuating the dark. He played all the hits on the honky-tonk piano in the clubhouse for them and this compensated for his missing years. He played and he watched, afraid to say too much, listening to their jokes and their talk about girls, becoming most venal when it centred on her.

He laughed with them, that special thin laugh that can be stopped as soon as it's begun.

There was a raft they would swim out to on the beach. His skin was light and his arms were thin and he had no Adam's apple to speak of, no hair creeping over his togs, but he would undress all the same with them and swim out. They would spend a day on it while the sun browned their backs and coaxed beads of resin from the planks. When they shifted too much splinters of wood shot through their flesh. So mostly they lay inert, on their stomachs, their occasional erections hidden beneath them, watching on the strand the parade of life.

It galled his father what he played.

'What galls me', he would say, 'is that you could be so good.'

But he felt vengeful and played them incessantly and even sang the tawdry lyrics. Some day soon, he sang, I'm going to tell the moon about the crying game. And maybe he'll explain, he sang.

'Why don't you speak to her?' he asked his sister when they passed her again. It was seven o'clock and it was getting dark.

'Because,' she said. 'Because I don't'.

But he turned. He saw her down the road, her yellow cardigan making a scallop round her fattening buttocks.

'Rita', he called. 'Rita'.

She turned. She looked at him blankly for a moment and then she smiled, her large pouting lips curving the invitation she gave to any boy that shouted at her.

He sat at the broken-keyed piano. The light was going down over the golf links and his sister's paperback novel was turned over on the wooden table. He heard her in her room, her shoes knocking off the thin wooden partition. He heard the rustling of cotton and nylon and when the rustles stopped for a moment he got up quickly from the piano and opened the door. She gave a gasp and pulled the dress from the pile at her feet to cover herself. He asked her again did she remember and she said she didn't and her face blushed with such shame that he felt sorry and closed the door again.

The sea had the movement of cloth but the texture of glass. It flowed and undulated, but shone hard and bright. He thought of cloth and glass and how to mix them. A cloth made of glass fibre or a million woven mirrors. He saw that the light of twilight was repeated or reversed at early morning.

He decided to forget about his sister and join them, the brashness they were learning, coming over the transistors, the music that cemented it. And the odd melancholy of the adulthood they were about to straddle, to ride like a Honda down a road with one white line, pointless and inevitable.

His father on his nights off took out his Selmer, old loved talisman that was even more shining than on the day he bought it. He would sit and accompany while his father stood and played – 'That Certain Feeling', 'All The Things You Are', the names that carried their age with them, the embellishments and the filled-in notes that must have been something one day but that he had played too often, that he was too old now to get out of. And to please his father he would close his eyes and play, not knowing how or what he played and his father would stop and let him play on, listening. And he would occasionally look and catch that look in his listening eyes, wry, sad and loving, his pleasure at how his son played only marred by the knowledge of how little it meant to him. And he would catch the look in his father's eyes and get annoyed and deliberately hit a bum note to spoil it. And the sadness in the eyes would outshine the wryness then and he would be sorry, but never sorry enough.

He soon learnt that they were as mistrustful of each other as he was of them and so he relaxed somewhat. He learnt to turn his silence into a pose. They listened to his playing and asked about his sister. They lay on the raft, watched women on the strand, their eyes stared so hard that the many shapes on the beach became one, indivisible. It made the sand dunes and even the empty clubhouse redundant. Lying face down on the warm planks, the sun burning their backs with an aching langour. The blaring transistor, carried over in its plastic bag. Her on the beach, indivisible, her yellow cardigan glaring even on the hottest days. He noticed she had got fatter since he came. Under them on the warm planks the violent motions of their pricks. She who lived in the chalet all the year round.

The one bedroom and the two beds, his father's by the door, his by the window. The rippled metal walls. The moon like water on his hands, the bed beside him empty. Then the front door opening, the sound of the saxaphone case lied down. His eyes closed, his father stripping in the darkness, climbing in, long underwear and vest. The body he'd known lifelong, old and somewhat loved, but not like his Selmer, shining. They get better with age, he said about instruments. His breath scraping the air now, scraping over the wash of the sea, sleeping.

The tall thin boy put his mouth to the mouth of the french letter and blew. It expanded, huge and bulbous, with a tiny bubble at the tip.

'It's getting worked up', he said.

He had dark curling hair and dark shaven cheeks and a mass of tiny pimples where he shaved. The pimples spread from his ears down-wards, as if scattered from a pepper-canister. His eyes were dark too, and always a little closed.

'We'll let it float to England', he said, 'so it can find a fanny big enough for it'.

They watched it bobbing on the waves, brought back and forwards with the wash. Then a gust of wind lifted it and carried it off, falling to skim the surface and rising again, the bubble towards the sky.

He had walked up from the beach and the french letter bound for England. He had seen her yellow cardigan on the tennis court from a long way off, above the strand. He was watching her play now, sitting on the white wrought-iron seat, his hands between his legs.

She was standing on the one spot, dead-centre of the court, hardly looking at all at her opponent. She was hitting every ball cleanly and lazily and the sound that came from her racquet each time was that taut twang that he knew only came from a good shot. He felt that even a complete stranger would have known, from her boredom, her ease, that she lived in a holiday town with a tennis court all the year round. The only sign of effort was the beads of sweat round her lips and the tousled blonde curls round her forehead. And every now and then when the man she was playing against managed to send a shot towards the sidelines, she didn't bother to follow it at all. She let the white ball bounce impotent towards the wire mesh.

He watched the small fat man he didn't recognise lose three balls for every ball won. He relished the spectacle of a fat man in whites being beaten by a bored teenage girl in sagging high heels. Then he saw her throw her eyes upwards, throw her racquet down and walk from the court. The white ball rolled towards the wire mesh.

She sat beside him. She didn't look at him but she spoke as if she had known him those three years.

'You play him. I'm sick of it.'

He walked across the court and his body seemed to glow with the heat generated by the slight touch of hers. He picked up the racquet and the ball, placed his foot behind the white line and threw the ball up, his eye on it, white, skewered against the blue sky. Then it came down and he heard the resonant twang as his racquet hit it and it went spinning into the opposite court but there was no one there to take it. He looked up and saw the fat man and her walking towards a small white car. The fat man gestured her in and she looked behind at him once before she entered.

And as the car sped off towards Mornington he swore she waved.

The car was gone down the Mornington Road. He could hear the pop-pop of the tennis balls hitting the courts and the twang of them hitting the racquets as he walked, growing fainter. He walked along the road, past the tarmac courts and past the grass courts and past the first few holes of golf course which angled in a T round the tennis courts. He walked past several squares of garden until he came to his. It wasn't really a garden, a square of sand and scutch. He walked through the gate and up the path where the sand had been trodden hard to the green corrugated door. He turned the handle in the door, always left open. He saw the small square room, the sand fanning across the line from the doorstep, the piano with the sheet-music perched on the keys. He thought of the midday sun outside, the car with her in the passenger seat moving through it, the shoulders of the figure in the driver's seat. The shoulders hunched and fat, expressing something venal. He thought of the court, the white tennis ball looping between her body and his. Her body relaxed, vacant and easeful, moving the racquet so the ball flew where she wished. His body worried, worrying the whole court. He felt there was something wrong, the obedient ball, the running man. What had she lost to gain that ease, he wondered. He thought of all the jokes he had heard and of the act behind the jokes that none of those who told the jokes experienced. The innuendos and the charged words like the notes his father played, like the melodies his father willed him to play. The rich full twang as the ball met her racquet at the centre.

He saw the alto saxaphone on top of the piano. He took it down, placed it on the table and opened the case. He looked at the keys, remembering the first lessons his father had taught him when it was new-bought months ago. The keys unpressed, mother-of-pearl on gold, spotted with dust. He took out the ligature and fixed the reed in the mouthpiece. He put it between his lips, settled his fingers and blew. The note came out harsh and childish, as if he'd never learnt. He heard a shifting movement in the inside room and knew that he'd woken his father.

He put the instrument back quickly and made for the tiny bathroom. He closed the door behind him quietly, imagining his father's grey vest rising from the bed to the light of the afternoon sun. He looked into the mirror that closed on the cabinet where the medicine things were kept. He saw his face in the mirror looking at him, frightened, quick glance. Then he saw his face taking courage and looking at him full-on, the brown eyes and the thin fragile jawline. And he began to look at his eyes as directly as they looked at him.

'You were playing', his father said, in the living room, in shirtsleeves, in uncombed afternoon hair, 'the alto—'

'No', he said, going for the front door, 'you were dreaming—'

And on the raft the fat asthmatic boy, obsessed more than any with the theatre on the strand, talking about 'it' in his lisping, mournful voice, smoking cigarettes that made his breath wheeze more. He had made classifications, rigid as calculus, meticulous as algebra. There were girls, he said, and women, and in between them what he termed lady, the lines of demarcation finely and inexorably drawn. Lady was thin and sat on towels, with high-heels and suntan-lotions, without kids. Woman was fat, with rugs and breasts that hung or bulged, with children. Then there were girls, his age, thin, fat and middling, nyloned, short-stockinged—

He lay on his stomach on the warm wood and listened to the fat boy talking and saw her walking down the strand. The straggling, uncaring walk that, he decided, was none of these or all of these at once. She was wearing flat shoes that went down at the heels with no stockings and the familiar cardigan that hid what could have classified her. She walked to a spot up the beach from the raft and unrolled the bundled towel from under her arm. Then she kicked off her shoes and pulled off her cardigan and wriggled out of the skirt her cardigan had hidden. She lay back on the towel in the yellow bathing suit that was too young for her, through which her body seemed to press like a butterfly already moulting in its chrysalis. She took a bottle then and shook it into her palm and began rubbing the liquid over her slack exposed body.

He listened to the fat boy talking about her – he was local too – about her father who on his stretches home came back drunk and bounced rocks off the tin roof, shouting 'Hewer'.

'What does that mean?' he asked.

'Just that', said the asthmatic boy. 'Rhymes with sure'.

He looked at her again from the raft, her slack stomach bent forward, her head on her knees. He saw her head lift and turn lazily towards the raft and he stood up then, stretching his body upwards, under what he imagined was her gaze. He dived, his body imagining itself suspended in air before it hit the water. Underwater he held his breath, swam through the flux of tiny bubbles, like crotchets before his open eyes.

'What did you say she was', he asked the fat boy, swimming back to the raft.

'Hewer', said the fat boy, more loudly.

He looked towards the strand and saw her on her back, her slightly plump thighs towards the sky, her hands shielding her eyes. He swam to the side of the raft then and gripped the wood with one hand and the fat boy's ankle with the other and pulled. The fat boy came crashing into the water and went down and when his head came up, gasping for asthmatic breath, he forced it down once more, though he didn't know what whore meant.

His father was cleaning the alto when he came back.

'What does hewer mean?' he asked his father.

His father stopped screwing in the ligature and looked at him, his old sideman's eyes surprised, and somewhat moral.

'A woman', he said, 'who sells her body for monetary gain'.

He stopped for a moment. He didn't understand.

'That's tautology', he said.

'What's that?' his father asked.

'It repeats', he said, and went into the toilet.

He heard the radio crackle over the sound of falling water and heard a rapid-fire succession of notes that seemed to spring from the falling water, that amazed him, so much faster than his father ever played, but slow behind it all, melancholy, like a river. He came out of the toilet and stood listening with his father. Who is that, he asked his father. Then he heard the continuity announcer say the name Charlie Parker and saw his father staring at some point between the wooden table and the wooden holiday-home floor.

He played later on the piano in the clubhouse with the dud notes, all the songs, the trivial mythologies whose significance he had never questioned. It was as if he was fingering through his years and as he played he began to forget the melodies of all those goodbyes and heartaches, letting his fingers take him where they wanted to, trying to imitate that sound like a river he had just heard. It had got dark without him noticing and when finally he could just see the keys as question-marks in the dark, he stopped. He heard a noise behind him, the noise of somebody who has been listening, but who doesn't want you to know they are there. He turned and saw her looking at him, black in the square of light coming through the door. Her eyes were on his hands that were still pressing the keys and there was a harmonic hum tiny somewhere in the air. Her eyes rose to his face, unseeing and brittle to meet his hot, tense stare. He still remembered the rough feel of the tartan blanket over them, three of them, the grass under them. But her eyes didn't, so he looked everywhere but on them, on her small pinched chin, ridiculous under her large face, on the yellow linen dress that was ragged round her throat, on her legs, almost black from so much sun. The tiny hairs on them glistened with the light behind her. He looked up then and her eyes were still on his, keeping his fingers on the keys, keeping the chord from fading.

He was out on the burrows once more, he didn't know how, and he met the thin boy. The thin boy sat down with him where they couldn't be seen and took a condom from his pocket and masturbated among the bushes. He saw how the liquid was caught by the antiseptic web, how the sand clung to it when the thin boy threw it, like it does to spittle.

He left the thin boy and walked down the beach, empty now of its glistening bodies. He looked up at the sky, from which the light was fading, like a thin silver wire. He came to where the beach faded into the mouth of a river. There was a statue there, a Virgin with thin fingers towards the sea, her feet layered with barnacles. There were fishermen looping a net round the mouth. He could see the dim line of the net they pulled and the occasional flashes of white salmon. And as the boat pulled the net towards the shore he saw how the water grew violent with flashes, how the loose shoal of silver-and-white turned into a panting, open-gilled pile. He saw the net close then, the fishermen lifting it, the water falling from it, the salmon laid bare, glutinous, clinging, wet, a little like boiled rice.

He imagined the glistening bodies that littered the beach pulled into a net like that. He imagined her among them, slapping for space, panting for air, he heard transistors blare 'Da Doo Run Run', he saw suntan-lotion bottles crack and splinter as the fisher up above pulled harder. He imagined his face like a lifeguard's, dark sidelocks round his muscular jaw, a megaphone swinging from his neck, that crackled.

He saw the thin band of light had gone, just a glow off the sea now. He felt frightened, but forced himself not to run. He walked in quick rigid steps past the barnacled Virgin then and down the strand.

'Ten bob for a touch with the clothes on. A pound without'.

They were playing pontoon on the raft. He was watching the beach, the bodies thicker than salmon. When he heard the phrase he got up and kicked the dirt-cards into the water. He saw the Queen of Hearts face upwards in the foam. As they made for him he dived and swam out a few strokes.

'Cunts', he yelled from the water. 'Cunts.'

On the beach the wind blew fine dry sand along the surface, drawing it in currents, a tide of sand.

His sister laid the cups out on the table and his father ate with long pauses between mouthfuls. His father's hand paused, the bread quivering in the air, as if he were about to say something. He looked at his sister's breasts across a bowl of apples, half-grown fruits. The apples came from monks who kept an orchard. Across the fields, behind the house. He imagined a monk's hand reaching for the un-plucked fruit, white against the swinging brown habit. For monks never sunbathed.

When he had finished he got up from the table and idly pressed a few notes on the piano.

'Why do you play that?' his father asked. He was still at the table, between mouthfuls.

'I don't know', he said.

'What galls me', said his father, 'is that you could be good'.

He played a bit more of the idiotic tune that he didn't know why he played.

'If you'd let me teach you', his father said, 'you'd be glad later on.'

'Then why not wait till later on and teach me then.'

'Because you're young, you're at the age. You'll never learn as well as now, if you let me teach you. You'll never feel things like you do now.'

He began to play again in defiance and then stopped.

'I'll pay you,' his father said.

His father woke him coming in around four. He heard his wheezing breath and his shuffling feet. He watched the grey, metal-coloured light filling the room that last night had emptied it. He thought of his

father's promise to pay him. He thought of the women who sold their
bodies for monetary gain. He imagined all of them on the dawn golf
course, waking in their dew-sodden clothes. He imagined fairways full
of them, their monetary bodies covered with fine drops of water. Their
dawn chatter like birdsong. Where was that golf course, he wondered.
He crept out of bed and into his clothes and out of the door, very
quietly. He crossed the road and clambered over the wire fence that
separated the road from the golf course. He walked through several
fairways, across several greens, past several fluttering pennants with
the conceit in his mind all the time of her on one green, asleep and
sodden, several pound notes in her closed fist. At the fourteenth green
he saw that the dull metal colour had faded into morning, true
morning. He began to walk back, his feet sodden from the dew.

SISTER IMELDA

Edna O'Brien

Sister Imelda did not take classes on her first day back in the convent but we spotted her in the grounds after the evening Rosary. Excitement and curiosity impelled us to follow her and try to see what she looked like, but she thwarted us by walking with head bent and eyelids down. All we could be certain of was that she was tall and limber and that she prayed while she walked. No looking at nature for her, or no curiosity about seventy boarders in gaberdine coats and black shoes and stockings. We might just as well have been crows, so impervious was she to our stares and to abortive attempts at trying to say 'Hello, Sister.'

We had returned from our long summer holiday and we were all wretched. The convent, with its high stone wall and green iron gates enfolding us again, seemed more of a prison than ever – for after our spell in the outside world we all felt very much older and more sophisticated, and my friend Baba and I were dreaming of our final escape, which would be in a year. And so, on that damp autumn evening when I saw the chrysanthemums and saw the new nun intent on prayer I pitied her and thought how alone she must be, cut off from her friends and conversation, with only God as her intangible spouse.

The next day she came into our classroom to take geometry. Her pale, slightly long face I saw as formidable, but her eyes were different, being blue-black and full of verve. Her lips were very purple, as if she had put puce pencil on them. They were the lips of a woman who might sing in a cabaret, and unconsciously she had formed the habit of turning them inward, as if she, too, was aware of their provocativeness.

She had spent the last four years – the same span that Baba and I had spent in the convent – at the university in Dublin, where she studied languages. We couldn't understand how she had resisted the temptations of the hectic world and willingly come back to this. Her spell in the outside world made her different from the other nuns; there was more bounce in her walk, more excitement in the way she tackled teaching, reminding us that it was the most important thing in the world as she uttered the phrase 'Praise be the Incarnate World.' She began each day's class by reading from Cardinal Newman, who was a favourite of hers. She read how God dwelt in light unapproachable, and how with Him there was neither change nor shadow of alteration. It was amazing how her looks changed. Some days, when her eyes were flashing, she looked almost profane and made me wonder what events inside the precincts of the convent caused her to be suddenly so excited. She might have been a girl going to a dance, except for her habit.

'Hasn't she wonderful eyes,' I said to Baba. That particular day they were like blackberries, large and soft and shiny.

'Something wrong in her upstairs department,' Baba said, and added that with make-up Imelda would be a cinch.

'Still, she has a vocation!' I said, and even aired the idiotic view that I might have one. At certain moments it did seem enticing to become a nun, to lead a life unspotted by sin, never to have to have babies, and to wear a ring that singled one out as the Bride of Christ. But there was the other side to it, the silence, the gravity of it, having to get up two or three times a night to pray and, above all, never having the opportunity of leaving the confines of the place except for the funeral of one's parents. For us boarders it was torture, but for the nuns it was nothing short of doom. Also, we could complain to each other, and we did, food being the source of the greatest grumbles. Lunch was either bacon and cabbage or a peculiar stringy meat followed by tapioca pudding; tea consisted of bread dolloped with lard and occasionally, as a treat, fairly green rhubarb jam, which did not have enough sugar. Through the long curtainless windows we saw the conifer trees and a sky that was scarcely ever without the promise of rain or a downpour.

She was a right lunatic, then, Baba said, having gone to university for four years and willingly come back to incarceration, to poverty, chastity and obedience. We concocted scenes of agony in some Dublin hostel, while a boy, or even a young man, stood beneath her bedroom window throwing up chunks of clay or whistles or a supplication. In our version of it he was slightly older than her, and possibly a medical student, since medical students had a knack with women, because of studying diagrams and skeletons. His advances, like those of a sudden storm, would intermittently rise and overwhelm her, and the memory of these sudden flaying advances of his would haunt her until she died, and if ever she contracted fever, these secrets would out. It was also rumoured that she possessed a fierce temper and that, while a postulant, she had hit a girl so badly with her leather strap that the girl had to be put to bed because of wounds. Yet another black mark against Sister Imelda was that her brother Ambrose had been sued by a nurse for breach of promise.

That first morning when she came into our classroom and modestly introduced herself, I had no idea how terribly she would infiltrate my life, how in time she would be not just one of those teachers or nuns but rather a special one, almost like a ghost who passed the boundaries of common exchange and who crept inside one, devouring so much of one's thoughts, so much of one's passion, invading the place that was called one's heart. She talked in a low voice, as if she did not want her words to go beyond the bounds of the wall, and constantly she stressed the value of work both to enlarge the mind and to discipline the thought. One of her eyelids was red and swollen, as if she was getting a sty. I reckoned that she overmortified herself by not eating at all. I saw in her some terrible premonition of sacrifice which I would have to emulate. Then, in direct contrast, she absently held the stick of chalk between her first and second fingers, the very same as if it were a cigarette, and Baba whispered to me that she might have been a smoker when in Dublin. Sister Imelda looked down sharply at me and said what was the secret and would I like to share it, since it seemed so comical. I said, 'Nothing, Sister, nothing,' and her dark eyes exuded such vehemence that I prayed she would never have occasion to punish me.

November came and the tiled walls of the recreation hall oozed moisture and gloom. Most girls had sore throats and were told to suffer this inconvenience to mortify themselves in order to lend a glorious hand in that communion of spirit that linked the living with the dead.

It was the month of the Suffering Souls in Purgatory, and as we heard of their twofold agony, the yearning for Christ and the ferocity of the leaping flames that burned and charred their poor limbs, we were asked to make acts of mortification. Some girls gave up jam or sweets and some gave up talking, and so in recreation time they were like dummies making signs with thumb and finger to merely say 'How are you?' Baba said that saner people were locked in the lunatic asylum, which was only a mile away. We saw them in the grounds, pacing back and forth, with their mouths agape and dribble coming out of them, like melting icicles. Among our many fears was that one of those lunatics would break out and head straight for the convent and assault some of the girls.

Yet in the thick of all these dreads I found myself becoming dreadfully happy. I had met Sister Imelda outside of class a few times and I felt that there was an attachment between us. Once it was in the grounds, when she did a reckless thing. She broke off a chrysanthemum and offered it to me to smell. It had no smell, or at least only something faint that suggested autumn, and feeling this to be the case herself, she said it was not a gardenia, was it? Another time we met in the chapel porch, and as she drew her shawl more tightly around her body, I felt how human she was, and prey to the cold.

In the classroom things were not so congenial between us. Geometry was my worst subject, indeed, a total mystery to me. She had not taught more than four classes when she realised this and threw a duster at me in a rage. A few girls gasped as she asked me to stand up and make a spectacle of myself. Her face had reddened, and presently she took out her handkerchief and patted the eye which was red and swollen. I not only felt a fool but felt in imminent danger of sneezing as I inhaled the smell of chalk that had fallen onto my gym frock. Suddenly she fled from the room, leaving us ten minutes free until the next class. Some girls said it was a disgrace, said I should write home and say I had been assaulted. Others welcomed the few minutes in which to gabble. All I wanted was to run after her and say that I was sorry to have caused her such distemper, because I knew dimly that it was as much to do with liking as it was with dislike. In me then there came a sort of speechless tenderness for her, and I might have known that I was stirred.

'We could get her defrocked,' Baba said, and elbowed me in God's name to sit down.

That evening at Benediction I had the most overwhelming surprise. It was a particularly happy evening, with the choir nuns in full soaring form and the rows of candles like so many little ladders to the golden chalice that glittered all the more because of the beams of fitful flame. I was full of tears when I discovered a new holy picture had been put in my prayer book, and before I dared look on the back to see who had given it to me, I felt and guessed that this was no ordinary picture from an ordinary girlfriend, that this was a talisman and a peace offering from Sister Imelda. It was a pale-blue picture, so pale that it was almost grey, like the down of a pigeon, and it showed a mother looking down on the infant child. On the back, in her beautiful ornate handwriting, she had written a verse:

> Trust Him when dark doubts assail thee,
> Trust Him when thy faith is small,
> Trust Him when to simply trust Him
> Seems the hardest thing of all.

This was her atonement. To think that she had located the compartment in the chapel where I kept my prayer book and to think that she had been so naked as to write in it and give me a chance to boast about it and to show it to other girls. When I thanked her next day, she bowed but did not speak. Mostly the nuns were on silence and only permitted to talk during class.

In no time I had received another present, a little miniature prayer book with a leather cover and gold edging. The prayers were in French and the lettering so minute it was as if a tiny insect had fashioned them. Soon I was publicly known as her pet. I opened the doors for her, raised the blackboard two pegs higher (she was taller than other nuns), and handed out the exercise books which she had corrected. Now in the margins of my geometry propositions I would find 'Good' or 'Excellent', when in the past she used to splash 'Disgraceful'. Baba said it was foul to be a nun's pet and that any girl who sucked up to a nun could not be trusted.

About a month later Sister Imelda asked me to carry her books up four flights of stairs to the cookery kitchen. She taught cookery to a junior class. As she walked ahead of me, I thought how supple she was and how thoroughbred, and when she paused on the landing to look out through the long curtainless window, I too paused. Down below, two women in suede boots were chatting and smoking as they moved along the street with shopping baskets. Nearby a lay nun was on her knees scrubbing the granite steps, and the cold air was full of the raw smell of Jeyes Fluid. There was a potted plant on the landing, and Sister Imelda put her fingers in the earth and went 'Tch tch tch,' saying it needed water. I said I would water it later on. I was happy in my prison then, happy to be near her, happy to walk behind her as she twirled her beads and bowed to the servile nun. I no longer cried for my mother, no longer counted the days on a pocket calendar until the Christmas holidays.

'Come back at five,' she said as she stood on the threshold of the cookery kitchen door. The girls, all in white overalls, were arranged around the long wooden table waiting for her. It was as if every girl was in love with her. Because, as she entered, their faces broke into smiles, and in different tones of audacity they said her name. She must have liked cookery class, because she beamed and called to someone, anyone, to get up a blazing fire. Then she went across to the cast-iron stove and spat on it to test its temperature. It was hot, because her spit rose up and sizzled.

When I got back later, she was sitting on the edge of the table swaying her legs. There was something reckless about her pose, something defiant. It seemed as if any minute she would take out a cigarette case, snap it open and then archly offer me one. The wonderful smell of baking made me realise how hungry I was, but far more so, it brought back to me my own home, my mother testing orange cakes with a knitting needle and letting me lick the line of half-baked dough down the length of the needle. I wondered if she had supplanted my mother, and I hoped not, because I had aimed to outstep my original world and take my place in a new and hallowed one.

'I bet you have a sweet tooth,' she said, and then she got up, crossed the kitchen, and from under a wonderful shining silver cloche she produced two jam tarts with a crisscross design on them where the pastry was latticed over the dark jam. They were still warm.

'What will I do with them?' I asked.

'Eat them, you goose,' she said, and she watched me eat as if she herself derived some peculiar pleasure from it, whereas I was embarrassed about the pastry crumbling and the bits of blackberry jam staining my lips. She was amused. It was one of the most awkward yet thrilling moments I had lived, and inherent in the pleasure was the terrible sense of danger. Had we been caught, she, no doubt, would have had to make massive sacrifice. I looked at her and thought how peerless and how brave, and I wondered if she felt hungry. She had a white overall over her black habit and this made her warmer and freer, and caused me to think of the happiness that would be ours, the laissez-faire if we were away from the convent in an ordinary kitchen doing something easy and customary. But we weren't. It was clear to me then that my version of pleasure was inextricable from pain, that they existed side by side and were interdependent, like the two forces of an electric current.

'Had you a friend when you were in Dublin at university?' I asked daringly.

'I shared a desk with a sister from Howth and stayed in the same hostel,' she said.

But what about boys? I thought, and what of your life now and do you long to go out into the world? But could not say it.

We knew something about the nuns' routine. It was rumoured that they wore itchy wool underwear, ate dry bread for breakfast, rarely had meat, cakes or dainties, kept certain hours of strict silence with each other, as well as constant vigil on their thoughts; so that if their minds wandered to the subject of food or pleasure, they would quickly revert to thoughts of God and their eternal souls. They slept on hard beds with no sheets and hairy blankets. At four o'clock in the morning while we slept, each nun got out of bed, in her habit – which was also her death habit – and chanting, they all flocked down the wooden stairs like ravens, to fling themselves on the tiled floor of the chapel. Each nun – even the Mother Superior – flung herself in total submission, saying prayers in Latin and offering up the moment to God. Then silently back to their cells for one more hour of rest. It was not difficult to imagine Sister Imelda face downward, arms outstretched, prostrate on the tiled floor. I often heard their chanting when I wakened suddenly from a nightmare, because, although we slept in a different building, both adjoined, and if one wakened one often heard that monotonous Latin chanting, long before the birds began, long before our own bell summoned us to rise at six.

'Do you eat nice food?' I asked.

'Of course,' she said, and smiled. She sometimes broke into an eager smile, which she did much to conceal.

'Have you ever thought of what you will be?' she asked.

I shook my head. My design changed from day to day.

She looked at her man's silver pocket watch, closed the damper of the range and prepared to leave. She checked that all the wall cupboards were locked by running her hand over them.

'Sister,' I called, gathering enough courage at last – we must have some secret, something to join us together – 'what colour hair have you?'

We never saw the nuns' hair, or their eyebrows, or ears, as all that part was covered by a stiff white wimple.

'You shouldn't ask such a thing,' she said, getting pink in the face, and then she turned back and whispered, 'I'll tell you on your last day here, provided your geometry has improved.'

She had scarcely gone when Baba, who had been lurking behind some pillar, stuck her head in the door and said, 'Christsake, save me a bit.' She finished the second pastry, then went around looking in kitchen drawers. Because of everything being locked, she found only some castor sugar in a china shaker. She ate a little and threw the remainder into the dying fire, so that it flared up for a minute with a yellow spluttering flame. Baba showed her jealousy by putting it around the school that I was in the cookery kitchen every evening, gorging cakes with Sister Imelda and telling tales.

I did not speak to Sister Imelda again in private until the evening of our Christmas theatricals. She came to help us put on make-up and get into our stage clothes and fancy headgear. These clothes were kept in a trunk from one year to the next, and though sumptuous and strewn with braiding and gold, they smelled of camphor. Yet as we donned them we felt different, and as we sponged pancake make-up onto our faces, we became saucy and emphasised these new guises by adding dark pencil to the eyes and making the lips bright carmine. There was only one tube of lipstick and each girl clamoured for it. The evening's entertainment was to comprise scenes from Shakespeare and laughing sketches. I had been chosen to recite Mark Antony's lament over Caesar's body, and for this I was to wear a purple toga, white knee-length socks and patent buckle shoes. The shoes were too big and I moved in them as if in clogs. She said to take them off, to go barefoot. I realised that I was getting nervous and that in an effort to memorise my speech, the words were getting all askew and flying about in my head, like the separate pieces of a jigsaw puzzle. She sensed my panic and very slowly put her hand on my face and enjoined me to look at her. I looked into her eyes, which seemed fathomless, and saw that she was willing me to be calm and obliging me to be master of my fears, and I little knew that one day she would have to do the same as regards the swoop of my feelings for her. As we continued to stare I felt myself becoming calm and the words were restored to me in their right and fluent order. The lights were being lowered out in the recreation hall, and we knew now that all the nuns had arrived, had settled themselves down, and were eagerly awaiting this annual hotchpotch of amateur entertainment. There was that fearsome hush as the hall went dark and the few spotlights were turned on. She kissed her crucifix and I realised that she was saying a prayer for me. Then she raised her arm as if depicting the stance of a Greek goddess; walking onto the stage, I was fired by her ardour.

Baba could say that I bawled like a bloody bull, but Sister Imelda, who stood in the wings, said that temporarily she had felt the streets of Rome, had seen the corpse of Caesar, as I delivered those poignant, distempered lines. When I came off stage she put her arms around me and I was encased in a shower of silent kisses. After we had taken down the decorations and put the fancy clothes back in the trunk, I gave her two half-pound boxes of chocolates – bought for me illicitly by one of the day girls – and she gave me a casket made from the insides of matchboxes and covered over with gilt paint and gold dust. It was like holding moths and finding their powder adhering to the fingers.

'What will you do on Christmas Day, Sister?' I said.

'I'll pray for you,' she said.

It was useless to say, 'Will you have turkey?' or 'Will you have plum pudding?' or 'Will you loll in bed?' because I believed that Christmas Day would be as bleak and deprived as any other day in her life. Yet she was radiant as if such austerity was joyful. Maybe she was basking in some secret realisation involving her and me.

On the cold snowy afternoon three weeks later when we returned from
our holidays, Sister Imelda came up to the dormitory to welcome me
back. All the other girls had gone down to the recreation hall to do barn
dances and I could hear someone banging on the piano. I did not want
to go down and clump around with sixty other girls, having nothing
to look forward to, only tea and the Rosary and early bed. The beds
were damp after our stay at home, and when I put my hand between
the sheets, it was like feeling dew but did not have the freshness of
outdoors. What depressed me further was that I had seen a mouse in
one of the cupboards, seen its tail curl with terror as it slipped away
into a crevice. If there was one mouse, there were God knows how
many, and the cakes we hid in secret would not be safe. I was still
unpacking as she came down the narrow passage between the rows of
iron beds and I saw in her walk such agitation.

'Tut, tut, tut, you've curled your hair,' she said, offended.

Yes, the world outside was somehow declared in this perm, and for
a second I remembered the scalding pain as the trickles of ammonia
dribbled down my forehead and then the joy as the hairdresser said
that she would make me look like Movita, a Mexican star. Now
suddenly that world and those aspirations seemed trite and I wanted
to take a brush and straighten my hair and revert to the dark gawky
sombre girl that I had been. I offered her iced queen cakes that my
mother had made, but she refused them and said she could only stay
a second. She lent me a notebook of hers, which she had had as a pupil,
and into which she had copied favourite quotations, some religious,
some not. I read at random:

> Twice or thrice had I loved thee,
> Before I knew thy face or name.
> So in a voice, so in a shapeless flame,
> Angels affect us oft . . .

'Are you well?' I asked.

She looked pale. It may have been the day, which was wretched and
grey with sleet, or it may have been the white bedspreads, but she
appeared to be ailing.

'I missed you,' she said.

'Me too,' I said.

At home, gorging, eating trifle at all hours, even for breakfast, having little ratafias to dip in cups of tea, fitting on new shoes and silk stockings, I wished that she could be with us, enjoying the fire and the freedom.

'You know it is not proper for us to be so friendly.'

'It's not wrong,' I said.

I dreaded that she might decide to turn away from me, that she might stamp on our love and might suddenly draw a curtain over it, a black crepe curtain that would denote its death. I dreaded it and knew it was going to happen.

'We must not become attached,' she said, and I could not say we already were, no more than I could remind her of the day of the revels and the intimacy between us. Convents were dungeons and no doubt about it.

From then on she treated me as less of a favourite. She said my name sharply in class, and once she said if I must cough, could I wait until class had finished. Baba was delighted, as were the other girls, because they were glad to see me receding in her eyes. Yet I knew that the crispness was part of her love, because no matter how callously she looked at me, she would occasionally soften. Reading her notebook helped me, and I copied out her quotations into my own book, trying as accurately as possible to imitate her handwriting.

But some little time later when she came to supervise our study one evening, I got a smile from her as she sat on the rostrum looking down at us all. I continued to look up at her and by slight frowning indicated that I had a problem with my geometry. She beckoned to me lightly and I went up, bringing my copybook and the pen. Standing close to her, and also because her wimple was crooked, I saw one of her eyebrows for the first time. She saw that I noticed it and said did that satisfy my curiosity. I said not really. She said what else did I want to see, her swan's neck perhaps, and I went scarlet. I was amazed that she would say such a thing in the hearing of other girls, and then she said a worse thing, she said that G. K. Chesterton was very forgetful and had once put on his trousers backward. She expected me to laugh. I was so close to her that a rumble in her stomach seemed to be taking place in my own, and about this she also laughed. It occurred to me for one terrible moment that maybe she had decided to leave the convent, to jump over the wall. Having done the theorem for me, she marked it '100 out of 100' and then asked if I had any other problems. My eyes filled with tears, I wanted her to realise that her recent coolness had wrought havoc with my nerves and my peace of mind.

'What is it?' she said.

I could cry, or I could tremble to try to convey the emotion, but I could not tell her. As if on cue, the Mother Superior came in and saw this glaring intimacy and frowned as she approached the rostrum.

'Would you please go back to your desk,' she said, 'and in future kindly allow Sister Imelda to get on with her duties.'

I tiptoed back and sat with head down, bursting with fear and shame. Then she looked at a tray on which the milk cups were laid, and finding one cup of milk untouched, she asked which girl had not drunk her milk.

'Me, Sister,' I said, and I was called up to drink it and stand under the clock as a punishment. The milk was tepid and dusty, and I thought of cows on the fair days at home and the farmers hitting them as they slid and slithered over the muddy streets.

For weeks I tried to see my nun in private; I even lurked outside doors where I knew she was due, only to be rebuffed again and again. I suspected the Mother Superior had warned her against making a favourite of me. But I still clung to a belief that a bond existed between us and that her coldness and even some glares which I had received were a charade, a mask. I would wonder how she felt alone in bed and what way she slept and if she thought of me, or refusing to think of me, if she dreamed of me as I did of her. She certainly got thinner, because her nun's silver ring slipped easily and sometimes unavoidably off her marriage finger. It occurred to me that she was having a nervous breakdown.

One day in March the sun came out, the radiators were turned off, and, though there was a lashing wind, we were told that officially spring had arrived and that we could play games. We all trooped up to the games field and, to our surprise, saw that Sister Imelda was officiating that day. The daffodils in the field tossed and turned; they were a very bright shocking yellow, but they were not as fetching as the little timid snowdrops that trembled in the wind. We played rounders, and when my turn came to hit the ball with the long wooden pound, I crumbled and missed, fearing that the ball would hit me.

'Champ . . .' said Baba, jeering.

After three such failures Sister Imelda said that if I liked I could sit and watch, and when I was sitting in the greenhouse swallowing my shame, she came in and said that I must not give way to tears, because humiliation was the greatest test of Christ's love, or indeed *any* love.

'When you are a nun you will know that,' she said, and instantly I made up my mind that I would be a nun and that though we might never be free to express our feelings, we would be under the same roof, in the same cloister, in mental and spiritual conjunction all our lives.

'Is it very hard at first?' I said.

'It's awful,' she said, and she slipped a little medal into my gym-frock pocket. It was warm from being in her pocket, and as I held it, I knew that once again we were near and that in fact we had never severed. Walking down from the playing field to our Sunday lunch of mutton and cabbage, everyone chattered to Sister Imelda. The girls milled around her, linking her, trying to hold her hand, counting the various keys on her bunch of keys, and asking impudent questions.

'Sister, did you ever ride a motorbicycle?'

'Sister, did you ever wear seamless stockings?'

'Sister, who's your favourite film star – male?'

'Sister, what's your favourite food?'

'Sister, if you had a wish, what would it be?'

'Sister, what do you do when you want to scratch your head?'

Yes, she had ridden a motorbicycle, and she had worn silk stockings, but they were seamed. She liked bananas best, and if she had a wish, it would be to go home for a few hours to see her parents and her brother.

That afternoon as we walked through the town, the sight of closed shops with porter barrels outside and mongrel dogs did not dispel my refound ecstasy. The medal was in my pocket, and every other second I would touch it for confirmation. Baba saw a Swiss roll in a confectioner's window laid on a doily and dusted with castor sugar, and it made her cry out with hunger and rail against being in a bloody reformatory, surrounded by drips and mopes. On impulse she took her nail file out of her pocket and dashed across to the window to see if she could cut the glass. The prefect rushed up from the back of the line and asked Baba if she wanted to be locked up.

'I am anyhow,' Baba said, and sawed at one of her nails, to maintain her independence and vent her spleen. Baba was the only girl who could stand up to a prefect. When she felt like it, she dropped out of a walk, sat on a stone wall, and waited until we all came back. She said that if there was one thing more boring than studying it was walking. She used to roll down her stockings and examine her calves and say that she could see varicose veins coming from this bloody daily walk. Her legs, like all our legs, were black from the dye of the stockings; we were forbidden to bathe, because baths were immoral. We washed each night in an enamel basin beside our beds. When girls splashed cold water onto their chests, they let out cries, though this was forbidden.

After the walk we wrote home. We were allowed to write home once a week; our letters were always censored. I told my mother that I had made up my mind to be a nun, and asked if she could send me bananas when a batch arrived at our local grocery shop. That evening, perhaps as I wrote to my mother on the ruled white paper, a telegram arrived which said that Sister Imelda's brother had been killed in a van while on his way home from a hurling match. The Mother Superior announced it, and asked us to pray for his soul and write letters of sympathy to Sister Imelda's parents. We all wrote identical letters, because in our first year at school we had been given specimen letters for various occasions, and we all referred back to our specimen letter of sympathy.

Next day the town hire-car drove up to the convent, and Sister Imelda, accompanied by another nun, went home for the funeral. She looked as white as a sheet, with eyes swollen, and she wore a heavy knitted shawl over her shoulders. Although she came back that night (I stayed awake to hear the car), we did not see her for a whole week, except to catch a glimpse of her back, in the chapel. When she resumed class, she was peaky and distant, making no reference at all to her recent tragedy.

The day the bananas came I waited outside the door and gave her a bunch wrapped in tissue paper. Some were still a little green, and she said that Mother Superior would put them in the glasshouse to ripen. I felt that Sister Imelda would never taste them; they would be kept for a visiting priest or bishop.

'Oh, Sister, I'm sorry about your brother,' I said in a burst.

'It will come to us all, sooner or later,' Sister Imelda said dolefully.

I dared to touch her wrist to communicate my sadness. She went quickly, probably for fear of breaking down. At times she grew irritable and had a boil on her cheek. She missed some classes and was replaced in the cookery kitchen by a younger nun. She asked me to pray for her brother's soul and to avoid seeing her alone. Each time as she came down a corridor towards me, I was obliged to turn the other way. Now Baba or some other girl moved the blackboard two pegs higher and spread her shawl, when wet, over the radiator to dry.

I got flu and was put to bed. Sickness took the same bleak course, a cup of hot senna delivered in person by the head nun, who stood there while I drank it, tea at lunchtime with thin slices of brown bread (because it was just after the war, food was still rationed, so the butter was mixed with lard and had white streaks running through it and a faintly rancid smell), hours of just lying there surveying the empty dormitory, the empty iron beds with white counterpanes on each one, and metal crucifixes laid on each white, frilled pillow slip. I knew that she would miss me and hoped that Baba would tell her where I was. I counted the number of tiles from the ceiling to the head of my bed, thought of my mother at home on the farm mixing hen food, thought of my father, losing his temper perhaps and stamping on the kitchen floor with nailed boots, and I recalled the money owing for my school fees and hoped that Sister Imelda would never get to hear of it. During the Christmas holiday I had seen a bill sent by the head nun to my father which said, 'Please remit this week without fail.' I hated being in bed causing extra trouble and therefore reminding the head nun of the unpaid liability. We had no clock in the dormitory, so there was no way of guessing the time, but the hours dragged.

Marigold, one of the maids, came to take off the counterpanes at five and brought with her two gifts from Sister Imelda – an orange and a pencil sharpener. I kept the orange peel in my hand, smelling it, and planning how I would thank her. Thinking of her I fell into a feverish sleep and was wakened when the girls came to bed at ten and switched on the various ceiling lights.

At Easter Sister Imelda warned me not to give her chocolates, so I got her a flashlamp instead and spare batteries. Pleased with such a useful gift (perhaps she read her letters in bed), she put her arms around me and allowed one cheek to adhere but not to make the sound of a kiss. It made up for the seven weeks of withdrawal, and as I drove down the convent drive with Baba, she waved to me, as she had promised, from the window of her cell.

In the last term at school, studying was intensive because of the examinations which loomed at the end of June. Like all the other nuns, Sister Imelda thought only of these examinations. She crammed us with knowledge, lost her temper every other day, and gritted her teeth whenever the blackboard was too greasy to take the imprint of the chalk. If ever I met her in the corridor, she asked if I knew such and such a thing, and coming down from Sunday games, she went over various questions with us. The fateful examination day arrived and we sat at single desks supervised by some strange woman from Dublin. Opening a locked trunk, she took out the pink examination papers and distributed them around. Geometry was on the fourth day. When we came out from it, Sister Imelda was in the hall with all the answers, so that we could compare our answers with hers. Then she called me aside and we went up towards the cookery kitchen and sat on the stairs while she went over the paper with me, question for question. I knew that I had three right and two wrong, but did not tell her so.

'It is black,' she said then, rather suddenly. I thought she meant the dark light where we were sitting.

'It's cool, though,' I said.

Summer had come; our white skins baked under the heavy uniform, and dark violet pansies bloomed in the convent grounds. She looked well again, and her pale skin was once more unblemished.

'My hair,' she whispered, 'is black.' And she told me how she had spent her last night before entering the convent. She had gone cycling with a boy and ridden for miles, and they'd lost their way up a mountain, and she became afraid she would be so late home that she would sleep it out the next morning. It was understood between us that I was going to enter the convent in September and that I could have a last fling, too.

Two days later we prepared to go home. There were farewells and outlandish promises, and autograph books signed, and girls trudging up the recreation hall, their cases bursting open with clothes and books.

Baba scattered biscuit crumbs in the dormitory for the mice and stuffed all her prayer books under a mattress. Her father promised to collect us at four. I had arranged with Sister Imelda secretly that I would meet her in one of the summerhouses around the walks, where we would spend our last half hour together. I expected that she would tell me something of what my life as a postulant would be like. But Baba's father came an hour early. He had something urgent to do later and came at three instead. All I could do was ask Marigold to take a note to Sister Imelda.

> Remembrance is all I ask,
> But if remembrance should prove a task,
> Forget me.

I hated Baba, hated her busy father, hated the thought of my mother standing in the doorway in her good dress, welcoming me home at last. I would have become a nun that minute if I could.

I wrote to my nun that night and again the next day and then every week for a month. Her letters were censored, so I tried to convey my feelings indirectly. In one of her letters to me (they were allowed one letter a month) she said that she looked forward to seeing me in September. But by September Baba and I had left for the university in Dublin. I stopped writing to Sister Imelda then, reluctant to tell her that I no longer wished to be a nun.

In Dublin we enrolled at the college where she had surpassed herself. I saw her maiden name on a list, for having graduated with special honours, and for days was again sad and remorseful. I rushed out and bought batteries for the flashlamp I'd given her, and posted them without any note enclosed. No mention of my missing vocation, no mention of why I had stopped writing.

One Sunday about two years later, Baba and I were going out to Howth on a bus. Baba had met some businessmen who played golf there and she had done a lot of scheming to get us invited out. The bus was packed, mostly mothers with babies and children on their way to Dollymount Strand. We drove along the coast road and saw the sea, bright green and glinting in the sun, and because of the way the water was carved up into millions of little wavelets, its surface seemed like an endless heap of dark-green broken bottles. Near the shore the sand looked warm and was biscuit-coloured. We never swam or sunbathed, we never did anything that was good for us. Life was geared to work and to meeting men, and yet one knew that mating could only lead to one's being a mother and hawking obstreperous children out to the seaside on Sunday. 'They know not what they do' could surely be said of us.

We were very made up; even the conductor seemed to disapprove and snapped at having to give change of ten shillings. For no reason at all I thought of our make-up rituals before the school play and how innocent it was in comparison, because now our skins were smothered beneath layers of it and we never took it off at night. Thinking of the convent, I suddenly thought of Sister Imelda, and then, as if prey to a dream, I heard the rustle of serge, smelled the Jeyes Fluid and the boiled cabbage, and saw her pale shocked face in the months after her brother died. Then I looked around and saw her in earnest, and at first thought I was imagining things. But no, she had got on accompanied by another nun and they were settling themselves in the back seat nearest the door. She looked older, but she had the same aloof quality and the same eyes, and my heart began to race with a mixture of excitement and dread. At first it raced with a prodigal strength, and then it began to falter and I thought it was going to give out. My fear of her and my love came back in one fell realisation. I would have gone through the window except that it was not wide enough. The thing was how to escape her. Baba gurgled with delight, stood up, and in the most flagrant way looked around to make sure that it was Imelda. She recognised the other nun as one with the nickname of Johnny who taught piano lessons. Baba's first thought was revenge, as she enumerated the punishments they had meted out to us and said how nice it would be to go back and shock them and say, 'Mud in your eye, Sister,' or 'Get lost,' or something worse. Baba could not understand why I was quaking, no more than she could understand why I began to wipe off the lipstick. Above all, I knew that I could not confront them.

'You're going to have to,' Baba said.

'I can't,' I said.

It was not just my attire; it was the fact of my never having written and of my broken promise. Baba kept looking back and said they weren't saying a word and that children were gawking at them. It wasn't often that nuns travelled in buses, and we speculated as to where they might be going.

'They might be off to meet two fellows,' Baba said, and visualised them in the golf club getting blotto and hoisting up their skirts. For me it was no laughing matter. She came up with a strategy: it was that as we approached our stop and the bus was still moving, I was to jump up and go down the aisle and pass them without even looking. She said most likely they would not notice us, as their eyes were lowered and they seemed to be praying.

'I can't run down the bus,' I said. There was a matter of shaking limbs and already a terrible vertigo.

'You're going to,' Baba said, and though insisting that I couldn't, I had already begun to rehearse an apology. While doing this, I kept blessing myself over and over again, and Baba kept reminding me that there was only one more stop before ours. When the dreadful moment came, I jumped up and put on my face what can only be called an apology of a smile. I followed Baba to the rear of the bus. But already they had gone. I saw the back of their two sable, identical figures with their veils being blown wildly about in the wind. They looked so cold and lost as they hurried along the pavement and I wanted to run after them. In some way I felt worse than if I had confronted them. I cannot be certain what I would have said. I knew that there is something sad and faintly distasteful about love's ending, particularly love that has never been fully realised. I might have hinted at that, but I doubt it. In our deepest moments we say the most inadequate things.

THE KEY

John McGahern

They cut the tongues out of the dead foxes brought to the barracks and threw them out to the grey cat or across the netting wire into the garden. They cut the tongues out of the foxes so that they couldn't be brought back again for the half-crown the government gave for each dead fox in its campaign for the extermination of foxes. Dry mornings they put out the 'Recruitment' and 'Thistle Ragwort Dock' posters on their boards and took them in again at nightfall and when it rained.

The Sergeant and his policeman, Bannon, had other such duties, for the last crime had been four years before when Mike Moran stole the spare wheel of Guinea McLoughlin's tractor, but as he threw it in the river they'd not enough evidence to obtain a conviction. As an army in peacetime their main occupation was boredom, and they had similar useless exercises. The Sergeant inspected the solitary Bannon on parade at nine each morning. They'd spent a certain number of hours patrolling local roads on their bikes. One or other of them had always to be on BO duty in the dayroom beside the phone that seldom rang. These regulations the Superintendent in the town tried to enforce by surprise inspections. These inspections usually found the Sergeant at work in his garden. As he'd almost certainly have been signed out in the books on some fictitious patrol, he'd have to run for cover of the trees along the river and stay hidden until the car left. Then he'd saunter in nervously chewing a grass stalk to inquire what had taken place.

All this changed the day he bought one of the lucky dips at

Moroney's auction. The lucky dips was a way to get rid of the junk at the end of the auction. They came in large sugar bags. His bag concealed two canisters of nuts and bolts and a yellowed medical dictionary.

Bannon was now sent out on the bike to patrol the local roads. The Sergeant sat all day in the dayroom poring over the yellowed pages detailing diseases and their remedies. The weeds in the garden started to choke the young lettuce, the edges of the unsprayed potato leaves to fritter black, and when the summer thunder with its violent showers made the growth more rapid he called me down to the dayroom.

'Sit down.' He offered a chair by turning it towards the empty fireplace. The dictionary was open among the foolscap ledgers on the table, *Patrick Moroney MD 1893* in faded purple copperplate on its flyleaf.

'You're old enough to know that nobody can be expected to live for ever?' he began.

'Yes.'

'If you expect something it's only common intelligence to prepare for it, isn't that right?'

'Yes.'

'Our ages being what they are, it's no more than natural to expect me to be the first to go?'

'That'll be years yet.'

'We thought that once before and we were wrong. One never knows the day or the hour. The foolish virgins are our lesson.'

I sat stiffly on the wooden chair.

'If I go you're the oldest and you'll have to look after the others. I think now is the time to begin to learn to fend for yourselves. This summer I expect you to look after the garden and timber as if I no longer existed. That way there'll be no danger you'll be caught napping when the day comes.'

'But you do exist.'

'Have I to spell it out?' he suddenly shouted. 'As far as the garden and timber goes I won't exist. And I'll see to the best of my ability that you'll learn not to depend on me for ever. It's no more than my Christian duty. Is that clear now?'

'Yes.'

'Begin by informing the others of the state of affairs. There has to be some beginning somewhere. Is that clear now?'

'Yes.'

I left to go up the long hallway to the living quarters, the noise of the children at play on its stone floor growing louder. 'I exist, I don't exist,' repeated itself over and over as I tried to find words to tell them the state of affairs, bewildered as to what they were.

They laughed when I tried to explain, and then I shouted, 'I'm no longer joking. He said he'd give us no help. He said we'd have to learn to live without him. That's what he said we'd have to do.'

It took long tedious hours to weed the garden, our hands staining black with the weeds. The excitement of bringing the timber down by boat from Oakport compensated for the tedium of the gardens and when the stack grew by the water's edge he approved: 'The hard way is the only way.'

On hot days he sat outside on one of the yellow dayroom chairs with the dictionary, the young swallows playing between their clay nests overhead under the drainpipe. The laughter from the garden disturbed him. The children were pelting each other with clay. He put down the book to come out where I was backing up the matted furrows, pumping half-canfuls of spray out on the potato stalks.

'It's not enough for you to work. You have to keep an eye on the others as well,' he said.

'What'll I do if they won't heed?' I was wet and tired backing up the rows of dripping stalks.

'Get a stick to them, that's what you'll do,' he said and left, anxious to return to the book. 'I have to get some peace.'

The circuit court saw him in Carrick, and he took home a thermometer in a shining steel case, senna leaves, sulphur, cascara, various white and grey powders, rose water, and slender glass flagons, in which he began to keep samples of his urine, each morning holding the liquid in the delicate glass to the window light to search for trace of sediment. His walk grew slow and careful.

From the autumn circuit he brought a cow's head, blood staining the newspaper, and a bomb box, the colour of grass and mud, war surplus. He showed us how to open the head down its centre, scrape out the brains, cut the glazed eye out of the sockets and the insides of the black lips with their rubber-like feelers.

Before going to bed we put it to stew over a slow fire. The next morning he remained in bed. He knocked with his shoe on the boards and told us to inform Bannon that he was going sick. After signing the ledgers at nine Bannon climbed the stairs to see how he was, and on coming down rang Neary, the police doctor.

Neary called on his way to his noon dispensary. Bannon climbed with him to the bedroom door. Only the low murmur of question and answer, the creak of moving shoes on the boards, came at first, but then the voices rose. They lulled again, while the doctor apparently made some additional examination, only to rise again worse than ever. The voices brought Bannon to the open door at the foot of the stairs to listen there with hands behind his back. Each time the voices died he returned to his patient surveyal of the road from the dayroom window, only to be brought back to the foot of the stairs by a fresh bout of shouting. He was visibly uneasy, straightening down the front of his tunic, stuffing the white hankie farther up his sleeve, when the bedroom door opened and closed sharply, and the doctor's quick steps were on the stairs. Bannon waited out of sight inside the open doorway until the doctor was at the foot of the stairs, then appeared obsequiously to unbolt the heavy front door of the porch, and followed Neary out on the gravel. The examination had lasted well past the noon of the doctor's dispensary.

'I hope there's nothing serious?' Bannon ventured on the gravel.

'As serious as it can be – apparently mortal,' the doctor answered with angry sarcasm as he put his satchel on the passenger seat of his car. 'And he knows all about it. Why he needs to see me is the one puzzlement.'

'How long will I mark him in the sick-book for?' Bannon shied away.

'Till kingdom come,' the doctor answered; but, before he closed the car door, changed: 'Till Wednesday. I'll come on Wednesday.'

We brought him broth of the cow's head and milk pudding, the air stale in the room with the one window shut tight on the river and half blinded; and Bannon, morning and evening, brought him local gossip or report, in which he took no interest. Every hour he spooned a concoction he'd made for himself from the juice of senna leaves and white powders.

On Wednesday Neary appeared well before his dispensary hour. This time the room upstairs was much quieter, though the door did close on, 'What I want is to see a specialist, not a bunch of country quacks.' The doctor was more quiet this time as he came down to the waiting Bannon at the foot of the stairs. When they passed through the heavy door on to the gravel, thick-veined sycamore leaves blowing towards the barrack wall from the trees of the avenue, Neary tentatively asked, 'Had you noticed any change in the Sergeant before he took to bed?'

'How do you mean, Doctor?' Bannon was as always cautious.

'Any changes in his behaviour?'

'Well, there was the book.'

'The book?'

'The book he spent the whole summer poring over, a book he bought at the auction.'

'What kind of book?'

'Medical book, it was.'

'Medical book' – the doctor moved stones of the gravel slowly with his shoes as he repeated. 'I might have known. Well, I won't deny him benefit of specialists if that's what he needs,' and in the evening the doctor rang that a bed was available in the Depot Hospital. The Sergeant was to travel on the next day's train. A police car or ambulance would meet him off the train at Amiens Street Station.

When Bannon climbed the stairs with the news, the Sergeant immediately rose and dressed.

'It took him a long time to see the light,' he said.

'I hope they won't keep you long there,' Bannon answered carefully.

'Tell the girls to get my new uniform out of the press,' he asked the policeman. 'And to get shirts and underwear and pyjamas out for packing.'

When he came down he told Bannon he could go home for the night. 'You'll have to mind this place for long enough on your own. I'll keep an eye on the phone for this evening,' he said with unusual magnanimity.

The packing he supervised with great energy, only remembering later that he was ill, and then his movements grew slow and careful again, finally shutting himself away with the silent phone behind the dayroom door. Before he did, he told me he wanted to see me there after the others had gone to bed.

A low 'Come in' answered my knock.

His feet rested on the bricks of the fireplace, a weak heat came from the dying fire of ash, and beside him, on another yellow chair, was the bomb box, the colour of mud and grass. A tin oil lamp was turned low on the trestle table, on the black and red ink stains, on the wooden dip pens standing in their wells, on the heavy ledgers and patrol books, on an unsheathed baton. A child muttering in its sleep from the upstairs room came through the door I'd left open. 'Shut it. We're not in a field,' he said.

Early, in the summer, we talked about you managing without me. And you did a good job in the garden and bringing the timber down. Well, it looks as if we prepared none too soon.'

'How?'

'You know what clothes and feeds you all – my pay. The police own the roof above your head. With my death that comes to a full stop. We all know how far your relatives can be depended on – as far as the door.'

He'd his greatcoat on over his uniform, the collar turned up but unbuttoned, his shoulders hunched in a luxury of care as if any sudden movement might quench the weak flame of life the body held.

'Fortunately I have made provisions for the day,' he said, turning to the bomb box on the chair, and with the same slow carefulness unlocked it. Inside, against the mud and grass camouflage over the steel, was a green wad of money in a rubber band, two brown envelopes and a large package.

'You see this money,' he said. 'It's one hundred pounds. That's for the immediate expenses when they take the body home. It won't cross the bridge, it'll go to Aughoo, to lie with your mother, no matter what your relatives try.

'Then open this envelope, it has your name,' he lifted the thin brown envelope, 'all instructions for the immediate death, what to do, are down there one by one.

'This other envelope has the will and deeds,' he continued. 'Lynch the solicitor in Boyle has the other copy, and the day after the funeral take this copy into him.

'I have discussed it all with Lynch, he'll help you with the purchase of a small farm, for after the death you'll have to get out of the barracks if you don't all want to be carted off to the orphanage, and if you dither the saved money'll go like snow off a rope. Paddy Mullaney wants to sell and Lynch and I agreed it's ideal if it comes at the right price. After the farm the first thing to get is a cow. You'll have to work from light to dark on that farm to keep these children but it'll be worth it and you have my confidence,' he said with great authority.

He locked the box, and handed me one of the keys.

'You have a key and I have a key. When news of the death comes you'll go first thing and open the box with your key. Is that clear?' he demanded.

What was to happen was taking clearer outline as I listened, eyes fixed on the bright metal of the key in the sweat of my palm.

'The bigger package is not for the time being of any importance. It's for when you grow older. Old watches, your mother's rings, photos, locks of hair, medals, albums, certificates. It's for when you all grow older.' Then he remembered again that he was ill, and sank back at once into the dark blue greatcoat.

What he'd been saying was that he was going to die. He'd be put in a coffin. The coffin would be put in the ground and covered with clay. He'd give no answer to any call.

Mullaney's farm where we'd go to live, small slated house of the herd, fields sloping uphill to the mound, wet ground about the mound where once they'd startled a hare out of its form in the brown rushes; it had paused in the loop of its flight as the shot blasted its tense listening into a crumpled stillness.

Stone walls of those fields. Drudge of life from morning to night to feed the mouths, to keep the roof above their heads. The ugly and skin shapes of starlings, beaks voracious at the rim of the nest, days grown heavier with the burden of the carrying.

'But you're not going to die.'

'All the symptoms point to the one fact that it's certain.'

'But the symptoms may be wrong.'

'No. It's as certain as anything can be in this life.'

'Don't, don't . . .'

'Do you love me, then?'

'Yes.'

'If you love me then you must do your best for the others. We can't order our days. They are willed. We have to trust in the mercy of God.'

'I'll have nobody.'

'You have the key. You'll open the box with the key when the news comes? Now we have to go to bed. It matters not how long the day.' He lifted the box by its handle, moved towards the stairs, its weight dragging his right shoulder down. 'Blow out the lamp. I'll wait for you.'

Painfully the slow climb of the stairs began. His breathing came in laboured catches. He leaned on the banister rail. Three times he paused, while I kept pace below, the key in my palm, weak moonlight from the window at the top of the stairs showing the hollowed wood in the centre of the steps, dark red paint on the sides of the way.

'I want you to come to my room to show you where to find it when the news comes.'

He opened the door of his room that stank from the stale air and senna leaves and sweat. The moon from the river window gave light enough, but he gave me matches to light the glass lamp, and grew impatient as I fumbled the lighting.

'Under the wardrobe,' he said as he pushed the box between the legs of the plywood wardrobe, its brass handle shining and the silver medallions of the police caps on its top.

'You'll pull it out from under the wardrobe when the news comes. You have the key?'

'But I don't want you to die.'

'Now,' he put his hand on my head, 'I love you too, but we can't control our days, we can only pray. You have the key?'

The key lay in the sweat of the palm.

'You'll open the box with the key when the news comes.'

The train took him to the hospital the next day but before the end of the same week he was home again. He asked at once if his room was ready and immediately went there. He said he didn't want anything to eat and didn't want to be called the next morning. No one ventured near the door till Bannon climbed the stairs. When no answer greeted the timid twice-repeated knock he opened it a small way.

'You're home, Sergeant. Are you any better?'

The Sergeant was sitting up in bed with spectacles on, going through the medical dictionary. He looked at Bannon over the spectacles but didn't answer.

'I just came up to see if there was anything I could do for you? If you wanted me to ring Neary or anything?'

'No. I don't want you to do anything. I want you to get to hell down to the dayroom and leave me in peace,' he shouted.

A scared and bewildered Bannon closed the door, came down the stairs, and there was no sound from the bedroom for several hours till suddenly a loud knocking came on the floorboards.

'He wants something.' 'You go up.' 'No, you go up.' 'No.' It spread immediate panic.

The next knock was loud with anger, imperative.

'Nobody'll do anything in this house.' I spoke almost in his voice as I went up to the room.

It had been relief to see him come home, even joy in the release. None of us knew what to make of him shutting himself away in the upstairs room. The shouts at Bannon had been loud. I still had the key.

'It took you long enough to come.'

He was lying down in the bed, and the medical book was shut on the eiderdown to one side.

'I was in the scullery.'

'You weren't all in the scullery.'

'They didn't want to come.'

'I want something to eat,' he said.

'What would you like?'

'Anything, anything that's in the house.'

'Bacon and egg or milk pudding?'

'Bacon and eggs'll do.'

I held the key in my hand. I wanted to ask him what to do with the key, if he wanted it back; and my eyes kept straying under the plywood wardrobe where the bomb box must be; but the face in the bed didn't invite any questions.

That day and the next he stayed in the room, but at five o'clock the third morning he woke the whole house by clattering downstairs and even more loudly opening and closing cupboard doors and presses, muttering all the time. When we came down he'd gone out. We saw him outside examining the potato and turnip pits, the rows of winter cabbage.

After his breakfast he shaved at the old mirror and carefully combed his receding hair over the bald patches of the scalp, polished his boots, gathered the silver buttons and medallions of the tunic on the brass stick and shone them with Silvo.

On the stroke of nine he went down to the dayroom. I heard his raised voice within minutes. 'Nothing done right. I've told you time in and time out that these records must never be let fall behind,' and the unfortunate Bannon's low excuses.

For several weeks I kept the key in my pocket, but each time I tried to ask him what to do with it and if he wanted it back, I wasn't able. Eventually, one warm evening, with some anxiety, I threw it as far away towards the river as I was able, watching its flight curve between the two ash trees to fall into the sedge and wild nettles a few feet from the water.

A PRIEST IN THE FAMILY

Colm Tóibín

She watched the sky darken, threatening rain.

'There's no light at all these days,' she said. 'It's been the darkest winter. I hate the rain or the cold, but I don't mind it when there's no light.'

Father Greenwood sighed and glanced at the window.

'Most people hate the winter,' he said.

She could think of nothing more to say and hoped that he might go now. Instead, he reached down and pulled up one of his grey socks, then waited for a moment before he inspected the other and pulled that up too.

'Have you seen Frank lately?' he asked.

'Once or twice since Christmas,' she said. 'He has too much parish work to come and visit me very much, and maybe that's the way it should be. It would be terrible if it was the other way around, if he saw his mother more than his parishioners. He prays for me, I know that, and I would pray for him too if I believed in prayer, but I'm not sure I do. But we've talked about that, you know all that.'

'Your whole life's a prayer, Molly,' Father Greenwood said and smiled warmly.

She shook her head in disbelief.

'Years ago the old women spent their lives praying. Now, we get our hair done and play bridge and go to Dublin on the free travel, and we say what we like. But I've to be careful what I say in front of Frank, he's very holy. He got that from his father. It's nice having a son a priest who's very holy. He's one of the old school. But I can say what I like to you.'

'There are many ways of being holy,' Father Greenwood said.

'In my time there was only one,' she replied.

When he had gone she got the *RTE Guide* and opened it for the evening's television listings; she began to set the video to record *Glenroe*. She worked slowly, concentrating. In the morning, when the *Irish Times* had been read, she would put her feet up and watch this latest episode. Now in the hour she had to spare before she went out to play bridge, she sat at the dining-room table and flicked through the newspaper, examining headlines and photographs, but reading nothing, and not even thinking, letting the time pass easily.

It was only when she went to fetch her coat in the small room off the kitchen that she noticed Father Greenwood's car still in front of the house; as she peered out, she could see him sitting in the driver's seat.

Her first thought was that he was blocking her car and she would have to ask him to move. Later, that first thought would stay with her as a strange and innocent way of keeping all other thoughts at a distance; it was something which almost made her smile when she remembered it.

He opened the car door as soon as she appeared with her coat held distractedly over her arm.

'Is there something wrong? Is it one of the girls?' she asked.

'No,' he said, 'no, there's not.'

He moved towards her, preparing to make his way back into the house. She wished in the second they locked eyes that she could escape now to an evening of cards and company, get by him quickly and walk to the bridge club at the hotel, if she had to. Anything, she thought, to stop him saying whatever it was he had come to say.

'Oh, it's not the boys! Oh, don't say it's the boys have had an accident and you're afraid to tell me!' she said.

He shook his head with certainty.

'No, Molly, not at all, no accident.'

As he reached her he caught her hand as though she would need his support nonetheless.

'I know you have to go and play bridge,' he said.

She believed then that it could not be anything urgent or important.

If she could still play bridge then clearly no one was dead or injured.

'I have a few minutes,' she said.

'Maybe I can come back another time. We can talk more,' he said.

'Are you in any trouble?' she asked.

He looked at her as though the question puzzled him.

'No,' he said.

She put her coat down on a chair in the hallway.

'No,' he said again, his voice quieter.

'Then we'll leave it for another time,' she said calmly and smiled as best she could. She watched him hesitate, and she became even more determined that she would go immediately. She picked up her coat and made sure the keys were in the pocket.

'If it can wait, then it can wait,' she said.

He turned away from her, walking out of the hallway towards his car.

'Right you be,' he said. 'Enjoy your night. I hope I didn't alarm you.'

She was already moving away from him, her car keys in her hand, having closed the front door firmly behind her.

The next day, when she had finished her lunch, she took her umbrella and her raincoat and walked to the library on the Back Road. It would be quiet, she knew, and Miriam the new girl would have time for her, she hoped. There was already a molly@hotmail.com, Miriam had told her on her last visit to learn how to use the library computer, so for her first email address she would need to add something to the word 'Molly' to make it original, like a number maybe, hers alone.

'Can I be Molly80?' she had asked.

'Are you eighty, Mrs O'Neill?'

'Not yet, but it won't be long.'

'Well, you don't look it.'

Her fingers had stiffened with age, but her typing was as accurate and fast as when she was twenty.

'If I could just type, I'd be fine,' she said now as Miriam moved an office chair close to the computer and sat beside her, 'but that mouse will be the end of me. It doesn't do what I want it to do at all. My grandsons can make it do whatever they want. I hate having to click. It was much simpler in my day. Just typing. No clicking.'

'Oh, when you're sending emails and getting them, you'll see the value of it,' Miriam said.

'Yes, I told them I was going to send them an email as soon as I could. I'll have to think of what to put into it.'

She turned her head when she heard voices and saw two women from the town returning books to the library. They were studying her with immense curiosity.

'Look at you, Molly. You've gone all modern,' one of them said.

'You have to keep up with what's going on,' she said.

'You never liked missing anything, Molly. You'll get all the news from that now.'

She faced the computer and began to practise opening her Hotmail account, as Miriam went to attend to the women, and she did not turn again when she heard them browsing among the stacks of books, speaking to one another in hushed voices.

Later, when she felt she had used enough of Miriam's patience, she walked towards the cathedral and down Main Street into Irish Street. She greeted people she met on the street by name, people she had known all of her life, the children of her contemporaries, many of them grown middle-aged themselves, and even their children, all familiar to her. There was no need to stop and talk to them. She knew all about them, she thought, and they about her. When news spread widely that she was learning how to use the computer in the library, one or two of them would ask her how it was going, but for the moment she would be allowed pass with a kind, brisk greeting.

Her sister-in-law sat in the front room of her house where the fire was lighting. Molly tapped on the window and then waited while Jane fumbled with the automatic system.

'Push now!' She could hear her voice through the intercom.

She pushed the door, which was stiff, and, having closed it behind her, let herself into Jane's sitting room.

'I look forward to Monday,' Jane said, 'when you come down. It's lovely to see you.'

'It's cold outside, Jane,' she said, 'but it's nice and warm in here, thank God.'

It would be easier, more relaxing somehow, she thought, if one of them made tea, but Jane was too frail to move very much and too proud to want her sister-in-law in her kitchen. They sat opposite each other as Jane tended the fire almost absent-mindedly. There was, she thought, nothing to say, and yet there would never be a moment's silence between them.

'How was the bridge?' Jane asked.

'I'm getting worse at it,' Molly replied, 'but I'm not as bad as some of them.'

'Oh, you were always a great card player,' Jane said.

'But for bridge you have to remember all the rules and the right bids and I'm too old, but I enjoy it, and then I enjoy when it's over.'

'It's a wonder the girls don't play,' Jane said.

'When you have young children, you've enough to think about. They never have a minute.'

Jane nodded distantly and looked into the fire.

'They're very good, the girls,' she said. 'I love it when they come down to see me.'

'You know, Jane,' Molly replied, 'I like seeing them and all that, but I wouldn't care if they didn't visit from one end of the week to the next. I'm one of those mothers who prefers her grandchildren to her children.'

'Oh, now,' Jane replied.

'It's true, Jane. I'd go mad if a week went by and my lovely grand-sons didn't come down on a Wednesday for their tea, and I'm always raging when their mothers come to collect them. I always want to keep the boys.'

'They're nice when they're at that age,' Jane said. 'And it's so handy that they live so close together and they get on so well.'

'Has Frank been here?' Molly asked.

Jane glanced up at her, almost alarmed. For a moment a look of pain came on her face.

'Oh Lord no,' she said.

'I haven't seen him much since Christmas either,' Molly said, 'but you usually know more about him. You read the parish newsletter. He gave up sending it to me.'

Jane bowed her head, as though searching for something on the floor.

'I must tell him to call in to you,' Molly said. 'I don't mind him neglecting his mother, but neglecting his aunt, and she the holiest one in the family . . .'

'Oh, don't now!' Jane said.

'I will, Jane, I'll write him a note. There's no point in ringing him. You only get the machine. I hate talking into those machines.'

She studied Jane across the room, aware now that all the time her sister-in-law spent alone in this house was changing her face, making her responses slower, her jaw set. Her eyes had lost their kind glow.

'I keep telling you,' she said, as she stood up to go, 'that you should get a video machine. It would be great company. I could bring you down videos.'

She noticed Jane taking a rosary beads from a small purse and wondered if this were being done deliberately as a way of showing that she had more important things to consider.

'Think about it anyway,' she said.

'I will, Molly, I'll think about that,' Jane replied.

Darkness was falling as she approached her bungalow, but she could clearly make out Father Greenwood's car parked again in front of her car. She realised that he would have seen her in one of the mirrors just as soon as she saw him, so there would be no point in turning back. If I were not a widow, she thought, he would not do this to me. He would telephone first, minding his manners.

Father Greenwood got out of the car as she came close.

'Now, Father Greenwood, come in,' she said. 'I have the key here in my hand.' She brandished the key as though it were a foreign object.

She had put the heating system on a timer so the radiators were already warm. She touched the radiator in the hallway for a moment and thought of taking him into the sitting room, but felt then that the kitchen would be easier. She could stand up and make herself busy if she did not want to sit listening to him. In the sitting room, she would be trapped with him.

'Molly, you must think it strange my coming back like this,' Father Greenwood said. He sat down at the kitchen table.

She did not answer. She sat down opposite him and unbuttoned her coat. It struck her for a moment that it might be the anniversary of Maurice's death and that he had come to be with her in case she needed his support and sympathy, but she then remembered just as quickly that Maurice had died in the summer and that he had been dead for years and no one paid any attention to his anniversary. She could think of nothing else as she stood up and took her coat off and draped it over the armchair in the corner. Father Greenwood, she noticed, had his hands joined in front of him at the table as though ready for prayer. Whatever this was, she thought, she would make sure that he never came to her house unannounced again.

'Molly, Frank asked me—'

'Is there something wrong with Frank?' she interrupted.

Father Greenwood smiled at her weakly.

'He's in trouble,' he said.

Immediately she knew what that meant, and then thought no, her first reaction to everything else had been wrong, so maybe this too, maybe, she thought, maybe it was not what had automatically come into her mind.

'Is it . . .?'

'There's going to be a court case, Molly.'

'Abuse?' She said the word which was daily in the newspapers and on the television, as pictures appeared of priests with their anoraks over their heads, so that no one would recognise them, being led from courthouses in handcuffs.

'Abuse?' she asked again.

Father Greenwood's hands were shaking. He nodded.

'It's bad, Molly.'

'In the parish?' she asked.

'No,' he said, 'in the school. It was a good while ago. It was when he was teaching.'

Their eyes were locked in a sudden fierce hostility.

'Does anyone else know this?' she asked.

'I came down to tell you yesterday but I didn't have the heart.'

She held her breath for a moment and then decided she should stand up, push her chair back without caring whether it fell over, not moving her eyes from her visitor's face for one second.

'Does anyone else know this? Can you answer a straight question?'

'It's known about all right, Molly,' Father Greenwood said gently.

'Do the girls know?'

'They do, Molly.'

'Does Jane know?'

'The girls told her last week.'

'Does the whole town know?'

'It's being talked about all right,' Father Greenwood said. His tone was resigned, almost forgiving. 'Would you like me to make you a cup of tea?' he added.

'I would not, thank you.'

He sighed.

'There will be a court hearing before the end of the month. They tried to have it postponed, but it looks as if it will be Thursday week.'

'And where is Frank?'

'He's still in his parish, but he's not going out much, as you can imagine.'

'He abused young boys?' she asked.

'Teenagers,' he replied.

'And they're now grown up? Is that correct?' she asked.

'He'll need all—'

'Don't tell me what he'll need,' she interrupted.

'It's going to be very hard for you,' he said, 'and that's killing him.'

She held the side of the table with her hands.

'The whole town knows? Is that right? The only person who hasn't known is the old woman? You've all made a fool out of me!'

'It was not easy to tell you, Molly. The girls tried a while ago and I tried yesterday.'

'And them all whispering about me!' she said. 'And Jane with her rosary beads!'

'I'd say people will be very kind,' he said.

'Well, you don't know them, then,' she replied.

He left her only when she insisted that he go. She checked the newspaper for the evening television and made her tea as though it were an ordinary Monday and she could take her ease. She put less milk than usual into the scalding tea and made herself drink it, proving to herself that she could do anything now, face anything. When a car pulled up outside, she knew that it would be the girls, her daughters. The priest would have alerted them and they would want to come now, when the news was raw, and they could arrive together so that neither of them would have to deal with her alone.

Normally, they walked around the side of the house and let themselves in the kitchen door, but she moved quickly along the short

corridor towards the front door and turned on the light in the porch
and opened the door. She stood watching them as they came towards
her, her shoulders back.

'Come in,' she said, 'from the cold.'

In the hallway, they remained for a second uneasily, unsure which
room they should go into.

'The kitchen,' she said drily and led the way, glad that she had left
her glasses on top of the open newspaper on the table so that it would
be clear to them that she had been occupied when they came.

'I was just going to do the crossword,' she said.

'Are you all right?' Eileen asked.

She stared at her daughter blankly.

'It's nice to see the two of you together,' she said. 'Are the boys well?'

'They're fine,' Eileen said.

'Tell them I'm nearly ready to take messages from them on an
email,' she said. 'Miriam said one more lesson and I'll be away.'

'Was Father Greenwood not here?' Eileen asked.

Margaret had begun to cry and was fumbling in her handbag
looking for tissues. Eileen handed her a tissue from her pocket.

'Oh yes, today and yesterday,' Molly said. 'So I have all the news.'

It struck her then that her grandsons would have to live with
this too, their uncle on the television and in the newspapers, their
uncle the paedophile priest. At least they had a different surname,
and at least Frank's parish was miles away. Margaret went to the
bathroom.

'Don't ask me if I want tea, I don't want tea,' Molly said.

'I don't know what to say,' Eileen replied. 'It's the worst thing.'

Eileen moved across the kitchen and sat in the armchair.

'Have you told the boys?' she asked.

'We had to tell them because we were afraid they'd hear in school.'

'And were you not afraid I'd hear?'

'No one would say it to you,' Eileen said.

'You didn't have the courage, either of you.'

'I still can't believe it. And he's going to be named and everything.'

'Of course he's going to be named,' Molly said.

'No, we hoped he wouldn't be. He's pleading guilty. So we thought
he mightn't be named. But the victims are going to ask that he be
named.'

'Is that right?' Molly asked.

Margaret came back into the room. Molly noticed her taking a colour brochure from her handbag. She put it on the kitchen table.

'We spoke to Nancy Brophy,' Eileen said, 'and she said that she would go with you if you wanted to go to the Canaries. The weather would be gorgeous. We looked at prices and everything. It would be cheap enough, and we'd pay the flight and the hotel and everything. We thought you'd like to go.'

Nancy Brophy was her best friend.

'Did you now?' Molly asked. 'Well, that's lovely, I'll look at that.'

'I mean when the case is on. It'll be all over the papers,' Eileen continued.

'It was good of you to think of it anyway. And Nancy too,' Molly said and smiled. 'You're all very thoughtful.'

'Would you like me to make you a cup of tea?' Margaret asked.

'No, Margaret, she wouldn't,' Eileen said.

'It's the boys you both should be worrying about,' Molly said.

'No, no,' Eileen replied. 'We asked them if anything had ever happened. I mean if Frank . . .'

'What?' Molly asked.

'Had interfered with them,' Margaret said. She had dried her eyes now and she looked at her mother bravely. 'Well, he hasn't.'

'Did you ask Frank as well?' Molly enquired.

'Yes, we did. It all happened twenty years ago. There was nothing since, he says,' Eileen said.

'But it wasn't just a single episode,' Margaret added. 'And I read that you can never tell.'

'Well, you'll have to look after the boys,' Molly said.

'Would you like Father Greenwood to come back and see you again?' Eileen asked.

'I would not!' Molly said.

'We were wondering . . .' Margaret began.

'Yes?'

'If you'd like to come and stay with one of us for a while,' Margaret continued.

'What would I do in your house, Margaret?' she asked. 'And sure Eileen has no room.'

'Or even if you wanted to go to Dublin,' Eileen said.

Molly went to the window and looked out at the night. They had left the parking lights on in the car.

'Girls, you've left the lights on and the battery'll be run down and one of your poor husbands will have to come and bail you out,' she said.

'I'll go out and turn them off,' Eileen said.

'I'm going out myself,' Molly said. 'So we can all go.'

'You're going out?' Eileen asked.

'I am, Eileen,' she said.

Her daughters looked at each other, puzzled.

'But you usually don't go out on a Monday night,' Eileen said.

'Well, I won't be able to go out until you move the car, because you're blocking the drive. So you'll have to go first. But it was nice to see you, and I'll enjoy looking at the brochure. I've never been in the Canaries.'

She saw them signalling to each other that they could go.

The town during the next week seemed almost new to her. Nothing was as familiar as she had once supposed. She was unsure what a glance or a greeting disguised, and she was careful, once she had left her own house, never to turn too sharply or look too closely in case she saw them whispering about her. A few times, when people stopped to talk to her, she was unsure if they knew about her son's disgrace, or if they too had become so skilled at the plain language of small talk that they could conceal every thought from her, every sign, as she could from them.

She made clear to her daughters that she did not wish to go on any holidays or change her routine. She played bridge on Tuesday night and Sunday night as usual. On Thursday she went to the gramophone society, and on Wednesday, after school, she was visited, as always, by her four grandsons, who watched videos with her, and ate fish fingers and chips and ice cream, and did part of their homework until one of their mothers came to collect them. On Saturday she saw friends, other widows in the town, calling on them in her car. Her time was full, and often, in the week after she had received the news of what was coming, she found that she had forgotten briefly what it was, but never for long.

Nancy Brophy asked her one day when she had called to Nancy's house if she was sure she did not want to go to the Canary Islands.

'No, I'm going on as normal,' Molly said.

'You'll have to talk about it, the girls say you'll have to talk about it.'

'Are they ringing you?'

'They are,' Nancy said.

'It's the children they should be worrying about,' Molly said.

'Well, everyone is worried about you.'

'I know. They look at me wondering how to get by me quickly enough in case I might bite them, or I don't know what. The only person who came up to me at the bridge club was Betty Farrell, who took my arm and asked me, with them all watching, to phone her or send word or call around to her if I needed anything. She looked as if she meant it.'

'Some people are very good,' Nancy said. 'The girls are very good, Eileen and Margaret. And you'll be glad now to have them so close.'

'Oh, they have their own lives now,' Molly said.

They sat for a while without speaking.

'Well, it's an awful shock the whole thing,' Nancy continued eventually. 'That's all I'll say. The whole town is shocked. Frank was the last person you would expect . . . You must be in a terrible state about it, Molly.'

'As long as it's the winter I can manage,' Molly said. 'I sleep late in the mornings and I'm kept busy. It's the summer I dread. I'm not like those people who suffer from that disorder when there's no light. I dread the long summer days when I wake with the dawn and think the blackest thoughts. Oh, the blackest thoughts! But I'll be all right until then.'

'Oh Lord, I must remember that,' Nancy said. 'I never knew that about you. Maybe we'll go away then.'

'Would you do something for me, Nancy?' Molly said, standing up, preparing to leave.

'I would, of course, Molly.'

'Would you ask people to talk to me about it, I mean people who know me? I mean, not to be afraid to mention it.'

'I will, Molly. I'll do that.'

As they parted, Molly noticed that Nancy was close to tears.

Two days before the trial, as she was walking back to her house with the morning newspaper, Frank's car drew alongside her and stopped.

She noticed a pile of parish newsletters on the back seat. She got into the front passenger seat without looking at him.

'You're out early,' he said.

'I'm just up,' Molly replied. 'I go out and get the paper before I do anything. It's a bit of exercise.'

When they reached the house, he parked the car and they both walked into the kitchen.

'You've had your breakfast, I'd say,' she said.

'I have,' he replied. He was not wearing his priest's collar.

'Well, you can look at the paper now while I make toast and a cup of tea.'

He sat in the armchair in the corner and she could hear him fold and unfold the pages of the newspaper as she moved around the kitchen. When the toast and tea were ready, she set them out on the table, with a cup and saucer for each of them.

'Father Greenwood said he was down,' Frank said.

'He was,' she replied.

'He says you're a lesson to everyone of your age, out every night.'

'Well, as you know, I keep myself busy.'

'That's good.'

She realised that she had forgotten to put butter on the table. She went to the fridge to fetch some.

'The girls are in and out to see you?' he asked.

'If I need them, I know where they are,' she said.

He watched her spreading the butter on the toast.

'We thought you might go away for a bit of a holiday,' he said.

She reached over for the marmalade, which was already on the table, and said nothing.

'Do you know, it would spare you,' he added.

'So the girls said.'

She did not want the silence that began then to linger for too long, yet everything she thought of saying seemed unnecessary. She wished he would go.

'I'm sorry I didn't come in and tell you myself what was happening,' he said.

'Well, you're here now, and it's nice to see you,' she replied.

'I think it's going to be . . .' He didn't finish, merely lowered his head. She did not drink the tea or eat the toast.

'There might be a lot of detail in the papers,' he said. 'I just wanted to warn you myself about that.'

'Don't worry about me at all, Frank,' she said.

She tried to smile in case he looked up.

'It's been bad,' he said and shook his head.

She wondered if they would let him say Mass when he was in prison, or have his vestments and his prayer books.

'We'll do the best we can for you, Frank,' she said.

'What do you mean?' he asked.

When he lifted his head and took her in with a glance, he had the face of a small boy.

'I mean, whatever we can do, we will do, and none of us will be going away. I'll be here.'

'Are you sure you don't want to go away?' he asked in a half-whisper.

'I am certain, Frank.'

He did not move. She put her hand on the cup; the tea was still hot. Frank smiled faintly and then stood up.

'I wanted to come in anyway and see you,' he said.

'I'm glad you did,' she said.

She did not stand up from her chair until she heard him starting the car in the drive. She went to the window and watched him reversing and turning the car, careful as always not to drive on her lawn. She stood at the window as he drove away; she stayed there until the sound of his car had died down in the distance.

THE SUPREMACY OF GRIEF

Hugo Hamilton

One eye is half shut while the other is open. So we don't know whether it's drunkenness or whether he is looking out with deep anger. He hasn't said a word for a while. His arms and legs are limp, restrained by the shape of the armchair. We don't know whether he is about to fall asleep or whether he will soon begin to mutter or talk, or even shout. Whether he might say something terribly funny or terribly tragic or whether he is building up a general resentment of all around him. One eye is ajar, but the other is fully open looking across the room at the opposite wall. Anyone looking at his eyes might draw upon himself the full force that lies behind them.

He's had a lot to drink of course. Not without reason. His wife Sarah died only five days ago. Even at the funeral, he was unpredictable, showing little sign of emotion and listening to the many semi-sincere condolences either with too much interest or an obvious lack of it. He looked at people's shoes. At the graveside, he nudged his brother to point out the extraordinary hat which one of Sarah's relatives wore. 'Would you ever look at that hat, for Christ sake,' he said almost for everyone to hear. And later in the day, there was the row with the same brother for turning his wife's funeral into a party. 'It's just an excuse for a party. Have you forgotten that my wife has just died?' The outburst was enough to return a degree of solemnity to the gathering and to remind everyone that nobody had more right than he to find solace in laughter. That all mirth was at his discretion.

The next day it was decided that he should spend a few days in

Dublin. Nobody knows when the real grief sets in. Nobody knows what a man alone in his grief might do. They had no children and it was considered better or safer for him to be in company for a while longer.

At his own instructions, his two sisters Grainne and Marita had gone through Sarah's possessions sharing what clothes and jewellery they could use and arranging for the rest to be disposed of so that no trace of his wife except the wedding photo and the well-kept gardens would remain on his return. Then he was brought to Dublin in the car, stopping frequently for drinks to hold back the emptiness. Arriving well after seven in the evening, he began to embrace and kiss everyone excessively saying, 'What a feckin' life?' 'What a shagging life, eh?'; to which nobody knew how to respond, not knowing whether he was serious or not, other than to hand him a further gin and tonic and direct him to the armchair where he has been sitting ever since. The drink is on a small table beside him, virtually untouched.

His two sisters sit on the sofa together discussing the details of the funeral with their cousin Deirdre. They throw occasional glances over at Damien in the armchair. Grainne or Auntie Grainne has just shifted her position in order to cross her legs and, feeling the renewed comfort in her muscles, continues to describe the funeral. 'It was magnificent.' To emphasise, she shakes her head very slowly while looking earnestly into the listener's eyes.

The two children in the house keep running from the kitchen into the sitting room and back. At one point, they stop to look at Uncle Damien's watch. Without altering the one-and-a-half ratio in his eyes, he smiles at them and urges them to try the watch on themselves. One of them walks around proudly with the large watch while the other clamours to have a go. They are wearing their best dresses with ribbons at the back. Their father, Paul, who sits on the other side of the fireplace, tells them to give the watch back before they break it. In doing this, they giggle because Uncle Damien makes it difficult by spreading his fingers out. The girls look intensely at the tufts of hair on his fingers and along the side of his hand. They look at his buttons, his face and his ears. They soon disappear again into the kitchen where their mother is cooking.

Uncle Damien looks at a large drink stain below Paul's chair without seeing it. He stares at the two objects on the mantelpiece without absorbing them. The miniature wooden snake emerging from a basket and the brass tortoise which can be used as an ashtray.

Auntie Grainne has just glanced at Uncle Damien and turns to Paul.

'Paul, you haven't told Damien about your new job.' Turning to Damien, she repeats the catalyst. 'Did you know that Paul had a fantastic new job with IBM?'

'Yah bugger!' Uncle Damien looks over at Paul. 'Well, congratulations. I always knew you were marked out for it.'

Paul is like most people. He talks about his job. He prefers to talk about anything but Uncle Damien's wife. He doesn't want to stir the heavy sediment of grief. His conversation ignores the most prominent issue on Uncle Damien's mind. The two sisters on the couch have also been avoiding any mention of Sarah. They don't talk about her face. They don't talk about her things. They won't quote her. They won't mention her absence or her former presence. It is almost as if Sarah had been a very bad woman.

Every time the children open the door of the sitting room, a faint smell of soup comes in with them from the kitchen. The smell is foreign.

Uncle Damien's mouth is sealed. It looks as though he is about to make a very serious observation. It also looks as though he is about to say something very funny. When the children interrupt to look at his watch again, he continues to look at Paul without listening. He waits for a moment and turns to the girls.

'I want you to do something for me. Will you go in to your mummy and tell her that if it's not duck à l'orange, I'm not eating it. Duck à l'orange, have you got that?'

Uncle Damien looks at them seriously. His speech is slow and deliberate. The children repeat 'Duck à l'orange' and run away into the kitchen from where the vague smell of food is impossible to identify.

The two sisters, Auntie Grainne and Auntie Marita, are both angled slightly towards Deirdre who is telling them about a recent burglary at her house. Above the mantelpiece hangs a painted picture of a boat leaning to one side on a strand, the tide having receded far away into the distance. Behind Uncle Damien there are green plants, bushy ferns and drooping stalks; enough for him to hide in thick undergrowth if he were to move back. The curtains are a mass of falling leaves.

Uncle Damien moves forward to speak to Paul, much in the same way as he might talk about something he read in the paper.

'Do you know that I had a very, very beautiful wife called Sarah?'

Paul is surprised at the words. Uncle Damien is looking at him and the pause demands a response. Paul searches and rejects all the possible answers. 'She was indeed!' or 'She must have been!' or 'No doubt about it!' After a moment, when it's almost too late, Paul says: 'I think everybody knows that.'

'Do you think so really?' Uncle Damien preserves the equilibrium between a joke and something very serious on his face. It seems as though he doesn't need to blink.

In an effort to punctuate the conversation, Paul adds 'Definitely.' But Uncle Damien continues.

'There's only one serious regret that I have.' He pauses again.

'There's something I should have told her. I always wanted to tell her, even as far back as ten years ago. I kept meaning to tell her about it but I always stopped myself when the moment came. I thought I would save her the trouble.

'Do you know that even on her deathbed, I had a great urge to tell her everything but I just couldn't. And now it's too late. It's the one thing that kills me.'

Paul wants to ask him what it was but won't let himself. He doesn't want to appear inquisitive. He expects Uncle Damien to tell him anyway. But the children rush in the door saying, 'She said you're very, very bold. You have to come in for your dinner now.'

'Is it duck à l'orange? If it isn't, I'm not eating.'

'Come in for your dinner,' they shout.

'I can't! I'm stuck in this chair. You're going to have to pull me out.'

His left eye remains half shut. His arms are still limp along the armrests. The girls make an effort to pull them but they only make him look heavier and sleepier.

'Look, girls, stop friggin' about. One of you pull this arm and you pull the other.'

Paul stands up and waits by the door, smiling at the effort his daughters need to extract Uncle Damien from the chair. With a little more success, they manage to pull him forward. They believe that their own strength has achieved this and pull even harder.

'Come on, girls, you'll have to do better than that,' Uncle Damien says. They pull again and he moves forward a little more. But instead of standing up, he begins to sink deliberately and heavily to his knees and when they keep pulling, he finally collapses on to his back on the floor. The older of the girls says, 'Oh no,' and giggles.

They try to pull him up again but Uncle Damien is playing dead. One eye is still half open but the other is still completely shut now. Paul discovers by looking at his head why Uncle Damien always carries a half-funny, half-serious expression. It's the shape of the head. It's still a schoolboy's head.

Dara has come in from the kitchen to tell everyone to sit down for dinner. When she finds Uncle Damien on the floor, she laughs and says, 'Uncle Damien, come on now, time for dinner.' One of the children lets go of an arm which falls loosely to the floor.

Aunt Marita gets up from the sofa followed by the others. Deirdre walks straight out to go to the bathroom. Aunt Marita begins to talk to Damien like a child.

'Damien, what are you doing on the floor? Up you get now, dinner's ready.'

But Uncle Damien seems to ignore everyone and continues to play dead. Nobody believes him. Everybody is sure he's only putting it on. Even though he looks completely lifeless, they know he's alive. Dead people generally look like they're grinning underneath. Aunt Marita doesn't like it. It's beneath his dignity to act dead like that. She reaches down and begins to pull at his arm.

'Come on, Damien, up you get now. You're keeping everybody waiting.'

Dara joins in and begins to pull at the other arm saying, 'The food is going cold.' But Uncle Damien even ignores this plea for courtesy and remains lifeless with his dead man's grin. Aunt Marita almost stumbles with the effort. 'Damien, you're too heavy,' she says. They manage to pull his shoulders up but his head falls back and his Adam's apple is pointing at the ceiling.

Nobody knows the difference between a dead man and a man who wants to play dead. They look the same. Perhaps they also feel the same. Nobody knows the difference between a dead man and a man whose wife is dead and who himself is acting dead.

The two women pull energetically. They have given up pleading with Uncle Damien and have begun to plead with Paul to help them.

Paul declines and remains at the door with one hand in his pocket. He doesn't want to help a man who doesn't want help. If he were to join in, it would make Uncle Damien look helpless.

Auntie Marita is breathless. Everybody is now concerned with getting Uncle Damien up. His half-closed eye still stares up at nothing. The more they pull the heavier he seems to get. They have stopped depending on Uncle Damien's own strength and demand help from Paul. Dara looks up at Paul seriously.

'Paul, come on now. All the food is going cold. Give us a hand.'

Paul capitulates under this renewed pressure and goes over to join in. But as he takes hold of Uncle Damien's wrist and begins to pull slowly, the eyes open wide and look straight up at Paul. We don't know whether the eyes are opened in anger or in disbelief. Whether he opened them to see something or say something. To perceive or transmit. Whether they are open to find out if he's alive or whether to tell Paul that there was never any doubt about it. Paul immediately releases his hold on the wrist and steps back. Uncle Damien gets up of his own accord.

As they walk in to take their places at the table, the thought of food makes them forget. Nobody remembers what Uncle Damien looks like dead.

THE SWING OF THINGS

Jennifer C Cornell

You go answer it, my father said when the doorbell rang. I was up to my elbows in lemon bubbles, a butcher's apron around my waist, but he took the pot and scrubber off me and held a clean towel while I dried my hands. Go on, luv, he said. I'll finish these.

Brian and Jack were my honorary uncles, and though I'd just seen them the previous evening they still hugged me close when I opened the door, the scent of cologne fresh on their collars, their cheeks newly shaven and smooth against mine. My father came from the kitchen and stood behind us with folded arms.

Is he ready? Brian asked me, before he saw him. I ordered a taxi.

I'm not going, my father said.

You are, Jack said.

Now look, said Brian, we've been through this already. He unbuttoned his coat with determination and aimed his voice at the other room. You don't mind, do you, Mr Scully?

Of course he doesn't, Jack said. He went over to where the old man sat in his chair by the fire and crouched down in front of him, eye-to-eye. Alright, Grandad? he said. What's the forecast?

There's too many chickens, the old man said.

So there are, Jack said, straightening up, I've always said so. See – what d'I tell you? Sharp as a tack.

For God's sake, said my father. Can't you see I can't go?

Listen, comrade, Jack said, it's not immigration; it's one night on the town. We'll have you back here within twenty-four hours.

I don't know, said my father. What about the child?

She's a good big girl, aren't you, luv? How old are you now? Seventeen? Twenty-one?

She's nine, my father said. Too young to be left in the house on her own.

But she's not on her own, Brian said, she's with her granda. You'll look after her, won't you, Mr Scully?

He's got to get out, the old man answered, but my father shook his head.

He doesn't know what he's saying. That's not about this.

He knows more than you do, Brian told him. They looked at each other in silence for a moment. C'mon, now, Brian said finally. You'll be in by midnight, earlier if you want. And you don't have to do a damn thing you don't want to, alright? Just get out of the house for once, that's all, have a few pints and watch the match.

My father sighed. Who d'you say's playing?

Liverpool, Jack said. And this time they'll win.

For the next twenty minutes they stood beside him in the downstairs toilet watching his razor move in the mirror, lifting their chins with the same squint and pout as he scraped the blade carefully across his throat. Then they followed him up to the back bedroom to help him match a clean shirt and tie, where they shook out his suit and condemned its condition, spit-polished his shoes and vetoed his socks until my father gave up and let them choose a pair. I heard them arguing about financial matters – who'd pay for the pints and the grub if they got any, how much to save for the cab fare home – until my father came in for his jacket and cap and the spare set of keys, kissed the old man on the top of his head, and said, Alright, luv, I suppose we're away.

A man was closing our front gate behind him when we stepped outside looking up, testing the odds in the blush of clouds above us of another summer evening ending in rain.

Hiya, the man said, and shook hands with Brian because he was the closest. Gus Holden. Is one of you a John Scully? I was told I could find him at this address.

Is that right? said Jack.

What for? Brian said.

Your name's not Holden, my father said. You're a McCulla. Pascal McCulla, from the Ligoniel Road.

Not any more, the man said. I've been Gus Holden for ten years now.

Your father owned a sweetie shop when I was a boy, my father continued. Remember, Brian? Across from the post office, near Leroy Street. How's he doing, your dad? Does he still have that shop?

No, no, it burned down years ago. He and my ma live in England now.

McCulla's a good name, Brian said. Why'd you change it?

Part of the job, the man said. You do what they tell you or you don't get paid.

Listen, Pascal, my father said, John Scully's my father, but he's not very well; I don't like to disturb him. Can I help you at all?

The thing is, the man said, it's your da won the prize. I don't think it's transferrable.

Jack shook his head like a man clearing water.

He's done what did you say?

He won a prize, the man repeated uncertainly. He was in a competition. He won a day out with me.

And who are you?

I do stunts, the man answered. He seemed embarrassed. For the cinema, mostly. Sometimes just for show.

What kind of stunts?

Lots of things. Get set on fire, jump off of buildings. The usual stuff.

That's not true, Brian said. You do that thing with the catapult, don't you? Off an eighty-foot bridge with a plane going by. You catch hold of it. I saw it on TV.

Yes, that's right, the man said. But I do the other stuff, too.

You should see that one, Brian said generally. That's really something.

It's a bit late for a day out, isn't it? my father said. It's almost seven now.

Aye, I know, the man said. But youse aren't on the phone, and I have a cousin in Velsheda Park I haven't seen for a while, so I reckoned I'd stop by here first and make plans for tomorrow or whatever day suits.

Jesus, Jack said. How about that.

A competition, my father repeated. What kind of competition? What did he have to do to win?

Oh, I don't know, said the stuntman. Just be a fan, I suppose.

No offence, Jack said, but that's just not possible. You sure you have the right address?

It says John Scully here, right enough, Brian answered, examining the letter the stuntman had taken from inside his coat. And it's your street and number. He refolded the letter and returned it, shrugged and shook his head. Looks like it's him.

Have a look in his room, Jack suggested. He might have the rule sheet or something up there.

No, said my father, he's got to have privacy. This is his house, too, after all.

So what do you want to do? Brian asked quietly.

We were on our way out, see, Jack told the stuntman.

Oh sorry! he said. I can come back tomorrow.

You're here now, Jack said. Hold on – you wouldn't mind staying here for a while, would you? Just for a couple of hours, to keep an eye on things. You'd be doing us a real favour, letting this fella have a night out for a change. He grinned at the stuntman and patted his back. Don't worry; you'll understand everything when you've met the old man.

Now wait a minute, my father protested, that's not on.

What about your cousin? Jack asked, ignoring him. Is she expecting you?

No, not at all. She doesn't know I've arrived.

Well that's it, then! Jack said. We'll be down at the Joxer for a couple of pints. They're showing the match on the big screen. You can see it yourself, if you want to. He's got a TV.

I don't feel good about this, my father said.

Don't be silly, Brian said, it's a great idea. As long as you don't mind, of course.

It's alright, the stuntman said, really. I don't mind.

When they were gone I led him inside. The old man was sitting just as I'd left him, and I went over and collected his plate from the table beside him and removed the napkin from his lap. His fingers shook as I wiped them clean.

What's all this for? said the stuntman, looking round him.

For him, I explained, so he doesn't get lost.

I'd written the first set myself, one for every door in the house. But bright colours confused him so my father made new ones, simple black letters on white, unlined card – one to say TOILET, another, COAT CLOSET, the three bedrooms upstairs identified by occupant, the back of both exits reading, THIS LEADS OUTSIDE. In our kitchen too everything was labelled. A note on the bread-basket reminded the old man where to find butter, another on the kettle told him how to make tea. TURN THIS OFF! said a sign on the cooker. My father had changed it over to electric after he found the old man still looking for matches an hour after he'd switched on the gas. The following week he'd stepped through the gate the postman had left open and struck out for Carnmoney, where he used to live. He'd gotten as far as the city centre, had even managed to find the right bus, but the coins in his pocket had made no sense to him, and though he'd lived all his life within a twelve-mile radius he was disoriented completely when the driver pulled away. He'd entered a shop but lost sight of the exit, had drawn the attention of a security guard, then stood in front of the Linen Hall Library counting the same fifty-pence piece over and over until the thought of the sum he believed he was carrying had paralysed him with dread. A whole afternoon of pedestrian traffic had moved him gradually to the opposite side of Donegall Square, where Brian walked into him on his way home from work. From then on we kept the gate bolted beyond compre-hension, and he carried a card on his person printed in large letters with his name and address.

I checked the carriage clock on the mantel, stoked the fire and switched on the pump.

It's time for his bath, I told the stuntman. Do you want to come up?

We followed the same procedure each evening. The first thing was to sit him down on the toilet, get his clothes off, and then fill the tub. I'm going to unbutton your shirt now, Da, my father would tell him while I got the old man's toothbrush ready and tested the water against my wrist – Lift your feet up now, let's pull off those socks. After the bath there were ointments to use for poor circulation and swollen joints, plus an assortment of tablets and liquids which had to be taken before going to bed.

I took everything off him but his vest and pants, then I opened my mouth so he'd open his and pulled my lips back in the grimace necessary for the brushing of teeth. My father shaved him every morning but by teatime his chin bristled against my palm, the short white stubble on his jowls too sparkling like frost in the bright light of the bathroom.

I don't think they cleaned it, he said as I wiped his lips. It's gone now, anyway. Audrey, luv, did I give you that one? There was something else the last time, you tell him. Did he take that one away with him, too?

Okay, I said, stand up a minute. I fastened a towel around his waist, reached up underneath it and pulled down his briefs. As he stepped into the bathtub I took the towel away and helped him sit down, and when he let go of the handrails I lifted his arms up and pulled off his shirt.

Aren't you going to answer him? the stuntman asked me.

No, I said, he's not talking to me. It's your hair, I explained. Audrey's my mother. She used to wear hers that way, too.

Hers had been thicker than his, however, and even longer, and when she tied it behind her the dark strands moved in lazy unison, like the tail of a horse. Who do I look like? I'd asked her one evening when my father and I were sitting beside her, one on either edge of the bed. We were looking through a shoe box of photos he'd come upon earlier while searching the closets for something to have ready for Mrs Mercer, who collected donations on behalf of the church. Like your father, she'd answered promptly, but he'd disagreed. He'd lifted the soft rope of hair from her pillow and tousled his own head next to mine. Look at that colour, he'd said, there's your answer. You see that, wee girl? You're a bit of us both.

The stuntman examined the ends of his own hair curiously, as if he'd only just realised how long they'd grown. I gave him the soap to hold so I wouldn't lose it, and the shampoo to pour when the time came for that.

Listen, he said, can he go outside?

I recalled the forecast, the violet horizon, the mild breath of the evening on me as I'd waved Brian and Jack and my father goodbye.

I think so, I said. But not for too long.

It's just that he did win this competition, the stuntman continued. He deserves something for it. There's got to be something outside I could do.

I dressed the old man in the clothes my father had already set out for him to wear the next day, a combination of garments he'd been fond of once. To be on the safe side I put a cardigan on him, then I led him downstairs and out into the garden where the stuntman stood, contemplating the house.

He was in his bare feet and he'd taken his shirt off. White gauze bound him from mid-waist to abdomen, swift movement seemed difficult, and I don't know why but I thought of my father, whom I'd happened to see once stepping into the bath. The door to the bathroom had been slightly open and I'd caught a thick glimpse of flank and buttock before he sank in, lifted the sponge from the water beside him and squeezed its load slowly over his head; all the strength with which he'd been fooling us drained away from him then. Some time before that I'd observed the woman who lived across from us step into her garden perfectly nude. Her body was a nest of soft folds and deflations, like those of the models who posed for night classes in Life Drawing and Sculpture in the art room at school. The first time I saw them disrobe with such confidence and then mount the platform to pass the interminable hours outstretched on cushions or straddling a chair, I'd been with friends – we'd just finished Swimmers, and waiting for someone to come fetch us home we were wandering the corridors, intrigued by all that the building was home to after school hours, independent of us. From then on I watched regularly the Adult Ed students seated at easels, the hesitant strokes of their pencils and chalk, the thoughtful perambulations of the silent instructor and the all the while oblivious expression of whatever naked man or woman was in front of them that week. The old man had recently moved in with us then, my mother had only a few months to live, and I already had doubts about my own body, already imagined I could see proof of its impermanence in my own face and limbs. The woman's husband, returning from work as she stepped from the house, had dropped the plastic box he was carrying which still held his crusts and wrappers from lunch. He'd put his arms around her and held her, and it occurred to me then that this is why we fall in love: because we need another's eyes to convince us we remain things of beauty, because without another's tongue to tell us we assume such words can not be said.

The stuntman touched his bandages gently.

Bad back, he told the old man as if he owed him an apology. It's going to catch up to me one of these days.

How'd you get it? I asked.

I'm not sure, to be honest. The littlest thing can cause an injury. Bobby Dunn knocked an eye out doing a high dive – there was a match on the surface and he hit it coming in. I've been doing a lot lately with airplanes and ladders; that kind of thing can throw your spine out of whack.

He carried a chair out from the kitchen and I had him put it where the old man could see, then he excused himself and returned to his survey, tugging briefly at the drainpipe, gauging the likely strength of the gutters, testing the soundness of the moulding and quoins.

I don't know, he confessed finally. I haven't done anything like this in ages. Everything's so high tech these days. I used to work a lot with animals, too, but I hardly do anything like that now. That's how I got started, actually – training horses in Connemara. The first film I did was with Peter O'Toole.

Sargano wrestled lions, the old man said, Bostock boxed with kangaroos.

The stuntman stared at him. That's right, he said. So they did.

I put money on the barber, the old man went on. I'd've liked to've been there. Your uncle, he was living in Lancashire, he wrote me about it, but it wasn't the same.

Not Tom Helme, the stuntman said cautiously, but the old man was plucking at the cuffs on his cardigan and didn't respond. Helme shaved a man in a cage with six lions, the stuntman told me, must be forty, fifty years ago now. He was a barber; he did it on a dare.

So what do you think? I inquired at length. He'd inspected the house now from every direction, and I'd seen him eyeing the distance to the roof of the garage from one of the windows on the second floor. By now dusk had dulled the edges of everything, and although his fingers were as warm as ever still I worried about the old man.

I could make up a rig if I had some boxes, the stuntman offered.

There's a Spar round the corner, I told him. You might find boxes there.

I'd need a lot of them, but, he said, his eyes on our chimney. That drop's thirty foot if it's an inch.

There weren't enough but he took what was there. A cardboard wall rose quickly in front of him, its layers compact and orderly, printed with CORNFLAKES, WHITE CLOUD and ARIEL AUTOMATIC. He found the old sheets my father had used to cover the furniture when preparing a room for the old man's arrival; the cotton still smelled of turps and was stiff as rubber where the paint had congealed. He threw these over the boxes and bound it all loosely with twine.

Don't try this at home, he said when he'd finished, then climbed easily up the drainpipe onto the short roof of our scullery, turned, and sat down.

Not to worry, he said. When I first started out I worked with this fella who used to say there's no such thing as a more dangerous stunt. That was true then, it still is, a little, but there are some stunts now that're more easy than others.

They told him he was finished, never lift'm again, the old man said. In some places they were half an inch deep.

Jesus, the stuntman said. Dick Grace. Now he was one of the greats. Outlived eighteen professional rivals; another four had to quit cuz of injury. He was a mess himself after that accident, right enough – 786 square inches, burned so badly his arms ended up webbed to his sides – but he cut the scar tissue with a razor so he could keep on working. It was him used to talk about outwitting gravity. The stuntman laughed softly, then shook his head. Jesus, he was fearless. It just didn't trouble him, the thought he might die.

When I was much smaller my mother told me that should we ever be separated in a shop or department store I was to stand by an exit, and she would come and look for me there. You still remember that? she'd said when I reminded her of it – though I suppose, she'd added, it's not so long ago. She'd been weak, however, and a doctor was coming, so I never did explain the reason I mentioned it – the conclusion I'd come to regarding death. The way I see death, I had wanted to tell her, it's a circular room in which I'm at the centre, and though I fight hard through the people to get to a wall, though I travel along it and feel for a door, the same faces keep passing with the slow regularity of unclaimed luggage, and I end up repeatedly where I began. But no other opportunity ever presented itself, and later I realised what I'd been describing was not death at all, but the waiting room outside it where all the rest of us are.

That's madness, I said.

The stuntman shrugged. We have to go sometime. I suppose he reckoned with the end coming at him it'd do him no harm to meet it halfway.

He stood up. I heard the sound of scuttling gravel, a clump of moss dislodged from our shingles fell swiftly past and vanished into a flower bed, then I spotted his head and shoulders, his elbows cocked on either side, and in an instant he'd levered himself over and was coming towards us across the roof of the house.

It's okay, he called down from the edge. The rig's a wee bit smaller than I'd like it, but you can fall fifty feet on dry land without damage if you know what you're doing. He crossed his arms over his breastbone, his fingers clasping the back of his neck. Backwards and sideways, he explained over his shoulder, and spread-eagled on impact. That's the safest way, usually, for this kind of thing.

He described the mathematics of arcs and projectiles, the various forces that determine a fall, but all I understood of what he was saying was the margin of error, something they'd tried to teach us in school. An explosion in town the previous evening had damaged a gas main near the building, and as we were already facing evacuation we'd gone on a field trip to the Ulster Museum to see an exhibit on the concept of chance. The rest of the group moved on without me while I lingered at one of the first displays, an upright contraption of transparent plastic through which a torrent of ball bearings perpetually bounced down from a single opening into a row of compartments below. Though their descent was described by the force of gravity, it was the force of their knocking against the short, even pegs which were there to obstruct them that shunted them into a bell-shaped curve – and I thought as I watched them repeating the pattern how everything in life was this accidental. Despite all the care of the hands that place us, trying to centre us so we fall just right, still our paths remain unpredictable, we're so easily sent veering by a single peg – success, disaster and recovery all equally uncontrollable, whatever the odds and calculations.

All set below? the stuntman said.

Out of sight around the corner I heard our gate hum.

All set, I answered. The stuntman nodded and stepped back with long strides, disappearing in sections from the bottom up. Then my father was beside me, our front door key ready between his fingers.

I thought I heard your voice, he said. What are you two doing out here? He touched the old man's forehead with the back of his hand. Are you alright, Da? he demanded. Where's Pascal?

Again the gate groaned and shuddered. My father, glancing back to see who was coming, said Ah, no, and shook his head.

Now, what did you think? Brian replied before he could say anything.

I told you, my father said. I just wasn't up for it. Why didn't youse stay there, enjoy the match?

Who needs football when there's home entertainment? Jack answered. Just in time, by the look of it. Have a look up there.

It seemed he spun from the edge in slow motion, off by many inches and almost certain to miss the rig, and I thought of the way glass shatters, the regal burst of liquids when they land. The cord around the boxes snapped when he struck them, the sheets leaped up with the sound of someone heavy elbowed out of slumber into turning over in bed, and flattened bits of cardboard shot out from under, scattering leaves and twigs. Grit and plaster pattered softly on the bushes as the pieces stopped revolving and slowly came to rest.

Jack was the first to reach him. He pulled the sheets and cardboard away like a man in a hurry rifling through drawers while my father and Brian followed behind him, stepping gingerly into the path he'd cleared. What I saw first when they finally reached him was the stuntman's chest heaving, the careful way he drew up his knees.

Easy, now, my father said urgently – Hold on! Don't move.

I'm alright, the stuntman said, sitting up. A thin strip of bandage grew taut behind him and he stopped abruptly.

Just wait a minute, for God's sake! Brian said. We'll ring for an ambulance. There's a hospital just down the road.

It's okay, the stuntman said, I feel fine. With an effort he stood and brushed the dust from his trousers. Miscellaneous joints clattered irritably as he stretched.

You are one daft bastard, Jack told him with admiration.

C'mon inside, my father said. I don't care what you say – you ought to have someone look you over.

I'm alright! the stuntman insisted. But I could do with a drink.

Good idea, Jack said, we'll go to the local. I'd very much like to buy this man a Bass.

Not me, thanks, said my father, youse three go. I want to get that child to bed. Da? he called, and they all turned with him to look back at us. You okay?

The old man had risen when the stuntman fell. The last time I'd seen him move so quickly I'd been much younger and spending the day with him at his house. A year before that he'd tackled the bare, uneven land that lay behind him and created a pond, and I was keen to see proof of what he'd told me, that from the first bucket of silver he'd spilled into the water had come a whole population of healthy fish. We'd approached the bank quietly but still the pond's rhythms had been disturbed; it was many minutes before they returned. There he is, he'd whispered finally, pointing to the source of that retching bellow whose tremor I'd felt in my own throat and chest. He'd eased himself off the log on which we'd been sitting, I saw his arm strike with a heron's speed, and all at once he was crouching beside me, his shirtfront splattered, the frog with its large golden eyes and vulnerable belly afraid but uninjured between his hands.

I put my hand on the old man's shoulder. He said, You're a good girl, Audrey, and placed his hand over mine.

We're alright, I answered. We're okay.

TRAIN TRACKS

Aidan Mathews

Timmy leans across the armrest of his window seat and tells the airhostess that he's sick. He might have told the cabin steward, the one who brought him the magnetic chess set with the missing bishop ten minutes before, but he didn't; he may be only twelve, twelve and a bit, but he's learned already from his mother and his sister that secrets are best shared with women.

The hostess smiles at him. Her smile is brisk, professional; her eyes are tired. A little fluid is oozing from her left earlobe where the pearl stud ought to be. He wonders whether it's tender, remembers his sister having her ears pierced by the ex-nun on her thirteenth birthday. Did the Germans take the earrings as well as the gold fillings from the men and women they killed in the camps he couldn't pronounce?

'Sick?'

'A bit.'

'In your head or your tummy?'

'In my stomach,' he says.

'Maybe you drank that Coke too fast. Would you feel better if you put your seat back? Or if you got sick? Sick into the bag.'

'No.' He has already stowed the sick-bag and the in-flight magazine and the sugar sachet from the lunch that was served, in the pocket of his school blazer as souvenirs of the flight.

'We'll be in Dusseldorf soon,' she tells him; and she reaches across the other, elderly passenger to rumple his hair with her red fingernails.

Now that she's touched him, he has to confess. He hopes the other passenger won't overhear, but the man seems to be asleep, his mouth open, a dental brace on his bottom teeth as if he were a child again, and a slight smell of hair-oil from his button-down collar.

'I can't go,' Timmy tells the airhostess. 'I've tried to go ever since I woke up at home this morning. I tried at the airport, in the departure lounge, and I've tried twice since the plane took off, but I had to stop because I was afraid that there'd be other people waiting outside. And it gets more sore all the time.'

She laughs; it's meant kindly.

'That's only constipation,' she tells him. 'It'll pass. And now you know how women feel when they're having babies.'

She begins to move away as the elderly passenger comes to.

'I could report her,' he says to Timmy. 'I could report her for saying things like that.'

Timmy doesn't answer. Instead, he stares out the window, tilting his glasses slightly on the bridge of his nose to bring the countryside beneath him into sharper definition. What do women feel when they're having babies, and why is it wrong to say so? His stomach tightens again, the pressure to pass a motion makes him gasp.

'Are you all right?'

'Yes. Thank you.'

The elderly passenger in the next seat holds a Ventolin inhaler to his mouth and sucks sharply on it. After ten or fifteen seconds, he exhales again slowly, as if he were blowing invisible smoke rings. He glances at Timmy.

'The good life,' he says.

'Were you in the army during the war?'

'Yes. I was.'

Timmy's delighted. He puts the bottoms of two pawn pieces together, and their magnets meet precisely.

'In the commandos?'

'In catering.' The boy's face falls. 'Don't despise it. An army marches on its stomach.'

But Timmy looks away at the window. Far below him, he can see a river that must be the Rhine, a thin tapeworm the colour of concrete; and near it a road, perhaps an autobahn, a relic of the Reich. But where are the train tracks? Surely there must be train tracks between Dusseldorf and the city of Krefeld where the Sterms have their home.

After all, there are train tracks everywhere in this strange, sinister land; and the train tracks lead from the cities through the country to the concentration camps, and everybody knew that they did, knew at the time, and said nothing.

The boy thinks of the depots, of the huddled deportees. He thinks of the chemists, the teachers, the mezzo-sopranos, squeezed into stifling cattle-trucks, sealed carriages; men with beards who had lectured in anatomy, artists and actresses whose dressing rooms were lavish with insect-eating plants from Argentina; people who could talk in three languages, yet who had to pull their dresses up or their trousers down and squat over straw while the train roared towards the watchtowers.

'Would you like to see the cockpit?'

The hostess beams at him. She seems revived. Or is she coming back because of what the elderly man said? Could she lose her job because of him?

'No, thank you.'

'Don't you want to be a pilot when you grow up?'

He looks at her, at the weeping earlobe, a wisp of brown hair black at the roots.

'No,' he says. 'I want to be a Jew.'

She frowns, the elderly passenger turns to stare at him; and the plane begins its descent.

His classmates troop through the shallow chlorine pools back into the men's dressing room. They peel off their swimming togs and wring them out over the basins, excitedly chattering in this vast wooden space with its lockers like baskets. One of them whistles the theme song from *The Monkees*; another pushes a hair-clip up his nostril to scrape out a scab.

'I'm dying for a drink. Water, water.'

One of the boys, pretending to be thirsty, lets his tongue loll. A taller child volunteers the tiny pink nipple on his chest, and the thirsty one nibbles greedily at it.

'There you go, my child. Suck away.'

Timmy twists his regulation gym shorts, twists and tightens them until the last little strings of water drip down on to the floor. He'll have to wear them again on the bus journey back to the school, because he forgot his togs today, for the third time in a single term. As a penalty, he has to write out the Our Father twelve times, once for each year of his life.

'Into the showers! Into the showers! Quickly, quickly!'

It's Mr Madden, standing in the doorframe, shouting. He's carrying the large Tayto crisps carton where he puts the boys' glasses and watches for safe-keeping while they're in the pool. Timmy hurries into the shower, jostling, being jostled in turn, the hips and buttocks of the other boys grazing against him. He lifts his face to the hard hail of the water.

'Do it now, Hardiman. Come on. Do it now.'

One voice, two, then many, all of them. Timmy joins in, though he doesn't quite know what it is that Hardiman must do. The boy beside him lifts his wrist. There's a phone number written on it, a five-letter phone number; it looks like a camp tattoo, it looks like—

'You all have to pay me sixpence. All of you.'

They nod solemnly; they're hushed now. Hardiman folds his arms across his chest and stares at his penis. One of the boys stops the shower; the others surround Hardiman to shield him from the door. Outside they can hear the shrieks of the prep class, dog-paddling on their yellow floats, and a distant whistle. Timmy wishes he had his glasses. Things are blurred without them. He has to squeeze the edges of his eyelids with his fingers in order to make anything out.

'You look a bit Chinese that way,' says the boy beside him.

'Do I?'

'A bit. Listen, Tim, when you go to Germany next week, will you bring me back some Hitler stamps?'

'Any moment now,' says Hardiman; and, sure enough, his penis begins to grow: slowly at first, then more swiftly, it stiffens, straightens and stands up. The boys stare at it in silence, at its beauty, its lack of embarrassment.

'And I didn't even have to stroke it,' says Hardiman. 'Most people have to stroke it. But I can make it big just by thinking.'

'Thinking what?' says Timmy. 'What do you think?'

'Never you mind,' Hardiman says.

They've left the airport, arrived at the station, boarded the train and found a compartment before Timmy has an opportunity to examine

Frau Sterm closely. Modest and mild, she doesn't much mind such inspection. Instead, she smiles benignly out the window, watching the long, low barges on the river.

'The Rhine,' she tells him. 'The Rhine.' And she laughs, laughs because this strawberry-blond boy is looking at her so seriously, as if she were an ichthyosaurus or some other creepie-crawlie in the Natural History Museum where she brings her own son, Claus, on rainy Saturdays. She laughs, and lifts her hands to her forehead to flick back her fringe. The two boys will hit it off, she thinks: they're different, and difference, despite what universities may say, is the fountainhead of friendship. That was the aim and outcome of these programmes, a pairing of peers, of boys whose fathers had fought as enemies but whose sons, she thinks, whose sons will build rabbit hutches together.

Timmy's intrigued by the hair under her arms. He's never seen it before. Neither his mother nor his sister have anything like it. He hasn't even come across it in the *National Geographic* or in his father's large, forbidden volume called *Diseases of the Breast*. Is it restricted to Germans or to German-speaking countries? Or is it found in Italy and France as well? Frau Sterm doesn't seem shy or secretive. After all, she's wearing a sleeveless dress. Besides, Europeans are different. In Spain, his sister wouldn't be allowed out without an escort; in Greece, she'd have to wear a black frock if her husband went and died. The world is peculiar.

'Are you afraid?'

She grins at him, showing her teeth. She has many gold fillings. If she were a Jew when she was little, they would have torn the gold out of her mouth with mechanics' tools. But she can't be Jewish, and not because the Jews are dead now, but because she's married to a man who served in the Wehrmacht, to a man who got frostbite in Russia. So perhaps the gold is from a Jew, perhaps it's migrated from one mouth to another; perhaps it was used to the sound of Lithuanian, to the taste of kosher sweetbread, and now it hears German greetings, and chews sausage.

'No,' he says. 'I'm not afraid.' And then, because he can't bear her to look at him without speaking, he decides to tell her about the presents.

'I have duty-free bottles for you,' he says. He can't remember what they are; his parents chose them. 'I have a model airplane for Claus. I have a Heinkel, a Heinkel bomber. There are a hundred and fifty bits. Do you know Heinkels?'

'Yes,' she tells him. 'Yes, I know Heinkels.' She becomes silent again.

Timmy's got to go to the toilet. It's the same problem, the need to shit something strong and solid that seems stuck inside him, the inability to shift it. He leaves the compartment, squeezes past a woman holding a hat-stand like a stag's antler in the passageway. He excuses himself as the two of them manoeuvre, excuses himself and wonders whether she'll think he's English, and, if so, whether she'll hate him, remembering perhaps a charred torso under masonry.

'Thank you,' he says.

'You're welcome.'

In the toilet, he's alone. The seat is plastic, not wooden like at home. And the lever for flushing is attached to the cistern behind; it doesn't hang from a chain. Timmy lowers his trousers, studies his underpants to ensure that they're not stained, but they are, slightly. How is he going to clean them without Frau Sterm finding out; and if she does, what can he tell her? His mother's warned him twice, three times that a boy is judged by the state of his shirt-collar and the condition of his underpants. He sits and strains, sits and strains. He feels behind him with his fingers, between his cheeks, to where the tip of the shit is wedged, but he can't pass it. The pain is too much.

The toilet is dry. Timmy can see down through it, though there's a loop in the exit pipe. Sleeper after sleeper after sleeper, thin strips of gravel and grass, a whirling monochrome, a rush of field-grey grey-ness. They would have seen the same, the ballerinas and the butchers, their eyes pressed to the chinks in the shoddy wooden goods trains.

The boy tears the identification tag from the lapel of his blazer, the one with his name and flight number on it, the one the air hostess with the red fingernails had written. He holds it over the bowl for a moment, feels it flap in the uprush of the breeze, and then he lets it go.

'*Voilà*,' says Mr McDonagh; and he whisks the sheet away. '*Voilà*. That's German, I think, or maybe it's French.'

Timmy fumbles with his glasses, blows the short hairs from the lenses, and puts the glasses on. Mr McDonagh has followed his father's instructions to the letter. His hair is more closely cropped than it's ever been before. He looks denuded, ridiculous. His cheeks flush pinker.

'I was only obeying my orders,' Mr McDonagh says.

The customer in the next chair chuckles.

'Jesus,' he says. 'You look like something that walked in out of the camps. When is it you're off anyway?'

'In three days.'

'Bring us back some reading material,' says the other man. 'Will you do that?'

'A bit of culture,' Mr McDonagh tells Timmy. 'The Rhine maidens out of Wagner.'

'*Die grossen Frauen*, more like. Do you know what I'm getting at?'

Timmy shakes his head.

'Leave him be,' says Mr McDonagh, blowing quietly on Timmy's bent neck. 'The child's a holy innocent.'

Timmy peers up at Mr McDonagh's reflection in the mirror.

'The boy I'm going to,' he explains, 'his father was in the German army. He was in Russia. He got wounded there. It was the same year Mum and Dad got married. So while he was sheltering behind some tank during snowstorms, my parents were on honeymoon down in Parknasilla, except that the hotel was full of priests. Isn't that strange?'

'Not really,' says Mr McDonagh. 'Priests had a lot of money twenty years ago.'

'Do you remember the invasion of Russia, Mr McDonagh?'

'Do I remember the day I got engaged? Of course I do. I was in the army myself at the time.'

'Where? Whereabouts?'

'I was stationed in Limerick. I was in the Irish army.'

'Who did you want to win?'

'The Allies, of course. I wanted the Allies to win. But . . .'

'But what?'

Mr McDonagh cleans his glasses with the end of his navy-blue tie.

'I wanted the Allies to get a bloody good thrashing first. After what the British done to us.'

The boy looks down at his lap, around at the floor. Thick tufts of his own hair litter the lino. It was strange to think that your own bits and pieces, toenails, fingernails, follicles of skin, strands of hair, an assortment of your own bodily parts, could be sorted out and swept away, like dog dirt or a broken salt cellar. And it was still stranger to imagine the small, sodden mounds of human hair that the barbers of

Belsen and Buchenwald had shaved from schoolchildren, from tots whose first teeth were still intact, from teenagers who cycled bikes without holding the handlebars.

'What about the Jews, Mr McDonagh? Did you know about the Jews?'

'Ah, the Jews,' he says, shaking the sheet he has taken from Timmy. 'The Jews. A very versatile people. Sure, every second actor is a Jew; and they're all over Hollywood. What happened to the Jews was such a pity.'

The other customer clears his throat. A soft ball of phlegm sits on his underlip.

'There's some lovely Jewish women as well,' he says. 'Not so *grossen* now, but every bit as *frauen*. Now why the fuck wasn't I born in Munich?'

Frau Sterm shows Timmy round the house. She shows him the kitchen, the living room, the study where Herr Sterm works on his legal cases, the narrow ground-floor bedroom for any visitors. He doesn't notice much at first, because the whole house has a strange smell he can't identify. Aerosol sprays are new to him; back home, the maid cleans the bookshelves and the tabletops and the brass canopy over the fireplace with sponge and spittle, the elbow grease of ages. Here it's different, a bright, brittle world.

'You like it?'

Frau Sterm lets the bed down by pressing a catch. It emerges from the wall and folds away slowly to the floor. Timmy's never seen one like it before, or the double-glazed windows that overlook the front lawn, a lawn without a fence or a stone wall to protect it, a lawn that slopes unselfconsciously to the public pavement.

'Yes,' he says. 'It's very nice.'

She stretches out her hand to him.

'Come. I have more to show.'

The boy follows her back into the kitchen. There's a low whine, like the noise of a mosquito, from the overhead light. The skeleton of a fish sits on the draining board. Across at the window there's a bowl piled with grapes and pale bananas, but when he looks more closely he finds they're made of glass. And beside him on the polished counter he can see a weighing scales with the brand name Krupps, loose flour in a circle round its stand. He has seen that name somewhere before; he can almost retrieve it, but not quite.

'I have a letter for you,' she tells him. 'A letter from your family. It was here two days.'

Timmy takes it, tears it open. It contains one sheet of paper, paper so thin it's almost transparent. The writing is his sister's.

Dear Timmy,
It is now about nine o'clock, and I am going to bed. You are already asleep upstairs, and Mummy is choosing your trousers for the journey. It is strange to think that when you read this, you will be in the land of Hansel and Gretel. That is why I am writing.

I will go to the shop each Wednesday, and collect your comics, so that when you come home again in ten weeks' time, you will not have missed anything. Isn't that typical of
Your Adorable Sister.

Frau Sterm is folding laundry at the other end of the kitchen. Timmy thinks that it's kind of her to have turned her back while he was reading his letter; it's the first thing she's done that has made him less panicked and petrified. If only the smells were not so different, if only there were one smell which reminded him of the hot-press or the scullery at home. He wants to sit down straightaway and write to his sister, telling her that he travelled on a jet plane without any propellers, that he saw strange magazines at the kiosks in the airport, magazines with sneering women sticking out their bottoms; that he lost his German phrase book somewhere between Dublin and Dusseldorf, and he can't remember how to say that he's having a lovely time; that there's a weighing scales in the kitchen, made by Krupps, and weren't they the same factory that built the crematoria; and that he's tried, and tried, and tried, but he still can't go big ways.

Frau Sterm pounds the kitchen window very precisely with a twisted kitchen towel, and a bluebottle staggers for a moment around the juices of its stomach before dropping to the ledge. But the blow has activated the sensors on the ultra-modern burglar alarm system. The bell wails through the house like an old-style air-raid alarm. Timmy cannot hear her at first when Frau Sterm tries to explain, and anyhow she hasn't the words.

'I understand,' he says.

His father tucks him in, brushes a few shavings of wood from a pencil off the side of the bedspread. Timmy puts his sketch pad down. They kiss. His father switches off the light.

'I can always talk more easily in the darkness. Why do you think that is? I often wonder.'

Timmy doesn't say. He works himself more comfortably into the sheets. And waits.

'About this trip. You mustn't be frightened. People are kind the world over. You'll see. That bloody Italian you have for Latin's been filling your head with all sorts of nonsense, just because his brother got a bayonet in the bottom somewhere in Sicily. And the comics you read are no better – Boche this, Boche that, Boche the other. Officers with monocles, infantry like wart-hogs. The Germans are no better and no worse than anyone else. Do you believe me?'

'Yes.'

'Most of the music I play is German. Don't you like Mozart and Mahler? Don't you like Beethoven?'

'Yes.'

'So you see. Herr Sterm's a lovely man. If he seems a bit . . . remote, well, that's the way Germans are. Until you get to know them, of course. Then it's party-time. You remember playing mushroom billiards with Herr Sterm last year, over in Connemara, and how he let you win all the time. Now I never let you win, not if I can help it.'

His father moves towards the door, a dark sculpture in the soft light from the landing.

'Remember this. To begin with, the Germans didn't invent anti-semitism; they inherited it. And who did they inherit it from? I'll tell you. They inherited it from the different Christian churches. That's who. You couldn't say these things ten years ago, or people would think you were an out-and-out Communist. But now with the Vatican Council going on, folk are finding out that a mouth is for more than sucking spaghetti.'

'Yes.'

'If anyone annoys you, just tell them this: in the middle of 1944, the

Allies precision-bombed a munitions factory outside Auschwitz.
Precision-bombed it. Pulverised the whole complex. But they didn't
bomb the train tracks leading to the camp. They knew perfectly well
that the camp was there; they knew perfectly well what was happening
inside it. Flame-throwers turned on pregnant women; newborn babies
kicked like footballs. But they didn't bomb the train tracks. And now
after twenty years, they talk about preserving the otter.'

The door swings open.

'I had a patient this morning. On the table. He was different.'

'Why?'

'He died. He died on me. I had to . . . rip open his ribcage. I had to
hold his heart in my hand, and pump it with my fingers until it started
to beat again. I worked his heart with my own hand, something I use
to pick my nose with.'

He stretches out his hand.

'Want to touch it?'

'No.'

His father grins.

Timmy stands up, holding his shorts with one hand at his knees, and
turns to stare into the toilet bowl. He has finally managed to empty his
bowels. It has never taken longer to do so, never been so distressing
before. His bottom aches. He wipes it gently, inspects the paper before
he discards it. It only partly covers the massive turd lying in the
shallow bowl. The sheer size of it fascinates the boy. How can there be
room for such a thing inside one's stomach?

But he mustn't delay. He's been inside the bathroom for almost
fifteen minutes. Frau Sterm may come knocking. He presses the plunger
firmly, and blue water gushes down the rim of the bowl. It swirls in a
frothy fashion round the turd, spitting and bubbling; but then, slowly
and silently, it ebbs away, it drains and disappears, it leaves the brown,
bloated mass where it is. Timmy tugs the lever desperately. Nothing
happens. The cistern is empty. It may take minutes to fill again. He
hoists up his shorts, buttons the fly, washes his hands, runs them
through the stubble on his scalp. Where is Frau Sterm? How long has
he been now? How long? The room may be smelly. He opens the
window, scatters toilet water on the cork floor. How long?

The cistern has filled again. It must have, because the noise of gurgling has stopped. Timmy forces the lever, more slowly this time, and again the blue water cascades in. He waits, he watches it settle. The waters clear.

The turd has not budged.

The boy runs out of the bathroom. There's a door to the left-hand side, but he hasn't been shown the rooms upstairs. Perhaps it's where the Sterms sleep; perhaps Frau Sterm is in there now. He stops, starts towards it again, reaches it, peers round the door. It's a child's room, a boy's room, Claus's room. There are Disney transfers on the walls, a beachball in the corner, a thin Toledo sword; and on the floor immediately in front of him, there's a model train set, stacked train tracks, little level crossings, carriages, tenders, engines, miniature porters and stokers.

The boy listens. He can hear nothing. He leans forward, snatches a long length of train track and rushes back to the bathroom. He locks the door, listens again. Then he drives the train track fiercely into the huge shit, working it this way and that, stabbing and slashing at it until the motion begins gradually to disintegrate. But he doesn't stop. He pounds and pummels, pounds and pummels again. At last, at long last, he's satisfied; he adds another mighty jab for good measure, and flushes. Piece by piece, fragment by fragment, the turd is swallowed up, swept down.

Timmy begins to cry; but he can't allow himself, not yet, not now. There's still the train track, the train track. How long has he been here now? He fumbles with the tap, turns it full on, holds the track beneath its blast of water, picks at the particles of shit with his fingernails; but it's no use. The thing is sodden, it stinks, he can't clean it. He stands for seconds, staring at the toy piece; then he rushes out of the bathroom, down the stairs to the ground floor, and stops, straining for a footfall, the least sound. Where is Frau Sterm?

When he reaches the garden, he hurls the track with all his strength into the air and over the low wooden stockade behind the rhododendrons and the raspberry bushes. It lands among rosebeds in the neighbouring garden. Timmy has thrown it with such force that the muscle under his armpit hurts him. Now he can let himself cry.

'I won't hurt you.'

Timmy is standing in his pyjamas in front of his mother. It's late, the last night before he leaves for Germany. His bag is packed.

'I put a scapular inside the suitcase,' his mother says as she takes his penis out of his pyjamas. 'Do you know what a scapular is?'

'No.'

His mother pulls his foreskin up and down, up and down. She tries to be very gentle.

'A scapular will protect you,' she says. 'My mother gave me a scapular when I went on my honeymoon with Daddy.'

'Did it protect you?'

She laughs.

'What protection did I need?'

Timmy decides to tell her.

'I had a dream last night. A dream about you. I was sitting in a deckchair somewhere, and a whole herd of cows walked up to me. Their udders were dragging on the ground. They wanted to be milked.'

'And did you milk them?'

'Yes. I milked them with my bare hands, on to the grass. There was no end of milk.'

'And where did I come in?'

'You didn't. But I felt the way I always feel when I'm with you.'

His mother kisses the tip of his nose. She slips his penis back into his pyjamas.

'I want you to ask Frau Sterm to do that for you. Will you do that? It's very important. You'll understand when you're bigger.'

'Will you write to me?'

'Of course I'll write to you. Of course I will. And you must write back. But don't just write to me. Write to your daddy. Write to him at his hospital. He'd love that.'

'All right.'

The mother looks at her son, the son at his mother.

'Germany's not that bad. You remember how I told you I was there with Granny, just before the war.'

'You were getting better.'

'I was getting better. I was recovering. I'd been ill.'

'With pleurisy.'

'With pleurisy. That's right. And lots of people had it. It was rampant.'

'What's rampant?'

'Everywhere. All over. An epidemic. Many people died from it.'

'But you got better.'

'I got better. I got better in Germany. Or at least I finished getting better there. And I met some lovely people.'

'Who?'

'I met a woman. A girl, I mean. She owned her own café, a coffee-house. You could order the most beautiful cakes. And a cellist played there in the afternoons. She was a sweet person, but she wore too much make-up. She looked a little like a cake herself.'

'Did you ever meet a man you liked?'

'Yes, I did. He was very like Daddy, except smaller.'

'Was he a Nazi?'

'He was in the army. But his real ambition in life was to become a bee-keeper.'

'Did he?'

His mother gets off her knees and brushes the wrinkles on her kneecaps.

'I don't know. Perhaps he died. Perhaps he died in the war. His name was Nikki.'

Timmy burrows down in the bed. He shifts his weight to one side, leaving enough room on the other, as he has always done and will always continue to do, for Bernard, his guardian angel.

Claus and Timmy have hit it off. Frau Sterm is certain of it. There may be a little diffidence on either side, but that sort of shyness is only to be expected. Dublin is not quite Dusseldorf, nor Krefeld Killarney. Frau Sterm rather likes the alliterative parallelism. She'll try it on her husband later.

Out in the garden, the two boys are smiling, circling each other. Claus opens his English phrase book, picks sentences at random, reads them.

'This is not the room I asked for at reception.'

Timmy laughs, more loudly than he needs to.

'Is the museum open on Sundays as well?'

'*Jawohl*,' says Timmy, and salutes in the old style favoured by fascists. Claus looks at him closely. His face frowns. Timmy's unsettled, uneasy. He brings his arm down.

'I had a phrase book too,' he tells him. 'Only I lost it. I don't know where. On the plane perhaps, or in the airport. But I'll get another. Then we can talk all the time. Can't we?'

Claus hasn't understood. He starts leafing through the Berlitz guidebook again. Thumbing the sections, looking up and over at his new acquaintance every so often. Eventually he finds what he's searching for.

'Can we reserve accommodation on this train?'

Timmy thinks of the train track under the rosebed, of the train set scattered on the bright carpet upstairs. Is it remotely possible that Frau Sterm would collect the pieces into their box, counting them as she went along? Or that Claus would remember the exact number, the precise tally? Certainly the missing strip would never be found, but what if the whole Sterm family were to realise that, since the arrival of the stranger in their midst, things had been thieved? The word itself they might forgo, they might speak instead of disappearance, but thieving would be what they meant. He would be sent straight home, he might meet the same hostess on the Dublin flight. She might have to serve him breakfast, but she wouldn't look into his eyes. Instead she would look away.

'Is there a couchette available on this train?'

No one could have seen him do what he had done. The window in the bathroom was frosted, the door had been locked or at least he had tried to lock it. Frau Sterm had been nowhere to be found. The neighbouring house with the rosebed didn't overlook the garden. In fact, now that he saw it for the second time, he realised it was a bungalow. He could breathe easy.

'Or even standing room?'

Claus smiles at him. He's been saving the one bad English word he knows, learned from a mischievous scatterbrain in his *Mittelschule*.

'Shit,' he says.

Before Timmy can answer him, Claus bounds across the garden and bends down at a forsythia tree. Moments later, he's back with a tortoise in his hands. Timmy steps forward a foot or two, and makes to touch the shell; but Claus throws the unfortunate creature high into the air, then catches it again. Timmy can't believe what he's seen, so Claus repeats the trick, then chucks the tortoise deftly to his new-found friend and penpal. Timmy returns it; it's tossed back. The tortoise has edged out of his shell. The boys can see its face and feet emerge. They go on throwing it, back and forth, one to the other, as if it were a rugby ball. But soon the inevitable happens. Claus fumbles a catch, drops the tortoise on the concrete walk, steps back and stares in horror. Neither boy is sure whether the tortoise is still alive or, if alive, whether it's harmed. Neither speaks. A slight breeze darkens the lawn; sunflowers bob in their beds.

'Claus.'

But Claus doesn't answer. He walks the two steps to the tortoise and nudges it with the toe of his sandal, nudges it in under the cover of a bush. No one will see it there. He'll come out later, after dinner, to examine it again. Timmy wonders if a tortoise has a spine. Perhaps a chip or even a hairline fracture in the shell won't matter.

'Shit,' says Claus again. 'Very shit.'

Father Eddy lines up his shot and putts the ball briskly into the hole. Timmy claps.

'When I was a lad,' Father Eddy says as he moves to the next Latin numeral on the clockwork golf course at the bottom of Timmy's garden, 'Luther was another word for Lucifer. He was the Devil himself, every bit as bad as Hitler, and worse.'

'Really?'

'I kid you not. He divided Christendom against itself. He made war on the Church. You couldn't reason with him. And terrible things happened. Famine, assassinations, sacrilege. So, of course, when I was in the seminary, everybody looked on Luther as an utter blackguard. A bandit.'

The priest putts again, more cautiously this time.

'But now, with the Council and everything that Pope John tried to show us, we know different. We can see with the eyes of charity, the eyes of compassion. We can see that Luther wasn't all bad. He was just bonkers. Stark, raving mad.'

The ball wobbles on the edge of the hole, but it doesn't go in. Father Eddy's vexed.

'Even so, if the Sterms do ask you along to one of their services, say no. Say you're only allowed to attend the Catholic church. And if there isn't one in the area, don't fret. The obligation doesn't bind you when you're abroad. I was in Greece one time, a couple of years before I was ordained, and I went a month without mass. I was a spiritual skin-and-bones case by the time I got home.'

Timmy toes the golfball in, then takes it out again and hands it back to Father Eddy. The priest crouches over his putter, practising.

'If anybody asks you, tell them you're Irish but that you learned English at school.'

'Yes.'

'Mind you, when you're away out of the country, your real nationality is Catholicism. The Faith. Think of the Irish monks who went out to convert Germany. Columbanus, Cillian. Holy men, whole men, men with a mission. You're following in their footsteps. You see what I'm saying?'

'Yes.'

Father Eddy looks around him at the twelve Latin numerals embedded in the lawn.

'Which is that?' he asks, pointing with his putter to the large metal 'V' under the plum tree.

'Five,' Timmy says.

'And that?'

'Nine. I know them up to a hundred. A hundred is C.'

'Good man yourself.'

It's getting late. Only the upper windows of the glasshouse catch the sunlight. The priest and the boy walk back towards the house.

'Isn't it a strange thing all the same,' Father Eddy says. 'Those Latin numerals were used by Julius Caesar. Augustus used them. House-wives in Pompeii were counting them on their fingers the day Vesuvius burst. And that's not today, nor the day before it either. That's a long time ago.'

'How many popes ago?'

'Many, many, many. And yet, two thousand years later, you can come upon them laid out in a circle at the end of a private garden. Do you know who made that possible?'

'No.'

'Well, you should know. It was the Church. The Church preserved Latin, the language of the very soldiers who crucified Our Lord. That's called an irony.'

'What's that?'

'A wound that gives pleasure.'

The priest stoops to pick a bird's feather from the lawn.

'You could talk to Claus in the Latin you have,' he tells Timmy. 'I imagine he learns it in his school. You know the verb "to love" backwards. And that's enough to start with. It's enough for anyone. Or it should be. You're not nervous? There's no reason to be nervous. Sure, the two of you will be thick as thieves before the plane's refuelled.'

Behind them, out of the cypress trees, magpies circle the clockwork golf course, land, and begin to pick at the glinting metal letters.

Herr Sterm leans back from the dining table and tilts his chin towards the ceiling. Almost from the moment that he entered the house, his nose has been bleeding. Already the front of his shirt is stained, the green tie that he wore to honour Timmy is flecked with red. Yet Frau Sterm continues to tell the boy that this is no unusual occurrence. It happens all the time, it's a sign of health, not illness. It passes after a while, as all things pass. And she ladles more vegetables on to Timmy's plate, and sets the plate before him.

The food is unintelligible. There are strange, anonymous entities Timmy's never seen before. Shape, size, flavour and taste are all new. He rummages with his knife and fork, sorts and separates the mess, but he can't bring himself to swallow the stuff. He can see fragments of his own reflection on the broad blade of the knife; his lower lip with the scrap of dead skin, his teeth in a white wobble, his eyebrows, eyelashes, eyes. His eyes stare back at him, confessing, concealing.

'Would you like to see a film tomorrow?'

He looks up at Frau Sterm. She seems distant, diminished.

'Yes. Thank you.'

'Would you like to see *The Sound of Music*?'

'Yes.'

Herr Sterm settles his chair back on its four legs again. He holds a large handkerchief to his nose as he speaks in a muffled way to his wife. He speaks first in German, then in English.

'*The Sound of Music* is not a good film. It is anti-German. The music is pretty, but the message, the message is propaganda. But there are other films. There are others; and these we will see.'

They eat in silence. Timmy forces a few mouthfuls of the green and purple rubbish into his mouth. Claus is in another world, playing soccer with the peas on his plate. Perhaps he's thinking about the

324

Aidan Mathews

tortoise; perhaps he's frightened. Herr Sterm begins to bleed again, over the napkin and the napkin ring. He swears in an undertone. His wife shushes him. Silence again for a spell . . . and then the bell rings.

The hall doorbell, its two tones, a little phrase.

The whole table tenses. Mother and father glance at each other. The husband rises, goes out. Frau Sterm peers out the window at the louvre doors into the kitchen.

'I think it is a neighbour,' she says.

And Timmy knows, knows in the pit of his stomach; deep in the boy's belly, there is certain knowledge. Why did the elderly passenger complain about the air hostess? Why had he said he wanted to be a Jew? What made him refuse to visit the cockpit? And how did Hardiman make his penis stand up straight? What was he thinking of when he did that? What was in his mind?

The door swings open. Herr Sterm walks back in. He says nothing. He's holding the train track. Why had he thrown his identification label into the toilet on the train? There must have been a reason. His father is always telling him there is a reason for everything. If so, why were the women sneering on the magazine covers? Herr Sterm begins to beat Claus around the shoulders and neck with the dirty train track. His wife screams. But Claus, Claus doesn't cry, doesn't cry out. He doesn't even try to cover his head. What did Mr McDonagh feel about Jews? What did he really feel? What did 'grossen Frauen' mean? Why was it funny?

Frau Sterm punches her husband in the side. She pleads with him; he doesn't answer. His nose has begun to bleed again. It drips on to Claus's T-shirt, runs down the back. The boy sobs and shudders. Herr Sterm raises the train track one last time, a soiled stretch, still filthy from the toilet and the garden; raises it, looks at it, lowers it. He runs his hand through his hair.

'I bought this . . . machinery for Claus yesterday. It is a new present. For him, but also for you. To play together.'

Why had he not touched his father's hand? And why had the Allied bombers not bombed the train tracks leading to Auschwitz? Why? And when would he know the answers? All the answers to everything, everything that made him feel scared and strange and examined. He looks at Herr Sterm, at Frau Sterm, at Claus. He feels sick in his stomach, sick and sore. The lenses of his glasses have begun to mist from the heat of his sweat. They start to slip forward down the bridge of his nose until the half of his field of vision is a blur, the other half is sharper than italics.

He says nothing. He says nothing at all.

SEE THE TREE,
HOW BIG IT'S GROWN

Kevin Barry

He turned to check his reflection in the window of the Expressway bus and some old quarehawk turned to look back at him. He appeared to be a man of about fifty. He did not appear to have set the world on fire. He looked beyond himself, and it had the look of South Tipp out there, lush and damp-seeming, with good-sized hills rising to the east, which would be the Comeraghs. He knew more about the hills than he knew about himself, but lush, yes, as if it was May, a savage growth that made each small copse of trees livid with bunched ferocity. The face seen dully in the window was a sad face, certainly, with a downcast mouth and emotional eyes, but it was strangely calm too. He took a glance south and found he was wearing an anorak long past its day, a pair of jeans with diesel stains caked into them and shoes straight off an evidence table. There was a bag, he noticed, in the rack overhead and he reached to take it down, breathing heavily. It was a Reebok holdall, scuffed and torn, and by no means a classy piece of luggage. He sat on the Expressway as it motored north through Tipperary this afternoon in the apparent summer with the bag in his lap. What kind of condition are you in at all, he wondered, when you wake up on a bus in the middle of countryside and you have no idea of who you are, or what your name is even?

The bus was quiet, with just a handful of sad cases thrown here and there, the elderly and the infirm, the free-pass brigade with their jaunty afflictions. He hefted the holdall, tested its weight. Come on now, what could be inside there? The head of John the Baptist? He opened it and with relief found just a sweatshirt and another pair of jeans. There was a box of fags, Bensons, and a yellow plastic lighter in a pocket of the jeans. There was a wallet in the other pocket, it held six hundred euro in cash and a scrap of paper folded over twice. The scrap of paper said 'Rooney's Auctioneers, 5pm.' It was at this point that he got the first of the tremors. This is what he would come to call them: the tremors. A tremor was when a flash of something came to him. The nature of this was visceral, more a feeling than a thought, and this first tremor came in the form of music, a snatch of music, five sad slow notes played on a recorder.

'Of course,' said an old fella in the seat opposite, looking across, 'I have the bus pass myself, I'd be going up and down the country on a regular basis.'

'Is that right?' he said, and his own voice was a surprise to him, a husky baritone.

'Oh yes. I do be bulling for road, you see. And I find that the B&Bs these days are excellent value for money. They serve you a powerful breakfast. And at this stage, most of the rooms have tea- and coffee-making facilities. And the cable as well. You can be watching Sky News.'

'I see.'

'And where'll you stay above?'

'The chances are', he said, 'I'll be in a B&B myself.'

'Very good!' said the old fella, as if this was the best decision a man could ever hope to make.

There were certain pieces of information available. He knew, for example, that the course of Irish history was besmirched with treacheries and suppressions. He knew this because in some foggy classroom at the back of his mind he had been made to read it aloud to the rest of the children, despite or maybe even because of his terrible stammer. T-t-t-the course of I-I-Irish history is b-b-b-besmirched . . . You wouldn't likely forget the treacheries and suppressions after that.

'The old boy looked over again, with rheumy eyes and gummy mouth, and he winked:

'Listen, there's every chance now we'll get in before five. You'll be able to get down to Rooney's, get a hold of them keys.'

'Do you reckon?' he said, and there was more than a sliver of fear in him.

'Ah we'll be in before five easy.'

A childish notion came. He thought that maybe he had died, and was in limbo, and that this old boy was some manner of gatekeeper. He shucked himself free of this sensation as best as he could, looked out the window: gloom floated down from morbid hills. The Expressway passed through a village, really more of a crossroads than a village, just a collision of a few byways and houses, a shop and, finally, a pub. As the bus passed by this establishment, the eyes nearly came out of his head. Was this, he wondered, a clue as to the character of the individual? He swivelled in his seat and looked desperately back down the road as the pub went out of view again. The throat was after going pure dry. He straightened himself and cast a wary glance across the aisle.

'He's making good time today,' said the old fella.

'He is.'

A bigger town announced itself with garden centres and DIY warehouses and a large sign in the middle of a new roundabout that read:

BULMER'S CIDER WELCOMES YOU TO CLONMEL

'He's sucking diesel today,' said the old fella. 'Twenty to five!'

'Faith, he is,' he said.

Taking the Reebok holdall, he stood as the bus eased into the bleak station and he made a whistling attempt at nonchalance.

'Listen to me,' said the old fella, 'the best of luck to you now with everything. Something tells me you might have done a good deal here. And don't mind what the crowd below are saying.'

'Thanks very much,' he said, and he stepped off the Expressway and into the mysteries of Clonmel.

He wasn't long getting directions to Rooney's – Davitt Street, first left – and he wasn't long noticing that it was beside a small pub name of The Dew Drop Inn. He had a few minutes to spare, and there was a strange draw from this place, a magnet drag. The next thing he knew, he was inside at the counter, in the dank half-light, throwing the holdall down to his feet and putting his elbows up on the bar.

'What'll it be?' said the young one behind the bar.

'Pint b-bottle of B-Bulmer's,' he said, 'and a b-b-baby Powers.'

It appeared that he knew full well what he was doing in this type of situation. There was a bottle put down in front of him, and a pint glass filled with ice, and the small whiskey appeared as a cheerful companion. He made short work of this order, and he started to feel somewhat philosophical. What, after all, he said to himself, is an identity? Surely it is only a means of marking yourself out in time. And what is time in itself, only an arbitrary and entirely illusory system designed to remind us of death? To separate us from the eternal present enjoyed by the beasts of the fields. So why need you bother with either one, when you have the bones of six hundred euro in your fist and a fag lit in the corner of your mouth? The five o'clock news came on the radio. It said Orla was missing since March 14th and the one clue for investigators was a red baseball cap.

'That'll be me,' he said to the young one, and she responded with a lazy smile and a stretching movement like a cat would make. There might be sport to be had in this place yet.

He strode in the door of Rooney's like a man who owned the rights to the whole of love. There was another young lady there, neat behind her desk, with a poignant mouth and agreeable knees.

'Good afternoon,' he said. 'I had an appointment for five?'

'Oh,' she said. 'It must be Mr Tobin, is it?'

'Correct.'

'Mr Tobin,' she explained, 'Mr Rooney is actually out at present. He is showing a pig operation in the direction of Knockbawn, but listen now, I have the keys and the lease here for you.'

'Outstanding.'

'The money has cleared. Everything is ready to go. All you have to do is sign your name. So if you'd like to take a seat, you can have a quick read through and make sure everything is in order.'

'I will,' he said. 'I'll take the w-weight off my feet.'

He felt that he was doing very well. His manner was charming, and if he didn't look exactly dapper, than at least he had a benevolent aura. Unfortunately, he noted, there was a smell of drink off him, which was something he would have to watch, but still and all he was presented with the necessary document. The lease shook a little as he read through it. It turned out he was after buying a chipper in Clonmel.

With the keys swinging, he set off into a most pleasant evening: the town swooned with glow, like a back-lit ale. He searched out No. 15a McDermott Street, which turned out to be no more than a hundred yards around the corner from Rooney's. After some trial and error with the keys, he managed to get the shutters up and the door opened and he crossed the threshold into a new era for both himself – Mr R. K. Tobin, apparently – and for the Uptown Grill.

So what do you do? What do you do when you wake up on a bus in South Tipp, and you don't know who you are, or where you're going, and the next thing you're inside in an auctioneers being presented with keys and then you're stood in the Uptown Grill, which is fourteen foot long by ten wide and contains a large deep fat fryer, a griddle, a glass-doored fridge, a full stock of supplies, a counter and a cash register? What do you do?

You start peeling spuds.

It quickly became clear that R. K. Tobin was not without some experience in the catering trade. The operation of the Uptown Grill didn't seem to faze him in the slightest. He wasn't in the door a half hour and he had wire baskets of nicely cut chips waiting for the fryer, he had the burgers battered, he had the haddock in breadcrumbs, and the potato cakes rolled, he had a griddle full of onions frying up nice and slow, releasing their sweetness to the air. Everything was waiting for the off, and as he worked he whistled a selection of show tunes from the early 1950s: 'If I Knew You Were Coming I'd A Baked A Cake', 'Cherry Pink And Apple Blossom White', 'Moon River'. His domestic arrangements, as it turned out, were all to hand, for he had climbed a greasy stairway out back and found a room above the chipper, same size, with a sink, a couch, a half bottle of Cork gin and a selection of golf magazines. He felt utterly alive with entrepreneurial swagger, and who was to say he wouldn't be taking up the golf himself? He brought the gin down with him as he prepared to open up for the teatime crowd. It just seemed like the thing to do.

Business came in fits and starts but overall it didn't seem a bad trade. It was steady enough through to seven o'clock, then you had lads late from work coming in for feeds, then a good crew around half-nine or ten in severe need of soakage. Quiet moments, he took a hit of gin from under the counter, looked out the door, saw the town fall away down the slate rooftops of terraces, turn into farmland and fields, melancholy hills. The light was pleasing – a softness to it – and there was an amount of birds, though he did not know the names of birds.

How much did he know? You could say he had the broad strokes of things. He was only too well aware that he was an Irishman. He had a fair idea about the kind of lads who were coming in for burgers and chips: ordinary fellas, big eaters, red in the face from wind, hands like the buckets off JCBs, you'd imagine pulmonary disorders, midnight visitations. They were polite enough, made a certain amount of small talk. Nobody questioned or made direct comment on the fact of a new proprietor at the Uptown, but they were not unwelcoming of the stranger. One chap left a newspaper on the counter, which let him know he had a Tuesday on his hands. Somehow, this came as no great surprise. He had a quick look through the paper: odd, as if he knew things and, at the same time, did not know. The way that a cow looks at you in the moonlight. A cow will incline its head to one side, and it'll stare at you with big wet eyes, as if it is sure it has seen you somewhere before but can't quite place you. This is the way he was reading the paper. Captains of industry, streets of girls at dinner dances, young lads hurling, planning applications, weddings, births, deaths. All of it was strange but familiar.

According to a notice on the door, the Uptown closed early on week nights, at eleven bells, and stayed late the weekends. He wasn't going to argue with that and at eleven o'clock, he closed up and took to the quiet streets for a breath of fresh air. There was a spit of misty rain falling, which was nice after the heat of the fryer, and even at eleven o'clock there were still some flecks of daylight in the far western sky. It was May, alright, he'd been bang on the money there. He stood smoking outside a department store, cool as a breeze but when he looked in at the window display, he was hit by another tremor, and this one nearly laid him out. It was the mannequin of a lady that did it, she was got up in the latest gear, some kind of suede outfit, and the way the mannequin's face was set was kind of . . . off, kind of twisted. It was set in a kind of drunken leer. The brown, wavy hair falling to the shoulders just so, the green belligerent eyes, the suede jacket, the leer – he had seen this look before. It was the mother.

They are walking down College Road. It's the night-time. She is still a young woman, with a child on either side of her. He would be the

younger by a year or two, he might be seven years old. He has her by
one hand, and the other child, it has to be Denis, he has her by the
other. She can barely get along the street, she lurches, drags them
towards the railings. It's late, on a summer's night, and he has a bag of
groceries in his hand. They mustn't have had the tea yet. The woman
can't walk, she's crying, then she's laughing. She has a large brown bag
with chips wedged under her arm, the vinegar is oiling the paper, and
she almost drops it on the pavement as she misses her step.

'Mam,' he says, 'would you m-mind the chips, would yuh?'

The tremor passed on its way – down over the terraces of the town
it went, away into the melancholy hills – and he bolted for the first pub
he could find. By luck, it was quite a pleasant lounge bar and a handwritten notice on the door shakily announced that a pass-the-mike
session was in progress. Pint bottle of Bulmers, b-b-b-baby Powers,
times two, times three, and suddenly it was past midnight, and he was
in flying form. There was a chap had a Casio keyboard and he was
playing accompaniment to anybody who'd sing. A mike was passed
around the dim-lit lounge, left and right, left and right, now who has
the bar of a song for us? A woman called Mairead got up and
smoothed down her good blouse and did an outstanding version of
'Wind Beneath My Wings'. The landlord, a man called Johnny – big
sentimental face on him – came out over the bar and launched into
'The Day Billie Joe McAllister Jumped Off The Tallahatchie Bridge'.

'You'll learn a new one yet, Johnny!' somebody shouted, and
everybody laughed.

Pint b-bottle, please. Someone called Bob sang 'The Black Hills Of
Dakota', and wasn't asked to do another. After a while it got maudlin.
A lad called Michael Russell was asked to sing, and he sang 'The
Summer Wind', because that was some man called Coughlan's song
and half of the place couldn't handle this at all, the man of the
Coughlans was only a month in the ground.

'Fifty-two years of age!' cried Mairead.

Left and right, left and right, pass the mike.

'What about this gentleman here? What's your own name, sir?'

'Am . . . R-R-Richard,' he said.

'Will you sing one for us, Rich?'

'Ah stop!'

'Ah come on now, Richie!'

Where it came from, he did not know but he took that mike and he stood up square and he closed his eyes. He wasn't sweet – you couldn't say that – or melodic, no, but he was as big-voiced as they come, pure loud, a most powerful set of lungs. He sang 'Eternal Flame' by The Bangles.

'. . . cloh-ose yur eyes . . . gimme yur hand . . . darlin' . . . do you feel mah heart beat-iin' . . . do you unnerstan' . . . do you feel the PAAII-INN . . . am I own-lee dreeeamin' . . . or is this BURNIN' . . . an ee-ternal FLAME . . .'

There were people up off their stools howling for more. He pulled out a big one and let it rip – 'Crying' by Roy Orbison. He made a fair reach for the high notes even. From the corner of his good eye, he threw a shine in the direction of the lady Mairead. There didn't seem to be a husband in tow.

'It's hard to unnn-erstan' . . . how the touuuuuccch of yur haaan' . . . can star' me cryin' . . . cry-aye-ah-han . . . an' now ahm ohhh-furrrr yuh-hooooooo . . .'

There was no doubt about it but he had a big future ahead of him at the pass-the-mike session in Keogh's Lounge Bar on Clancy Street of a Tuesday night. They asked him to do a third one, but he said no, no, firmly. You got to know when to hold 'em, and know when to fold 'em.

And yes, one good eye. He was only walking away from Keogh's when it struck him that he was half blind. Leftie was firing blanks. He had a look up at the moon to be sure and he realised that the peripheries were indeed mightily skewed So. The clues were starting to come in. He was an R. K. Tobin, call him Richie. He had the lease of a chipper in Clonmel. He'd had a mother a demon drunk, and a brother by the name of Denis. He was half blind, and something told him there had been an accident, and he had got money from it, which was now down to less than six hundred euro. He knew his way around the inside of a deep-fat fryer, and home, for now, was a small unkempt room with a couch and a sink.

When he got there, he unscrewed the bottle of Cork gin and got good and familiar with it. He had the broad strokes of things and he knew that he had been drunk many thousands of times, mostly on account of the heebie jeebies. It was through no fault of his own but he was simply not the sort of man who was comfortable in the night-time. He was familiar with the motions of alcohol. The elevations of mood

were no news to him, nor the sudden dips. He knew what it was like
to drink big in small towns – it was hard work sometimes, you had to
have the same good time over and over again.

He picked up a golf magazine, then another, then noticed a
magazine near the bottom of the pile that did not seem to be in any
way, shape or form about golf. It was in fact a pornographic title and
as he flicked through it, sipping at the gin, he discovered its theme. It
was about women who dressed up by wearing animal tails. There was
mail order, even, where you could send off for a horse's tail attached
to a belt. Now maybe he was an innocent man for fifty, but this
was news to him and there in the grim room, at two in the morning,
it became an intense agitation. He got up off the couch and began
to pace.

'Is this what it's all about now?' he shouted. 'Is that what's supposed
to be going on around the place? Somebody's mother or somebody's
daughter? Hah? Going around a kitchen in a horse's tail? Stood over
a pan of sausages? Hah?'

He caught sight of the old quarehawk reflected in the window,
pacing and ranting, and that shut him up lively. He turned off the light
and lay down on the couch. He drew the malodorous anorak over his
head. An unquiet sleep came. There were images full of dark portent,
images of mountains and still water. It was an enormous relief when
he woke to grey light in the window. He went immediately downstairs – though it was just gone five in the morning – and he got busy
sorting out the grease traps. He looked out onto the street and it was
familiar but odd, as if streets were running into the wrong streets, as
if the hills were wrong, and the sky at a crooked slant, it was the
amalgam place of a dream out there. A tremor arrived with the rise of
the morning.

This student has been coming around Wednesdays for three or four
weeks now. He is doing a project about low-income families. Richie
thinks it's a disgrace, this fella is just a snoop, but his mother and father
put up with it because they're bored, is what it is, because they're on
the wagon, and they'll talk to just about anybody to escape the
monotony. The student has all these daft bloody questions. Tonight it's
about God and Mass and all that.

'Do you go to Mass yourself, Mrs Tobin?'

'Sometimes,' she says. 'Not that I believe that much in Jesus and stuff but it's just lovely sometimes, you know, if there's a choir and the way things are said.'

'The ritual, you mean,' he says. 'It's the ritual of the thing you admire?'

'Yeah.'

'And what about yourself, Mr Tobin?' he says. 'Do you have beliefs?'

'I don't know, really. I mean if you're asking me do I believe in miracles and walking on water and bread and fishes, I couldn't look you in the face and say oh I do, yeah. But if you're asking me when we're dead do we just lie around and rot in the ground like cabbage, well, I don't know that I believe that either.'

'And what about you, Richard?'

'Oh don't be asking him,' says the Da. 'Richie's a fucking pagan.'

He put a mop to the floor of the chipper. There was some relief in laying the suds down, squeezing the mop out in the wringer of the bucket, taking the suds up again. The day had arrived into Clonmel like a morbid neighbour, dour and overcast, the sky was low and dense, it was close in. As he swung the mop back and forth across the linoleum, things started to come apart altogether. He would begin to get a clear image, then somebody would drop a rock into the middle of the pool. Tremors queued up.

'Ah stop it for fuck sake,' he said.

But it's the Ummera Wood, he's fifteen years old and pustular, a hank of hair and hormones, and Denis is a year or two older. They're bush drinking – naggins of vodka. They sneak up on her quiet and she freaks out and screams, then laughs with relief 'cause she knows them – Denis and Richie. The three of them sit around drinking, and she's slagging them off because they're younger than she is. They drink the vodka. Denis gets quiet and moon-faced for a while, then he strikes up, he says Linda would you snog Richie, would yuh? Fuck off, she says, he's only a baby! Snog me so, he says. Nah, she says, you're too fucking ugly! And he has her by the hair then and she's down on the ground. What are yuh crying for, he says, we're only having a mess? And he's on top trying to screw her and Richie kneels down and puts his in her face and he says b-bite me and I'll fucking b-b-bate yuh.

He peeled spuds. He made batter for the burgers. He rolled out the potato cakes. He filleted the fish. He wondered where Denis had got to, and then he saw him: he was on his back underneath a Subaru Legacy at a garage outside a small town on a trunk road to Cork. He was covered in oil and diesel, there was junk everywhere, tarpaulin piles, dead Fiestas, tyres and wrenches, scrap iron, and Denis found that life was very hard sometimes because you cannot take a spanner to it.

(And love is very hard to do.)

Richie locked up the chipper for a while and he walked through the town to clear his head of all the crap that was building. He would stay in Clonmel for a time at least, nobody seemed to know him here – they say God looks after drunks and children. He walked to the town's far edge and there in the small garden of a house on a new-build estate, he saw a boy and a girl holding hands and crying and he went to them. He said, what's the matter? The dog is dead, she told him, and he asked the dog's name and she said the dog was called Honey, we had to bury Honey. He said I know a song about Honey and he sang the old Bobby Goldsboro number. A mother appeared at the front door, arms folded, thin smile, and he made a move back towards the centre of the town.

It was coming to life just then. Trim old ladies busied along towards the shops. Men were going into the ESB to talk about bills and easi-payment plans. He hummed to it all as he walked and then he thought that maybe if you tried hard enough you could transmit the thing itself out into the world and each time he passed somebody new he said lightly under his breath just the single word 'love', he said it to the postman and he said it to the guard, he said it to the old ladies and to the cats on the walls. The sun was making a good effort to come through the low banks of cloud; traffic streamed down for the new roundabout. Five sad slow notes played on a recorder. It was turning into June.

VISIT

Gerard Donovan

The first weekend in April began cloudy but broke into splinters of sunlight and gusts by afternoon on the Friday. I had driven the hundred or so miles from Galway to the nursing home that housed almost thirty residents, a recently built long T-shaped bungalow on the outskirts of Mullingar, and walked the long hall and read the book of familiar pages through open doors: the eyes that looked for someone familiar, and failing that, for a conversation. Those eyes held voices and followed you until you passed and sometimes called after you. I could not breathe my way along that hall. When I came to her door it was open as always, but slightly, and her face filled the narrow space; she was asleep, but lightly, and when I opened it wider, an expression I knew filled in the dormant spaces of that face with the person I knew. Left to their own devices, a few months alone can drain people of themselves, but here she was, and still herself. I bent to kiss her forehead.

A nurse looked into the room, smiled at me and closed the door. My mother turned her head on the pillow to the box of Cadbury's chocolates by the television.

Take one, Luke, there's plenty of them.

I adjusted the pillow at her neck. She lived in the armchair now because she was afraid of lying on her back, what would happen, how she might suffocate, never rise again. At a certain stage illness must take a shape and a name and move into the room with the sick, preferring a particular corner, and utterly silent, wait with an equal malaise. So she watched too and slept in the armchair, ate in it, and the pillow gave her little comfort, but she was lost without something to put behind her. At night the nurses piled a couple more on a footstool to elevate her legs. That was the routine, I wondered what thoughts occupy a body for months in an armchair when there's nothing to fan them away, no distraction, no business elsewhere. They must crowd close.

She asked me to open a window and we watched a show on the television before both falling asleep in the sharp light. I still hadn't recovered from the jet lag and woke after her, an hour or so later. She saw me move and laughed.

Looks like we were both out for the count.

I was out alright. I noticed that the sun had crept to the top corner of the window.

She turned. It's a lovely day.

A little over a long time had quickened to a lot over a short time. A few of our neighbours, the ones who made the trip from Galway to visit her, sometimes met in the hall, and I once heard them whisper how she looked so different recently. I wondered why people whispered when they wanted to keep things secret since whispers draw far more attention than ordinary speech. Who wants to listen to people talk? But whispers, now that must be important. I played my own part in the passage: I checked on her health with the nurses on the way out each time, and they answered, sometimes without looking up: She's fine and comfortable, which is what they said about every resident in the home. These are the best answers to the questions people ask to make themselves feel comfortable before they open the doors back to the sunlight and the fresh air of their own lives, the town they live in that is far away from there. A nursing home is after all a business: if you run one you want people sending their own parents there in time. You want people to leave feeling that they have done all they can, because it is a question of time.

I said to her, Do you want to go out?

She laughed. I haven't been out in ages. Months.

I opened the window and checked for clouds. Well it's fine, I said.

Okay then, she said.

I went down the hall and told the nurse on duty that I wanted to take my mother for a walk. I could see the nurse taking it in. She asked questions and answered them herself.

A walk? You mean outside to the lawn? Under the tree? Yes, we'll be right there.

Escape is also a matter of time. At a certain age and when the cities of the body no longer accept emissaries and require advance notice for anything, movement becomes a ritual like a king's procession, it builds into ceremonies of delay, whether to the bathroom or to the window, both of which are thousands of miles away. I waited in the lounge in front of the loud television while two nurses removed her from the armchair, dressed her, placed her in a wheelchair, and handed her the small plastic purse without which she would not leave. Twenty minutes later they brought her in a cardigan to the door of the waiting room. A blanket covered her legs, the smile had always been there.

Now there, she's ready, one of them said. Enjoy your walk, Mary.

I stood behind and wheeled her outside the building as we moved from shade to the bright late afternoon.

Where do you want to go? I said. Over there, by the tree?

Let's go out the gate, she said.

Out the gate – you mean out onto the road? I said.

Why not.

A car tore by. It was the busy route from the west into Mullingar.

Right or left?

Right, towards town.

The town centre was a mile along the freshly tarred road, and there was no pavement to it yet but flattened piles of stones from the construction, probably because no one was expected to be walking along it. I wheeled her beyond the white wall and immediately the wheelchair sank an inch into gravel that lined the edge for about a hundred yards. Up ahead a hard shoulder waited, but not here, and to the side of the gravel the high, untended grass pocked the dirt mounds. Back in the fields lay the undiscovered foundations of many houses to come, the rough magic of building sites, the cold cauldron of pools and cement.

I think the tyres are a bit light on air, I said, and dug my legs in for purchase and a sustained push to get the wheelchair moving; by coming at it from either side and shoving hard onto the handles or lifting them I was able to shift it onto the harder mix of dry clay and stones. I felt the sun and sweat on my neck, remembered when I worked in gardens, and why I hadn't done that in so long, the smell of a lifted shovel and clay, the promise of flowers, what you bury that soon waves effortlessly in the wind. We were moving now. Three cars sped by us in a group, and the breeze lifted the blanket off her legs.

I saw her nightdress under the cardigan. Are you cold?

Not at all, I'm fine. Let's keep going.

I leaned down and pushed in the right place. A little rocking along the uneven surface and jammed rocks held us back, but after five minutes – about a hundred yards – we reached the hard-shoulder section and moved easier until we passed where the river came close to the road. The water creased into a fan and we watched the white of a swan filter through the reeds. It did not weigh anything. A red wildflower leaned out of the grass on a stem that held it above the weeds. A bird sang from nearby, close enough to be invisible, and I didn't recognise the type of song. Perhaps for once the flower was singing and the bird was a blade of grass.

So keep going? I said.

Yes.

Another few hundred yards and the traffic thickened, people glancing out of their cars at this man pushing a woman along a road in a wheelchair, nothing but blank faces in glass fleeting by with glances that could be read in that instant, what this must be, what is happening, why is that woman on the road and who is that man and where could he be going; but they drove steadily on under the shifting cloud of the late afternoon sky probably because others were following right behind. Rolling easy on the smooth surface and picking up to walking speed I felt her weight in my hands, yet my hands held no weight. We were two parts of an enterprise only a half mile from town, and the going was good from there until we reached the first path and soon after that came to a petrol station, the briquettes stacked, the gas containers chained, the sign for prices, the first locals buying milk and bread.

I slowed. I'm going to put some air in the tyres. Is that okay?

That's fine.

I wheeled her into the station past the petrol pumps, past the shop and across to the machine off at the side where you put in your coin; a car stopped to let us pass – I waved thanks and lined the wheelchair up and waited as my mother found a coin in her purse, then fitted the hose to the valve of the right wheel, ratcheting until I heard the air sizzle like a morning fry. A man filling his tank gave us a second, a third turn of the head. Another car slowed as it pulled out, two faces stuck like old questions to the right rear window. When the first wheel felt firm, I filled the other. She looked ahead.

That's better, I said.

Meanwhile the entire station became one face that watched a woman in a wheelchair getting some air. It was possible that they did not see me as I was bent down to the wheel. Yes, a lady of some years had apparently stopped for air. As we rolled out of the station, wheels hard and ready for town, the attendant signalled out at us from the line of customers, his face connecting a laugh and a question in the recognition or hope that shows itself whenever something different comes your way and releases the handle of the ordinary. It was the closest anyone came to a word.

I was glad to be moving again. Even April can be chilly.

I said, Are we still going into town?

I think so. Feels much better, she said.

We made a left and reached a row of houses, and half an hour after we left the gate of the nursing home we passed a sweet shop on the other side of the main street in Mullingar. I pulled the wheelchair to the side to give my arms a rest. We were in the countryside of the town now, and people walked with shopping bags, stood aside and said good day.

I said, Would you like something?

She pulled the purse from under her blanket again. Not really, but you get something for yourself.

No, I've got enough.

She held out a wad of notes. Here, Luke. And get me some jelly babies.

She said she would be okay, and the chair was parallel to the road and not on any kind of slope. I folded the money and locked the wheels, crossed the road and walked into dark aisles of a small shop looking for jelly babies, stepping carefully and palming the packets for detail in the dark, like a cinema. The bags and wrappers rustled under my fingers, the same food that had passed a hundred playtimes and to which a hundred times we bent in rows of desks at school, slipping in a sweet under a teacher's gaze with a flick of the finger, then back up with the head to myths or triangles, whatever it was. The dim containers woke as my eyes got used to the light and recited their names: wine gums, jelly babies, fruit pastilles. I held a bag up to smell it.

Is that everything?

I looked behind me to the boy with the question who lingered at the cash register looking down the aisle at me. He had asked well, the right mix of suspicion and help. I waited at the counter as he rang me up and slid the coins out, placing them before me in a small stack. Outside I saw her sitting in the wheelchair, hands folded on her lap, and knew I was living the moment that says nothing, that will allow nothing said of consequence. I walked out of the shop and to the edge of the road, waited for the traffic to pass, holding the change she would insist I keep.

The cars kept coming. It was getting on in the day and after work. Dinners were ready, lights flooding rooms. The afternoon dramas like *Emmerdale Farm* were at an end, and soon it would be time for the news.

I looked again and put a foot out to cross but stepped back as more cars like black and red drops rose out of the nowhere at one end of the street and slid to the nowhere at the other end, each hiding her a second so that she disappeared and appeared like a film on reel. Then the string of traffic passed and the way was clear, and though it was time, I held the sweets and the change and still waited to cross.

My mother faced west where the sky breached the uneven rooftops and the early evening light pressed the orange doors of the houses. She was smiling. Her eyes were closed and her face was calm, turned to the sun.

EVERYTHING IN THIS COUNTRY MUST

Colum McCann

A summer flood came and our draft horse got caught in the river. The river smashed against stones and the sound of it to me was like the turning of locks. It was silage time and the water smelled of grass. The draft horse, Father's favourite, had stepped in the river for a sniff maybe and she was caught, couldn't move, her foreleg trapped between rocks. Father found her and called *Katie!* above the wailing of the rain. I was in the barn waiting for drips on my tongue from the ceiling hole. I ran out past the farmhouse into the field. At the river the horse stared wild through the rain maybe she remembered me. Father moved slow and scared like someone travelling deep through snow except there was no snow, just flood, and Father was frightened of water, always frightened. Father told me, *Out on the rock there girl*. He gave me the length of rope with the harness clip and I knew what to do. I am taller than Father since my last birthday, fifteen. I stretched wide like love and put one foot on the rock in the river middle and one hand on the tree branch above it and swung out over the flood.

Behind me Father said, *Careful now hai*. The water ran warm and fast and I held the tree branch, still able to lean down from the rock and put the rope to the halter of the lovely draft horse.

The trees bent down to the river in a whispering and they hung their long shadows over the water and the horse jerked quick and sudden and I felt there would be a dying, but I pulled the rope up to keep her neck above water, only just.

Father was shouting, *Hold the rope girl!* and I could see his teeth

clenched and his eyes wide and all the big veins in his neck, the same
as when he walks along the ditches of our farm, many cows, hedgerows, fences. Father is always full of fright for the losing of Mammy
and Fiachra and now his horse, his favourite, a big Belgian mare that
cut the soil in the fields long ago.

The river split at the rock and jumped fast into sprays coming up
above my feet into my dress. But I held tight to the rope, held it like
Father sometimes holds his last Sweet Afton at mealtime before
prayers. Father was shouting, *Keep it there girl good!* He was looking at
the water as if Mammy was there, as if Fiachra was there, and he
gulped air and he went down in the water to free the draft horse's hoof,
and he was gone so long he made me wail to the sky for being alone.
He kept a strong hold of one tree root but all the rest of his body went
away under the quick brown water.

The night had started stars. They were up through the branches. The
river was spraying in them.

Father came up spluttering for air with his eyes all horsewild and
his cap lost down the river. The rope was jumping in my hands and
burning like oven rings, and he was shouting, *Hold it girl hold it hai for
the love of God hold it please!*

Father went down in the water again but came up early, no longer
enough in his lungs to keep down. He stayed in the river holding the
root and the water was hitting his shoulders and he was sad watching
the draft horse drown, so I pulled hard again on the halter rope and the
horse gave a big scream and her head rose up.

One more try, Father said in a sad voice like his voice above
Mammy's and Fiachra's coffins long ago.

Father dipped under and he stayed down as long as yesterday's
yesterday, and then some headlights came sweeping up the town road.
The lights made a painting of the rain way up high and they put
shadows on the hedgerows and ditches. Father's head popped out of
the water and he was breathing heavy, so he didn't see the lights. His
chest was wide and jumping. He looked at the draft horse and then at
me. I pointed up the road and he turned in the flood and stared. Father
smiled, maybe thinking it was Mack Devlin with his milk truck or
Molly coming home from the sweet shop or someone come to help
save his favourite horse. He dragged on the tree root and struggled out

from the river and stood on the bank and his arms went up in air like he was waving, shouting, *Over here over here hai!*

Father's shirt was wet under his overalls and it was very white when the headlights hit it. The lights got closer and in the brightening we heard shouts and then the voices came clear. They sounded like they had swallowed things I never swallowed.

I looked at Father and he looked at me all of a sudden with the strangest of faces, like he was lost, like he was punched, like he was the river cap floating, like he was a big tree all alone and desperate for forest. They shouted out, *Hey mate what's goin' on?* in their strange way and Father said, *Nothing*, and his head dropped way low to his chest and he looked across the river at me and I think what he was telling me was, *Drop the rope girl*, but I didn't. I kept it tight, holding the draft horse's neck above the water, and all the time Father was saying but not saying, *Drop it please Katie drop it, let her drown*.

They came right quick through the hedge with no regard for their uniforms and I could hear the thorns ripping back against their jackets. One took off his helmet while he was running and his hair was the colour of winter ice. One had a moustache that looked like long grasses and one had a scar on his cheek like the bottom end of Father's barn hayknife.

Hayknife was first to the edge of the river and his rifle banged against his hip when he jumped out to the rock where I was halter holding. *Okay luv you're all right now*, he said to me and his hand was rain wet at my back. He took the halter and shouted things to the other soldiers, what to do, where to stand. He kept a hold of the halter and passed me back to LongGrasses who caught my hand and brought me safely to the riverbank. There were six of them now, all guns and helmets. Father didn't move. His eyes were steady looking at the river, maybe seeing Mammy and Fiachra staring back at him.

One soldier was talking to him all loud and fast, but Father was like a Derry shop window dummy and the soldier threw up his arms and turned away through the rain and spat a big spit into the wind.

Hayknife was all balance on the rock with the halter, and he didn't even hold the branch above his head. Icehair was taking off his boots and gun and shirt and he looked not like the boys from town who come to the barn for love, he looked not like Father when Father cuts hay without his shirt, no, he looked not like anybody, he was very skinny and strong with ribs like sometimes a horse has after a long day in the field. He didn't dive like I think now I would have liked him to, he just stepped into the water very slow and not show-offy and began making his way across, arms high in the air, getting lower. But the river got too deep and Hayknife was shouting from the rock saying, *Stay high Stevie, stay high side mate.*

And Stevie gave a thumb up to Hayknife and then he was down under the water and the last thing was the kick of the feet.

LongGrasses was standing beside me and he put Stevie's jacket on my shoulders to warm me, but then Father came over and he pushed LongGrasses away. Father pushed hard. He was smaller than Long-Grasses but LongGrasses bashed into the trunk of the tree and hit against it. LongGrasses took a big breath and stared hard at him. Father said, *Leave her alone can't you see she's just a child?* I covered my face for shame like in school when they put me in class at a special desk bigger than the rest, not the wooden ones with lifting lids, except I don't go to school any more since what happened with Mammy and Fiachra. I felt shame like the shame of that day in school and I covered my face and peeped instead through my fingers.

Father was giving a bad look to LongGrasses. LongGrasses stared at Father for a long time too and then shook his head and walked away to the riverbank where Stevie was still down in the water.

Father's hands were on my shoulders keeping me warm and he said, *It'll be all right now love*, but I was only thinking about Stevie and how long he was under water. Hayknife was shouting at the top of his voice and staring down into the water and I looked up and saw the big army truck coming through the hedgerows and the hedge was broken open with a big hole and Father screamed *No!*

The extra lights of the truck were on and they were lighting up all the river. Father screamed again *No!* but stopped when one of the soldiers stared at him, *Your horse or your bloody hedge mate.*

Father sat down on the riverbank and said, *Sit down Katie*, and I could hear in Father's voice more sadness than when he was over Mammy's and Fiachra's coffins, more sadness than the day after they were hit by the army truck down near the Glen, more sadness than the day when the judge said, *Nobody's guilty it's just a tragedy*, more sadness than even that day and all the other days that follow.

Bastards, said Father in a whisper, *bastards*, and he put his arm around me and sat watching until Stevie came up from the water swimming against the current to stay in one place. He shouted up at Hayknife, *Her leg's trapped*, and then, *I'm gonna try and get the hoof out*. Stevie took four big gulps of air and Hayknife was pulling on the halter rope and the draft horse was screaming like I never heard a horse before or after. Father was quiet and I wanted to be back in the barn alone waiting drips on my tongue. I was wearing Stevie's jacket but I was shivering and wet and cold and scared because Stevie and the draft horse were going to die, since everything in this country must.

Father likes his tea without bags like Mammy used to make and so there is a special way for me to make it – put cold cold water in the kettle and only cold then boil it then put a small boiling water in the teapot and swish it around until the bottom of the teapot is warm. Then put in tea leaves not bags and then the boiling water and stir it all very slowly and put on the teacosy and let it stew on the stove for five minutes making sure the flame is not too high so the teacosy doesn't catch flame and burn. Then pour milk into the cups and then the tea followed at last by the sugar all spooned around into a careful mix.

My tea fuss made the soldiers smile even Stevie who had a head full of blood pouring down from where the draft horse kicked him above his eye. Father's face went white when Stevie smiled but Stevie was very polite. He took a towel from me because he said he didn't want to get blood on the chair. He smiled at me two times when I put my head around the kitchen door and he held up one finger meaning *One sugar please* and a big O from fingers for *No milk please*. Some blood was drying in his hair and his eyes were bright like the sky should be, and I could feel my belly sink way down until it was there like love in the barn, and he smiled at me number three.

Everyone felt good for saving a life even a horse life, but Father was silent in the corner. He was angry at me for asking the soldiers to tea and his chin was long to his chest and there was a puddle at his feet. Everybody was towel drying except Father because there was not enough towels.

LongGrasses sat in the armchair and said, *Good thing ya had heat lamps guvnor*.

Father just nodded.

How was it under the water Stevie? said LongGrasses.

Wet, said Stevie and everybody laughed but not Father. He stared at Stevie then looked away.

The living room was bright now. I liked the green of the uniforms and even the red of Stevie's blood. But Stevie's head from the horse kick must have been very sore. The other soldiers were talking about how maybe the army truck should take Stevie straight off to hospital and not get dry, just get stitches, and not get tea, just come back later to see about the draft horse if she survives under the heat lamps. But Stevie said, *I'm okay guys, it's just a scrape, I'd kill for a cuppa*.

The tea tasted good from long brewing and we had biscuits for special visitors, I fetched them from the pantry. I bit one to make sure they were fresh and I carried out the tray.

I was sneezing but I was very careful to sneeze away from the tray so as to have politeness like Stevie. Stevie said, *God bless you* in his funny way and we were all quiet as we sipped on the tea but I sneezed again three four five times and Hayknife said, *You should change out of them wet clothes luv.*

Father put down his teacup heavy on the saucer and it was very quiet.

Everyone even the soldiers looked at the floor and the mantelpiece clock was ticking and Mammy's picture was staring down from the wall and Fiachra when he was playing football and the soldiers didn't see them but Father did. The long silence was longer and longer until Father called me over, *Come here Katie*, and he stood me by the window and he took the long curtain in his hands. He turned me around and wrapped the curtain around me and he took my hair and started rubbing not tender but hard. Father is good, he was just wanting to dry my hair because I was shivering even in Stevie's jacket. From under the curtain I could see the soldiers and I could see most of all Stevie. He sipped from his tea and smiled at me and Father coughed real loud and the clock ticked some more until Hayknife said, *Here, guv, why don't you use my towel for her?*

Father said, *No thanks*.

Hayknife said, *Go on guv*, and he put the towel in a ball and made to about throw it.

Father said, *No!*

Stevie said, *Take it easy*.

Take it easy? said Hayknife.

Maybe you should all leave, said Father.

Hayknife changed his face and threw the towel on the ground at Father's feet and Hayknife's cheeks were puffing and he was breathing hard and he was saying, *Fat lot of fucken thanks we get from your sort Mister*.

Hayknife was up on his feet now and pointing at Father and the light shone off his boots and his face was twitching so the scar looked like it was cutting his face. LongGrasses and Stevie stood up and they were holding Hayknife back, but Hayknife was saying, *Risk our fucken lives and save your fucken horse and that's all the thanks we get, eh?*

Father held me very tight with the curtain wrapped around me and he seemed scared and small and trembly. Hayknife was shouting lots and his face was red and scrunched. Stevie kept him back. Stevie's face was long and sad and I knew he knew because he kept looking at Mammy and Fiachra on the mantelpiece beside the ticking clock. Stevie dragged Hayknife out from the living room and at the kitchen door he let go. Hayknife turned over Stevie's shoulder one last time and looked at Father with his face all twisted but Stevie grabbed him again and said, *Forget it mate*.

Stevie took Hayknife out through the kitchen and into the yard towards the army truck and still the rain was coming down outside and then the living room was quiet except for the clock.

I heard the engine of the army truck start.

Father stood away from me and put his head on the mantelpiece near the photos. I stayed at the window still in Stevie's jacket which Stevie forgot and hasn't come back for yet.

I watched the truck as it went down the laneway and the red lights on the green gate as it stopped and then turned into the road past where the draft horse was lifted from the river. I didn't hear anything then just Father starting low noises in his throat and I didn't turn from the window because I knew he would be angry for me to see him. Father was sniffling, maybe he forgot I was there. It was going right down into him and it came in big gulps like I never heard before. I stayed still but Father was trembling big and fast. He took out a handkerchief and moved away from the mantelpiece. I didn't watch him because I knew he would be shamed for his crying.

The army truck was near out of sight, red lights on the hedgerows.

I heard the living room door shut then the kitchen door then the pantry door where Father keeps his hunting rifle then the front door and I heard the sound of the clicker on the rifle and him still crying going further and further away until the crying was gone and he must have been in the courtyard standing in the rain.

The clock on the mantelpiece sounded very loud so did the rain so did my breathing and I looked out the window.

It was all near empty on the outside road and the soldiers were going around the corner when I heard the sounds, it wasn't like bullets, it was more like pops one two three.

The clock still ticked.

It ticked and ticked and ticked.

The curtain was wet around me but I pulled it tight. I was scared, I couldn't move. I waited it seemed like for ever.

When Father came in from outside I knew what it was. His face was like it was cut from stone and he was not crying anymore and he didn't even look at me, just went to sit in the chair. He picked up his teacup and it rattled on the saucer so he put it down again and he put his face in his hands and stayed like that. The ticking was gone from my mind and all was quiet everywhere in the world and I held the curtain like I held the sound of the bullets going into the draft horse, his favourite, in the barn, one two three, and I stood at the window in Stevie's jacket and looked and waited and still the rain kept coming down outside one two three and I was thinking oh what a small sky for so much rain.

CURFEW

Sean O'Reilly

There were four other men in the room apart from his Da and his big brother Eamon. They were all finishing off their cans of beer, not talking. It was cold and some of them were still wearing their coats. With the curtains left open, the room was darker than the street but nothing was moving out there. Fergal could see as far as the corner where The Frankie and the rest of that crowd used to hang about before all this started.

– Glad you're back then?

That was Mr Harley's voice, only you couldn't be sure which one he was of the shadows in the dark room. His Da was the one near the fireplace. Eamon was a dead cert with the wagging leg on the sofa. There was a sigh from his big brother which could have either meant yes or no, and he raised the can and dipped back his head to drain it.

– It's always hard.

Eamon crushed the tin in his hand. There was some laughing. His Da was laughing too loud.

– Did you come to that conclusion on your bed Fluff or some other place of permanent repose? Mr Deaney said. Mr Deaney always spoke as if he thought he was at a funeral. Mr Harley was laughing as well. Fergal didn't know the man Fluff. The laughing stopped when Eamon struck a match and their faces appeared and their shadows stretched up the walls.

His Da got out of the chair and stood in front of the fireplace. He took something out of his trouser pocket and left it on the mantelpiece.

He put his hands behind his back and sighed and shook his head. This was a room for important occasions. There used to be ornaments in the glass cabinet under the window. No fire was ever lit in the grate.

– Go and fucken ask wee Jimmy Glyn if you want to know about doubt.

That was his Da, like he couldn't keep it to himself any longer.

After a while Mr Deaney said, almost whispering, We can't be sure, that's all I'm trying to say. Nothing more.

– Who the fuck else would do it? Tell me that one, his Da answered straight away.

– There's no other way of thinking about it, Mr Walsh said from the chair in the corner. Mr Walsh sang at Mass some Sundays with his eyes closed.

Mr Deaney stayed quiet. In the dark his Da made noises of disbelief. Mr Harley leaned forward and put his elbows on his knees. The man beside Eamon changed his position on the sofa a few times.

– Sure who knows anything for sure? If you ask me, some things are impenetrable and we'd be in some state if they weren't.

That was Fluff again.

– Our Fergal's laughing at you there, Fluff, Eamon the bastard came out with. He's sitting there and he thinks it's wile funny what you jist said.

– Is he now? Fluff said, pushing himself up to the edge of the sofa.

– Leave the wee fella alone, went Mr Deaney's voice.

– Aye, and that's another thing, James, Eamon went on to Mr Deaney. Y'know this wee brother here of mine. Well, I've been hearing stories about him and your wee girl Nuala. They're a big item from what I've heard. Always hanging about together and sneaking off y'know like. You'd need to watch him so you would.

His Da let out a big roar like it had come down the chimney and that was the sign for them all to start shouting and cheering. Fluff clapped his hands like it was the first time he had learned. Mr Deaney put his fingers in his mouth and made a whistle. Eamon threw the squashed can across the room at Fergal's head.

He went out of the room and up the stairs. Behind him, his Da was calling and them all laughing and whistling. Fergal sat on the bed and put his feet into his boots still soft from the polishing he had given them the night before. No way was he staying in now whoever was giving the orders. All day dobbing around the docks he wished he had gone to school instead of having to listen to Harkin going on about the big slaughter and the spoils. He was glad when he got home and lay down on the bed and he must have fallen asleep with his coat on. He woke sweating. It would be a better laugh to stay in he decided, with the house all to himself, and he could wait for them to come back to hear the stories. There would probably be a crowd and he could stay up late listening to the stories and maybe he'd be slipped a tumbler of whiskey. Fuck all that now. He was going out this night and it was their bloody problem if he was caught or kidnapped by whoever it was.

He put a knife down his boot and went over to the window to watch for the men leaving. The black sky seemed to slant down into the street. Stars crawled up it. The lights were out in the houses along the street except Downey's where the da gave out marbles up the town and called them gifts. The men's voices came up through the floor; they were arguing by the sound of it. Thinking again, Fergal took off the boots and pushed them under the bed. He went back to the window. A few nights before he had been standing in the same spot when Walker and two men called at the door. Walker had the dogs with him. His Da was out of his sight in the doorway, apart from his arm that stuck out once and pointed up into the sky. Walker did most of the talking and he patted the dogs on the head. Fergal went down the stairs and asked who it was but his Da started shadow boxing and laughing and Fergal got a bad punch on the ear.

The bedroom door opened and Eamon was there with one arm in his coat. Fergal kept his back to him and tried to stare at the snapped lamp post at the corner like it was his own staring that had the power to break it. Eamon said something and pulled the zip up on his coat.

– You going to be a good wee boy then? You huffing?

– Fuck off, Fergal mouthed silently to the window.

– Don't you fucken move out this house. Right. You hear me?

Fergal turned to face his brother. You think you can jist come back and . . .

Eamon stared him down. Aye I do, he said.

– I hope somebody knocked your head off one night.

Eamon did his sarcastic laugh and put up his fists for a mock fight.

– Put on your pyjamas now wee boy, he said, and I'll be back in a while to read you a story. Once upon a time there was this wee shithead who didn't listen to what his big brother told him. You can make the rest up yourself.

Running through the streets at night, with the curtains flicking open in the blacked-out houses, like he was charging the darkness itself, Fergal let a scream out of him which made the hair on his neck move. A dog howled back and he screamed again. A man in a vest appeared at a window who was the da of that wee lad Brown who was always too sick to come out of the house. He picked up stones on the move. He took aims and drew back his arm at an old cooker in the street, a lamp post, the window of an empty house, a car door in a tree, some shape at a corner, a beer keg, a coat lying over a gate and launched stones at the darkness itself.

Outside a group of three wrecked houses which stood alone above an embankment, he gave the whistle, like the sound of a bomb dropping. Harkin didn't answer. He climbed in through a window hole and whistled again and then he moved into the next house through a gap in the wall and looked up at bony rafters all pointing to the same spot in the sky where there was nothing. The third house had a roof and half of the upper floor but you had to climb up the back of the chimney to get to the supply of weapons and blankets stored up there. He drifted back into the middle house and sat on a mound of bricks under the rafters which were like hands about to pray. No matter what Harkin said, it was safer on the ground and easier to escape if somebody came after you and you wouldn't be cornered. Up above you were stuck and had just to wait if you heard a noise and grip your wee knife and hope and it might be something you'd have no chance of tackling all along.

It was the same in the hut. A twig breaking or a rustle and you had to charge out and attack, not just sit there holding your breath and hoping like Harkin. Huts are for hiding, Harkin always says. They are invisible under the ground. That's the point of them. Nobody will find you if it's a good hut and the ground's well camouflaged. Fergal believed most of this was right but you would never know if it was a bad hut until it was too late. A hut is about the person or thing outside being as afraid to come tearing in as you are to rush out. But what if they didn't have the same fear? And the things without fear? There might be things without fear.

It must be more than two months now since they were both down there the last time. The hut was in a clearing behind the trees and bushes on Hunch Lane. This was the biggest hut they had built and there were different rooms with walls made out of muck which they smoothed flat and candles and carpet they found near the reservoir. The roof was corrugated sheets from a shutdown pub, supported by bricks and stakes of wood and they replaced the sods on top of it in the same order they were cut. They carried bramble bushes from out the back roads and covered the entry.

That last time was just before all the trouble started and they were drinking a bottle of cider and Harkin was talking about what he was going to do with his life as though it mattered and Fergal was listening and asking himself why he never thought about questions like this. The bottle got emptied and Harkin shut up for a while. They heard laughter outside the hut then. Right outside the entrance, and moving across the roof above their heads where the bramble was packed tight. Harkin grabbed him by the arm to wait.

The laughter went on and on without fading or getting louder. A midget man out walking in the dark, laughing away to himself for the sake of it – that's what it sounded like. Harkin whispered something and shook his head at the same time not to chance it. Fergal elbowed him out of the way and threw himself towards the opening and screamed with the knife out. He stood up in the brambles swiping his knife and there was nothing to be seen. It was quiet. Harkin crawled out with a sewer rod. A moon was up and nothing was escaping through the brambles and trees. They waited and watched for a long while and then they walked home without talking about it. Fergal went into the backyard and looked in the window and he saw Eamon had come back and he was sitting in the chair near the fire with his coat still on.

Now, squatting on the bricks in a roofless house, he heard a girl's voice say his name. The face of Nuala Deaney was looking in at him through the window hole.

– You were dreaming.

– I was like fuck.

– I could have got you there.

– What you doing out?

– Same as you, she said. Enjoying myself.

She disappeared from the window and Fergal dragged his feet through the bricks on the floor and jumped out into the street after her.

– Does your da know? he called to her.

– Does my da know what?

– He was round at ours.

– I wouldn't put it past him.

Nuala Deaney was still in her school uniform which they called a pinafore with a baseball cap on her head and her ponytail pulled through the space in the back. The cap was new. IHS was written along the front in white letters and he wanted to ask about those letters. He watched her skim some broken slates over the wire. She picked up a bit of wood.

– So did you hear? she started to question him, flipping a stone into the air and batting it over the wire that ran down one side of the embankment. About the cows up on the hill? WACK. Drained all the blood out of them. And that wee girl WACK in the stream? They – shite

– I thought you'd be with your Eamon.

– He's a fucken bastard jist.

– So do you think WACK it's the gypsies or not?

– It has to be. Dead cert.

– Why? She turned to look at him.

– Who else is it going to be? Aul Mrs Kerrigan like? He pulled himself up on the windowsill.

– Harkin WACK doesn't think it is.

– Does he? He didn't say that to me. He's showing off jist. And where is he now the slabber?

WACK.

Fergal watched the stone vanish into the darkness like that was where it belonged all the time.

– Is your Eamon – shite – going to stay then?

– Fucken hope not.

– Shite, that's two in a row.

– Not a good sign, Fergal said. I wouldn't chance another one.

– I have to, Nuala said, but as she was searching for the right stone they both noticed the movement of lights among the trees away out across the fields they knew were there in the darkness. Fergal jumped down off the window and walked over to the edge of the embankment. They watched the lights. Nuala threw the bit of wood up into the air and neither of them moved when it landed behind them among the old slates.

The tall wooden gates into Frederick Farm were tied back to the trees. Torch beams flashed and lopped and swiped through the dark and the trees and the muck and men's faces at all angles. Cars and vans made a line on each side of the lane. Up ahead, a tractor stood in the greenish light from the open farmhouse door. Fergal thought he had caught a glimpse of his Da at the front of the crowd. He heard Mad Hugo's laugh before he spotted him, along with Eamon, drinking from a bottle. Slanty was looking down at the muck, probably worrying about his shoes and wondering whether to give his hair a quick comb before the action. There were many faces and cars he didn't recognise.

Nuala wouldn't stop talking no matter how many times he told her. He gave up waiting for Harkin at the houses and ran across the fields, followed by Nuala talking and trying to be stupid by falling over or pretending she'd broken her ankle. The crowd was faced towards the gates and the farmhouse so the two of them hid behind a shed at the back. The branches lay on the shed roof like they were exhausted. Nuala scraped the moss off the corner of the shed with her bangle. She was saying something about Harkin now.

Harkin was a mouth. After all his talk about the spoils, he was too scared to sneak out. He was always making plans he never stuck to. If Harkin went to the shop for you, he came back with something different and if it was his idea to cut brambles out the back roads, he'd dander off and start fishing with his hands in a stream.

– Well that's what he told me, Nuala was saying. That there was this girl and she came to your hut some nights.

– Our hut?

– Naw, aul Mrs Kerrigan's. Harkin told me she was older and he didn't know who she was.

– A girl?

– She might have been a gypsy for all he knew, that's what he told me.

– He's a fucken mouth. When like? Sure we haven't been down there in ages. He's fucken slabbering so he is.

Nuala hissed at him to keep his voice lower.

– He's a fucken lying bastard.

– Maybe you weren't there.

– What? I'd know jist. Sure what's a girl going to be doing in our hut? He's making it up. He is.

Nuala was pointing now.

– He's jist making it up, Fergal went on. Sure where is he now and he wouldn't shut up all week?

Nuala elbowed him.

Four men were coming down the path from the farmhouse. One of them held a torch aimed at the ground. The crowd went silent and closed together and their torches were lowered, lighting up the legs in the muck and the sky and trees went darker. The four men stopped at the gate as if it was the edge of a cliff. The crowd waited way below. The one in the hat who was definitely Walker took a step forward over the edge the same as on Sundays when he stood out in the aisle with the collection baskets or was coming towards you with his hand out to tell you to stop talking. The dogs followed him. Half Kerry Blue and half greyhound. They hung and cowered at his heels like things that knew they were strange and beyond pain and they sat upright in the muck with their ears pointed to the sound of his voice.

– How are we the night boys? Smell the soil on the air, boys. The aroma of solitude. Black honey. Drink it in, boys. The heart aches and the blood burns to be at peace. Even the animals know this. Even an animal knows the time to act. And bear in mind there are ones at home tonight, men with nothing to do. We have sat around for long enough, watching the shadows cross the windows, listening to the scratchings behind the door, where there is no window and where there has never been a door. We have all been hiding, boys. Hiding our heads in the sand. But fear is no compass. There is no map for the wilderness before us. What does the soul call out across the wilderness?

– I'm thirsty, Mad Hugo let him hear. Some of the crowd laughed and the talking swelled and ceased suddenly.

– Very true, said Walker, shifting the brim of his hat. But we need clear heads, boys, not moonshine. Not the wildness of men who do not even recognise their own front door. The faces of friends. Where is the moon tonight, boys? The moon is the light of fools and cowards. The dream of men without a home. But bear one thing in mind, boys: they are not afraid of us. Do not break off on your own. I want us all to go home to our beds tonight and sleep without regret or shame. Now, before I hand you over to Frederick here, I would ask that young lad over yonder, maybe two of them, to step out from behind that shed and show himself. Or on their own heads be it.

With the words a hundred torch beams seemed to grab hold of them among the trees. For a few seconds there was only a blazing light in the world like it must have been at the very beginning of things. Fergal looked into the glare and wondered at the sense of having seen it before. He thought he heard his name said. Hurried streaks of lights broke away from the bright source and then he heard voices. Even then, he might not have moved out of the path of the lethal wands if he had not recognised his brother's voice near him. He ran for it. Keeping low, he made it through the trees and across a path into bushes and through the long grass at the edge of a field. He remembered Nuala. All he had to do was keep out of sight for long enough and they would give up in case they missed the action at the farm. He wondered if they had got Nuala.

Eamon was the first out into the field, slashing the torch around like a sword, across the ground, the trees and up into the sky. Someone else limped out next who was Mad Hugo. Eamon ran further on into the field, slicing and stabbing the dark with the torch. Mad Hugo shouted. Eamon was moving in circles. Mad Hugo shouted again and headed back into the bushes. Fergal watched his older brother kick the ground. He put the torch under one arm and cupped his hands around his mouth. If that's who I think it is, you're dead meat, wee brother.

Fergal closed his eyes in the long grass and laughed. Whatever happened when he went back to the house, who caught him, what punishments, even if the worst gypsies got their hands on him, it wouldn't matter because they would never be able to beat the image out of him of Eamon in the dark field jabbing with his torch. Since that night in the backyard when he saw Eamon sitting there with his coat still on, the house seemed to grow bigger and bigger like a castle you couldn't find a way out of. The rooms were so big you had to whisper. He went in and he could tell from the light and the air that Eamon and his Da had been sitting there for hours without a word. The thing was, Eamon didn't seem to be changed by being away. Four years should do something to you. Fergal had always imagined his brother in big cities crowded with people and noise. Sometimes he hoped they would hear about his death in mysterious circumstances and everyone would ask him and no funeral was possible. He searched his brother's face and his accent and his clothes and under the bed and followed him about the streets and waited outside pubs and in rooms with him for some sign or mark or bit of evidence of a story. His brother might as well have been living under the ground for those years. Even the ornaments on the mantelpiece changed over the years. The wall around the backyard was different. Even a man in jail has a story to tell. He asked his Da and his Da said, You jist get sick of it. It's only yourself you're kidding.

He ran towards a paler patch in the dark where he could see through the high branches to the stars. The heavy whiffs of pine stung his eyes. He was sweating already and the sweat smelled of the pine and took it under his skin. He was working towards the reservoir. When he circled back to the farm he found the cars in the empty clearing, the gates closed and the footprints in the muck filling with water and reflecting the stars. He climbed through bushes into wet mossy ground and on into a grove of ferns and up a slope on the trunk of a tree to a stony area where a foundation pit had been dug in the past and the cement powder was hard in the bags.

Still there were no voices or signs of people. He looked back but there was nothing to see. He found himself wishing he had stayed in the house like he wanted and waiting for them to come back to tell him all about it. He ran on to put a stop to the thought. Near where the stream should be, he halted and lay down on the hollow-feeling ground.

Over on the right, he saw a shaking glow between the columns of the trees of a fire about a good stone's throw away. For a long while he watched for movement. The fire was weakening in a ring of stones. The ground around was stirred up and scattered like there were plenty of feet. Somebody had taken a piss against a tree. Lifting a hot stick, he sifted through the pieces in the fire. Deep in the ash, he turned something over and hooked it clear to get a better look. He was a long time finding it again. He kicked the smoking thing back towards the light of the fire and saw it was a blackened skull and hairy with cinders and needles.

He dropped the branch and knife and ran, trying to listen past the thumping of his feet for another sound in pursuit of him. To the left, he saw a barbed wire fence with a slope down to the over-flow basin. Straight ahead were trunks of different sizes and some had fallen into the arms of others. Beyond that leaves whipped his face. He went over a hidden wall and found himself surrounded by nettles taller than him. He pulled the jumper up over his face and charged in.

At the brambles he stopped. He was running without a notion of what he wanted and he knew that was a mistake. He told himself to think. He could try the hut or get back out on to the path and head for the farm along the lanes. There were weapons in the hut they had never collected. The sky was greener now, the stars grey. He made a move for the hut and stopped. He let a shout out of him because he couldn't decide. While the shout was still in the air, the back of his knees caved in and he dropped forward into the brambles. A boot to the arms brought him face down into the scalding thorns and hooks. Another one under the ribs made him wretch. He saw his Da looking up into the morning sky and a bird flying past with a clump of his youngest son's hair in its bloody beak. He saw Eamon chasing burning dogs around the streets with bits of his brother tied to their tails. Harkin and Nuala hid his tongue in a box under the bed and Harkin told her stories about the gypsies.

– Sweet mother of fuck I didn't know it was you, Fergal hi. You alright? Fuck me I hadn't a clue who it was. That shout just scared the life out of me.

That was Mad Hugo's voice.

A boot turned him over and the light slammed into his eyes and the cuts.

– I fucken warned you didn't I eh? What the hell are you up to ya wee fucker?

So Eamon was there too.

– Who is it? said Slanty from further away.

– It's wee fucken Fergal so it is, said Mad Hugo. I nearly killed him the wee man.

Eamon knelt on his chest and put the torch in his face.

– What the fuck you up to?

– I can't see. Move the torch.

– I don't give a fuck. What are you up to?

– Is he on his own?

– I don't know, Fergal tried to tell them. I can't see with that in my eyes. I was over in the forest. There was this fire.

– Who were you with in the forest?

– I don't know. There was this fire and then I ran over here to the hut and – Fergal got a slap on the side of the head.

– What hut? Eamon said.

– In there. Move the light.

Eamon's mouth was right against his ear now. Y'see if you're up to anything, y'see if you are wee bro, I'm going to beat your head in non-stop for a fortnight.

It went dark and he lay there on his back listening to the three talking. They had chased somebody into the brambles. Slanty wanted to give up and find the rest. Eamon was all set for staying. Mad Hugo told him to take it easy. Slanty wanted reinforcements and Eamon told him to wise up. They were carrying crowbars.

Mad Hugo pulled Fergal up to his feet and slapped him on the back.

– You'll be alright wee lad.

Fergal touched the blood on his face. He sniffed the pine smell from the blood on his finger.

– Who else knows about this hut then?

– Nobody. Me and Harkin just.

The torchlight hit him in the face again.

– What about our wee Nuala?

– Naw.

– Y'sure? Where is she the night then?

– I don't know. I can't fucken see.

– And nobody else knows.

– Naw. I haven't showed it to anyone anyway.

– Just you and Harkin and nobody else ever set foot in it?

– Naw. Harkin might of but I didn't.

A hand gripped him by the neck. Eamon's face was there in front of him.

– Harkin might of what?

– I don't know.

– Harkin might of fucken what?

– He said this girl knew about it but he was only fucken lying. He was just making it up.

– What girl?

– I don't know.

– Say I don't know again and I'll ram this down your throat.

The cold claw of the crowbar touched his swollen lip.

– I fucken don't. He said he didn't know her either. He was jist fucken slabbering so he was. He said it was this gypsy girl but he —

Fergal felt himself falling backwards into the brambles again. He couldn't tell where he had been hit, in the stomach or across the head. Eamon was battering the brambles with the crowbar. Mad Hugo said he knew all along it was a girl they had seen. Fergal thought of the old kings burned on the top of bonfires. He thought of boats on fire crossing the horizon. For every star there was a cut in his face. He was floating on a cloud of burning brambles. He closed his eyes and drifted like smoke across the fields and through the streets.

They made him stand up and told him he was going into the hut to see who was there and any funny business and they would strip the skin off him. Fergal asked for a torch but Eamon stopped Mad Hugo handing him one. They wouldn't give him a weapon to protect himself. He felt a jab from the crowbar between his shoulders and he stepped forward through the brittle cloud at his feet. He saw the underground rooms of the huts and the smoke filling the dark if he didn't come out again. But what if it wasn't empty and this girl was inside? Maybe there was a mad horde of them in there. Harkin might be involved with it and that's why he had told Nuala as a sort of warning. Fergal looked back at the three of them and a light struck his face. One of them spoke, probably Eamon. What if it was them? Eamon might be in on it. Where was everybody else? Eamon came back around the time it all started. They must bloody know already who was in there.

He sucked in his breath for the pain and made a jump to the right and ran towards the gap in the hedges. He knew exactly where it was. They were after him straight away. Eamon was shouting. Mad Hugo laughed. There was a low strip of barbed wire you had to avoid. Another jump and he landed in the ditch and crawled out of there into the lane on his hands and knees. He slid back in again and gripped the grass to pull himself out. His brother landed in there behind him just as Fergal made the path again. Another light exploded in his face and a boot pressed him down into the muck. He was ordered to stay very still and he lay feeling the cold muck against the hacked face. A dog was growling. Above him he could hear the low voices like these were

men meeting any night on the street under his window. Something
sharp with a thick point scraped the side of his neck but it wasn't
metal. Then in his ear an animal panted and sniffed up his smell.

What's the joke there, Paddy?
– Talk about half hung.
– You could see right through.
– Some handful.
– What's the word for it?
– I missed that bit.
– More's the power to him.

Nuala was sitting beside him on the floor with her knees up. Her hat
was lost. He had some whiskey in a tumbler from Mad Hugo. His Da
started off being against any drink but then he forgot. When he sipped
it, the cuts stung on his lip and up his face. Nuala wanted him to go
into the hall with her or up the stairs to tell him something important
she said. Imagine them all laughing and jeering if he went out of the
room and Nuala behind him. He couldn't tell her that. Harkin was
looking at him and trying to wink at him from the other side of the
room, on the scran for butts. With the lights on, the window was wet
black now like a puddle. Eamon and Mad Hugo were taking the hand
out of Fluff in the corner. Walker was in for a while. There were a lot
more people in the room than there were chairs for. The smoke drifted
past the two lamps on the wall and up to the ceiling and he wondered
if it was warmer up there and the voices were louder up there. Where
do voices go? he said to Nuala and she banged her head with the palm
of her hand at him. Harkin's da was pouring a can of stout into a glass
on the arm of the sofa. Muck was hardening on the carpet with bits of
grass stuck in the prints. The men's shoes were steaming which made
him want to laugh. You see their shoes, he said to Nuala. She elbowed
him and gave him that stare which meant listen to me with my hair
hanging over my face. His Da was standing in front of the fireplace
with his elbow on the mantelpiece between the clock that never
worked and the fiddle player in the cage.
– Have a bet on it then? Put your money where your whatever you
call it is. There was about six of us and he was still kicking about. Aye,
up near the reservoir. Didn't give in easy, I'll tell you that. Naw, on past

that. Sure I had him by the leg. Aye, so I heard. He shouldn't have been out of the bloody house in the first place. That's what you get. Sure if you look at him the wrong way he goes up the stairs to huff. Aye. Hi Dandy, where's the wee woman the night? Aw aye. That's not what I heard. Who you kidding? Aye, Tony said it, some dogs alright. For fuck's sake, it was dripping off them when they came out. Aye, one of them was limping, I saw that myself. Aye, the younger one. Aye, Walker'll be fucken sore if he's forced into it. I'd bet you my front teeth if I had any. Aye, but at least I didn't fucken sell mine, eh Larkey, and for what, eh for what?

The laughing.

Huala was shaking her head in front of his face and her hair was flying around like she was falling down a hole. He took another taste of the whiskey. There must still be a thorn in his lip. Eamon helped him wash his face when they got back to the house. They walked home together through the streets only he couldn't remember all of it. There was nothing between Baldrick Hill and Florence Street. Nuala put her face right up to his ear and he saw the skull lying in the fire covered with pine needles the way her hair danced across the cuts on his face. She was saying she was there as well, hiding in the trees, and she saw the dogs go in and they came out again and nothing happened and they tore the roof off the hut and it was empty and nothing happened. Do you hear me Fergal? she was saying, there was nothing there. He heard her but he was thinking about the walk back with Eamon and whether it was an order from Walker or Eamon had put himself forward. That didn't matter anyway. An order is like a puddle in the street. The dog might drink from it but that doesn't mean it's thirsty. Eamon said that on Rosemount Avenue when they saw two mongrels bent over a puddle. One of them stopped first and then the other one ran back and started slurping beside it. Eamon stood watching them like it was important. The dogs ran on and the puddle settled and then the second one returned and had another drink, looking around like it thought it was being crafty. Eamon winked at him and talked about a dog they used to have called Sundance, a wee golden retriever. Fergal didn't remember it but Eamon insisted that he did and kept stopping in the streets and telling him. Fergal wondered that maybe he was making it up for a laugh but the way Eamon went on about it made it hard not to believe him. He said Sundance could do loads of tricks and you could never leave it alone in the house or it wouldn't look at you for days. Fergal didn't remember. Eamon went on about it the rest of the way down Rosemount and they never saw a single person. One day they let the dog out and it never came back he said, dabbing Fergal's face in the kitchen. It was probably running wild in the hills somewhere. Mad Hugo and a few others turned up with drink and sat down at the kitchen table. Mad Hugo made toast and gave Fergal a slice, but he didn't say anything. They were all talking about different things and the stories started up.

LANGUAGE, TRUTH
AND LOCKJAW

Bernard MacLaverty

Norman sat in the dentist's waiting room. Outside, the rain needled down from a grey sky. The wet shining roofs descended like steps to the sea. Because he was an emergency he had to wait for over an hour while people with appointments filed past him.

Then the dentist's bespectacled head appeared round the door and said,

'Mr Noyes?'

There were two dentists on the island and it was immediately obvious to Norman that he had picked the wrong one. As he called out his secret codes to his assistant he breathed halitosis. He dug into the molar that was causing the trouble and Norman yelled, his voice breaking embarrassingly.

'That seems to be the one,' said the dentist. 'I don't think we can save it. It's a whited sepulchre.'

He went to the window and filled a large syringe. Before he approached the chair he considerately hid it behind his back.

'Open up,' he said. 'That should go dead in a minute. On holiday?'

'Yes.'

'The weather has been poor.'

'You can say that again.'

He had known from the minute the trip had been proposed that everything would go wrong. Patricia said that he had helped in no small measure to *make* it go wrong by his bloody-minded attitude.

When *she* was a child on holiday her father, when it rained, had dressed them up in bathing suits and wellies and Pakamacs and taken them for riotous walks along the beach. He had litten – her own word – blue smoke fires with damp driftwood. But now when it rained he, Norman, retreated to the bedroom with his books. His defence was that he had work to do and that he had agreed to the trip only on condition that he could finish his paper on Ryle.

'What do you do?' asked the dentist.

'I teach. Lecturing at the University.'

'Oh. What in?'

'Philosophy.'

'That's nice.'

Things were beginning to happen in his jaw like pins and needles.

'Where are you staying?'

'We have a bungalow up at Ard-na-something.'

'Oh yes. Beside the old Mansion House. Interesting neighbours.'

Norman supposed he was referring to the mentally handicapped men he had seen staring at him over the wall. They stood for hours in the rain, immobile as sentries, watching the house. At night he heard hooting laughter and yelps and howls which previously he had only associated with a zoo.

'Open wide.' He hung a suction device like a walking stick in Norman's mouth. 'Relax now. Sometimes I think it would be better to hook that thing down the front of your trousers. Some patients sweat more than they salivate.'

The assistant smiled. She was plain but from where he lay Norman could see that the middle button of her white coat was undone and he could just see the underslope of her breast in a lacy bra.

The dentist leaned on Norman's bottom jaw and began working inside his mouth. There was a cracking sound and the dentist tut-tutted and went to a cupboard behind the chair. He's broken it, thought Norman.

'How long are you here for?' asked the dentist.

'A ort igh.'

'That's nice.'

'I cank cose i jaw.'

'What?'

Norman pointed to his lower jaw making foolish noises.

'Oh,' said the dentist. He manipulated the jaw and clicked it back into place. 'The muscle must be weak.'

'Is it broken – the tooth?'

'No, it's out.'

Norman was astonished. He had felt nothing.

Patricia shouted out from the kitchen.

'Well, love, how did it go?'

Norman had to step over the children, who were playing with a brightly coloured beach-ball on the carpet of the hallway. Although it was five o'clock on a summer's afternoon the light had to be switched on.

'OK. He pulled it.' Norman produced a Kleenex with its soggy red spot and offered it to his wife. She refused to look at it, telling him to throw it in the bin. She asked,

'Did you expect something from the fairies for it?'

'I just thought you might be interested, that's all.'

'Aww you poor thing,' she said, kissing him lightly on the cheek. 'Did you feel that? Perhaps I should kiss you on the side that's not numb.' She had a levity and a patronising approach to him in sickness which he did not like.

'I think I'll lie down for a while. One *ought* to after an extraction.'

'Whatever you say. Will you want something to eat?'

'What are you making?'

'Spaghetti.'

'We'll see.'

In the bedroom he kicked off his shoes and stood at the rain-spotted window. They were there again, standing amongst the trees at the wall. Their heads were just visible, hair plastered wet and flat. After enquiring at the shop they had found out that the Mansion House was a holiday home for the region and that a party of mentally retarded men was staying there. A mixture of mongols and cretins and God knows what. When they saw Norman appear at the window they faded back into the trees.

He lay down on the bed and got beneath the coverlet. The room smelled damp. It had probably been empty over the summer months as well as the winter. Who in their right mind would want to stay beside a madhouse? He closed his eyes and his left ear began to whine

like a high-pitched siren in the distance. He wondered if this was
normal. With relief he heard the noise fade as his ear tingled back to
ordinary sensation. He knew he was a hypochondriac. At night when
he couldn't sleep, usually after working on a lecture or a paper, he
would become aware of his heart-thud and lie awake waiting for it to
miss. A discomfort in his arm, in time, would become a definite pain
and a symptom of an impending heart attack. A discomfort anywhere
else in his body would lead to thoughts of cancer. Laziness could be
mistaken for debility, which would become a sure sign of leukaemia.
This laziness could last for days and gave him much to worry about.

Although he did not say these things out loud somehow Patricia
knew his nature and treated him in an offhand way like a child. Before
he married her she had been a primary school teacher and there was
always a hint of it in the way she talked to him when he was ill or said
he was feeling unwell. She had spotted the medical dictionary he had
slipped in among his other books to be taken on holiday but he had
made an excuse, saying that in remote places, like an island off the
Scottish coast, anything could happen to her or the kids. She had
pointed out to him that there was an air-ambulance service straight to
the nearest fully equipped hospital on the mainland at any time of the
day or night. At his insistence she had checked with the tourist board
by phone that this was so.

Without articulating it they both knew that they had reached a stale
point in their nine-year-old marriage. They no longer talked or argued
as they once did and sarcasm coloured most of the things they said to
one another.

Each year they went to the same place for a month's holiday along
with other families they knew. In March Norman had been sitting
reading the paper when Patricia said,

'I think we should go away for a holiday just by ourselves.'

'What about the children?'

'Oh, we would take *them*.'

'How can we be by ourselves if the children are there?'

'It would get us away from the same old faces. The same old
interminable conversations. Get away somewhere isolated. We would
be by ourselves at night.'

'But I have this paper to finish . . .'

'You're at the sports page already,' she squawked and fell about laughing. It was something which had endeared her to him when they first met, but now after ten years of knowing her it was something he couldn't understand – how something she considered funny seemed to take over her whole body and flop it about. One night at a party someone had told her a joke and she had slid down the wall, convulsing and spilling her drink in jerking slops on the floor. In the morning when he asked her she couldn't remember what the joke was about.

His tendency was to smile, a humour of the mind, something witty rather than funny affected him. There were times when the company about him were in fits of laughter and he couldn't see the joke.

The children in the hallway began to fight, then one of them broke into a howl of tears. Norman turned his good ear to the pillow. Children, especially of their age, were totally irrational. The younger was Becky, a gap-toothed six-year-old who refused to eat anything which was good for her and insisted on everything which was sweet and bad. John was two years older and had his mother's loud sense of humour. At least he ate cauliflower. He must have fallen asleep because the children wakened him with whispers, creeping round the bed.

'Mum says tea,' they shouted, seeing him awake.

Norman got up. His mouth tasted awful and he washed what remained of his teeth ruefully with peppermint toothpaste, thinking about old age. He sucked some spaghetti into the unaffected side of his mouth and crushed it carefully with his tongue against the roof of his mouth.

'How do you feel now, dear?' asked Patricia.

'So-so,' he said, 'I think the dentist must have served his time in an abattoir. My jaw is sore.'

'Look, Mum, there they are again,' said Becky.

'Who, dear?'

'The loonies.'

'So they are, God love them,' said Patricia.

Norman looked over his shoulder out of the dining room window. They were standing at the wall again, six of them. They had moved from the bedroom to the dining room. When they saw Norman turn his head they ducked down, then slowly came up again. The one who stood with his mouth hanging open shouted something unintelligible and the others laughed.

'You shouldn't call them loonies,' said Norman.

'Spacers, then,' said John.

'You shouldn't call them that either.'

'That's what they are, isn't it?'

Norman looked at his wife.

'I suppose it didn't mention this fact in the brochure for the house?'

'No, dear, it didn't. Four minutes from the beach was enough for me. Shall I pull the blind for you?'

'No, but it's something animal in me. I don't like to be watched while I'm eating.'

'It's good to know there's some animal in you.'

Norman gave her a look then switched his gaze to his son.

'John, is that the way to hold your fork?'

The rest of the evening the children spent watching the black and white television set which they had scorned when they first arrived. Norman went to the bedroom to do some work. He was writing a paper sparked off by Ryle's distinction between pleasure and pain – that they were not elements on the same spectrum, that positive quantities of one did not lead to minus quantities of the other. He had become involved in tortuous arguments about sadism and masochism. He had shown his draughts to the Prof who had said, after some consideration, that the paper was tending more to the physiological than the philosophic. He had added, looking over his glasses, that he much preferred a wank. 'Marriage is all right,' he had said, 'but there's nothing like the real thing.'

Norman never knew how to take him, never knew when he was serious. The man could be guilty of the most infantile jokes. He repeatedly accused Norman of talking a lot of hot Ayer and of being easily Ryled. What could you say to a man like that? He was always goosing and patting his young secretary – and she didn't seem to mind. He was a woolly existentialist who spoke about metaphysical concepts that could not be defined. He said that, with its pernickety approach to language, British philosophy was disappearing up its own arse while the world around it was in chaos. Also that British philosophy – including Norman – was like a butcher sharpening his knives. Eventually the knives would wear away but the meat would still be there to be cut. Norman thought, what more could you expect from the son of a County Derry farmer?

Norman had just written the first sentence of the severe rewriting the Prof had suggested when Patricia came into the room.

'Norman, the rain's gone off. Let's go for a walk.'

'But the writing is just beginning to go well.'

She put her arms around his neck.

'Don't be so solemn. It has stopped piddling for the first time since we arrived. There is even some blue in the sky. Come for a walk to the pier with us.'

Outside, the light had an eerie translucent quality. It was about ten o'clock and the low white sun had come through the cloud out over the Atlantic and was highlighting the gable ends of houses. The road was still wet and shining. The children in anoraks ran on ahead, leaving Norman and Patricia walking together.

'How's the toofy-peg?' Patricia asked.

'How is its absence, you mean.'

'Well, if you insist.'

'Not too bad now.'

'As night approaches.'

'You could put it that way.' He smiled. 'What do you think?'

'Yes. Holidays I feel like it more often.'

'Tomorrow this socket will begin to heal – usually that's bad news. Isn't it funny how you can never smell your own breath?'

He reached out and took her by the hand. Her face showed mock surprise but she responded by squeezing his fingers.

'Of course we don't have to kiss,' he said, smiling.

'Like an egg without salt. A total perversion.'

She leaned over and kissed him as they walked. They stopped in the middle of the road and kissed mouth to mouth lightly, friendly. John whistled *wheet-weeo* at them from a distance and they laughed. Norman was much taller than she and it was easy for him to put his arm around her shoulder as they walked.

At eleven Patricia turned on the ancient electric blanket at its highest – it had gears, almost, instead of settings – to try to get rid of the damp smell. Norman was reading a journal by the fire. She sat opposite him, her hands empty. A grandfather clock ticked loudly in the corner.

'One of the ideas of this holiday was that we should talk,' she said.

'Uh-huh.' He turned the page.

'You don't talk to me any more.'

'I'm sorry, what's that?'

'We don't talk any more.'

He closed the journal with a smile but kept his place with a finger.

'OK. What would you like to talk about?'

'Anything.'

The grandfather clock worked itself up to a long whirr before striking a quarter past.

'The more I think of it,' began Norman, 'the more I am convinced that there might be something in what the Prof says – that British philosophy is trying to commit hara-kiri. And I'm not sure that that is such a good thing. I would hate to end up believing the same things as that man.'

'I would like to talk about us. What we think, what we feel.'

'Hard words, Trish. "Think" and "feel". It's difficult to know what we mean by them. It's essential that we get our concepts straight.'

'Bollocks, Norman. Let's talk about something else.'

'Why? You said we could talk about anything.'

'OK.' She thought for a moment, then said. 'Those people who stare over the wall. Do you think because they are less intelligent they have less vivid emotions?'

'What are "vivid" emotions?'

'You know what I mean.'

'Seriously I don't.'

'The kind of thing you find in Lawrence.'

'That man is a fog of urges. He's groping all the time – making up words. Blood consciousness; the dark forest of the human soul. Patricia, if you can't put a thing into language, it doesn't exist.'

'Norman, what utter . . .'

'To answer your question. It's a problem for physiologists or neurologists or somebody like that. I don't know what loonies feel.'

'It's no wonder we don't talk any more.'

'Why's that?'

'Because you talk such utter balls. That someone should dismiss Lawrence with a wave of . . .'

'Trish.'

'What?'

'Trish. Let's have a cup of tea and go to bed. Arguing will put us off. You can't make love when you're seething. Besides, this tooth of mine is beginning to hurt.'

'Absence of tooth.'

'OK. If we sit up much longer you'll go sleepy on me.'

Patricia sighed and made a cup of tea while Norman finished reading the article in his journal.

'It's a good question,' he said, softening his biscuit in his tea and sucking it into the good side of his mouth, 'but I honestly don't know the answer to it. Taken logically it would mean that the most intelligent men have the – as you call them – the most vivid emotional responses. That is obviously not true.'

'Not in your case anyway.' She smiled or sneered at him, he couldn't tell which because he only caught the end of it.

'But I thought we weren't going to argue.'

On holidays they had agreed to do equal shares of the housework. It was Norman's turn to wash the cups, which he did even though he had had a tooth out. While he was in the kitchen Patricia took a burning peat from the fire with a pair of tongs and incensed the bedroom.

'I love that smell,' she said. 'Do you want to come to bed now?'

'I'll just wait till the smoke clears.'

As he slowly dried the cups and tidied up, his tongue sought out the jellied cavity and he touched and tasted its coppery acidity. There was no pain in it now. Perhaps he was a better dentist than he gave him credit for. Just in case, he took three Disprin dissolved in water before he locked up and turned out the lights.

In the bedroom Patricia lay reading with her bare arms outside the counterpane. Her hair was undone. A strange ululating cry came from the direction of the Mansion House. Norman looked out between the drawn curtains, half expecting to see six heads lined up at the window-sill to watch, but the Mansion House was in darkness. The sound, like a child's version of a long Red Indian war cry, came again, chilling him.

'Woolawoolawoolawoolawoolawoolwoola.'

'God, what a place.'

He undressed and slipped in naked beside her nakedness. She was still a beautiful woman and, although he had come to know her body, he never ceased to be awed by it in total nakedness. She told him how aroused she was. A simple thing like holding hands earlier in the evening had been the start of it. Her voice was hushed. Her arousal touched him and they made love. Because of his condition he suggested that she did not put her tongue in his mouth. Nevertheless, Norman got the feeling that this was good sex in this strange, lightly creaking bed. When they came together he made an involuntary animal noise far back in his throat and his mouth fell wide open.

'Agggghrrrrr,' he said.

The noise he made was followed by an audible click. Patricia, with her eyes closed, was listening to her own breathing subside and touching his shoulders with her fingertips. She opened her eyes and looked at him. His mouth was open and his eyes were staring wide in fright.

'i aws gust,' said Norman.

'What?'

'i aw. It's gust.'

Patricia began to laugh, shaking and cupping her ear to him as if she couldn't hear properly.

'What are you saying?'

Norman pointed to his yawning mouth and said as clearly as he was able,

'ock jaw.'

'I thought you were having a heart attack.'

Now that she understood she advised him with amused concern that the best thing he could do in the circumstances would be to get off her. Norman struggled into a pair of pyjama bottoms and regarded himself in the mirror. He kept trying to close his mouth but nothing happened. Somewhere in his jaw the circuits had fused again. Over his shoulder he saw his wife's reflection sitting up in bed heaving in suppressed bare-breasted laughter. When he turned to face her with his mouth agape her laughter became sound. Loud, whinnying and vulgar.

'Oh Norman, you look so *stupid*. You're like one of the loonies,' she managed to say between wheezes. 'Are you kidding me?'

He turned away from her and tried to remember what the dentist had done. He took his lower jaw in his left hand and pushed. Nothing happened. He tried to push upwards and sideways and sideways and downwards but with no effect.

Patricia had put on her nightdress and was now standing looking at him in the mirror. She turned him and looked into his mouth.

'You look like the man in the moon,' she said, giggling. She tried to put it back into place. He had to bend his knees to let her reach up and he had his arms hanging loose by his sides. Patricia stepped back and looked at him, then subsided into peals of laughter again. 'Better still. One of those monkey moneyboxes.' She clapped her hands. 'You put a penny in his hand and he went – gulp.' She demonstrated. 'We had one with its jaw broken.' Norman turned away from her and scrabbled about in the cardboard box of his philosophy books until he found his medical dictionary. He wondered what heading would be the most helpful to read. With his jaw locked open he couldn't swallow his saliva and it drooled over his bottom lip on to the page. He pored over the book.

'anky.'

Patricia gave him a handkerchief from the open case on the dresser and he staunched his dribbles.

'I'm getting to interpret your grunts quite well,' she said. Norman could find nothing which related to his case except under tetanus which he was fairly sure he didn't have. He thought of going to the square and phoning from a callbox for the ambulance plane, until he remembered that he couldn't even speak and they would think he was drunk. Patricia would have to do it. He imagined arriving alone in the infirmary at Glasgow or somewhere in his pyjama bottoms and trying with gestures and groans to explain the complexities of what had happened. With great difficulty he told his wife the thought.

'If you're going out,' she said wiping the tears from her cheeks, 'we'll have to put a coffee-tin lid in your mouth to keep the draught out.' She fell on the bed and rolled about. 'You're agog,' she shrieked. 'Agog describes you perfectly. Norman, you're the perfection of agogness.'

'or ucks ake Trish,' he said, 'ee serious.'

The noise from the Mansion House came again, ridiculing him.

'Woolawoolawoolawoolawoolawoola.'

Patricia was by now as inarticulate as he was. She was becoming almost hysterical and Norman, even in the midst of his trouble, wondered if he should slap her face to bring her out of it. It was obviously a nervous reaction to what had happened. As if he didn't have enough to cope with.

He went to the bathroom to see if a change of mirror would help. Sexual pleasure had reduced him to a slavering moron. He thought of D. H. Lawrence and Patricia's admiration for him. He pulled and pushed and wiggled at his bottom jaw. He looked and felt like the mental defectives who had peered at him over the wall. To be like this for ever. In the distance the grandfather clock tolled midnight. He had been like this for the best part of half an hour. He would *have* to go to hospital. There was the dentist but he didn't know where he lived. He didn't even know his name. Then suddenly he remembered that the Prof's wife had been a practising dentist at one time. He could phone him long distance and ask her advice. Again he remembered that he couldn't speak. It would only give the Prof another chance to say, 'Noyes, you're full of sound and fury signifying nothing.' The bastard.

All Patricia's squawking and hooting had wakened John and he came, puffy-faced with sleep, to the bathroom. He peed, forgot to flush it and walked past his father as he stared in the mirror.

'Hunggh,' said Norman. The boy turned. Norman pointed to the lavatory.

'What?'

'uh it.'

The child stood not understanding, holding up his pyjama trousers by the loose waist. Norman took him by the shoulders and led him back to the lavatory. A little saliva spilled on to John's head and Norman rubbed it.

'uh it.'

'Daddy, what's wrong?'

Norman lifted the child's hand and rested it on the handle – then pressed both hand and handle. The lavatory flushed noisily and the child staggered sleepily back to his bedroom.

'What's wrong with Daddy?' Norman heard him ask in the hallway.

'He's having a long yawn, dear. Now go back to bed.'

Patricia came in with the medical dictionary opened at a page.

'Look, this is it,' she said pointing to a diagram, 'down and out and *then* up. Here, let me try.'

She set the book on the Vanitory unit, stood on tiptoe, still consulting it over her shoulder, and took his jaw firmly in her hands. She pulled downwards and towards herself. Norman agghed and she pushed hard. There was a gristle-snapping sound and his mouth closed. He tried it tentatively, partially opening and closing it, like a goldfish.

'You've done it,' he said. He wiggled it laterally just to make sure. 'I was imagining all kinds of terrible things.' He laughed nervously.

'But you looked *so* funny, Norman. I'm sorry for laughing.' Her shoulders were still shaking.

'You have a strange sense of humour.' He wiped the shine off his chin with the handkerchief. 'The next time I get my foreskin caught in my zip I'll let you know and we can have a night's entertainment.

Back in the bedroom Patricia imitated a chimpanzee with her mouth open and arms dangling and said,

'Poor Norm.'

When they were settled in bed he sighed.

'I thought I was a goner. The dentist says I must have a weak muscle.'

'There's nothing wrong with your muscle, darling,' she said and snuggled in to his side. The fine rain had begun again and he heard it hiss off the roof and the surrounding trees. He would never understand this crazy woman he was married to. It was hurtful to be laughed *at*. But he was grateful to her for putting his jaw back and, in a kind of thanksgiving, he resolved to take the whole family for a walk along the beach the next day to light bonfires, whether it rained or not.

He turned out the light. The yelling from the Mansion House seemed to have stopped but he couldn't be sure it would not begin again. In the dark, as they were drifting off to sleep, Patricia shook the bed with giggles in the same way as shudders remain after a long bout of crying.

MIDWIFE TO THE FAIRIES

Éilís Ní Dhuibhne

We were looking at the *Late Late*. It wasn't much good this night, there was a fellow from Russia, a film star or an actor or something – I'd never heard tell of him – and some young one from America who was after setting up a prostitutes' hotel or call-in service or something. God, what Gay wants with that kind I don't know. All done up really snazzy, mind you, like a model or a television announcer or something. And she made a mint out of it, writing a book about her experiences if you don't mind. I do have to laugh!

I don't enjoy it as much of a Friday. It was much better of a Saturday. After the day's work and getting the bit of dinner ready for myself and Joe, sure I'm barely ready to sit down when it's on. It's not as relaxing like. I don't know, I do be all het up somehow on Fridays on account of it being such a busy day at the hospital and all, with all the cuts you really have to earn your keep there nowadays!

Saturday is busy too of course – we have to go into Bray and do the bit of shopping like; and do the bit of hoovering and washing. But it's not the same, I feel that bit more relaxed, I suppose it's on account of not being at work really. Not that I'd want to change that or anything. No way. Sixteen years of being at home was more than enough for me. That's not to say, of course, that I minded it at the time. I didn't go half-cracked the way some of them do, or let on to do. Mind you, I've no belief in that pre-menstrual tension and post-natal depression and what have you. I come across it often enough, I needn't tell you, or I used to, I should say, in the course of my duty. Now with the maternity unit gone, of course all that's changed. It's an ill wind, as they say. I'll say one thing for male patients, there's none of this depression carry-on with them. Of course they all think they're dying, oh dying, of sore toes and colds in the head and anything at all, but it's easier to put up with than the post-natals. I'm telling no lie.

Well, anyway, we were watching Gaybo and I was out in the kitchen wetting a cup of tea, which we like to have around ten or so of a Friday. Most nights we wait till it's nearer bedtime, but on Fridays I usually do have some little treat I get on the way home from work in The Hot Bread Shop there on the corner of Corbawn Lane, in the new shopping centre. Some little extra, a few Danish pastries or doughnuts, some little treat like that. For a change more than anything. This night I'd a few Napoleons – you know, them cream slices with icing on top.

I was only after taking out the plug when the bell went. Joe answered it of course and I could hear him talking to whoever it was and I wondered who it could be at that hour. All the stories you hear about burglars and people being murdered in their own homes . . . there was a woman over in Dalkey not six months ago, hacked to pieces at ten o'clock in the morning. God help her! . . . I do be worried. Naturally. Though I keep the chain on all the time and I think that's the most important thing. As long as you keep the chain across you're all right. Well, anyway, I could hear them talking and I didn't go out. And after a few minutes I could hear him taking the chain off and letting whoever it was in. And then Joe came in to me and he says:

'There's a fellow here looking for you, Mary. He says it's urgent.'

'What is it he wants? Sure I'm off duty now anyway, amn't I?'

I felt annoyed, I really did. The way people make use of you! You'd think there was no doctors or something. I'm supposed to be a nurse's aide, to work nine to five, Monday to Friday, except when I'm on nights. But do you think the crowd around here can get that into their heads? No way.

'I think you'd better have a word with him yourself, Mary. He says it's urgent like. He's in the hall.'

I knew of course. I knew before I seen him or heard what he had to say. And I took off my apron and ran my comb through my hair to be ready. I made up my own mind that I'd have to go out with him in the cold and the dark and miss the rest of the *Late Late*. But I didn't let on of course.

*

*There was a handywoman in this part of the country and she used to be called
out at all times of the day and night. But one night a knock came to her door.
The woman got up at once and got ready to go out. There was a man standing
at the door with a mare.*

He was a young fellow with black hair, hardly more than eighteen or
nineteen.

'Well,' says I, 'what's your trouble?'

'It's my wife,' he said, embarrassed like. He'd already told Joe, I
don't know what he had to be embarrassed about. Usually you'd get
used to a thing like that. But anyway he was, or let on to be.

'She's expecting. She says it's on the way.'

'And who might you be?'

'I'm her husband.' Didn't believe in names. Oh well.

'I see,' says I. And I did. I didn't come down in the last shower. And
with all the carry-on that goes on around here you'd want to be thick
or something not to get this particular message straight away. But I
didn't want to be too sure of myself. Just in case. Because, after all, you
can never be too sure of anything in this life. 'And why,' says I to him
then, 'why isn't she in hospital, where she should be?'

'There isn't time,' he said, as bold as brass.

'Well,' says I then, 'closing maternity wards won't stop them having
babies.' I laughed, trying to be a bit friendly like. But he didn't see the
joke. So, says I, 'and where do you and your wife live?'

'We live on this side of Annamoe,' he said, 'and if you're coming
we'd better be off. It's on the way, she said.'

'I'll come,' I said. What else could I say? A call like that has to be
answered. My mother did it before me and her mother before her, and
they never let anyone down. And my mother said that her mother had
never lost a child. Not one. Her corporate works of mercy, she called
it. You get indulgence. And anyway I pitied him, he was only a young
fellow and he was nice-looking, too, he had a country look to him. But
of course I was under no obligation, none whatever, so I said, 'Not that
I should come really. I'm off duty, you know, and anyway what you
need is the doctor.'

'We'd rather have you,' he said.

'Well, just this time.'

'Let's go then!'

'Hold on a minute, I'll get the keys of the car from Joe.'

'Oh, sure I'll run you down and back, don't bother about your own car.'

'Thank you very much,' I said. 'But I'd rather take my own, if it's all the same to you. I'll follow on behind you.' You can't be too careful.

So I went out to start the car. But lo and behold, it wouldn't go! Don't ask me why, that car is nearly new. We got it last winter from Mike Byrne, my cousin that has the garage outside Greystones. There's less than thirty thousand miles on her and she was serviced only there a month before Christmas. But it must have been the cold or something. I tried, and he tried, and Joe, of course, tried, and none of us could get a budge out of her. So in the heel of the hunt I'd to go with him. Joe didn't want me to, and then he wanted to come himself, and your man . . . Sean O'Toole, he said his name was . . . said OK, OK, but come on quick. So I told Joe to get back inside to the fire and I went with him. He'd an old Cortina, a real old banger, a real farmer's car.

'Do not be afraid!' said the rider to her. 'I will bring you home to your own doorstep tomorrow morning!'

She got up behind him on the mare.

Neither of us said a word the whole way down. The engine made an awful racket, you couldn't hear a thing, and anyway he was a quiet fellow with not a lot to say for himself. All I could see were headlights, and now and then a signpost: Enniskerry, Sallygap, Glendalough. And after we turned off the main road into the mountains, there were no headlights either, and no house-lights, nothing except the black night. Annamoe is at the back of beyonds, you'd never know you were only ten miles from Bray there, it's really very remote altogether. And their house was down a lane where there was absolutely nothing to be seen at all, not a house, not even a sheep. The house you could hardly see either, actually. It was kind of buried like at the side of the road, in a kind of a hollow. You wouldn't know it was there at all until you were on top of it. Trees all around it too. He pulled up in front of a big five-bar gate and just gave an almighty honk on the horn, and I got a shock when the gate opened, just like that, the minute he honked. I never saw who did it. But looking back now I suppose it was one of the brothers. I suppose they were waiting for him like.

It was a big place, comfortable enough, really, and he took me into the kitchen and introduced me to whoever was there. Polite enough. A big room it was, with an old black range and a huge big dresser, painted red and filled with all kinds of delph and crockery and stuff. Oh you name it! And about half a dozen people were sitting around the room, or maybe more than that. All watching the telly. The *Late Late* was still on and your one, the call-girl one, was still on. She was talking to a priest about unemployment. And they were glued to it, the whole lot of them, what looked like the mother and father and a whole family of big grown men and women. His family or hers I didn't bother my head asking. And they weren't giving out information for nothing either. It was a funny set-up, I could see that as clear as daylight, such a big crowd of them, all living together. For all the world like in *Dallas*.

Well, there wasn't a lot of time to be lost. The mother offered me a cup of tea, I'll say that for her, and I said yes, I'd love one, and I was actually dying for a cup. I hadn't had a drop of tea since six o'clock and by this time it was after twelve. But I said I'd have a look at the patient first. So one of them, a sister I suppose it was, the youngest of them, she took me upstairs to the room where she was. The girl. Sarah. She was lying on the bed, on her own. No heat in the room, nothing.

After a while they came to a steep hill. A door opened in the side of the hill and they went in. They rode until they came to a big house and inside there were lots of people, eating and drinking. In a corner of the house there lay a woman in labour.

I didn't say a word, just put on the gloves and gave her the examination. She was the five fingers, nearly into the second stage, and she must have been feeling a good bit of pain but she didn't let on, not at all. Just lay there with her teeth gritted. She was a brave young one, I'll say that for her. The waters were gone and of course nobody had cleaned up the mess so I asked the other young one to do it, and to get a heater and a kettle of boiling water. I stayed with Sarah and the baby came just before one. A little girl. There was no trouble at all with the delivery and she seemed all right but small. I'd no way of weighing her, needless to say, but I'd be surprised if she was much more than five pounds.

'By rights she should be in an incubator,' I said to Sarah, who was sitting up smoking a cigarette, if you don't mind. She said nothing. What can you do? I washed the child . . . she was a nice little thing, God help her . . . I wrapped her in a blanket and put her in beside the mother. There was nowhere else for her. Not a cot, not even an old box. That's the way in these cases as often as not. Nobody wants to know.

I delivered the afterbirth and then I left. I couldn't wait to get back to my own bed. They'd brought me the cup of tea and all, but I didn't get time to drink it, being so busy and all. And afterwards the Missus, if that's what she was, wanted me to have a cup in the kitchen. But all I wanted then was to get out of the place. They were all so quiet and unfriendly like. Bar the mother. And even she wasn't going overboard, mind you. But the rest of them. All sitting like zombies looking at the late-night film. They gave me the creeps. I told them the child was too small, they'd have to do something about it, but they didn't let on they heard. The father, the ould fellow, that is to say, put a note in my hand . . . it was worth it from that point of view, I'll admit . . . and said, 'Thank you.' Not a word from the rest of them. Glued to the telly, as if nothing was after happening. I wanted to scream at them, really. But what could I do? Anyway the young fellow, Sean, the father as he said himself, drove me home. And that was that.

Well and good. I didn't say a word about what was after happening to anyone, excepting of course to Joe. I don't talk, it's not right. People have a right to their privacy, I always say, and with my calling you've to be very careful. But to tell the truth they were on my mind. The little girl, the little baby. I knew in my heart and soul I shouldn't have left her out there, down there in the back of beyonds, near Annamoe. She was much too tiny, she needed care. And the mother, Sarah, was on my mind as well. Mind you, she seemed to be well able to look after herself, but still and all, they weren't the friendliest crowd of people I'd ever come across. They were not.

But that was that.

Until about a week later, didn't I get the shock of my life when I opened the evening paper and saw your one, Sarah, staring out at me. Her round baby face, big head of red hair. And there was a big story about the baby. Someone was after finding it dead in a shoebox, in a kind of rubbish dump they had at the back of the house. And she was arrested, in for questioning, her and maybe Sean O'Toole as well. I'm not sure. In for questioning. I could have dropped down dead there and then.

I told Joe.

'Keep your mouth shut, woman,' he said. 'You did your job and were paid for it. This is none of your business.'

And that was sound advice. But we can't always take sound advice. If we could the world would be a different place.

The thing dragged on. It was in the papers. It was on the telly. There was questioning, and more questioning, and trials and appeals and I don't know what. The whole country was in on it.

And it was on my conscience. It kept niggling at me all the time. I couldn't sleep, I got so I couldn't eat. I was all het up about it, in a terrible state really. Depressed, that's what I was, me who was never depressed before in my life. And I'm telling no lie when I say I was on my way to the doctor for a prescription for Valium when I realised there was only one thing to do. So instead of going down to the surgery, didn't I turn on my heel and walk over to the Garda barracks instead. I went in and I got talking to the sergeant straight away. Once I told them what it was about there was no delaying. And he was very interested in all I had to say, of course, and asked me if I'd be prepared to testify and I said of course I would. Which was the truth. I wouldn't want to but I would if I had to. Once I'd gone this far, of course I would.

Well, I walked out of that Garda station a new woman. It was a great load off my chest. It was like being to confession and getting absolution for a mortal sin. Not that I've ever committed a mortler, of course. But you know what I mean. I felt relieved.

Well and good.

Well. You'll never believe what happened to me next. I was just getting back to my car when a young fellow ... I'd seen him somewhere before, I know that, but I couldn't place him. He might have been the fellow that came for me on the night, Sean, but he didn't look quite like him. I just couldn't place him at all ... anyway, he was standing there, right in front of the car. And I said hello, just in case I really did know him, just in case it really was him. But he said nothing. He just looked behind him to see if anyone was coming, and when he saw that the coast was clear he just pulled out a big huge knife out of his breast pocket and pointed it at my stomach. He put the heart crossways in me. And then he says, in a real low voice, like a gangster in *Hill Street Blues* or something:

'Keep your mouth shut. Or else!'

I was in bits. I could hardly drive myself home with the shock. I told Joe of course. But he didn't have a lot of sympathy for me.

'God Almighty, woman,' he said, 'what possessed you to go to the guards? You must be off your rocker. They'll be arresting you next!'

Well, I'd had my lesson. The guards called for me the next week but I said nothing. I said I knew nothing and I'd never heard tell of them all before, the family I mean. And there was nothing they could do, nothing. The sergeant hadn't taken a statement from me, and that was his mistake and my good luck I suppose, because I don't know what would have happened to me if I'd testified. I told a priest about the lie to the guards, in confession, to a Carmelite in White Friar Street, not to any priest I know. And he said God would understand. 'You did your best, and that's all God will ask of you. He does not ask of us that we put our own lives in danger.'

There was a fair one day at Baile an Droichid. And this woman used to make market socks and used to wash them and scour them and take them to the fair and get them sold. She used to make them up in dozen bunches and sell them at so much the dozen.

And as she walked over the bridge there was a great blast of wind. And who should it be but the people of the hill, the wee folk! And she looked among them and saw among them the same man who had taken her on the mare's back to see his wife.

'How are ye all? And how is the wife?' she said.

He stood and looked at her.

'Which eye do you see me with?' he asked.

'With the right eye,' she said.

Before he said another word he raised his stick and stuck it in her eye and knocked her eye out on the road.

'You'll never see me again as long as you live,' he said.

Sometimes I do think of the baby. She was a dawny little thing, there's no two ways about it. She might have had a chance, in intensive care. But who am I to judge?

MEN AND WOMEN

Claire Keegan

My father takes me places. He has artificial hips, so he needs me to open gates. To reach our house you must drive up a long lane through a wood, open two sets of gates and close them behind you so the sheep won't escape to the road. I'm handy. I get out, open the gates, my father free-wheels the Volkswagen through, I close the gates behind him and hop back into the passenger seat. To save petrol he starts the car on the run, gathering speed on the slope before the road, and then we're off to wherever my father is going on that particular day.

Sometimes it's the scrapyard, where he's looking for a spare part, or, scenting a bargain in some classified ad, we wind up in a farmer's mucky field, pulling cabbage plants or picking seed potatoes in a dusty shed. Sometimes we drive to the forge, where I stare into the water-barrel, whose surface reflects patches of the milky skies that drift past, sluggish, until the blacksmith plunges the red-hot metal down and scorches away the clouds. On Saturdays my father goes to the mart and examines sheep in the pens, feeling their backbones, looking into their mouths. If he buys just a few sheep, he doesn't bother going home for the trailer but puts them in the back of the car, and it is my job to sit between the front seats to keep them there. They shit small pebbles and say baaaah, the Suffolks' tongues dark as the raw liver we cook on Mondays. I keep them back until we get to whichever house Da stops at for a feed on the way home. Usually it's Bridie Knox's, because Bridie kills her own stock and there's always meat. The handbrake doesn't work, so when Da parks in her yard I get out and put the stone behind the wheel.

I am the girl of a thousand uses.

'Be the holy, missus, what way are ya?'

'Dan!' Bridie says, like she didn't hear the splutter of the car.

Bridie lives in a smoky little house without a husband, but she has sons who drive tractors around the fields. They're small, deeply unattractive men who patch their wellingtons. Bridie wears red lipstick and face powder, but her hands are like a man's hands. I think her head is wrong for her body, the way my dolls look when I swap their heads.

'Have you aer a bit for the child, missus? She's hungry at home,' Da says, looking at me like I'm one of those African children we give up sugar for during Lent.

'Ah now,' says Bridie, smiling for his old joke. 'That girl looks fed to me. Sit down there and I'll put the kettle on.'

'To tell you the truth, missus, I wouldn't fall out with a drop of something. I'm after being in at the mart and the price of sheep is a holy scandal.'

He talks about sheep and cattle and the weather and how this little country of ours is in a woeful state while Bridie sets the table, puts out the Chef sauce and the Colman's mustard and cuts big, thick slices off a flitch of boiled ham. I sit by the window and keep an eye on the sheep who stare, bewildered, from the car. Da eats everything in sight while I build a little tower of biscuits and lick the chocolate off and give the rest to the sheepdog under the table.

When we get home, I find the fire shovel and collect the sheep-droppings from the car and roll barley on the loft.

'Where did you go?' Mammy asks.

I tell her all about our travels while we carry buckets of calf-nuts and beet-pulp across the yard. Da sits in under the shorthorn cow and milks her into a bucket. My brother sits in the sitting room beside the fire and pretends he's studying. He will do the Inter-cert. next year. My brother is going to be somebody, so he doesn't open gates or clean up shite or carry buckets. All he does is read and write and draw triangles with special pencils Da buys him for mechanical drawing. He is the brains in the family. He stays in there until he is called to dinner.

'Go down and tell Seamus his dinner is on the table,' Da says.

I have to take off my wellingtons before I go down.

'Come up and get it, you lazy fucker,' I say.

'I'll tell,' he says.

'You won't,' I say, and go back up to the kitchen, where I spoon garden peas on to his plate because he won't eat turnip or cabbage like the rest of us.

Evenings, I get my school-bag and do homework on the kitchen table while Ma watches the television we hire for winter. On Tuesdays she makes a big pot of tea before eight o'clock and sits at the range and glues herself to the programme where a man teaches a woman how to drive a car. How to change gears, to let the clutch out and give her the juice. Except for a rough woman up behind the hill who drives a tractor and a Protestant woman in the town, no woman we know drives. During the break her eyes leave the screen and travel with longing to the top shelf of the dresser, where she has hidden the spare key to the Volkswagen in the old cracked teapot. I am not supposed to know this. I sigh and continue tracing the course of the River Shannon through a piece of greaseproof paper.

On Christmas Eve I put up signs. I cut up a cardboard box and in red marker I write THIS WAY SANTA and arrows, pointing the way. I am always afraid he will get lost or not bother coming because the gates are too much trouble. I staple them on to the paling at the end of the lane and on the timber gates and one inside the door leading down to the parlour where the tree is: I put a glass of stout and a piece of cake on the coffee table for him and conclude that Santa must be drunk by Christmas morning.

Daddy takes his good hat out of the press and looks at himself in the mirror. It's a fancy hat with a stiff feather stuck down in the brim. He tightens it well down on his head to hide his bald patch.

'And where are you going on Christmas Eve?' Mammy asks.

'Going off to see a man about a pup,' he says, and bangs the door.

I go to bed and have trouble sleeping. I am the only person in my class Santa Claus still visits. I know this because the master asked, 'Who does Santa Claus still come to?' and mine was the only hand raised. I'm different, but every year I feel there is a greater chance that he will not come, that I will become like the others.

I wake at dawn and Mammy is already lighting the fire, kneeling on the hearth, ripping up newspaper, smiling. There is a terrible moment when I think maybe Santa didn't come because I said 'Come and get it, you lazy fucker,' but he does come. He leaves me the Tiny Tears doll I asked for, wrapped in the same wrapping paper we have, and I think how the postal system is like magic, how I can send a letter two days before Christmas and it reaches the North Pole overnight, even though it takes a week for a letter to come from England. Santa does not come to Seamus any more. I suspect he knows what Seamus is really doing all those evenings in the sitting room, reading *Hit 'n Run* magazines and drinking the red lemonade out of the sideboard, not using his brains at all.

Nobody's up except Mammy and me. We are the early birds. We make tea, eat toast and chocolate fingers for breakfast. Then she puts on her best apron, the one with all the strawberries, and turns on the radio, chops onions and parsley while I grate a plain loaf into crumbs.

Seamus and Da come down and investigate the parcels under the tree. Seamus gets a dartboard for Christmas. He hangs it on the back door and himself and Da throw darts and chalk up scores while Mammy and me put on our anoraks and feed the pigs and cattle and sheep and let the hens out.

'How come they do nothing?' I ask her. I am reaching into warm straw, feeling for eggs. The hens lay less in winter.

'They're men,' she says, as if this explains everything.

Because it is Christmas morning, I say nothing. I come inside and duck when a dart flies past my head.

'Ha! Ha!' says Seamus.

'Bullseye,' says Da.

On New Year's Eve it snows. Snowflakes land and melt on the window ledges. It is the end of another year. I eat a bowl of sherry trifle for breakfast and fall asleep watching Lassie on TV. I play with my dolls after dinner but get fed up filling Tiny Tears with water and squeezing it out through the hole in her backside, so I take her head off, but her neck is too thick to fit into my other dolls' bodies. I start playing darts with Seamus. He chalks two marks on the lino, one for him and another, closer to the board, for me. When I get a treble nineteen, Seamus says, 'Fluke.'

'Eighty-seven,' I say, totting up my score.

'Fluke,' he says.

'You don't know what fluke is,' I say. 'Fluke and worms. Look it up in the dictionary.'

'Exactly,' he says.

I am fed up being treated like a child. I wish I was big. I wish I could sit beside the fire and be called up to dinner and draw triangles, lick the nibs of special pencils, sit behind the wheel of a car and have someone open gates that I could drive through. Vrum! Vrum! I'd give her the holly, make a bumper-sticker that would read: CAUTION, SHEEP ON BOARD.

That night we get dressed up. Mammy wears a dark red dress, the colour of the shorthorn cow. Her skin is freckled like somebody dipped a toothbrush in paint and splattered her. She asks me to fasten the catch on her string of pearls. I used to stand on the bed doing this, but now I'm tall, the tallest girl in my class; the master measured us. Mammy is tall and thin, but the skin on her hands is hard. I wonder if someday she will look like Bridie Knox, become part man, part woman.

Da does not do himself up. I have never known him to take a bath or wash his hair, he just changes his hat and shoes. Now he clamps his good hat down on his head and puts his shoes on. They are the big black shoes he bought when he sold the Suffolk ram. He has trouble with the laces, as he finds it hard to stoop. Seamus wears a green jumper with elbow-patches, black trousers with legs like tubes and cowboy boots to make him taller.

'Don't trip up in your high heels,' I say.

We get into the Volkswagen, me and Seamus in the back and Mammy and Da up front. Even though I washed the car out, I can smell sheep-shite, a faint, pungent odour that always drags us back to where we come from. Da turns on the windscreen wiper; there's only one, and it screeches as it wipes the snow away. Crows rise from the trees, releasing shrill, hungry sounds. Because there are no doors in the back, it is Mammy who gets out to open the gates. I think she is beautiful with her pearls around her throat and her red skirt flaring out when she swings round. I wish my father would get out, that the snow would be falling on him, not on my mother in her good clothes. I've seen other fathers holding their wives' coats, holding doors open, asking if they'd like anything at the shop, bringing home bars of chocolate and ripe pears even when they say no.

Spellman Hall stands in the middle of a car park, an arch of bare, multi-coloured bulbs surrounding a crooked 'Merry Christmas' sign above the door. Inside is big as a warehouse with a slippy wooden floor and benches at the walls. Strange lights make every white garment dazzle. It's amazing. I can see the newsagent's bra through her blouse, fluff like snow on the auctioneer's trousers. The accountant has a black eye and a jumper made of grey and white wool diamonds. Overhead a globe of shattered mirror shimmers and spins slowly. At the top of the ballroom a Formica-topped table is stacked with bottles of lemonade and orange, custard-cream biscuits and cheese-and-onion Tayto. The butcher's wife stands behind, handing out the straws and taking in the money. Several of the women I know from my trips around the country are there: Bridie with her haw-red lipstick; Sarah Combs, who only last week urged my father to have a glass of sherry and gave me stale cake while she took him into the sitting room to show him her new suite of furniture; Miss Emma Jenkins, who always makes a fry and drinks coffee instead of tea and never has a sweet thing in the house because of her gastric juices.

On the stage men in red blazers and candy-striped bow-ties play drums, guitars, blow horns, and The Nerves Moran is out front, singing 'My Lovely Leitrim'. Mammy and I are first out on the floor for the cuckoo waltz, and when the music stops, she dances with Seamus. My father dances with the women from the roads. I wonder how he can dance like that and not open gates. Seamus jives with teenage girls he knows from the vocational school, hand up, arse out, and the girls spinning like blazes. Old men in their thirties ask me out.

'Will ya chance a quickstep?' they say. Or: 'How's about a half-set?'

They tell me I'm light on my feet.

'Christ, you're like a feather,' they say, and put me through my paces.

In the Paul Jones the music stops and I get stuck with a farmer who smells sour like the whiskey we make sick lambs drink in springtime, but the young fella who hushes the cattle around the ring in the mart butts in and rescues me.

'Don't mind him,' he says. 'He thinks he's the bee's knees.'

He smells of ropes, new galvanise, Jeyes Fluid.

After the half-set I get thirsty and Mammy gives me a fifty-pence piece for lemonade and raffle tickets. A slow waltz begins and Da walks across to Sarah Combs, who rises from the bench and takes her jacket off. Her shoulders are bare; I can see the tops of her breasts. Mammy is sitting with her handbag on her lap, watching. There is something sad about Mammy tonight; it is all around her like when a cow dies and the truck comes to take it away. Something I don't fully understand is happening, as if a black cloud has drifted in and could burst and cause havoc. I go over and offer her my lemonade, but she just takes a little, dainty sip and thanks me. I give her half my raffle tickets, but she doesn't care. My father has his arms around Sarah Combs, dancing slow like slowness is what he wants. Seamus is leaning against the far wall with his hands in his pockets, smiling down at the blonde who hogs the mirror in the Ladies.

'Cut in on Da.'

'What?' he says.

'Cut in on Da.'

'What would I do that for?' he says.

'And you're supposed to be the one with all the brains,' I say. 'Gobshite.'

I walk across the floor and tap Sarah Combs on the back. I tap a rib. She turns, her wide patent belt gleaming in the light that is spilling from the globe above our heads.

'Excuse me,' I say, like I'm going to ask her the time.

'Tee-hee,' she says, looking down at me. Her eyeballs are cracked like the teapot on our dresser.

'I want to dance with Daddy.'

At the word 'Daddy' her face changes and she loosens her grip on my father. I take over. The man on the stage is blowing his trumpet now. My father holds my hand tight, like a punishment. I can see my mother on the bench, reaching into her bag for a hanky. Then she goes to the Ladies. There's a feeling like hatred all around Da. I get the feeling he's helpless, but I don't care. For the first time in my life I have some power. I can butt in and take over, rescue and be rescued.

There's a general hullabaloo towards midnight. Everybody's out on the floor, knees buckling, handbags swinging. The Nerves Moran counts down the seconds to the New Year and then there's kissing and hugging. Strange men squeeze me, kiss me like they're thirsty and I'm water.

My parents do not kiss. In all my life, back as far as I remember, I have never seen them touch. Once I took a friend upstairs to show her the house.

'This is Mammy's room,' I said. 'And this is Daddy's room.'

'Your parents don't sleep in the same bed?' she said in a voice of pure amazement.

The band picks up the pace. 'Oh hokey, hokey, pokey!'

'Work off them turkey dinners, shake off them plum puddings!' shouts The Nerves Moran and even the ballroom show-offs give up on their figures of eight and do the twist and jive around, and I shimmy around and knock my backside against the mart fella's backside and wind up swinging with a stranger.

Everybody stands for the national anthem. Da is wiping his forehead with a handkerchief and Seamus is panting because he's not used to the exercise. The lights come up and nothing is the same. People are red-faced and sweaty; everything's back to normal. The auctioneer takes over the microphone and thanks a whole lot of different people, and then they auction off a Charolais calf and a goat and batches of tea and sugar and buns and jam, plum puddings and mince pies. There's pebbles where the goat stood and I wonder who'll clean it up. Not until the very last does the raffle take place. The auctioneer holds out the cardboard box of stubs to the blonde.

'Dig deep,' he says. 'No peeping. First prize a bottle of whiskey.'

She takes her time, lapping up the attention.

'Come on,' he says, 'good girl, it's not the sweepstakes.'

She hands him the ticket.

'It's a – What colour is that would ya say, Jimmy? It's a salmon-coloured ticket, number seven hundred and twenty-five. Seven two five. Serial number 3x429H. I'll give ye that again.'

It's not mine, but I'm close. I don't want the whiskey anyhow; it'd be kept for the pet lambs. I'd rather the box of Afternoon Tea biscuits that's coming up next. There's a general shuffle, a search in handbags, arse pockets. The auctioneer calls out the numbers a few times and it looks like he'll have to draw again when Mammy rises from her seat. Head held high, she walks in a straight line across the floor. A space opens in the crowd; people step aside to let her pass. Her new high-heeled shoes say clippety-clippety on the slippy floor and her red skirt is flaring. I have never seen her do this. Usually she's too shy, gives me the tickets, and I run up and collect the prize.

'Do ya like a drop of the booze, do ya, missus?' the Nerves Moran asks, reading her ticket. 'Sure wouldn't it keep ya warm on a night like tonight. No woman needs a man if she has a drop of Power's. Isn't that right? Seven twenty-five, that's the one.'

My mother is standing there in her elegant clothes and it's all wrong. She doesn't belong up there.

'Let's check the serial numbers now,' he says, drawing it out. 'I'm sorry, missus, wrong serial number. The hubby may keep you warm again tonight. Back to the old reliable.'

My mother turns and walks clippety-clippety back down the slippy floor, with everybody knowing she thought she'd won when she didn't win. And suddenly she is no longer walking, but running, running down in the bright white light, past the cloakroom, towards the door, her hair flailing out like a horse's tail behind her.

Out in the car park snow has accumulated on the trampled grass, the evergreen shelter beds, but the tarmac is wet and shiny in the headlights of cars leaving. Thick, unwavering moonlight shines steadily down on the earth. Ma, Seamus and me sit into the car, shivering, waiting for Da. We can't turn on the engine to heat the car because Da has the keys. My feet are cold as stones. A cloud of greasy steam rises from the open hatch of the chip van, a fat brown sausage painted on the chrome. All around us people are leaving, waving, calling out 'Goodnight!' and 'Happy New Year!' They're collecting their chips and driving off.

The chip van has closed its hatch and the car park is empty when Da comes out. He gets into the driver's seat, the ignition catches, a splutter, and then we're off, climbing the hill outside the village, winding around the narrow roads towards home.

'That wasn't a bad band,' Da says.

Mammy says nothing.

'I said, there was a bit of life in that band.' Louder this time.

Still Mammy says nothing.

My father begins to sing 'Far Away in Australia'. He always sings when he's angry, lets on he's in a good humour when he's raging. The lights of the town are behind us now. These roads are dark. We pass houses with lighted candles in the windows, bulbs blinking on

Christmas trees, sheets of newspaper held down on the windscreens of parked cars. Da stops singing before the end of the song.

'Did you see aer a nice little thing in the hall, Seamus?'

'Nothing I'd be mad about.'

'That blonde was a nice bit of stuff.'

I think about the mart, all the men at the rails bidding for heifers and ewes. I think about Sarah Combs and how she always smells of grassy perfume when we go to her house.

The chestnut tree's boughs at the end of our lane are caked with snow. Da stops the car and we roll back a bit until he puts his foot on the brake. He is waiting for Mammy to get out and open the gates.

Mammy doesn't move.

'Have you got a pain?' he says to her.

She looks straight ahead.

'Is that door stuck or what?' he says.

'Open it yourself.'

He reaches across her and opens her door, but she slams it shut.

'Get out there and open that gate!' he barks at me.

Something tells me I should not move.

'Seamus!' he shouts. 'Seamus!'

There's not a budge out of any of us.

'By Jeeesus!' he says.

I am afraid. Outside, one corner of my THIS WAY SANTA sign has come loose; the soggy cardboard flapping in the wind. Da turns to my mother, his voice filled with venom.

'And you walking up in your finery in front of all the neighbours, thinking you won first prize in the raffle.' He laughs and opens his door. 'Running like a tinker out of the hall.'

He gets out and there's rage in his walk, as if he's walking on hot coals. He sings: 'Far Away in Australia!' He is reaching up, taking the wire off the gate, when a gust of wind blows his hat off. The gates swing open. He stoops to retrieve his hat, but the wind nudges it further from his reach. He takes another few steps and stoops again to retrieve it, but again it is blown just out of his reach. I think of Santa Claus using the same wrapping paper as us, and suddenly I understand. There is only one obvious explanation.

My father is getting smaller. It feels as if the trees are moving, the chestnut tree whose green hands shelter us in summer is backing away.

Then I realise it's the car. We are rolling, sliding backwards. No handbrake and I am not out there putting the stone behind the wheel. And that is when Mammy gets behind the wheel. She slides over into my father's seat, the driver's seat, and puts her foot on the brake. We stop going backwards. She revs up the engine and puts the car in gear. The gear-box grinds – she hasn't the clutch in far enough – but then there's a splutter and we're moving. Mammy is taking us forward, past the Santa sign, past my father, who has stopped singing, through the open gates. She drives us through the snow-covered woods. I can smell the pines. When I look back, my father is standing there watching our tail-lights. The snow is falling on him, on his bare head, and all he can do is stand there, clutching his hat.

MOTHERS WERE ALL THE SAME

Joseph O'Connor

I met Catriona again on the train in from Luton. I had noticed her on the plane, just before we came in to land, leafing through the lousy in-flight magazine – 'a great big top o'the morning from Delaney's Irish Cabaret' – while the old lady beside her worried about air disasters. The hostess told her to calm down and held her bony little hand. The old lady's hand, that is. Not Catriona's. Catriona's hands weren't bony at all. They were cute.

She said it was statistically impossible. She said you had more chance of being kicked to death by a mule than dying in an air crash. The old lady said to tell that to Yuri Gagarin, but the hostess just giggled and said, 'Who's he when he's at home? Something to do with glasnost, is it?' Catriona looked over at me. She grinned, and she rolled her beautiful eyes.

The plane screeched in, bucked as the wheels skimmed the ground, and shuddered to a halt outside the arrivals terminal. Catriona was ahead of me as we shuffled in off the tarmac, collars raised in the cold. Two police cars emptied. The plainclothes men stared and scribbled like crazy on their clipboards as we filed past them.

I told the customs guy I'd just arrived from Dublin, and I didn't know how long I'd be staying. That was true alright. He glared under his peaked cap, making me feel guilty. He had a face like the 'Spitting Image' puppet of Norman Tebbit, but without the charm. I mean, I hadn't done anything, but the way he looked at me made me feel like some kind of terrorist, just the same. Then he asked me to write down my full name, and he slouched off into a back room. That's it, I thought, I'm finished now. I gazed around the baggage lounge, full of wailing babies and neon signs. LUTON: GATEWAY TO THE SOUTH EAST. RYANAIR TO THE REPUBLIC OF IRELAND. LOADZA LUVVERLY LOOY IN THE SIZZLING SOARAWAY SUN. Then I saw her staring at me. Just for a second, but she was definitely looking at me. I smiled back, but she turned away to look for her bags. I made up my mind to ask her later, if I got the chance.

'Right,' said the customs man, and he told me to report my address to the local police as soon as I had one. I was going to ask why. But you don't bother, do you? You're so relieved that your name hasn't somehow crept into their bloody computer that you just smile politely and say thanks very much. He said he hoped I had a nice trip, and he was sorry for holding me up. But it was for everyone's good, if I knew what he meant. I knew what he meant.

I only had my rucksack, so I caught up with her on the other side of customs. I saw her immediately, looking in the window of the Sock Shop.

A troop of boy scouts was lined up at the burger counter, screaming curses and waving banknotes. Three football fans were drunk and singing in the corner, beer all over their England shirts. Soldiers walked up and down with machine guns in their hands. Actually, there were uniforms everywhere, now that I think of it. That's one thing I noticed straight away, everybody seemed to be wearing a uniform. Customs, police, pilots, cleaners, waitresses, delivery boys, hostesses, all rushing around the hall. Above it all was the sound of the loudspeaker, announcing late flights and missing passengers.

I said, 'Excuse me,' and she turned around, looking a little surprised. 'Yeah?' she said.

I asked if I had seen her somewhere before. I was hoping she wouldn't think this was some big corny pick-up line, but I really did think I had seen her somewhere before and I couldn't remember where. I said I couldn't help noticing her on the plane and she looked familiar. She said she really didn't think so, and she looked away. I said I was sure. She turned again and scrutinised me. Then she asked if I was a friend of Johnny Reilly, by any chance. I said, yeah, I was. Used to be anyway. Recognition dawned on her face. That party he had – last Christmas? I was there with a blond-haired girl. Susan. Yes. She remembered me now. I was pretty flattered, actually, until she pointed out the reason she remembered me. I was the one who had puked over the aspidistra in the hall.

I grinned. She pursed her lips and looked at her watch. I said it was a small world. She said, yeah, it was a small world, but she wouldn't like to have to paint it. There didn't seem to be much else to say. She'd just come over for the weekend. What about me? I was here looking for a job. Who wasn't? I told her I didn't know how long I'd stick it. She just kept staring at that watch so eventually I just said bye, and she wished me luck and dragged her case outside to the bus stop for Luton station.

I waited for the next bus. Well, if she wanted to be like that, fine, I didn't really feel like being friendly anyway. Too many things on my mind. I didn't feel like some big conversation. OK, OK, so I had Aunt Martha's place, but that was only good for a few weeks at most, the old bat. I'd have to get a job soon. Then my own place. I never knew the folks would be so upset about me going, either. When I told them first they were delighted. But the morning I left it was a different story. Tears and scribbled addresses and folded-up tenners in the suit pocket. The whole emigrant bit. You'd have sworn I was going to the moon, the way they went on. The whole thing was like some bloody Christy Moore song come to life in our front room. On the way out to the airport I actually thought my father was going to tell me the facts of life. It was that bad.

At least the suit wasn't too hick. Still fitted me, anyway. Just about. Though I'd really have to go on a diet. All the drinking I'd done in the weeks I was saying my goodbyes was catching up fast. I must have put on eight pounds. But everyone insists on buying you pints, so what can you do? Everyone except Johnny Reilly, of course, the tight shit. My father got me the suit the week I started college. It was hanging over the back of my door when I reeled in that night. He said I'd need a good suit. I wore it twice in three years. Once for Granny's funeral and once for my graduation. He said to bring it with me to London anyway. He said I'd need it for all the interviews.

On the bus I thought about Una Murray. I'd never known she was into me until it was too late. But after our farewell drink she lunged at me on Capel Street Bridge, with the wind from the Liffey blowing through her hair like in a movie or something. Shit. If only I'd known before. Well, it wouldn't have made any difference. Still, would have been nice to know. Susan would have been jealous as hell.

When I got to Luton station, the London train was just pulling in, and the scramble of passengers was milling around the doorways. I fought my way on, dragging the rucksack behind, and I made a rush for the one spare seat. There were posters everywhere, saying that unattended luggage would be removed by the cops and blown up.

There she was, sitting opposite me as I squeezed in. Catriona. She was reading a book. *The Ultimate Good Luck* by Richard Ford. She looked up and smiled again. She said we must stop meeting like this. I tried to think of something smart but nothing came. I just grinned back like an idiot and I think I blushed as I offered her a duty-free cigarette. She shook her head and took off her glasses and pointed to another sign. NO SMOKING. An old man with a moustache glared at me.

'Haven't you heard of King's Cross?' he said.

We got talking again. She asked me where I was staying in London. Strange, but I said I didn't know. I don't know why I said that. Because I did know. But as Johnny Reilly says, I can't give anyone a straight answer, and I must admit that much is true. I suppose I was afraid she'd have nowhere to stay and want to come to Aunt Martha's with me. Look, I know it's stupid, but I'm funny like that. I like my space. Crazy, I know, but what can you do? I think it's because everyone at home asks so many bloody questions. Where were you? Until when? Who were you with? And the great bloody existential conundrum of course: just who do you think you are? All that stuff is enough to make anyone defensive. I'm not saying it's right. I'm just saying that's the way it is.

I needn't have worried. She was fixed up already, staying in some hotel near the station. It was a small place, she said, but it was hunky-dory. I couldn't remember the last time I'd heard that expression. Hunky-dory. As the train pulled in I asked if she needed any help with her bags. I knew she didn't, but I thought I'd ask anyway. She said she could manage on her own. So I shook hands with her on the platform and said goodbye again. Her hand was cold. She smiled, because I was being so formal, I suppose, with the handshake and everything. She said she might see me around. I shrugged and said I hoped so. She told me she hoped I'd find somewhere to stay, and I said good luck, see you, and walked off.

'Eddie,' she shouted, as I walked through the ticket barrier. I turned and saw her trotting towards me, dragging her case, panting. She said she was sorry, that I must have thought she was really rude. I wondered what she meant. She said if I really had nowhere to stay why didn't I come with her? She said that was the obvious thing. She was sure they'd have another room. It was a really cheap place too, and if I needed somewhere to sleep for a few nights, until I found something else, it was probably OK. I hesitated. I knew I couldn't afford to stay in any hotel, no matter how cheap, not even for one night. Three nights would nearly clean me out. But then I thought, to hell with it. Why not? Nothing ventured, all of that. I just felt like doing something different. I don't know why. Something spontaneous after all the weeks of planning every last moment. That's what I wanted. And I suppose I have to admit I thought she was pretty cute, too. I asked whether she was sure she wouldn't mind. She said, of course not. She'd love the company. I could come with her now, and maybe she could show me some of the sights over the weekend. Alright. I said I would.

She was amazed that I'd never been to London before. She'd come over every summer for three years. She had a job over there whenever she wanted it, in some trendy lefty bookshop on Charing Cross Road. She might come over for good next year, she said. But she knew what it was like to be in London on your own. It was such an overwhelming place. So huge and anonymous and impersonal. So different from Dublin. Yeah, I told her, that's why I came over.

Then she wanted to know what Johnny Reilly was doing these days. I said I didn't know. I was going to tell her about our big falling out, but I didn't bother. I just said I hadn't seen him for a while, and I hadn't a clue what he was up to, but it was probably either illegal or a waste of time.

'That sounds like Johnny alright,' she said.

So we went over together to the El Dorado Hotel and we signed in. The Greek guy behind the counter told us he rented rooms by the hour. You didn't have to have them for the whole night. There were no questions asked here, not blooming likely. I blushed like a sap and she made some joke. The Greek laughed out loud and apologised. Then he said he did have separate rooms to spare and he'd show us the way. Creaking up the stairs I whispered that I wasn't so crazy about this kip.

But she told me not to be so silly, that old Zorba was only joking about the hourly rate. I said I thought he was pretty serious, and she sighed and said she knew, but for seven-fifty a night you couldn't expect The Ritz. I coughed knowledgeably and said I supposed she was right.

While she changed and unpacked, I slipped downstairs and outside and phoned Aunt Martha. The phone box was plastered with stickers advertising masseuses and prostitutes and kinky nuns and 'corporal punishment specialists'. I thought it must be great to be a specialist at something. Aunt Martha's businesslike voice buzzed down the line. I was to come over immediately. She had the dinner on and my cousins were just dying to meet me again. I imagined Uncle Frank and her and Alvin and Sharon sitting around the table. I could just see them all – waiting for me. I reconsidered, just for a second.

But I just couldn't face it. I told Aunt Martha I was sorry but I was still in Dublin Airport and I couldn't make it until Monday. It was the fog, I said. Everything was screwed up because of the fog. I felt bad about lying, but what can you do? She sounded so disappointed though. Soon as I'd said it, I regretted it, but it was too late then. She said they'd just have to wait. I said I was really sorry. She said she should think so too. All the trouble she'd gone too, not to mention the expense. I noticed her weird accent. She nearly didn't sound Irish at all.

The funny thing was, though, as soon as I put the phone down I knew in my heart that this whole thing was a big mistake. I really did. I just had this feeling, you know? Like God was going to get me for lying to Aunt Martha. Not that I believe in God. But still. You never know.

Back at the El Dorado things were looking up. My room was fine. It was small, but you could see Tower Bridge in the distance, and there was a television in the corner. I flicked the switch but nothing happened. You had to put a pound coin in the slot to make it work. Well, it looked good. And although I didn't want to watch anything, it made me feel good knowing that I could, if I wanted to, if I had a pound to spare.

I sat down and bounced on the bed. Gently. Yeah, this was great. God, I thought, if my mother could only see me now. Holed up with a strange woman in a King's Cross knocking shop. I felt like a Harold Robbins hero.

I said this to Catriona on the Tube up to Leicester Square that night.

She said she wasn't familiar with the Harold Robbins *oeuvre* – she was a little sarcastic really – but she knew what I meant about the El Dorado. It hadn't been quite as sleazy last time she was there. Still, never mind. It was all part of our little adventure, she said. We walked around the square for a while, looking at the lights and the posters in the cinema windows.

I bought her an ice cream in a little place in Soho. She said this was a really trendy area now, and the shops were way too expensive. I said she didn't have to tell me, the ice creams had cost six-fifty. She smiled and said she'd give me the money. I told her not to be so silly, but she insisted, so I took it. I gave the waiter a two-quid tip. Well, I didn't want her to think I was mean. She said, 'You only did that because you don't want me to think you're mean.' I tried to be as offended as possible but she just slipped her arm through mine and laughed again, and there was something about her made me want to be happy. So I admitted it and she sighed with mock desperation that men were so transparent.

Catriona was beautiful when she sighed. Wearing jeans and Doc Martens and a Public Enemy T-shirt, she was far more elegant than any of the women we watched swanning out of the opera house in pearls and fur. Her eyes were kind of soft and sparkling, the kind you read about in books. Her face was lightly freckled. She had a way of talking fast and avoiding my eyes that was just irresistible. And she was funny, too. In the wine bar she made sarcastic comments about the posers and yuppies in the corners.

I told her about home and Susan and everything. It's funny how much you can trust and say to a total stranger. And I told her I wasn't really sure what kind of job I was looking for, just something a bit more interesting than sitting in Dublin on the old rock and roll. She said she still had a year to go in art school, then she'd probably come over here and do some course or another. She had lots of friends over here already. In fact, she knew more people over here than she did in Dublin. Lots of people. Bucketloads of them. She'd never be stuck in London, she said.

The thing that got me was this. When we were talking about gigs and holidays and stuff I noticed she said 'we' all the time. We did this. We saw that. Some lucky bastard was obviously going out with her back home, and I suppose she kept dropping this 'we' shit to let me know that. Half-way through the second bottle of wine I plucked up the courage to ask her. She said he was a brilliant guy, Damien, they were really happy together and all that. A really wonderful pass-the-sickbag relationship.

'So, what's happening?' I asked her, pretending not to be jealous as hell. 'I mean, are we talking wedding bells or what?'

'Maybe,' she admitted, 'when he qualifies.'

'And kids and everything?'

'Yeah,' she said. 'I'm sure we'll have children. I mean, why wouldn't we?'

'I don't know,' I said, 'why would you? I mean, why?'

'What is this,' she said, 'twenty fucking questions?'

I suppose I shouldn't have been so pushy and everything. It's not good to pry. I know that, but you know, it was just the booze really. Booze makes some people happy or sad or horny. It makes me curious. Always has. Outside in the rain I felt uneasy and confused. She seemed very quiet now, like there was something on her mind. The mood of things had changed. The feel of the night was suddenly weird and different now. Maybe this hadn't been such a great idea. I told her I was sorry for asking so many personal questions. She just stood there outside the Hippodrome chewing her fingernails and saying nothing.

'Do you want me to go away?' I asked.

She smiled then. She slipped her hand into mine. She said she was sorry too. She didn't know what had come over her. She had things on her mind. She couldn't say. Maybe she'd tell me some other time. She was really sorry, though. Here she was spoiling my first night in London. I told her that was rubbish, and if it wasn't for her I'd be having an awful time. I said come on, here I was in London with a gorgeous woman and not a care in the world. She smiled and looked up at me then. She asked me if I meant the gorgeous bit.

'Yeah,' I said. I did. She said she'd been called beautiful before, but never gorgeous. 'They're not the same thing,' I said, 'not the same thing at all.'

'Charmer,' she said, in a sad voice, 'you're just like Damien.' I said I was sure I wasn't. She said I was, but for one night it didn't matter.

That night Catriona and I made love in the El Dorado Hotel. I had no condoms but she said it was safe. We held each other tight as the bedsprings gave us away. I didn't care. I didn't think about anything except her. I couldn't. Afterwards we lay in each other's arms. I asked her is she sure it was safe. She said yes. Her voice sounded weird. Like she was about to shout. Then I touched her face and she softened. She held my hand very hard.

When I woke up I didn't know where I was. My head hurt and my mouth was numb. She was sitting at the dressing table, putting her earrings in. She said she was going out for the day and wouldn't be back until teatime. She had to see this friend of hers. I asked if it was a guy. She laughed and said no. But she wouldn't let me come. It was just girl talk, she said.

'I'll probably tell her all about you,' she smiled, 'all about how I seduced you.' She kissed me before she slipped out of the room. She said she'd see me back here at eight.

'Yeah,' I said, 'mind yourself.' She said she would.

Down in the breakfast room the Greek grinned lasciviously as he ladled a large sausage onto my plate.

'Eat it all up,' he said. 'You will need all your strength, yes?'

I spent the day dossing around. On Oxford Street the shop windows were full of cheap suits and grim-looking dummies. A guy in sunglasses was selling gold chains from a cardboard box outside the HMV Megastore. 'Any shop in the West End, ladies and gents, they'd costya two hundred nicker straight up but here it's not two hundred, it's not one hundred and fifty, it's not seventy-five or fifty or even thirty. A pony, ladies and gents. First twenty-five pound down gets it.' Nobody moved. 'Come on now, loves,' he said, 'before Mister Plod comes back, who'll give me twenty-five for one of these lovely items?' I walked away and bought a postcard of Princess Diana for my mother. I wrote it over coffee in a little place on Russell Street. I told her I'd arrived safely, and that I was fine, and already making friends. I smiled when I wrote that. I couldn't find a post office open anywhere so I put the card in my pocket and forgot all about it. I never sent it. I still have it in my pocket somewhere, all crumpled up and torn. I've always kept it.

When Catriona came back that night she had an upset stomach. She was bleary-eyed and pale. She told me she'd eaten some awful burger or something, and it hadn't agreed with her at all. I told her to watch it. I told her catching salmonella is the national fucking sport over here. But when she tried to laugh it really creased her up. She had to lie down. She had to get some sleep. Soon as she said that she leaned over and vomited on the floor. I was worried. She walked into the room and flopped onto the bed, shivering and clutching her stomach. She really was in a bad way. When I put my arms around her she started all of a sudden – I mean for absolutely no reason – to cry. I asked her to tell me what was wrong. Had she had some row with her friend? She said, no, she hadn't even seen her. Why not? She snapped at me then. I mean, she nearly bit my fucking head off. She really got weird on me, started saying she had no friends and she was on her own. I said I was her friend and she laughed and said, yeah, things were that bad. Then she said she was sorry. I held her hand as she eased painfully under the sheets, with all her clothes still on. I asked if it was something to do with her period.

'Oh my God,' she sighed, 'spare me the new man bit.' She laughed out loud then, really laughed the bloody roof down. No, she said, if there was one thing it had nothing to do with, it was that. Then she told me she just had to get some sleep. I was to come back and see her later on.

In my room I walked up and down, chain-smoking and flicking ash all over the carpet. I didn't care. Then I lay on my bed and stared out at the lights on the street. What the hell was wrong? Would she be alright? Jesus, say if she bloody died or something. I got up and poured myself a glass of duty free. The tumbler was dirty and it tasted like toothpaste. But I drank it anyway. Then I had another one. Then I had a double. She'd probably be OK. Just some bug or something, that was all. In fact I wasn't feeling so terrific myself. I fed a pound into the television. I watched a documentary about a tribe in the Amazon that eat monkeys.

The bed was wet when I woke up. The stench of the whisky was everywhere. The clock on the wall said ten-past eleven. Shit. I must have dozed off holding the bottle. It was nearly all spilt. My jeans stuck to my legs. I splashed water over my face. I stared in the mirror. I looked awful. My face was pale and my tongue felt all furry. Maybe it was that ice cream we'd had the night before. I don't know. Six-quid-fifty for strawberry-flavoured botulism. Or too much cheap red wine. Yeah. That was probably what was wrong with her. Just a hangover.

When I stumbled in she was sitting up in the bed and wearing my pyjama top. I sat down beside her and asked how she was. She had been crying again. She wrapped her arms around me. The smell of drink filled my head. I told her not to worry. I said everything would be alright. She said my name a few times while I tried to kiss her. She was so beautiful. I couldn't help it.

'Please,' she said, taking my hands off her. She couldn't. It wasn't that she didn't want to. She just couldn't. 'Don't you understand anything?' she said, with tears in her eyes. 'I mean, do I have to paint you a picture?'

I said if she wanted to be like that she could stay on her own. It wasn't my bloody fault she was sick. I told her I bet old Damien wouldn't have stood for this bloody primadonna crap. Who the hell did she think she was, anyway? She told me to get out. I said I was sorry. She started screaming, 'Get out, you shit. Get out of my room.' She picked up a glass and pitched it at me; it smashed on the wall.

When I came back later and knocked on her door there was no answer. I stood in the corridor, apologising through the keyhole. No sound came from the room. The Greek came by and saw me on my knees.

'The ladies, my friend,' he shrugged, 'what can you do with them?' I said nothing.

Next morning Catriona was gone. She'd checked out at seven-thirty, taken all her stuff, ordered a cab for Luton airport. The Greek said he was terribly sorry. I said I hadn't known her that well anyway.

'Still,' he said, 'a very sad situation.' I asked him what he meant. He said no offence, but it was just very sad, a young girl like her.

Breathless, I stood in Catriona's room, staring at the made-up bed and the open windows. My pyjama top lay on the chair by the window. There was a brown bloodstain on it. The Greek's wife came in with an armful of clean white towels.

The young lady had been very ill in the night, she said. They were going to call me but Catriona had insisted that they shouldn't. She begged them not to. She couldn't let anyone find out. If her parents discovered, they would kill her. She explained everything and said it was nothing to worry about. The nurses had told her all this would happen. What she needed now was rest. No worry, and plenty of sleep. It was all over now. But a little discomfort was only to be expected.

The Greek's wife told me she was terribly sorry. She'd thought I would have been aware of things. If only she'd known, she would have broken it more gently. I felt like my whole body was turning to water. She asked me if I wanted a drink. I said no, I still had some duty free left.

I arrived at Aunt Martha's place at lunchtime on Sunday. The door opened and I fell in. She was furious with me. What did I mean, turning up in this drunken state? Did I think this was some kind of boarding house? And where had I been, anyway? She'd phoned Dublin on Friday night to see whether the fog had lifted. My mother had been worried sick about me. I'd better have a good explanation. They were just about to call the police. My father was searching the house for a photo to give them for *The News*. The only one he could find was the one they took the day of my graduation. They didn't know what kind of trouble I was in. Out in the hall I rang home. I said I'd bumped into Johnny Reilly, a guy I once knew in college, who was living over here now. I'd decided to stay a few nights with him. My mother said she wanted me back home on the next plane. She said it was patently obvious that I couldn't be trusted to look after myself.

Alvin and Sharon said it was good to see me. Sharon had purple hair now, and Alvin had a ring through his nose. I managed to croak that I was sorry for all the trouble I'd caused. They shrugged and said not to worry. They said London was all about enjoying yourself. They said I shouldn't let my mother guilt-trip me. In the kitchen someone made me a cup of strong coffee. Alvin said not to pay any attention to Aunt Martha either. He said mothers were all the same. Then Sharon put her arms around me and told me to stop crying. She was sure it would all blow over soon. We'd be laughing about it, she said, in a few weeks.

I went to bed and stared at the ceiling. I wrapped the blanket tight around me. Really tight. Over my head. So tight that it felt like a second skin. And the whole world was shut out now, on the other side of the darkness.

THE DRESSMAKER'S CHILD

William Trevor

Cahal sprayed WD-40 on to the only bolt his spanner wouldn't shift. All the others had come out easily enough but this one was rusted in, the exhaust unit trailing from it. He had tried to hammer it out, he had tried wrenching the exhaust unit this way and that in the hope that something would give way, but nothing had. Half five, he'd told Heslin, and the bloody car wouldn't be ready.

The lights of the garage were always on because shelves had been put up in front of the windows that stretched across the length of the wall at the back. Abandoned cars, kept for their parts, and cars and motor-cycles waiting for spares, and jacks that could be wheeled about, took up what space there was on either side of the small wooden office, which was at the back also. There were racks of tools, and workbenches with vices along the back wall, and rows of new and reconditioned tyres, and drums of grease and oil. In the middle of the garage there were two pits, in one of which Cahal's father was at the moment, putting in a clutch. There was a radio on which advice was being given about looking after fish in an aquarium. 'Will you turn that stuff off?' Cahal's father shouted from under the car he was working on, and Cahal searched the wavebands until he found music of his father's time.

He was an only son in a family of girls, all of them older, all of them gone from the town – three to England, another in Dunne's in Galway, another married in Nebraska. The garage was what Cahal knew, having kept his father company there since childhood, given odd jobs to do as he grew up. His father had had help then, an old man who was related to the family, whose place Cahal eventually took.

He tried the bolt again but the WD-40 hadn't begun to work yet. He was a lean, almost scrawny youth, dark-haired, his long face usually unsmiling. His garage overalls, over a yellow T-shirt, were oil-stained, gone pale where their green dye had been washed out of them. He was nineteen years old.

'Hullo,' a voice said. A man and a woman, strangers, stood in the wide open doorway of the garage.

'Howya,' Cahal said.

'It's the possibility, sir,' the man enquired, 'you drive us to the sacred Virgin?'

'Sorry?' And Cahal's father shouted up from the pit, wanting to know who was there. 'Which Virgin's that?' Cahal asked.

The two looked at one another, not attempting to answer, and it occurred to Cahal that they were foreign people, who had not understood. A year ago a German had driven his Volkswagen into the garage, with a noise in the engine, so he'd said. 'I had hopes it'd be the big end,' Cahal's father admitted afterwards, but it was only the catch of the bonnet gone a bit loose. A couple from America had had a tyre put on their hired car a few weeks after that, but there'd been nothing since.

'Of Pouldearg,' the woman said. 'Is it how to say it?'

'The statue you're after?'

They nodded uncertainly and then with more confidence, both of them at the same time.

'Aren't you driving, yourselves, though?' Cahal asked them.

'We have no car,' the man said.

'We are travelled from Ávila.' The woman's black hair was silky, drawn back and tied with a red and blue ribbon. Her eyes were brown, her teeth very white, her skin olive. She wore the untidy clothes of a traveller: denim trousers, a woollen jacket over a striped red blouse. The man's trousers were the same, his shirt a nondescript shade of greyish blue, a white kerchief at his neck. A few years older than himself, Cahal estimated they'd be.

'Ávila?' he said.

'Spain,' the man said.

Again Cahal's father called out, and Cahal said two Spanish people had come into the garage.

'In the store,' the man explained. 'They say you drive us to the Virgin.'

'Are they broken down?' Cahal's father shouted.

He could charge them fifty euros, Pouldearg there and back, Cahal considered. He'd miss Germany versus Holland on the television, maybe the best match of the Cup, but never mind that for fifty euros.

'The only thing,' he said, 'I have an exhaust to put in.'

He pointed at the pipe and silencer hanging out of Heslin's old Vauxhall, and they understood. He gestured with his hands that they should stay where they were for a minute, and with his palms held flat made a pushing motion in the air, indicating that they should ignore the agitation that was coming from the pit. Both of them were amused. When Cahal tried the bolt again it began to turn.

He made the thumbs-up sign when exhaust and silencer clattered to the ground. 'I could take you at around seven,' he said, going close to where the Spaniards stood, keeping his voice low so that his father would not hear. He led them to the forecourt and made the arrangement while he filled the tank of a Murphy's Stout lorry.

*

When he'd driven a mile out on the Ennis road, Cahal's father turned at the entrance to the stud farm and drove back to the garage, satisfied that the clutch he'd put in for Father Shea was correctly adjusted. He left the car on the forecourt, ready for Father Shea to collect, and hung the keys up in the office. Heslin from the courthouse was writing a cheque for the exhaust Cahal had fitted. Cahal was getting out of his overalls, and when Heslin had gone he said the people who had come wanted him to drive them to Pouldearg. They were Spanish people, Cahal said again, in case his father hadn't heard when he'd supplied that information before.

'What they want with Pouldearg?'

'Nothing only the statue.'

'There's no one goes to the statue these times.'

'It's where they're headed.'

'Did you tell them, though, how the thing was?'

'I did of course.'

'Why they'd be going out there?'

'There's people takes photographs of it.'

Thirteen years ago, the then bishop and two parish priests had put an end to the cult of the wayside statue at Pouldearg. None of those three men, and no priest or nun who had ever visited the crossroads at Pouldearg, had sensed anything special about the statue; none had witnessed the tears that were said to slip out of the downcast eyes when pardon for sins was beseeched by penitents. The statue became the subject of attention in pulpits and in religious publications, the claims made for it fulminated against as a foolishness. And then a curate of that time demonstrated that what had been noticed by two or three local people who regularly passed by the statue – a certain dampness beneath the eyes – was no more than raindrops trapped in two over-defined hollows. There the matter ended. Those who had so certainly believed in what they had never actually seen, those who had not noticed the drenched leaves of overhanging boughs high above the statue, felt as foolish as their spiritual masters had predicted they one day would. Almost overnight the weeping Virgin of Pouldearg became again the painted image it had always been. Our Lady of the Wayside, it had been called for a while.

'I never heard people were taking photographs of it.' Cahal's father shook his head as if he doubted his son, which he often did and usually with reason.

'A fellow was writing a book a while back. Going around all Ireland, tracking down the weeping statues.'

'It was no more than the rain at Pouldearg.'

'He'd have put that in the book. That man would have put the whole thing down, how you'd find the statues all over the place and some of them would be okay and some of them wouldn't.'

'And you set the Spaniards right about Pouldearg?'

'I did of course.'

'Drain the juice out of young Leahy's bike and we'll weld his leak for him.'

*

The suspicions of Cahal's father were justified: the truth had no more than slightly played a part in what Cahal had told the Spanish couple about Pouldearg. With fifty euros at the back of his mind, he would have considered it a failure of his intelligence had he allowed himself to reveal that the miracle once claimed for the statue at Pouldearg was without foundation. They had heard the statue called Our Lady of Tears as well as Our Lady of the Wayside and the Sacred Virgin of Pouldearg by a man in a Dublin public house with whom they had drifted into conversation. They'd had to repeat this a couple of times before Cahal grasped what they were saying, but he thought he got it right in the end. It wouldn't be hard to stretch the journey by four or five miles, and if they were misled by the names they'd heard the statue given in Dublin it was no concern of his. At five past seven, when he'd had his tea and had had a look at the television, he drove into the yard of Macey's Hotel. He waited there as he'd said he would. They appeared almost at once.

They sat close together in the back. Before he started the engine again Cahal told them what the cost would be and they said that was all right. He drove through the town, gone quiet as it invariably did at this time. Some of the shops were still open and would remain so for a few more hours – the newsagents' and tobacconists', the sweet shops and small groceries, Quinlan's supermarket, all the public houses – but there was a lull on the streets.

'Are you on holiday?' Cahal asked.

He couldn't make much of their reply. Both of them spoke, correcting one another. After a lot of repetition they seemed to be telling him that they were getting married.

'Well, that's grand,' he said.

He turned out on to the Loye road. Spanish was spoken in the back of the car. The radio wasn't working or he'd have put it on for company. The car was a black Ford Cortina with a hundred and eighty thousand miles on the clock; his father had taken it in part-exchange. They'd use it until the tax disc expired and then put it aside for spares. Cahal thought of telling them that in case they'd think he hadn't much to say for himself, but he knew it would be too difficult. The Christian Brothers had had him labelled as not having much to say for himself, and it had stuck in his memory, worrying him sometimes in case it caused people to believe he was slow. Whenever he could, Cahal tried to give the lie to that by making a comment.

'Are you here long?' he enquired, and the girl said they'd been two days in Dublin. He said he'd been in Dublin himself a few times. He said it was mountainy from now on, until they reached Pouldearg. The scenery was beautiful, the girl said.

He took the fork at the two dead trees, although going straight would have got them there too, longer still but potholes all over the place. It was a good car for the hills, the man said, and Cahal said it was a Ford, pleased that he'd understood. You'd get used to it, he considered; with a bit more practising you'd pick up the trick of understanding them.

'How'd you say it in Spanish?' he called back over his shoulder. 'A statue?'

'*Estatua*,' they both said, together. '*Estatua*,' they said.

'*Estatua*,' Cahal repeated, changing gear for the hill at Loye.

The girl clapped her hands, and he could see her smiling in the driving mirror. God, a woman like that, he thought. Give me a woman like that, he said to himself, and he imagined he was in the car alone with her, that the man wasn't there, that he hadn't come to Ireland with her, that he didn't exist.

'Do you hear about St Teresa of Ávila? Do you hear about her in Ireland?' Her lips opened and closed in the driving mirror, her teeth flashing, the tip of her tongue there for a moment. What she'd asked him was as clear as anyone would say it.

'We do, of course,' he said, confusing St Teresa of Ávila with the St Teresa who'd been famous for her humility and her attention to little things. 'Grand,' Cahal attributed to her also. 'Grand altogether.'

To his disappointment, Spanish was spoken again. He was going with Minnie Fennelly, but no doubt about it this woman had the better of her. The two faces appeared side by side in his mind's eye and there wasn't a competition. He drove past the cottages beyond the bridge, the road twisting and turning all over the place after that. It said earlier on the radio there'd be showers but there wasn't a trace of one, the October evening without a breeze, dusk beginning.

'Not more than a mile,' he said, not turning his head, but the Spanish was still going on. If they were planning to take photographs they mightn't be lucky by the time they got there. With the trees, Pouldearg was a dark place at the best of times. He wondered if the Germans had scored yet. He'd have put money on the Germans if he'd had any to spare.

Before they reached their destination Cahal drew the car on to the verge where it was wide and looked dry. He could tell from the steering that there was trouble and found it in the front offside wheel, the tyre leaking at the valve. Five or six pounds it would have lost, he estimated.

'It won't take me a minute,' he reassured his passengers, rummaging behind where they sat, among old newspapers and tools and empty paint tins, for the pump. He thought for a moment it mightn't be there and wondered what he'd do if the spare tyre was flat, which sometimes it was if a car was a trade-in. But the pump was there and he gave the partially deflated tyre a couple of extra pounds to keep it going. He'd see how things were when they reached Pouldearg crossroads.

When they did, there wasn't enough light for a photograph, but the two went up close to the Wayside Virgin, which was more lopsided than Cahal remembered it from the last time he'd driven by it, hardly longer than a year ago. The tyre had lost the extra pressure he'd pumped in and while they were occupied he began to change the wheel, having discovered that the spare tyre wasn't flat. All the time he could hear them talking in Spanish, although their voices weren't raised. When they returned to the car it was still jacked up and they had to wait for a while, standing on the road beside him, but they didn't appear to mind.

He'd still catch most of the second half, Cahal said to himself when eventually he turned the car and began the journey back. You never knew how you were placed as regards how long you'd be, how long you'd have to wait for people while they poked about.

'Was she all right for you?' he asked them, turning on the headlights so that the potholes would show up.

They answered in Spanish, as if they had forgotten that it wouldn't be any good. She'd fallen over a bit more, he said, but they didn't understand. They brought up the man they'd met in the public house in Dublin. They kept repeating something, a gabble of English words that still appeared to be about getting married. In the end, it seemed to Cahal that this man had told them people received a marriage blessing when they came to Pouldearg as penitents.

'Did you buy him drinks?' he asked, but that wasn't understood either.

They didn't meet another car, nor even a bicycle until they were further down. He'd been lucky over the tyre: they could easily have said they wouldn't pay if he'd had them stranded all night in the hills. They weren't talking any more; when he looked in the mirror they were kissing, no more than shadows in the gloom, arms around one another.

It was then, just after they'd passed the dead trees, that the child ran out. She came out of the blue cottage and ran at the car. He'd heard of it before, the child on this road who ran out at cars. It had never happened to himself, he'd never even seen a child there any time he'd passed, but often it was mentioned. He felt the thud no more than a second after the headlights picked out the white dress by the wall and then the sudden movement of the child running out.

Cahal didn't stop. In his mirror the road had gone dark again. He saw something white lying there but said to himself he had imagined it. In the back of the Cortina the embrace continued.

Sweat had broken on the palms of Cahal's hands, on his back and his forehead. She'd thrown herself at the side of the car and his own door was what she'd made contact with. Her mother was the un-married woman of that cottage, many the time he'd heard that said in the garage. Fitzie Gill had shown him damage to his wing and said the child must have had a stone in her hand. But usually there wasn't any damage, and no one had ever mentioned damage to the child herself.

Bungalows announced the town, all of them lit up now. The Spanish began again, and he was asked if he could tell them what time the bus went to Galway. There was confusion because he thought they meant tonight, but then he understood it was the morning. He told them and when they paid him in Macey's yard the man handed him a pencil and a notebook. He didn't know what that was for, but they showed him, making gestures, and he wrote down the time of the bus. They shook hands with him before they went into the hotel.

*

In the very early morning, just after half past one, Cahal woke up and couldn't sleep again. He tried to recall what he'd seen of the football, the moves there'd been, the saves, the yellow card shown twice. But nothing seemed quite right, as if the television pictures and snatches of the commentary came from a dream, which he knew they hadn't. He had examined the side of the car in the garage and there'd been nothing. He had switched out the lights of the garage and locked up. He'd watched the football in Shannon's and hadn't seen the end because he lost interest when nothing much was happening. He should have stopped; he didn't know why he hadn't. He couldn't remember braking. He didn't know if he'd tried to, he didn't know if there hadn't been time.

The Ford Cortina had been seen setting out on the Loye road, and then returning. His father knew the way he'd gone, past the unmarried woman's cottage. The Spaniards would have said in the hotel they'd seen the Virgin. They'd have said in the hotel they were going on to Galway. They could be found in Galway for questioning.

In the dark Cahal tried to work it out. They would have heard the bump. They wouldn't have known what it was, but they'd have heard it while they were kissing one another. They would remember how much longer it was before they got out of the car in Macey's yard. It hadn't been a white dress, Cahal realised suddenly: it trailed on the ground, too long for a dress, more like a nightdress.

He'd seen the woman who lived there a few times when she came in to the shops, a dressmaker they said she was, small and wiry with dark inquisitive eyes and a twist in her features that made them less appealing than they might have been. When her child had been born to her the father had not been known – not even to herself, so it was said, though possibly without justification. People said she didn't speak about the birth of her child.

As Cahal lay in the darkness, he resisted the compulsion to get up in order to go back and see for himself; to walk out to the blue cottage, since to drive would be foolish; to look on the road for whatever might be there, he didn't know what. Often he and Minnie Fennelly got up in the middle of the night in order to meet in the back shed at her house. They lay on a stack of netting there, whispering and petting one another, the way they couldn't anywhere in the daytime. The best they could manage in the daytime was half an hour in the Ford Cortina out in the country somewhere. They could spend half the night in the shed.

He calculated how long it would take him to walk out to where the incident had occurred. He wanted to; he wanted to get there and see nothing on the road and to close his eyes in relief. Sometimes dawn had come by the time he parted from Minnie Fennelly, and he imagined that too, the light beginning as he walked in from the country feeling all right again. But more likely he wouldn't be.

'One day that kid'll be killed,' he heard Fitzie Gill saying, and someone else said the woman wasn't up to looking after the kid. The child was left alone in the house, people said, even for a night while the woman drank by herself in Leahy's, looking around for a man to keep her company.

That night, Cahal didn't sleep again. And all the next day he waited for someone to walk into the garage and say what had been found. But no one did, and no one did the next day either, or the day after that. The Spaniards would have gone on from Galway by now, the memories of people who had maybe noticed the Ford Cortina would be getting shaky. And Cahal counted the drivers whom he knew for a fact had experienced similar incidents with the child and said to himself that maybe, after all, he'd been fortunate. Even so, it would be a long time before he drove past that cottage again, if ever he did.

Then something happened that changed all that. Sitting with Minnie Fennelly in the Cyber Café one evening, Minnie Fennelly said, 'Don't look, only someone's staring at you.'

'Who is it?'

'D'you know that dressmaker woman?'

They'd ordered chips and they came just then. Cahal didn't say anything, but knew that sooner or later he wasn't going to be able to prevent himself from looking around. He wanted to ask if the woman had her child with her, but in the town he had only ever seen her on her own and he knew that the child wouldn't be there. If she was it would be a chance in a thousand, he thought, the apprehension that had haunted him on the night of the incident flooding his consciousness, stifling everything else.

'God, that one gives me the creeps!' Minnie Fennelly muttered, splashing vinegar on to her chips.

Cahal looked round them. He caught a glimpse of the dressmaker, alone, before he quickly looked back. He could still feel her eyes on his back. She would have been in Leahy's; the way she was sitting suggested drunkenness. When they'd finished their chips and the coffee they'd been brought while they were waiting, he asked if she was still there.

'She is, all right. D'you know her? Does she come into the garage?'

'Ah no, she hasn't a car. She doesn't come in.'

'I'd best be getting back, Cahal.'

He didn't want to go yet, while the woman was there. But if they waited they could be here for hours. He didn't want to pass near her, but as soon as he'd paid and stood up he saw they'd have to. When they did she spoke to Minnie Fennelly, not him.

'Will I make your wedding dress for you?' the dressmaker offered. 'Would you think of me at all when it'll be the time you'd want it?'

And Minnie Fennelly laughed and said no way they were ready for wedding dresses yet.

'Cahal knows where he'll find me,' the dressmaker said. 'Amn't I right, Cahal?'

'I thought you didn't know her,' Minnie Fennelly said when they were outside.

*

Three days after that, Mr Durcan left his pre-war Riley in because the handbrake was slipping. He'd come back for it at four, he arranged, and said before he left: 'Did you hear that about the dressmaker's child?'

He wasn't the kind to get things wrong. Fussy, with a thin black moustache, his Riley sports the pride of his bachelor life, he was as tidy in what he said as he was in how he dressed.

'Gone missing,' he said now. 'The gardaí are in on it.'

It was Cahal's father who was being told this. Cahal, with the cooling system from Gibney's bread van in pieces on a workbench, had just found where the tube had perished.

'She's backward, the child,' his father said.

'She is.'

'You hear tales.'

'She's gone off for herself anyway. They have a block on a couple of roads, asking was she seen.'

The unease that hadn't left him since the dressmaker had been in the Cyber Café began to nag again when Cahal heard that. He wondered what questions the gardaí were asking; he wondered when it was that the child had taken herself off; although he tried, he couldn't piece anything together.

'Isn't she a backward woman herself, though?' his father remarked when Mr Durcan had gone. 'Sure, did she ever lift a finger to tend that child?'

Cahal didn't say anything. He tried to think about marrying Minnie Fennelly, although still nothing was fixed, not even an agreement between themselves. Her plump honest features became vivid for a moment in his consciousness, the same plumpness in her arms and her hands. He found it attractive, he always had, since first he'd noticed her when she was still going to the nuns. He shouldn't have had thoughts about the Spanish girl, he shouldn't have let himself. He should have told them the statue was nothing, that the man they'd met had been pulling a fast one for the sake of the drinks they'd buy him.

'Your mother had that one run up curtains for the back room,' his father said. 'Would you remember that, boy?'

Cahal shook his head.

'Ah, you wouldn't have been five at the time, maybe younger yet. She was just after setting up with the dressmaking, her father still there in the cottage with her. The priests said give her work on account she was a charity. Bedad, they wouldn't say it now!'

Cahal turned the radio on and turned the volume up. Madonna was singing, and he imagined her in the get-up she'd fancied for herself a few years ago, suspenders and items of underclothes. He'd thought she was great.

'I'm taking the Toyota out,' his father said, and the bell from the forecourt rang, someone waiting there for petrol. It didn't concern him, Cahal told himself as he went to answer it. What had occurred on the evening of Germany and Holland was a different thing altogether from the news Mr Durcan had brought, no way could it be related.

'Howya,' he greeted the school-bus driver at the pumps.

*

The dressmaker's child was found where she'd lain for several days, at the bottom of a fissure, partly covered with shale, in the exhausted quarry half a mile from where she'd lived. Years ago the last of the stone had been carted away and a barbed-wire fence put up, with two warning notices about danger. She would have crawled in under the bottom strand of wire, the gardaí said, and a chain-link fence replaced the barbed wire within a day.

In the town the dressmaker was condemned, blamed behind her back for the tragedy that had occurred. That her own father, who had raised her on his own since her mother's early death, had himself been the father of the child was an ugly calumny, not voiced before, but seeming now to have a natural place in the paltry existence of a child who had lived and died wretchedly.

'How are you, Cahal?' Cahal heard the voice of the dressmaker behind him when, early one November morning, he made his way to the shed where he and Minnie Fennelly indulged their affection for one another. It was not yet one o'clock, the town lights long ago extinguished except for a few in Main Street. 'Would you come home with me, Cahal? Would we walk out to where I am?'

All this was spoken to his back while Cahal walked on. He knew who was there. He knew who it was, he didn't have to look.

'Leave me alone,' he said.

'Many's the night I rest myself on the river seat and many's the night I see you. You'd always be in a hurry, Cahal.'

'I'm in a hurry now.'

'One o'clock in the morning! Arrah, go on with you, Cahal!'

'I don't know you. I don't want to be talking to you.'

'She was gone for five days before I went to the guards. It wouldn't be the first time she was gone off. A minute wouldn't go by without she was out on the road.'

Cahal didn't say anything. Even though he still didn't turn round he could smell the drink on her, stale and acrid.

'I didn't go to them any quicker for fear they'd track down the way it was when the lead would be fresh for them. D'you understand me, Cahal?'

Cahal stopped. He turned round and she almost walked into him. He told her to go away.

'The road was the thing with her. First thing of a morning she'd be running at the cars without a pick of food inside her. The next thing is she'd be off up the road to the statue. She'd kneel to the statue the whole day until she was found by some old fellow who'd bring her back to me. Some old fellow'd have her by the hand and they'd walk in the door. Oh, many's the time, Cahal. Wasn't it the first place the guards looked when I said that to the sergeant? Any woman'd do her best for her own, Cahal.'

'Will you leave me alone!'

'Gone seven it was, maybe twenty past. I had the door open to go into Leahy's and I seen the black car going by and yourself inside it. You always notice a car in the evening time, only the next thing was I was late back from Leahy's and she was gone. D'you understand me, Cahal?'

'It's nothing to do with me.'

'He'd have gone back the same way he went out, I said to myself, but I didn't mention it to the guards, Cahal. Was she in the way of wandering in her nightdress? was what they asked me and I told them she'd be out the door before you'd see her. Will we go home, Cahal?'

'I'm not going anywhere with you.'

'There'd never be a word of blame on yourself, Cahal.'

'There's nothing to blame me for. I had people in the car that evening.'

'I swear before God, what's happened is done with. Come back with me now, Cahal.'

'Nothing happened, nothing's done with. There was Spanish people in the car the entire time. I drove them out to Pouldearg and back again to Macey's Hotel.'

'Minnie Fennelly's no use to you, Cahal.'

He had never seen the dressmaker close before. She was younger than he'd thought, but still looked a fair bit older than himself, maybe twelve or thirteen years. The twist in her face wasn't ugly, but it spoilt what might have been beauty of a kind, and he remembered the flawless beauty of the Spanish girl and the silkiness of her hair. The dressmaker's hair was black too, but wild and matted, limply straggling, falling to her shoulders. The eyes that had stared so intensely at him in the Cyber Café were bleary. Her full lips were drawn back in a smile, one of her teeth slightly chipped. Cahal walked away and she did not follow him.

That was the beginning; there was no end. In the town, though never again at night, she was always there: Cahal knew that was an illusion, that she wasn't always there but seemed so because her presence on each occasion meant so much. She tidied herself up; she wore dark clothes, which people said were in mourning for her child; and people said she had ceased to frequent Leahy's public house. She was seen painting the front of her cottage, the same blue shade, and tending its bedraggled front garden. She walked from the shops of the town, and never now stood, hand raised, in search of a lift.

Continuing his familiar daily routine of repairs and servicing and answering the petrol bell, Cahal found himself unable to dismiss the connection between them that the dressmaker had made him aware of when she'd walked behind him in the night, and knew that the roots it came from spread and gathered strength and were nurtured, in himself, by fear. Cahal was afraid without knowing what he was afraid of, and when he tried to work this out he was bewildered. He began to go to Mass and to confession more often than he ever had before. It was noticed by his father that he had even less to say these days to the customers at the pumps or when they left their cars in. His mother wondered about his being anaemic and put him on iron pills. Returning occasionally to the town for a couple of days at a weekend, his sister who was still in Ireland said the trouble must surely be to do with Minnie Fennelly.

During all this time – passing in other ways quite normally – the child was lifted again and again from the cleft in the rocks, still in her nightdress as Cahal had seen her, laid out and wrapped as the dead are wrapped. If he hadn't had to change the wheel he would have passed the cottage at a different time and the chances were she wouldn't have been ready to run out, wouldn't just then have felt inclined to. If he'd explained to the Spaniards about the Virgin's tears being no more than rain he wouldn't have been on the road at all.

The dressmaker did not speak to him again or seek to, but he knew that the fresh blue paint, and the mourning clothes that were not, with time, abandoned, and the flowers that came to fill the small front garden, were all for him. When a little more than a year had passed since the evening he'd driven the Spanish couple out to Pouldearg, he attended Minnie Fennelly's wedding when she married Des Downey, a vet from Athenry.

The dressmaker had not said it, but it was what there had been between them in the darkened streets: that he had gone back, walking out as he had wanted to that night when he'd lain awake, that her child had been there where she had fallen on the road, that he had carried her to the quarry. And Cahal knew it was the dressmaker, not he, who had done that.

He visited the Virgin of the Wayside, always expecting that she might be there. He knelt, and asked for nothing. He spoke only in his thoughts, offering reparation and promising to accept whatever might be visited upon him for associating himself with the mockery of the man the Spaniards had met by chance in Dublin, for mocking the lopsided image on the road, taking fifty euros for a lie. He had looked at them kissing. He had thought about Madonna with her clothes off, not minding that she called herself that.

Once when he was at Pouldearg, Cahal noticed the glisten of what had once been taken for tears on the Virgin's cheek. He touched the hollow where this moisture had accumulated and raised his dampened finger to his lips. It did not taste of salt, but that made no difference. Driving back, when he went by the dressmaker's blue cottage she was there in the front garden, weeding her flower beds. Even though she didn't look up, he wanted to go to her and knew that one day he would.

CONTRIBUTORS

John Banville (b. 1945)

John Banville was born in 1945 in Wexford. His first book, *Long Lankin*, a collection of short stories, was published in 1970. His novels include *Doctor Copernicus*, which won the 1976 James Tait Black Memorial Prize; *Kepler* (1981), which won the *Guardian* Fiction Prize; and the 2005 Man Booker Prize winner *The Sea*. Banville has also adapted several plays by Heinrich von Kleist, including 1994's 'The Broken Jug'. He was the literary editor of the *Irish Times* from 1988 to 1999, and continues to contribute reviews frequently. He also reviews for the *New York Review of Books*, the *New Republic* and the *Guardian*.

Kevin Barry (b. 1969)

Kevin Barry is the author of the story collection, *There Are Little Kingdoms*, which was awarded the Rooney Prize for Irish Literature, and of the forthcoming novel, *City of Bohane*. His stories have appeared in the *New Yorker*, the *Best European Fiction* anthology, *Phoenix Irish Short Stories*, the *Stinging Fly* and the *Dublin Review*. He also writes plays and screenplays. He lives in County Sligo.

Elizabeth Bowen (1899–1973)

Elizabeth Bowen was born in Dublin in 1899, but moved to England with her mother at an early age, later dividing her adult life between Ireland and England. A prolific writer, Bowen's first collection of stories, *Encounters* (1923), was followed by eleven novels and seven short story collections, as well as essays and criticism. Her books include *The Hotel* (1927), *The Last September* (1929) and *The Death of the Heart* (1938). Bowen was awarded a CBE in 1948, and received honorary degrees from Trinity College Dublin in 1949, and from Oxford University in 1956. The Royal Society of Literature made her a Companion of Literature in 1965. She died in 1973.

Clare Boylan (1948–2006)

Clare Boylan was born in Dublin in 1948. A prominent journalist during the women's movement, she worked at the *Irish Press* and as Features Editor of *Image* magazine. She produced seven novels, including *Holy Pictures* (1993) and *Room for a Single Lady* (1997), three collections of short stories, two anthologies, and a large volume of criticism. Her last and most famous work was her completion of Charlotte Brontë's unfinished manuscript *Emma*, published as *Emma Brown* in 2003. She died of cancer in 2006, at the age of fifty-eight.

Patrick Boyle (1905–1982)

Patrick Boyle was born in County Antrim in 1905 and for much of his life worked for the Ulster Bank, primarily in Donegal. He began writing in his forties, and achieved recognition by winning the *Irish Times* Short Story Competition in 1965. His first book, the short story collection *At Night All Cats Are Grey* was published in 1966, and his debut novel *Like Any Other Man* was published the same year. This was followed by two further short story collections: *All Looks Yellow to the Jaundiced Eye* (1969) and *A View from Calvary* (1976).

Maeve Brennan (1917–1993)

Maeve Brennan was born in Dublin. At seventeen, she moved with her family to Washington DC, where her father was appointed the Republic of Ireland's first envoy to the United States. Brennan studied English Literature at the American University in Washington, later moving to New York where, in 1949, she became a staff writer for the *New Yorker*. There, she wrote criticism, essays and fiction, making her name with sketches of New York life, written under the pseudonym 'The Long-Winded Lady'. In 1950 she began to publish her short stories in the magazine. These are collected in *In and Out of Never-Never Land* (1969) and *Christmas Eve* (1974), and in the posthumously published *The Springs of Affection* (1997) and *The Rose Garden* (2000). Brennan's novella *The Visitor* was also published in 2000, after the only known copy of the typescript was discovered in the archives of the University of Notre Dame.

Jennifer C Cornell

Jennifer C Cornell's short story collection, *Departures*, was published in 1995 and won the Drue Heinz Literature Prize. Her work has appeared in *New Hibernia Review*, *TriQuarterly* and *New England Review*. She lives in Belfast, Northern Ireland.

Anne Devlin (b. 1951)

Anne Devlin was born in Belfast in 1951, and worked initially as a teacher. She won the Hennessy Literary Award in 1982 after David Marcus published her story 'The Journey to Somewhere Else' in the *Irish Press*. Her stories have adapted for award-winning film and television productions, and her short fiction was collected as *The Way-Paver* in 1986. She has written prize-winning drama for the Royal Court Theatre and the Royal Shakespeare Company, and her work for the big screen includes 'Wuthering Heights', 'Vigo' and 'Titanic Town'. Having lived in London for a decade, she returned to Belfast with her husband and son in 2007.

Gerard Donovan (b. 1959)

Gerard Donovan (b. 1959) grew up in Galway. He is the author of the novels *Schopenhauer's Telescope*, which won the 2004 Kerry Group Irish Fiction Award and was longlisted for the 2003 Booker Prize, *Doctor Salt* (2004), *Julius Winsome* (2006), as well as the short story collection *Country of the Grand* (2008). He lived in a converted railway station in New York for a decade and is now a Reader at the University of Plymouth in Devon, England.

Roddy Doyle (b. 1958)

Born in Dublin in 1958, Roddy Doyle worked for fourteen years as an English and Geography teacher before giving up his post to write full-time. His debut novel was published in 1987, when Doyle founded his own publishing company, King Farouk Press, and printed three thousand copies of *The Commitments*. The book, the first in Doyle's 'Barrytown Trilogy', was later republished to great critical acclaim by Heinemann, and adapted into a highly successful film. Doyle is the author of eight other novels, including *Paddy Clarke Ha Ha Ha*, which won the Booker Prize in 1993 and, most recently, *The Dead Republic*. He is also a playwright and screenwriter, and the author of several children's books. He lives in Dublin.

Hugo Hamilton (b. 1953)

Hugo Hamilton was born in Dublin in 1953 of a German mother and a fervent Irish nationalist father. He has written two memoirs, *The Speckled People* (2003), which won numerous prizes, including the Prix Femina Étranger in France, and *A Sailor in the Wardrobe* (2006), which continues his life story of growing up between two languages. His first novel *Surrogate City* (1990) was followed by six subsequent novels, including *The Last Shot* (1991) and *Disguise* (2008), and by a collection of short stories, *Dublin Where the Palm Trees Grow* (1996). He won the 1992 Rooney Prize for Irish Literature. His latest novel *Hand in the Fire* (2010) picks up the theme of trespassing from one culture into another by looking at Ireland through the eyes of a Serbian immigrant. He currently lives in Dublin.

Neil Jordan (b.1950)

Neil Jordan was born in Sligo in 1950 and studied Irish history and English literature at University College Dublin. After graduating, he co-founded the Irish Writers' Co-op, and worked with several theatre companies. His debut short story collection *Night in Tunisia* won the *Guardian* Fiction Prize in 1976, and he has subsequently published four novels: *The Past* (1979), *The Dream of a Beast* (1983), *Sunrise with Sea Monster* (1994) and *Shade* (2005). Jordan is an award-winning writer and director of films, including the *The Crying Game* (1992) and *Michael Collins* (1996). He lives Dublin and is a member of Aosdána.

Claire Keegan (b. 1968)

Claire Keegan was born in Wexford in 1968. She has written two collections of stories: *Antarctica (1999)* and *Walk the Blue Fields* (2007). *Antarctica* was a *Los Angeles Times* Book of the Year and won the Rooney Prize for Irish Literature. These stories have earned Keegan the William Trevor Prize (judged by Trevor), the Edge Hill Prize and the Macaulay Fellowship. Her story *Foster* won the Davy Byrnes Award, and was published in book form by Faber and Faber in 2010. Her stories have been published in the *Paris Review*, *Granta* and the *New Yorker*. She lives in rural Ireland.

Mary Lavin (1912–1996)

Mary Lavin was born in Massachusetts in 1912, the only child of Irish immigrants. She moved to Ireland as a child and later attended University College Dublin. In 1938, her first short story 'Miss Holland' appeared in the *Dublin Magazine*. Lavin's first published volume entitled *Tales from Bective Bridge*, including the short story 'Lilacs', was published in America in 1942, winning the James Tait Black Memorial Prize. Having published two novels, *The House in Clewe Street* (1945) and *Mary O'Grady* (1950), she became a regular contributor to the *New Yorker* magazine. She was the recipient of two Guggenheim Fellowships and the International PEN Katherine Mansfield Prize. She served as president of the Irish Academy of Letters and was a founder member of Aosdána, which elected her Saoi in 1992. Mary Lavin lived on a farm at Bective Abbey, County Meath, and at a Dublin mews in Lad Lane. She died in Dublin in 1996. *Tales from Bective Bridge* is to be re-issued in Faber Finds in 2011.

Eugene McCabe (b. 1930)

Eugene McCabe was born in Glasgow in 1930 to Ulster Irish parents who came back to Ireland at the outbreak of war. An Arts graduate of University College Cork, he later ran the family farm where he worked for the next fifty-five years, writing whenever possible. He is a renowned playwright and screenwriter, winning many international awards for his plays and for his television series *Victims*, set in Northern Ireland. He is the author of a novel, *Death and Nightingales* (1993) and of much short fiction, including *Victims: A Tale from Fermanagh* (1976), *Heritage and Other Stories* (1978), *Christ in the Fields: A Fermanagh Trilogy* (1993) and *Tales from the Poor House* (1999). His collected stories, *Heaven Lies About Us*, were published in 2005. Now retired from farming, he continues to live and write on the family farm on the Monaghan–Fermanagh border. He is a member of Aosdána.

Colum McCann (b.1965)

Colum McCann was born in Dublin in 1965 and began his career as a journalist in the Irish Press group. He left Ireland in the 1980s for North America and now lives in New York with his wife and children. McCann's writing has appeared in over thirty languages and numerous international publications. He is the author of two collections of short stories and five novels, including *This Side of Brightness*, *Dancer* and *Zoli*. In 2009 his novel *Let the Great World Spin* won the US National Book Award. Previous awards and honours include a Pushcart Prize, the Rooney Prize, the Hennessy Award for Irish Literature and the Hughes and Hughes/*Sunday Independent* Novel of the Year 2003. His short film adaptation for his story 'Everything in this Country Must' was nominated for an Academy Award in 2005. In 2009 McCann was elected a member of Aosdána and was awarded the Chevalier de l'Ordre des Arts et Lettres by the French government.

John McGahern (1934–2006)

John McGahern was born in Dublin and grew up in County Leitrim, the eldest of seven children. He worked as a primary school teacher but was dismissed from his post when his second novel *The Dark* was banned, for its sexual content, by the Irish Censorship Board. Much of his life was spent living and writing on his farm in County Leitrim. He is the author of six novels, including *The Barracks* (1963), *The Dark* (1965) and *Amongst Women* (1990) which was shortlisted for the Booker Prize. McGahern also published four highly acclaimed collections of short stories and wrote plays for radio, television and the stage. He received numerous awards and honours, including the *Irish Times* award, the American-Irish Award, the Prix Etrangère Ecureuil and the Chevalier de l'Ordre des Arts et des Lettres. *Memoir*, his last book, was published shortly before his death in 2006.

Bernard MacLaverty (b. 1942)

Bernard MacLaverty was born in Belfast and lived there until 1975 when he moved to Scotland. His first novels, *Lamb* (1980) and *Cal* (1983), were produced as films, and were followed by *Grace Notes* (1997), which was shortlisted for the Booker Prize, and *The Anatomy School* (2001). His short story collections are *Secrets*, *A Time to Dance*, *The*

Great Profundo, *Walking the Dog*, and in 2006 *Matters of Life and Death*. MacLaverty has written for film, radio and television, and was named Scottish Writer of the Year in 1988. His other awards include the RTÉ Jacobs Award for Best Play (1981), *Evening Standard* Award for Best Screenplay (1984) and Best First Director (BAFTA Scotland 2004) for the short film 'Bye-Child' which he also wrote. Recently he has written libretti for short opera. He lives and works in Glasgow and is a member of Aosdána.

Michael McLaverty (1904–1992)

Born in 1904 in County Monaghan, Michael McLaverty was five when his parents moved to Belfast. He was educated at Queen's University Belfast and then St Mary's University College, Twickenham. Having worked as a primary school teacher for thirty years, in 1957 McLaverty was appointed principal of Belfast's new St Thomas's Secondary School, where he employed Seamus Heaney on the faculty for several years. McLaverty was a prodigious writer, publishing eight novels and three short story collections, including *The White Mare and Other Stories* (1943), *The Game Cock and Other Stories* (1947) and *The Road to the Shore* (1976). His *Collected Short Stories* were published in 1978 and reissued in 2004 by Blackstaff Press. He died in 1992.

Aidan Mathews (b. 1956)

Aidan Mathews' first book of poems, published when he was twenty-one, was the Patrick Kavanagh Award-winning *Windfalls*. A second collection, *Minding Ruth*, appeared in 1983, and a third, *According to the Small Hours*, in 1998. His plays include *The Diamond Body* (1984), *The Antigone* (1984), *Exit-Entrance* (1988), which won the *Sunday Tribune* Theatre Award in that year, *Communion* (2002), *Walking Out Together* (2004) and translations of tragedies by Lorca and Euripides. He has written two short story collections, *Adventures in a Bathyscope* (1988) and *Lipstick on the Host* (1992), which received a Cavour Prize for Foreign Fiction in Italy, and the novel *Muesli at Midnight* (1990). A recipient of the Literature Award of the Irish Arts Council, his most recent work is *In the Poorer Quarters* (2007), a personal conversation with the Gospel of Mark.

Val Mulkerns (b. 1925)

The writer and freelance journalist Val Mulkerns was born in Dublin in 1925. After working for a few years in the civil service she moved to London but returned to Ireland in 1952 as Associate Editor of the literary journal *The Bell*. After two early novels Mulkerns published no further fiction for twenty-four years, until her sequence of short stories *Antiquities* appeared in 1978. Following this came the further collection *An Idle Woman* (1980) and two novels: *The Summerhouse* (1984) and *Very Like a Whale* (1986). Another collection of short stories, *A Friend of Don Juan*, was published in 1988. Val Mulkerns is also the author of two books for children which were published in Germany. In 1984 she was awarded the AIB Prize for Literature. She is a founder member of Aosdána.

Éilís Ní Dhuibhne (b. 1954)

Éilís Ní Dhuibhne was born in Dublin in 1954 and is a graduate of University College Dublin. She has written novels, collections of short stories, several books for children, plays and non-fiction works. She writes in both Irish and English. Her short story collections include *Blood and Water*, *Eating Women is Not Recommended*, *Midwife to the Fairies*, *The Inland Ice* and *The Pale Gold of Alaska*. Among her literary awards are the Bisto Book of the Year Award, the Readers' Association of Ireland Award, the Stewart Parker Award for Drama, the Butler Award for Prose from the Irish American Cultural Institute and several Oireachtas awards for novels and plays in Irish. Her novel *The Dancers Dancing* was shortlisted for the Orange Prize for Fiction. Éilís worked for many years as an assistant keeper in the National Library of Ireland and is now Writer Fellow at University College Dublin where she teaches on the MA in Creative Writing. She is a member of Aosdána.

Edna O'Brien (b. 1930)

Edna O'Brien was born in Twamgraney, County Clare, in 1930. Her first novel, *The Country Girls*, was published in 1960. A critical and popular success, it was banned in Ireland, along with her subsequent six novels, for the assumed frank portrayal of its characters' sex lives. O'Brien has since written more than twenty novels, short stories, biographies of James Joyce and Lord Byron and plays, which include

Virginia (on the life of Virginia Woolf), *Family Butchers* and *Haunted*. She has received numerous awards, including the 1990 *Los Angeles Times* Book Prize, the American National Arts Gold Medal for Lifetime Contribution and the Bob Hughes Lifetime Achievement in Irish Literature 2009, and is on Oprah Winfrey's *Book Club* as one of the top ten Irish writers of all time. She is a member of Aosdána and an honorary member of the American Academy of Letters.

Philip Ó Ceallaigh (b. 1968)

Philip Ó Ceallaigh has lived and worked in a number or countries, including Spain, Russia, the US, Egypt and Georgia. He is the author of the short story collections *Notes From a Turkish Whorehouse* (2006) and *The Pleasant Light of Day* (2009), both shortlisted for the Frank O'Connor International Short Story Prize and translated into a number of languages. Ó Ceallaigh was the editor of *Sharp Sticks, Driven Nails* (2010), an anthology of contemporary short stories. In 2006 he won the Rooney Prize for Irish Literature. He lives in Bucharest, Romania.

Frank O'Connor (1903–1966)

Frank O'Connor was born Michael John O'Donovan in Cork in 1903. An only child, born to a poor family, his formal education ended at thirteen. In 1923, he was interned after volunteering for the losing side in the Irish Civil War. He subsequently worked as a librarian, as well as for the Abbey Theatre and *The Bell* magazine. In 1951 he left Ireland for America where he taught at Harvard, Northwestern and Stanford universities. In a relatively short life, he wrote two novels, three books of literary criticism, a biography of Michael Collins, five books of translations of Irish poetry and more than twenty books of short stories. It is for these he is best known. The Frank O'Connor International Short Story Award is named in his honour. He died in Dublin in 1966.

Joseph O'Connor (b. 1963)

Joseph O'Connor was born in Dublin in 1963. He studied at University College Dublin and Oxford University, and as a student travelled to

Nicaragua, where he reported on the aftermath of the Sandinista revolution. His novels include *Cowboys and Indians*, which was nominated in the First Novel category for the Whitbread Prize (1991), *Desperadoes* (1993) and *The Salesman* (1998). In 2002, O'Connor published *Star of the Sea*, which became an international bestseller and won prizes and accolades around the world. Its sequel *Redemption Falls* was published in 2006. O'Connor has also written a collection of short stories, *True Believers* (1991), as well as non-fiction, stage plays and screenplays. In 2010 he published the novel *Ghost Light*.

Seán Ó Faoláin (1900–1991)

Born in 1900 in Cork, Seán Ó Faoláin was strongly influenced by the radical nationalism of the early 20th century. In 1921 he earned a BA in English from the University College at Cork, and later studied at Harvard University. He lectured for some years in the US before returning to Ireland and becoming a full-time writer. Ó Faoláin was a founder and editor of the prestigious literary journal *The Bell*. He wrote numerous plays, biographies and novels, but remained most well known for his short stories, published in twelve collections. He was a member of Aosdána, and was elected Saoi, its highest honour, in 1986.

Sean O'Reilly (b. 1969)

Born in Derry, Sean O' Reilly is the author of the short story collection *Curfew and other Stories* (2000), and the novels *Love and Sleep* (2002), *The Swing of Things* (2004) and *Watermark* (2006). He lives in Ireland.

Keith Ridgway (b. 1969)

Keith Ridgway was born in Dublin in 1965. He is the author of the novella *Horses*, the novels *The Long Falling* (1998), *The Parts* (2003) and *Animals* (2006), and the short story collection *Standard Time* (2001). *The Long Falling* was awarded the Prix Femina Étranger in 2001. He received the Rooney Prize for Irish Literature in 2001. He currently lives in London.

Colm Tóibín (b. 1955)

Colm Tóibín was born in 1955 in County Wexford. He graduated from University College Dublin and lived in Catalonia before returning to Dublin to work as a journalist. His novels include *The Heather Blazing* (1992), which won the Encore Award for best second novel and *The Blackwater Lightship* (1999) which was shortlisted for the Booker Prize. *The Master* (2004), also shortlisted for the Booker Prize, went on to win the International IMPAC Dublin Literary Award in 2006. His most recent novel, *Brooklyn*, won the Costa Novel Award in 2009. He has published many books of non-fiction, and two books of short stories: *Mothers and Sons* (2006), winner of the Edge Hill Prize, and *The Empty Family* (2010). A regular contributor to the *Dublin Review*, the *London Review of Books* and the *New York Review of Books*, he is a member of Aosdána.

William Trevor (b. 1928)

Born in County Cork in 1928, William Trevor studied history at Trinity College Dublin. He moved to England with his wife and worked as a sculptor for some years before becoming an advertising copywriter and in 1965 he turned to writing full-time. He has published many novels and short story collections, winning the Whitbread Prize three times (in 1976, 1983 and 1994) and being nominated five times for the Booker Prize, most recently for his novel *Love and Summer* (2009). He was awarded an honorary CBE in 1977, and the Bob Hughes Lifetime Achievement Award in Irish Literature in 2008. He is a member of Aosdána and lives in Devon, in south-west England.

ACKNOWLEDGEMENTS

Many thanks to my mother, Cora Enright, for the use of her bookshelves, for her suggestions, requests and clippings. Thanks also to my sister Mary Enright and to Colm Tóibín, for jogging my memory and trawling through their own. Thanks for advice and encouragement from Gill Coleridge, Robin Robertson and Peter Straus. Brendan Barrington and Declan Meade, who work closely with emerging writers, were particularly generous and helpful. Thanks also to the library staff in Trinity College Dublin, and to Sara Holloway, Amber Dowell and all at Granta.

PERMISSIONS

'Summer Voices' from Long Lankin by John Banville. Copyright © John Banville, 1984. Reprinted by permission of the author and The Gallery Press, Loughcrew, Oldcastle, County Meath, Ireland.

'See The Tree, How Big It's Grown' from *There Are Little Kingdoms* by Kevin Barry. Copyright © Kevin Barry, 2007. Permission granted c/o Lucy Luck Associates, 18–21 Cavaye Place, London SW10 9PT.

'Summer Night' from *The Collected Stories* by Elizabeth Bowen. Copyright © Elizabeth Bowen, 1923. Reproduced with permission of Curtis Brown Group Ltd, London on behalf of the Estate of Elizabeth Bowen.

'Villa Marta' from *Concerning Virgins* by Clare Boylan. Copyright © Clare Boylan. Reproduced by permission of the author c/o Rogers, Coleridge & White., 20 Powis Mews, London W11 1JN.

'Meles Vulgaris' from *The Port Wine Stains – Patrick Boyle's Best Stories* by Patrick Boyle. Copyright © Patrick Boyle. Reproduced by permission of The O'Brien Press Ltd, Dublin.

'An Attack of Hunger' from *The Springs of Affection: Stories of Dublin* by Maeve Brennan. Copyright © The Estate of Maeve Brennan, 1998. Reprinted by permission of Counterpoint Press.

'The Swing of Things' from *Departures* by Jennifer C Cornell. Copyright © Jennifer C Cornell, 1995. Reprinted by permission of the University of Pittsburgh Press.

'Naming the Names' from *The Way-Paver* by Anne Devlin. Copyright © Anne Devlin 1986. Reprinted by permission of Faber and Faber Ltd.

'Visit' from *Country of the Grand* by Gerard Donovan. Reprinted in the UK by permission of Faber and Faber Ltd. 'Visit' from *Young Irelanders* by Gerard Donovan. Reprinted in the US by permission of The Overlook Press, New York, www.overlookpress.com.